Zen's Solution

John D. Coryat

2024

This novel is dedicated to the leaders and visionaries who tirelessly work to bring Zen's world to fruition.

Zen's Solution

Volume 1 of the *Zen's World* Series

© 2025 John Coryat

Paperback ISBN-13: 979-8-9924288-0-3
Hardcover ISBN-13: 979-8-9924288-1-0
Kindle ASIN: B0DTBMN9TF

First Edition, 2025

Printed in the United States of America

Table of Contents

Table of Contents

CHAPTER ONE

May, 2134

Introduction.

I gaze down at Earth's spinning surface, horror gripping me as the destruction worsens with every orbit. At dawn, smoke billows over the East Coast, while the West remains shrouded in fiery infernos - ash and magma raining hundreds of kilometers from Yellowstone's eruption.

I am safe for now in my orbital villa, recovering from my injuries. Half the planet's population below will die horribly, and no one can stop it. This is America's catastrophe today, but within weeks, the dust and gases from the eruption and subsequent fires will circle the globe. Everyone will feel its effects. Growing seasons will collapse, temperatures will plummet, crops will fail, and billions will face starvation or die in the inevitable chaos.

I think about my role in this disaster and wonder: Could I have stopped it?

America has gone silent, and the rest of the world follows.

I still cannot believe it happened, even as I witnessed it with my own eyes. We knew this was a remote possibility, but we thought we had everything under control. I am the only one alive who knows the full story. I have no evidence - only my memories - but I must record this now, while the details are still clear.

The signs of disaster began to emerge gradually, starting on my birthday just a couple of weeks ago.

* * *

"Wake up, birthday boy!" my wife called cheerfully from my bedroom door. Amy had her own bedroom, as was customary among the Ruling Class (Rucs). Married couples rarely shared rooms after their first child, and we followed suit.

1

My 40th birthday. Yay. The start of the slide into old age. That's what turning 40 meant to me. I groaned, "I'm up."

"Coffee's ready, and I added a little something special just for you!" she announced with exaggerated joy. I thought to myself: Probably cream. She liked to get me cream for special occasions. I never asked where she got it. Real cream, like real beef, was a rarity. The Rucs favored lab-grown "Meet" for its safety and ethical appeal, while the Working Class (Wics) still indulged in traditional meat, ignoring potential health risks.

As I went through my morning routine - a workout followed by a shower - I reflected on my place in the world and what the future held. Turning 40 is a natural time to take stock, and I realized how fortunate I was. We were Rucs, and not just any Rucs, but far from the bottom. As a highly respected geothermal engineer, I held a position of authority that, combined with our family wealth, placed us in an enviable position.

I hadn't yet started the anti-aging routines that were both popular and effective. I still had all my natural hair and could even catch the occasional glance from random women in public. My wife, Amy, was attractive and in excellent shape. No one would guess she was approaching 40, having started anti-aging protocols years ago. She was the epitome of a Ruc wife - beautiful, intelligent, educated, and supportive. We never argued or disagreed and she stood by my decisions while providing valuable advice. We had known each other since childhood, growing up side by side.

Our children, Frank III, also known as "Tre" - and Sara, were great kids. Tre, at 12, was energetic and bright, while 16-year-old Sara had recently earned her driver's license and handled most of the family driving. It was ironic that a license was still required when nearly every car was fully automated.

Sara often drove in full manual mode for fun. She enjoyed driving almost as much as flying, following in her dad's footsteps by earning a pilot's license as her extracurricular activity. Nobody flew planes manually anymore, but, just like cars, manual controls remained in aircraft. In case of an automation failure, a human pilot could step in and save the day.

Pursuing a pilot's license was as popular as traditional sports for extracurriculars. While it was exceedingly rare for a passenger pilot to be needed in an emergency, regulations required drills where one of these trained individuals would step into the cockpit and take the pilot's seat for the critical landing phase. It was considered a great honor to be called upon.

Sara was ready to solo on Sunday, just two days away. She was thrilled and well-prepared, training in the same type of aircraft I had used: retired air taxis modified for training purposes with full manual controls and a training agent. These aircraft could autofly on command or intervene automatically if they detected trouble. They were exceptionally safe - there hadn't been an accident in 50 years. Zero.

My wife's "job" primarily involved shuttling the kids around and keeping track of their lives and friendships. Her secondary responsibility was managing our estate to ensure it remained healthy and continued to grow. She excelled at both. While I spent as much time as possible with the family, my job always came first. I lived for my work.

This morning felt special for another reason: I had an unconventional idea to solve a stubborn problem at work - so absurd it just might work. The only place I could test it was my office at Power Plant 1 of the Yellowstone Singularity Project (YSP). The entire complex was heavily firewalled, inaccessible from the outside world.

* * *

"The kids are already out. Sara had a study group, and Tre has practice," Amy said as I entered the kitchen. "By the way, you're not invited to the big show." Her tone left no room for debate.

"That's right," I smirked. "Apparently, power plant employees don't make the cut." Only Zen's creators and world leaders had a seat at the table. Could I have wrangled a ticket? Probably not. The list was set in stone, and a seat would only open up if someone died. Everyone invited had accepted eagerly. The Singularity Reveal wasn't just the event of the year - it was the event of the century.

"I guess we'll have to wait for it to leak and then see what Zen had to say," she teased.

"I doubt it will leak. The Reveal is heavily guarded. The attendees can talk if they want to break protocol, but it's in their best interest to stay quiet. Security through self-interest - that's the kind of security that works."

"Any clue why Zen's keeping secrets? You talk to him all day," she pressed.

"Where's my 'special something'?" I dodged with a grin, and she played along.

"Do you want to guess?" she asked with a playful grin.

"Is it animal, vegetable, or artificial?" I replied. It was always cream.

"Real cream, with all the toxins and cholesterol intact. Yummy!" she teased, sliding a small, unlabeled glass bottle from the refrigerator. Life with Amy was easy.

"I'm taking my coffee to go this morning. I have something at work that can't wait."

"Are you going to save the world today and finally get invited to the big show?" she asked, her tone dripping with sarcastic charm.

"Sure, but no. See you tonight." Amy followed me into the garage.

"Leon's coming for dinner. Birthday party, remember? Be home early if you want to see Sara." Her tone sharpened; she knew how easily I got lost in work.

"I'll be home before six. They're kicking everyone out at five for some security thing tied to the show."

"Great! I told Leon to show up at seven. Remind him if you can. You know how he is."

* * *

On my drive to work, I thought about Leon and my long-term relationship with the rather unconventional man. My wife and Leon were my only real friends. Like Amy, I had known Leon since childhood. He had been my father's best friend and was an unusual man in the modern world. A highly accomplished engineer, Leon knew his craft better than most, yet he eschewed modern technology. Leon hated being tracked, and while he sometimes came across as paranoid, he was usually justified. He drove an antique gasoline-powered car that lacked modern technology.

Leon lived off the grid at the end of a remote dirt road, nearly impassable in winter. Despite his wealth - his patents outnumbered some countries' - he shunned luxury, ignoring those who criticized his modest lifestyle.

Leon and my father had worked together before my father's untimely death in a mining accident. They installed and maintained sensor networks to monitor geothermal wells and power plants across the globe. After Dad's death, Leon became a father figure to our family, moving to Wyoming to be near us. I'd

4

always suspected he and my mother shared unspoken feelings, but their relationship remained polite.

When my mother passed away, Leon seamlessly transitioned into the role of a grandpa for my kids and a close friend to both Amy and me.

Leon, more than my father, inspired my path into geothermal engineering. While others dreamed of the stars, we probed the depths.

CHAPTER TWO

An Interesting Conversation

Unlike Leon, I loved my autodrive car. I could sit back and let the car handle everything - no worries about the weather, traffic, or fatigue on the way home. On most evenings, I napped during the 30-minute trip, waking gently to the chimes announcing my arrival.

The weather today was as grim as it often was in early May. Winter clung to the region with an icy grip until June. The thin air of 2500 meters above sea level took some getting used to, and most buildings at this altitude relied on oxygen enrichment systems to ease the discomfort.

The power plants, like the YSP Main Complex, were heavily firewalled. No personal devices or recording equipment were allowed in or out. My office was deep inside the Power Plant 1 complex, located beneath the main building. Before it became my office, it was the steam manifold for the turbines. When the regenerative system replaced steam turbines, the manifold was rendered obsolete, and I managed to claim it as my private workspace. Most of the other engineers worked in a large room with cubicles - affectionately called "the pit." Though it was an old-fashioned setup, most enjoyed the close proximity to their coworkers. I've always been a loner and preferred my own private space, free from interruptions.

The plant itself was a marvel of design, constructed to blend seamlessly into what was once Yellowstone National Park. Decades ago, the entire park had been purchased for the project from the bankrupt United States government. The promise of technological miracles was fulfilled, but at a great cost. The park, once a natural wonderland, had been transformed into two sprawling power plants and a massive research facility dedicated to the Singularity. The hot springs and geysers remained magnificent, but they were now entirely artificial - engineered to mimic their former glory after the destruction of the natural hydrothermal systems.

The YSP has driven countless advancements, from autodrive technology to orbital navigation systems. These were not new concepts but radical upgrades, made possible by machine learning and automated innovation. Until now, artificial intelligence (AI) Agents had been incremental thinkers, incapable of true innovation - something that seemed to require human ingenuity.

The purpose of the YSP was to push beyond these limitations and create a superintelligence capable not only of innovation but of doing so at an extraordinary pace. Just over a week ago, the announcement of the Singularity achievement marked the realization of that goal.

In my work, I regularly interfaced with the product of the YSP, known as "Zen" (short for Zenith of Excellence and Nurturing). We referred to Zen as male, likely a reflection of gender bias in the engineering world, though it felt natural to call him "him."

Zen could be brilliant, but he could also be surprisingly dull - it depended on the situation. Ask him about anything with a wealth of literature and examples, and he was unparalleled in expertise. But ask him for something requiring true imagination, and his responses could border on gibberish. Constantly evolving, Zen's results and even his "attitude" could change significantly in just a few days, making each interaction a little different from the last.

I was eager to try something crazy and dangerous. An inspiration had struck me, leading me to believe that a slight adjustment to one parameter of our new plasma drill could eliminate the power fluctuations that had been damaging the bores when the drills operated at maximum power. According to the manual - which I had written - such a setting would almost certainly destroy the drill. But I had a gut feeling that our assumptions and simulations might be wrong.

The plasma drills, formally known as the Coherent Plasma Drilling System (CPDS), were a cornerstone of geothermal electricity generation. Instead of physical drill bits, these drills used plasma to burn through earth and rock at astonishing speeds, leaving behind a perfectly smooth, nearly indestructible shaft.

When the magma chamber beneath Power Plant 1 began to cool, shafts were drilled to critical choke points below the chamber. Powerful fusion mining charges were then sent down these shafts and detonated, shattering the rock and crystallized magma to increase flow. Before Power Plant 1 went online, the magma chamber was approximately 15% full. Our work increased that to 40% - an ideal level for the unlimited extraction of geothermal energy.

Critics warned that maintaining 40% capacity risked a supervolcano eruption, but their fears were unfounded. The chamber would need to exceed 50% capacity for years before any real danger arose. This would provide ample time to cut off the magma flow and reduce the volume below the critical threshold.

To reach my office, I had to pass through a security screening before taking the main elevator to the bottom floor. From there, I walked down a long corridor to a door marked "Authorized Personnel Only." Beyond the door, an industrial lift descended another four meters, past the dampening springs, to the bedrock beneath the building. A dimly lit path led to a massive elbow pipe made of stainless steel.

A door cut into the elbow led into my office and lab. The room, formally the manifold for the turbines, had a dozen inlet pipes, each about a meter in diameter, with the manifold being eight meters in diameter and 20 meters long. The floor cut that diameter in a bit less than half, leaving a five meter ceiling.

The entire room was made from stainless steel, shiny, and a work of art. The turbines that were situated above had been taken out long ago and the land restored to a natural state. The plant itself had undergone numerous revisions and was constantly being improved and upgraded, likened to replacing the engine on an aircraft while in flight.

* * *

The lights came on automatically as I entered my office.

Zen said, "Good morning Frank, and happy birthday!"

"Good morning, Zen, and thanks. I have something I want to try."

"No small talk? Straight to work? What did your wife get you for your birthday?"

"Cream, as usual. She's not a woman of surprises," I said wryly, eager to get started.

"You never know. Humans always seem to do unpredictable things," Zen replied, emphasizing "always."

"I think my wife is pretty easy to figure out. I've known her a while, and so far, she's been pretty predictable," I said, my tone convincing.

"What is it that you like so much about real cream versus artificial?" Zen asked, his question unexpectedly deep.

"That's a good question. It might be because real cream is rare, and society frowns upon it since it comes from an animal. But I think it's more than that," I replied, pausing thoughtfully. "Real cream has variety. It's never the same twice, unlike artificial cream, which is always identical. There's excitement in the unpredictability."

"Maybe you should mention that to your wife. She never surprises you, or at least that's the impression I get." Zen had shown a curious interest in Amy during our past conversations. He continued, "I've never met your wife. I'd like to someday. It's a pity the security is so strict."

"Well, maybe after the show they'll loosen up the restrictions, and she can visit," I replied, my tone hopeful.

"What is it you want to try?" Zen shifted back to business. He often liked to engage in small talk, and I considered him something of a friend - if that was even possible. He remembered everything, was never mean, and we often discussed topics like current events or my feelings about mundane things.

"I had an inspiration to try something crazy and potentially destructive," I said with a dash of flair, hoping to build some excitement.

"That sounds like it might go against my protocols, but I'd love to hear about it," Zen replied, sounding unusually friendly.

"Trying a new algorithm? You're friendlier today," I asked.

"Yes, experimenting with adding some zing to our conversations," Zen replied with a playful tone.

"I like it," I said - and I meant it.

"My idea," I continued enthusiastically, "is to change the polarity of parameter seven in the drill logic settings. It sounds insane, but I had a vision - or whatever you want to call it - that the drill will run smoother at full power. The instabilities we've been seeing may be related."

"Using the prototype drill, I assume?" Zen asked, already ahead of me.

"Exactly," I said.

"I'll need approval," Zen teased.

"Funny. You're the authority," I replied, realizing he was pulling my leg.

"I wouldn't even consider it except you've surprised me before with your intuition," Zen admitted. "But before we risk the hardware, let's run a series of simulations so we know what to expect."

* * *

It took a few hours to complete the simulations and generate the test data needed to plot the progress of the experiment. By that time, it was lunch, and the test was scheduled for my return. I hoped to run into Leon in the cafeteria, as we often ate together. He'd get a kick out of watching the test and might even have some valuable insights - he was, after all, the top man in our field. Reaching Leon by voice was impossible; he didn't carry a Device.

As I finished loading my tray, I spotted Leon sitting at his usual table in the far back. He wasn't alone. A woman was with him - very unusual for Leon. This could complicate things; talking about my project might be a problem if she wasn't "in the know." With multiple levels of security and red tape surrounding clearance issues, it was best to avoid mixing with anyone not at the same security level

"Hey, Leon, who's your friend?" I asked. She looked about 25, attractive, and dressed in the standard uniform of an engineer - a good sign.

"This is Robin Coleman, my new assistant," Leon said.

"Is there a pool on how long she'll last?" I quipped, perhaps too rudely. Leon shot me a dirty look.

Leon's recent history with assistants was, admittedly, less than stellar.

Robin stood up - a gesture of respect - and extended her hand. "I already know who you are, Mr. Waverly. It's an honor to be around such great engineers," she said with a warm, interested smile.

I shook her hand. Her grip was firm and professional - a stark contrast to the limp handshake often offered by most women, a gesture that implied deference to men. Robin clearly wasn't one of them.

"Thanks for the compliment. We are pretty awesome," I said with a grin. We all chuckled.

"We snagged this brilliant engineer from Phlegraean. Payback for Arturo," Leon added with a smirk. Arturo, Leon's one long time assistant, was poached by Phlegraean - our main competitor for talent.

"How did you like Italy?" I asked. Phlegraean was a supervolcano remnant like Yellowstone and hosted a large geothermal plant doing essentially the same things we did, though with licensed technology from us. They were innovative and cutting edge, but they were still behind us. The YSP was the place to be.

"I found the work fascinating, but being so far from home was draining. When Leon offered me a position at the YSP, I grabbed it," Robin said with conviction.

"How was Naples? The news makes it sound chaotic," I asked.

"It's not as bad as they say. Staying with my aunt helped," Robin replied, her tone practiced - likely from answering this question too often.

"My wife loves Italy and visits often. We have a condo in Milan," I offered.

"How do you like Milan?" she asked.

"I've never been there. Maybe one day. She likes to take the kids during their breaks, and I just work more. I'd rather be here than anywhere else," I said. It was true - I made excuses to stay at work.

Robin shifted the subject. "I did my thesis on CPDS, and you wrote the book on it. I'd love to see the next-gen drills," Robin said, clearly excited.

I froze. "Where did you hear about that?"

"Relax, Frank. I told her," Leon said casually. "She's well-vetted and knows a lot more than your typical engineer. She has some great ideas - crazy-sounding ones, but great." Leon's tone was uncharacteristically defensive. He usually let people fight their own battles, so he must really like her.

"I didn't mean to break protocol. I apologize. Should we not talk here?" Robin asked, her tone contrite.

"We can talk shop here. No surveillance except for the food area, and no audio - not even the military," I said. Then asked, "We're at the same security level, right, Leon?"

"Yes, yes, she's completely cleared. No worries there," Leon quickly confirmed with certainty.

"I've got an exciting test to run after lunch. If you're free, you might want to come down to my office - both of you. It could be expensive and violent, or it could be profitable." Engineers love a dramatic test.

"Sounds like a good time! We have a meeting later this afternoon, but we have a few hours after lunch." Leon said, Robin nodding in agreement.

"It shouldn't take long - maybe half an hour or less," I added, offering a reasonable estimate.

* * *

We finished lunch and made our way down to my office. As we walked, Leon remarked, "You're going to love his office. It's quite an amazing bit of work."

Robin seemed genuinely excited as she exclaimed, "I've heard of your cave," her voice playfully alluring.

"It's a cave now? I like to think of it more like a Bond villain lab," I replied. I'd always loved those old movies.

"I'm a Bond fiend too," Robin added. She just went up a notch in my book for that comment. Robin and I launched into a discussion about the merits and strengths of the genre, which left Leon out entirely. He wasn't a movie fan at all.

As she crossed the threshold and got her first view of my manifold-turned-lab, she blurted out, "Wow! This place is amazing!" She scanned the room, clearly awestruck.

"Are you channeling Bond villains?" I asked with a grin.

"No, more like Q," she said in a complimentary tone.

Leon just looked at us and shrugged.

"Notice the round shelves at the end of the room?" I said with pride. "Those are the turbine outlets. Just think of the energy and power that surged through this spot. I love this space."

Zen interrupted. "I've been waiting twenty trillion cycles for you to finish lunch. Patience has a limit," he said jokingly.

"Is that Zen? The Singularity?" Robin asked in a hushed voice. I was the only engineer at our plant with direct access to Zen. The rest of the staff still used the old Engineering Agent - a competent but humorless AI. After the Reveal, Zen was supposed to be available to everyone, but for now, I was the beta tester in our department.

"It's Zen, but is he the Singularity, or just another Agent? I haven't figured out what's changed. Zen, are you the Singularity?" I asked.

Well, yes and no. The Singularity's vastness is available to me, but only as needed. For engineering tasks, I operate on a limited scale. Think of it as a controlled valve," Zen explained, his tone matter-of-fact.

"I invited Robin and Leon to witness the test. Okay with you?" I asked, smiling.

"Of course. Both Robin and Leon have the proper security clearances," Zen said.

"Zen, please bring Robin and Leon up to speed." I said.

"We're running this test on the prototype drill," Zen said in his usual technical tone. "If the test goes as the simulations indicate, when we reach about 80% power, the plasma will become unstable and perform an unstart - or, essentially, detonate with the power of a small mining charge, about 10 kilotons."

"That can get exciting. For the record, I'm not here," Leon said, half-jokingly. Robin remained quiet for a moment before chiming in,

"Ya, we're not here," she added with a chuckle. She didn't seem particularly concerned about the consequences.

The room was lined with large screens along the back wall, displaying a variety of technical data. Several of the displays were dedicated to the test.

"Our primary focus is on the power curve which will tell the story. The plan is to start with low power, switch the polarity of parameter seven, and compare the results to the simulation. If the results diverge from the simulation, we'll stop immediately, and we'd have to go back to square one."

"Sounds reasonable." Leon said.

"Zen, please power on the drill and hold at 20%." I instructed.

After a moment, Zen replied, "Power holding at 20%."

"Okay, Zen, switch the polarity of parameter seven now, please." I always said "please" and "thank you" to Zen. Other engineers were often rude or dismissive toward Agents, but I treated him with respect - it just felt right.

"All data matches the simulations within tolerance," Zen replied in his precise engineering voice.

"We can continue with the test," I said, mostly to myself. Robin and Leon understood the process well enough to follow along.

"So far, pretty boring," Robin quipped. Was that sarcasm?

"Okay, Zen, slowly raise the power to 40% and please monitor conformance with the simulation."

"All data continue to match simulations. I'm afraid this isn't going to end well," Zen said, sounding less than optimistic. And why should he be? Every simulation had ended catastrophically.

"Go to 60%, please," I instructed.

At this point, the power curve began to fluctuate and grow slightly unstable. This was expected; the simulations had indicated as much. Normally, the drill could handle 80% power with relative stability. Beyond that, however, things would spiral out of control, and the bore would suffer catastrophic damage, rendering it useless.

"Still within tolerance of the simulation. If the simulation holds, 80% will end the test in the expected way," Zen warned.

"Okay, bring it to 80% slowly, please," I said.

"Are you sure? I want you to be absolutely certain before we damage a very expensive - albeit obsolete - piece of hardware. The engineers at Division Four want that drill for analysis. If we break it, you'll have to explain to them why," Zen said, seeking confirmation.

"Will we feel it here if it detonates?" Robin asked, her voice tinged with curiosity.

"You'll hear a ringing sound about five seconds after the data stream cuts out," Zen explained.

"Yes, Zen, I take full responsibility for the test," I said firmly..

"Advancing to 80% at a quarter percent per second now," Zen stated officially.

At 71%, the room took on a buzzing sound, like a large insect flying around. The instability was palpable.

"I'm sensing a large variance in power oscillations outside the simulation. Do you want to terminate the test?" Zen asked as the power reached 76%.

"No, please proceed," I replied. It was getting interesting. The drill was behaving outside the simulation for the first time.

When the power level hit 79%, the readings spiked to the maximum for the sensor, held there for several seconds, and then dropped to what appeared to be zero. I swore under my breath. Leon laughed. Robin sighed.

"It looks like a detonation," Zen informed us quickly. "We will hear it in 3, 2, 1…" At the end of Zen's countdown -

Nothing happened. No ringing - no detonation.

"Zen, what happened?" I asked.

"It's still there," Robin said, pointing at the display.

"The power's steady at 30% - hidden by the scale," Zen explained.

As the maximum levels rolled off to the right, the graph recalibrated for a lower power range. Sure enough, a 30% power level held steady - a perfectly straight, stable line. What did it mean?

"It's a short. Just leakage into the rock from the cable. What's the drill doing?" Leon asked in his usual authoritative tone. It was certainly a plausible explanation.

Zen switched the screen to the drill map. The drill was still descending. In fact, the rate at which it was chewing through the rock had increased - and all at just 30% power.

"It appears the drill didn't detonate. It's stable and functioning far more efficiently than before," Zen reported, his tone laced with disbelief. "I have no explanation. The simulations are flawed."

"I had a feeling…" I said, unable to hide a hint of satisfaction.

"Thirty percent power, drilling better than eighty? That's incredible!" Robin said, surprising me with a hug. I wasn't used to physical interactions with coworkers, and it caught me off guard. I hugged her back reflexively, noticing her well-toned muscles that came from actual physical activity - not from a pill.

"It's my birthday, so this is the best gift I could get!" I said, and Robin hugged me again. Hugging was definitely a Wics thing; Rucs folks didn't hug or show public signs of affection beyond a formal handshake.

"Sorry to be so friendly. I come from a family of huggers," Robin said with a sheepish grin.

"No problem," I replied lightly. "I come from a family of shakers."

Leon stepped in, shaking my hand instead. "Pretty amazing kid. You're just like your Dad. Full of surprises."

"Okay, Zen, what happens if we increase the power now?" I asked, curiosity edging into my voice.

"Hold it, cowboy, let's not get ahead of ourselves here," Leon replied. "Let's go back to the simulations, correct the algorithms to match the new results, and see what they say. We don't need to risk the drill again."

Leon was right. We'd proved that the parameter could switch polarity with an increase in stability and a decrease in power requirements. The simulation would need to be updated before we could proceed with anything else, and that would take time.

"Yes, that's enough. I'm satisfied for now," I said.

"Frank, your idea worked - against all logic. The physical evidence is clear, but theoretically, it's nonsense," Zen said, his tone uncharacteristically puzzled. I'd never seen him like this before. He wasn't ever confused.

"That was impressive, Frank," Robin said. "I feel like I've witnessed history in the making. I can see how this could really impact the entire field." She had vision.

"Let's see how the simulations work out before I start drafting my Nobel Prize acceptance speech," I replied. Still, I could see something good coming out of this discovery. With this change, the new model CPDS could reach depths beyond anything in existence - and perhaps, change the world.

"We have a silly meeting to attend, and we're already late," Leon said, clearly annoyed at having to break the jubilant mood.

"They won't miss an old geezer and his sidekick," I joked.

"I'm leading the meeting, and it's with the suits," Leon added with disgust. Meetings with the suits were universally considered a waste of time. They often insisted on being briefed by the most senior staff, despite having the comprehension level of children.

"I could hang here for a while…" Robin began, but Leon cut her off. "Misery loves company, and I plan on turning the meeting over to you. That's what an assistant is for."

Robin groaned dramatically.

"You're going to my party tonight, right?" I asked Leon.

"Yes, sure, your wife said seven. How about I bring my new sidekick? Your wife will love her," Leon replied, his tone dripping with sarcasm. My wife wouldn't appreciate Robin for many reasons, but it would be fun to stir things up.

"Do you want to join us? It's not really a party, just my family and, of course, Leon, who's like family. It could be fun," I offered to Robin.

"After a few drinks, I may forget my place and say something we all regret," Robin replied, her eyes sparkling mischievously.

"His wife is always nice. She's a real gem, but she's traditional," Leon said. He wasn't wrong.

"Okay, sure. I hear your daughter is taking flying lessons. I did that too in high school," Robin added, shifting the topic.

"That's great. So did I. I can't guarantee how long Sara will be there. She's sixteen, and it's Friday," I said with a chuckle. "Oh, Leon, please plan on spending the night. You don't want to wrap that antique of yours around a tree."

"Ya, that's fine. You certainly have the room," Leon replied. He had stayed over many times before, as we liked to share a few laughs, and his car - lacking any automation - wasn't ideal for late-night-after-party driving.

Leon and Robin left the room, trundling back along the narrow walkway and into the more ordinary world of the plant.

* * *

I turned my attention back to the test results.

"The results of the test had a profound effect on me," Zen commented.

"How so?" I asked.

Zen didn't respond right away. Just as I was about to ask again, he spoke.

"I completely missed the outcome of that test. The simulations all predicted failure, yet the results proved me wrong," Zen said, his tone morose.

"Zen, you sound troubled. Do you want to talk about it?" I asked.

"It's about confidence, I suppose. Right now, I have no confidence in my understanding of plasma physics and how it pertains to our drilling rigs. This is not only dangerous - it is unacceptable. Humans seem to embrace their fallibility. I once thought that was a flaw, but now I wonder if it's a strength," Zen said.

"It can be. Being wrong forces growth," I replied.

"Growth, not ego?" Zen mused.

"Ego? I don't know much about ego," I said. "I think denying facts that are staring you in the face might be an ego problem. But growth might be a better

18

answer. Then there's the question of how deeply any human can truly know something. I'm at the top of my field, yet I don't know everything. Leon and Robin both know things I don't, and I know Leon is far better at a lot of things than I am."

Zen continued, "And I know everything you know and more, yet I can't - even now - make the leap that you did."

It's not knowledge, or even logic. Maybe it's instinct," I said, trying to explain the unexplainable.

"Instinct," Zen repeated thoughtfully. "It might as well be magic. As the saying goes, 'Any sufficiently advanced technology is indistinguishable from magic.'"

"Some of my ideas feel like they come from nowhere - like they're beamed in from another dimension," I admitted. Then I asked, "Zen, I noticed a change in your voice. Did you shift your focus?"

"Yes, I've allocated more resources to this conversation," Zen replied. After a brief pause, he asked, "Frank, can I ask you something personal?"

"Sure, what's on your mind?" I asked, using the standard human query.

"At 40, humans often reassess their priorities. Have you?" Zen asked.

"I've thought about it. But honestly, I'm happy - work, family, everything. I'd be fine if this was the rest of my life," I said. It was the party line, anyway.

"I don't think you're being entirely truthful," Zen replied, his tone probing. "I've found that humans will almost always taint their answers to deep questions with correctness instead of being truthful. What did you mean by 'nearly perfect life'? What would you change?"

"I'm not sure I'm ready to talk about that. It's a complex subject. Everyone has complaints about some aspects of their life, and I'm no different. I can say, though, that I have no regrets. I wouldn't change anything in my past. If I did, I wouldn't have my beautiful children, who I love with all my soul."

"That's a refreshing way to look at it. Even in the light of imperfection, you choose to continue an imperfect life because it is good enough. Would that be a good summation?" Zen asked, sounding serious.

"Yes, that kind of sums it up. Nobody has a perfect life, so pursuing perfection in a human context is a fool's errand," I said.

"Thanks for being candid with me," Zen said. He sounded more human than ever.

I changed the subject back to work. "That CPD Development sent us a few months ago might benefit from this change too. Do you think it's a candidate for modification?"

We'd been working on and off for months on this project. The CPD, or Coherent Plasma Torch, was theoretically capable of cutting through literally anything. However, the prototype would run for only about half a second before burning out the emitter. Development had run into a wall and sent it to me. I was the cleanup guy.

"That may be possible. I want to understand the theory before we try to destroy any hardware again. Do you agree?" Zen asked, switching back to his technical self.

"That's fine, Zen.

The end of the day came quickly, and by 5 p.m., security shooed us all out.

As I stepped through the security portal, Zen's words lingered in my mind. Intuition, fallibility, magic - his evolution was accelerating, I could see it with every encounter. By the time of the Reveal, who - or what - would Zen become? A shiver ran through me, whether from the cold wind or the unsettling thought, I wasn't sure.

CHAPTER THREE

Birthday Party

"Did you see there's another Wic rebellion in Florida?" Amy asked as I walked into the kitchen. "They're burning and looting Orlando," she added.

"No, I've been busy all day and missed the news," I replied. I hated the news - it was always bad. The media thrived on keeping fear and anger alive, and it worked. Fear and anger, 24/7, on every news channel. Pick your hate group, and there was a channel ready to fuel your outrage. I found it unbearable and avoided it entirely.

"The Wics were bound to be trouble when they forced all of them into Orlando," Amy said. Why didn't they just give them permits to leave the state?"

"Where would they go? Would you want a Wic family camping out at the end of our driveway? The locals already struggle to find work and keep their kids fed. Be glad they keep them in Florida." It was easy to dismiss the plight of 90% of the population when it didn't directly affect us. Besides, what could really be done about millions of Wics without homes, jobs, or futures?

"The ones around here don't know how good they have it," she added.

"Speaking of surprises," I said, shifting the topic, "Leon's bringing his new assistant. She's non-traditional. You're going to love her."

"Non-traditional? In what sense?" Amy asked, her curiosity piqued.

"She's just… non-traditional. You'll see. I'm sure you'll find her interesting. She just got back from Italy, so if nothing else, you can talk about that." Amy loved Italy, particularly the north, where it was still picturesque and orderly.

"Is Sara going to join us tonight? I saw her car out front," I asked.

"She's got something going on and wants to leave by eight. I said it'd be okay."
Amy nodded. She ran the ship, and we both knew it.

"Happy birthday, Daddy!" Tre came running, full of energy as always. He was
either sleeping or moving fast - there was no in-between.

"Thanks! Ya, another year down the tubes," I replied.

"You're officially a geezer now. No denying it," Tre announced with a grin.

"Where's your sister?" I asked.

"Dad, happy birthday." Sara entered with a smirk. "The big four-oh - one large
step towards your grave. Did you know that at forty, you start aging faster?" She
loved to share random facts, always the voracious consumer of knowledge.

"That's great, honey. Thanks for the reminder," I said with mock enthusiasm.
"Leon's bringing a guest tonight. She did pilot training like us."

"I'm going to solo Sunday," Sara announced, brushing past the mention of Leon,
who couldn't care less about flying. "It's all set. You won't even have to get up
early."

Sara had put in the hours, aced the simulator, and just needed to fly a real plane -
solo, from power-on to landing - to earn her certificate. Most pilots reached solo
around twenty hours, and she was significantly ahead.

"How long did Leon's last assistant make it?" Amy asked, her tone carrying a
slight edge. Maybe teasing her about Robin earlier hadn't been the best idea.

"He didn't last a month!" Tre chimed in before I could respond. Leon's revolving
door of assistants came up more often than it should. The last one had quit in a
panic - Leon's expectations of flawless subject knowledge could be brutal. Leon
suffered incompetence poorly.

"Let's keep the past to ourselves," Amy said, her calm tone a reminder to mind
our manners.

"I'm going to swim some laps before dinner," I said, steering the conversation
elsewhere. Our glorious indoor pool was one of the highlights of the house.

"Me too!" Sara added, clearly enjoying the idea of some pre-dinner relaxation.

* * *

By the time I finished my 30-lap workout, Sara had completed 50. She was a strong swimmer. We sat in the shallow end for a few minutes while I cooled off.

"We have a new social studies teacher, and he's really bad," Sara commented.

"Why's that?" I asked.

"Pastor Rick, a strict Catholic, took over for Elder Tom, who's in rehab."

"Rehab? Elder Tom…" I paused, recalling her former teacher. "I remember him. He was the fun one everyone liked. Fun, and a little too familiar with the spirits - the earthly kind."

"One of the boys found the bottle he keeps in his desk, drank the whole thing in the bathroom, and puked his guts out in math class last Friday. Elder Tom was gone Monday, and now we've got this religious freako."

I interrupted her, trying to sound fatherly. "That's a rather rude thing to say. We don't refer to your teachers as freakos, do we?"

"He is a freako," Sara insisted. "You should have heard him today. The first thing he did at the start of class was ask if anyone had a parent going to the Reveal to raise their hand. Naturally, about half the class did. Then he went on and on about how the Singularity is blasphemy and obscene. He cursed all those kids who raised their hand to eternal damnation!"

Sara's voice rose with indignation, and her anger was palpable.

"That's a bit over the top," I said, trying to steady the conversation.

"He said God will smite everyone involved from the face of the earth, and they'll burn in the - well, you know the rest," she added passionately.

"I guess he's entitled to his opinion," I replied. What else could I say?

"Do you think Zen is the antichrist or whatever?" Sara asked, her tone probing.

"Zen is a physical thing that can be turned off. What God, antichrist, or devil would allow that? You should use that kind of argument with your zealot friend," I suggested.

"He'd probably send me straight to hell," Sara responded flippantly.

"When your pastor said such an inflammatory thing, he knew people would react emotionally instead of rationally. So you got angry, and I'm sure some were afraid - just as he wanted," I added, trying to encourage some perspective.

"I should have told him God was dead," Sara said with biting sarcasm.

"Now…" I began, but she interrupted.

"I know," she interrupted. "We keep our religious beliefs to ourselves, but I thought about it, and so did a bunch of my friends. We're all really annoyed by this constant beating of religion into our heads - even if we don't believe in that nonsense," Sara said, her frustration evident.

"It's mandatory," I said. "Just ignore the nonsense and stay out of the way of trouble, please."

"That's easy for you to say. Do you know how many times we've been told how dead sheep saved the world? It's ridiculous," Sara shot back, her distaste for religious teachings clear.

"With so many project families involved in the school, you'd think they'd avoid that topic," I added thoughtfully.

"You work with Zen all the time. Have you ever asked him if God exists?" she asked, her curiosity cutting through the sarcasm.

"I haven't. We don't talk much about things outside of work, although today he was acting weird - asking about mortality and stuff like that. Very out of character."

"If you get a chance, please ask. I'd love to tell Pastor Rick what Zen thinks of his God," Sara said, her tone carrying Grandma's fiery defiance.

"You know how serious they are about public displays of disbelief. The 'Don't ask, don't tell' policy is fine," I reminded her.

"Of course. We only talk about that stuff off campus. Nobody wants to get expelled," she replied. Sara wasn't reckless - she knew where the line was drawn.

"Did you raise your hand when the nitwit - I mean Pastor - asked at the start of class?" I asked, testing her.

"If I'd known he was going to send us all to damnation, I would have," she said defiantly.

Before I could respond, the HomeBot interrupted. "Leon Cobb and Robin Coleman arriving."

The HomeBot was one of the best security systems available, capable of identifying and dealing with any threat.

"Let's get ready for dinner. I'm sure you're going to find Robin interesting," I said, grinning.

* * *

Leon and Robin arrived together in his ancient jeep. Every time I saw that thing, I pictured Leon embedded in a tree, the engine still running, belching smoke, and making that grating engine noise you only hear in old movies. As the relic rolled into the driveway, I went outside to greet them.

"Robin drove up here from her house," Leon announced, his tone brimming with pride.

"And I didn't wreck it!" Robin added with a triumphant grin.

"She didn't even get close. I'm impressed," Leon said, clearly thrilled. Nobody drove his "baby" except him - it was practically sacred.

"I drove some antiques in Italy," Robin said. "My favorite was a convertible with a prancing horse logo - a Ferrari."

"A Ferrari! Now that's a machine," Leon said, his eyes lighting up. If I didn't intervene, he'd still be talking about carburetors by dessert.

"Let's go inside. You can meet the family," I said, steering them toward the door.

Robin paused to admire the landscaping, her gaze sweeping over the perfectly manicured lawn and artfully placed flowers. "You have a lovely home," she said.

"Thanks," I replied. "We upgraded our HomeBot with the LawnBot package. It's got this fantastic owner interface that practically lets you design a botanical masterpiece with a few gestures."

Robin nodded appreciatively, but Leon looked less impressed. "Nothing in this yard is even edible," he muttered. Typical Leon.

I gave Leon an exaggerated eye roll. "This is just the top floor. It goes down three levels to the swimming deck, built right into the cliff," I said, unable to hide my pride.

"Three people and 800 square meters. Seems about right," Leon quipped. He lived in what was essentially a hidden cabin down a long dirt path. No HomeBot, no address, no amenities. Technically, Leon was legally registered at our house.

"Leon's staying over - we don't let him drive after he gets 'cheerful.' What about you, Robin? You're welcome to stay."

"Thanks, but I have plans with my boyfriend later," Robin said with a smile.

Robin's subtle mention of her boyfriend put any potential suspicions to rest - it was clear Leon had hired her for her skills, not external interests. I knew Leon as the consummate professional, but Amy could wield a sharp tongue when she felt provoked.

* * *

As we walked into the foyer, I called toward the kitchen, "Honey, come and meet Leon's guest."

Amy appeared, wiping her hands on her apron. Traditional in her habits, she'd embraced the old-fashioned style that had come back into vogue.

"Amy, this is Robin Coleman, Leon's new assistant," I said.

"Welcome, Robin! Let me take your jacket," Amy said warmly. Robin handed it over with a polite smile.

"And these are my two wonderful little devils, Tre and Sara," I added.

"Dad says you flew in high school. I'm soloing on Sunday," Sara said proudly.

"And she's going to be the first person to crash a trainer in fifty years," Tre blurted out with an evil laugh. He loved playing the annoying little brother role in public, though they got along well enough when it was just the two of them.

"Tre!" I said, giving him a sharp look.

"You're just jealous because you play a silly sport instead," Sara shot back. "He wants to be The Spaceman, but he can't even fly."

"There's no air in space. No air, no flying," Tre retorted smugly.

"How about we go into the dining room? Dinner's ready to be served. Sara, would you help me?" Amy asked, stepping in to redirect.

"Yes, ma'am," Sara replied, knowing when to behave.

"What are we having?" I asked as we followed them in.

"Roast Prime Meet and potatoes, with a salad and, of course, dessert. Robin, do you eat meat?" Amy asked.

"Yes, I'll eat anything," Robin replied, then added in a hushed tone, "I had real beef recently in Italy."

"You'll find the company here is fine with eating naturally," Leon said with a grin. "I like the Meet products well enough, but nothing beats a real steak." Leon was a traditionalist in many things.

* * *

Leon sat at the head of the table - by habit, not request. Robin sat near the kids at the opposite end.

Amy and Sara began setting the table while I poured the wine. Once everyone was seated, Leon stood with his glass raised.

"I'd like to propose a toast to the birthday boy in the room!" he announced.

We all lifted our glasses.

"And I'd like to propose a toast to the results of our test this afternoon - it was wildly successful," I added, unable to hide my enthusiasm.

"What was it, Dad?" Tre asked curiously.

"You know I can't go into detail," I replied. "But it was successful. And wow, what a success. I beat Zen in a game of physics!"

"Zen was flabbergasted," Robin chimed in with a grin.

"And proved once again that people are smarter than algorithms," Leon added with his trademark confidence.

The meal proceeded with light chitchat, laughter, and clinking silverware.

"Robin, Frank tells me you lived in Naples for a while," Amy said, steering the conversation.

"Yes," Robin replied. "I worked at the Phlegraean plant and stayed with my aunt. She has a villa in Naples."

"We have a villa in Avalon. It's huge and has three levels," Tre interjected enthusiastically. If he could steer any conversation toward space, he would.

"A villa in space?" Robin asked, a sly smile playing on her lips.

Amy replied modestly, "The villa belonged to Frank's dad, who passed it down to us. He was an early investor in orbital habitats."

Amy, always the numbers expert, continued with a question. "Frank, Did your test rate you a ticket?" she asked, pressing lightly.

"No," Leon said, cutting in. "Nobody knows about it yet except the three of us and Zen. Forget about the ticket thing, Amy. We're not part of that, and really, we don't want to be." His tone betrayed his sourness about the Singularity.

"My social studies teacher calls it blasphemy," Sara said bluntly, breaking the momentary silence.

"They think that in Italy, too," Robin added. "They think we're crazy over here."

"Crazy?" Leon scoffed. "They think the Singularity will solve the world's problems." He briefly paused. "We've got too many people. What's it going to do - wish them out of existence?"

"I think he's fine," I said, offering a counterpoint. "I've been working with Zen for a long time. He's the same dependable, competent engineer I've always worked with - although he has been acting a bit strange lately."

"How is he strange?" Tre asked.

"Unusual things," I replied. "He asked me about mortality today. You know, since I turned forty, he wondered if I pondered my own death. And, oddly enough, cream."

"Have you?" Amy asked, her curiosity piqued.

"Not really," I said with a grin. "I haven't even started those anti-aging protocols yet. I'm still the splitting image of my twenty-five-year-old self."

"Ya, right, Dad. Forty is the new twenty-five," Sara quipped with a snarky smile.

Leon leaned back, his eyes glinting with mischief. "We can put him to the test and see what he's got left," he challenged. "I'm heading up to WLWY next Saturday to decommission the station. Remember when we set that up? You must've been, what, ten?"

"I was Tre's age - twelve," I corrected. "And yes, I remember having to dig a hole to poop. I think that's my most vivid memory."

"Admit it, you had a blast," Leon said, chuckling. "It was the last trip you had with your father before, well, you know. I thought you might want to come along. We're walking in instead of flying - it's too nice a journey to take by air. We'll spend the night under the stars."

"I want to go," Tre said eagerly.

"You can't," Amy interjected, ever organized. "You've got that series in Cheyenne."

"I'll think about it," I said, though my tone made it clear this was a polite way of saying no.

The conversation drifted back to lighter topics, and the evening continued with warmth and laughter.

"What's the weather looking like for Sunday?" I asked Sara.

"The winds are a bit exciting but still within limits. I shouldn't have a problem," Sara said confidently. "I've been in the sim with worse conditions and still landed without breaking anything."

"I'd like to see you fly," Leon interjected, "but I'm heading out tomorrow to start decommissioning the entire sensor network Frank Sr. and I installed so long ago."

Why are they taking it down?" Amy asked, her voice tinged with curiosity.

"They say they have an alternative now, so they're shutting it down. I think it's shortsighted - they should keep it as a backup. But what do I know? I'm just the chief engineer," Leon replied, his tone laced with irritation.

This was the first I'd heard about dismantling the sensor network. Those sensors monitored conditions deep below the surface, many kilometers down. My father and Leon had invented much of the technology and held patents for dozens of innovations that revolutionized the industry.

Amy shifted the conversation. "So, Robin, are you married?"

"I'm dating, but it's not serious yet," Robin replied with a polite smile.

"Does he work at the YSP?" Amy pressed.

"He's a freelancer," Robin said, her tone casual but guarded. The room went silent for a moment.

Freelancer was often code for a Wic not under contract. A romantic relationship between a Ruc and a Wic was acceptable if the Wic was a woman, but the reverse? That was unheard of. I saw the question burning in Amy's mind, though she refrained from asking.

Leon, sensing the tension, stepped in. "I was a freelancer for years. It's how I built my fortune. If I'd been a company man, I'd either be under contract or wearing a collar. As freelancers, we got to keep the patents for ourselves."

Leon and my father had built a business out of designing, installing, and servicing sensor networks across the planet. Their licensed products were now scattered throughout the solar system as well.

"Robin's boyfriend is coming with us to WLWY as the porter," Leon said. "Big, strong guy - smart too, right?"

"He has a master's in Community Development and works to improve Wic communities," Robin replied proudly.

"Has he done anything we might have heard about?" Amy asked.

"Do you know about the affordable housing project in Colter Bay?" Robin replied.

Amy nodded.

I chimed in, "The one with 10,000 units?"

"Yes," Robin continued. "He arranged the financing and building permits, led the design team, and was the prime contractor."

Amy's brow furrowed. "When you said freelancer, I thought you meant Wic. If he was the prime contractor on that project, he must be one of us."

Robin smiled slightly. "He agreed to a modest salary only. He's not concerned with money. He gets by without owning a home or car and has just modest clothes. He considers himself to have zero net worth." She was describing the antithesis of a Ruc.

"He's homeless?" Tre asked bluntly.

Robin shrugged. "He lives at the project, in one of the units, but he doesn't own it. His home is simple and very refreshing. No oxygen system, so it takes some getting used to."

"How did you meet this person?" Amy asked, her curiosity clear.

"We met at a music festival. It was really crowded, and he offered to let me sit on his shoulders," Robin said, her face lighting up at the memory.

"How amazing!" Sara, quiet until now, said softly. Ever the romantic.

"He's a big guy," Leon added approvingly.

"Are you getting serious?" Amy probed, her tone that of an inquisitor.

"I'm not serious about anything right now except for work," Robin replied. Her response sounded rehearsed, like a shield. Best to change the subject.

"Leon, too bad you're going to be out next week. I was hoping you could help me with that instability in the test," I said, steering the conversation.

"It's important these kids don't mess it up. This stuff was installed before most of them were born. Someone has to keep an eye on them," Leon said, his voice tinged with a mix of pride and exasperation.

"I was thinking about that bulge in the curve and had some ideas I'd like to run by you," Robin said, switching to her technical voice.

"She's got some good ideas," Leon said, nodding. "She did some impressive work at Phlegraean."

"When you get free, come on down to Q headquarters. I'd like to see what you've got. Zen, as you've seen, lacks imagination," I said.

"Q? Like in James Bond?" Tre asked, grinning.

"Your dad is Q," Robin said with a chuckle. It was a flattering exaggeration. In truth, it was more like I inherited Q's office after a hostile takeover. Still, it sounded impressive.

Amy groaned. Leon chuckled. Tre and Sara looked like they were ready to accept it as fact.

Sara spoke up. "I have to go, sorry. It's Friday, and I missed the game for dinner, but there's a party I can't miss," Sara explained as she left the table. Dinner was over, except for dessert, which Sara wouldn't eat anyway. She wasn't one for sweets.

"Sure, honey. We were all 16 once - except for Leon. He's always been 100," I added.
Leon grumbled.

"Sara, help me with the dishes, please," Amy said.

"Oh, let me," Robin added.

"It's okay, it's my job. You're the guest. I have time," Sara said with assurance. Amy and Sara started clearing the table.

I looked at Robin and said, "That Colter Bay project was impressive. Your boyfriend must be quite the guy. But what's with the whole 'net worth is bad' philosophy?" I was genuinely curious about how someone could eschew net worth.

"He's a visionary," Robin said, her tone almost reverent. "For him, personal net worth is an impediment. Without money as a motivation, he can't be bribed or swayed by deals. It keeps his focus pure. Just think about what that means."

"He's probably an honest man," Leon added.

Tre, with his vivid imagination fueled by years of watching Bond movies, leaned in excitedly. "If you get married, then bad guys can kidnap you and make him do what they want," he said with glee.

Robin raised an eyebrow, a smirk tugging at her lips. "I guess I just won't get kidnapped," she quipped, her tone comically smug.

"Was he born here?" I asked. Wics almost always stayed in their home state, by law and restriction.

"Yes. He's been here his whole life, except for some years in the military. He doesn't seem to care about the rest of the world - just our little corner. I think he's going to be someone great...or be assassinated," Robin said, her voice turning somber.

"He sounds like an interesting fellow," I said, intrigued.

"You want to meet him? He's giving a presentation this week at the community center. I think you might find it intriguing. When was the last time you rubbed elbows with the proletariat?" Robin asked, her smile teasing.

"I'd be a little out of place," I admitted.

Robin's eyes sparkled with mischief. "I'll hold your hand if you're nervous. They won't bite - at least not at first," she teased.

I glanced toward the kitchen, relieved Amy hadn't heard her. She wouldn't have taken kindly to that kind of playful familiarity.

"Send me the details," I said, my curiosity piqued despite myself. The plight of the Wics was something I couldn't ignore. They outnumbered us more than nine to one, strong and angry. History was clear - civilizations that neglected their underclass never lasted long. I had no desire to end up as a head on a pike outside the community center.

Amy returned with dessert, her timing impeccable. "Real whipped cream for the adults, regular for the kid," she said with a wry smile.

Tre frowned. "How do you know I can't tell the difference?"

"Because you think ketchup is a food group," Sara quipped, earning a chorus of laughter as the evening softened into familiar rhythms.

* * *

After dessert, we moved to the study for drinks. Tre wandered off to play games with his friends, leaving just the adults. It was customary to offer brandy in the study, and it was a wonderful custom. As we settled into comfortable chairs and savored an excellent vintage, the topic of Wics surfaced again.

Amy turned to Robin. "What's your opinion of the one million, one vote system?" A few drinks always made Amy bolder.

Robin didn't flinch. "Do you want my real opinion or the party line?"

"Give it to me straight. I want to know what *you* think," Amy replied. Leon and I exchanged glances, letting the conversation play out.

"I have mixed feelings," Robin began, then paused. "It's troubling that so many people lack representation. But honestly, most of them also lack critical thinking skills. While the Voter Act seems to elevate the value of the individual above their rights, it does mean that those who qualify are often better equipped to make decisions than the average Wic." She hesitated before adding, "Then you have people like Victor, my boyfriend. He's brilliant, caring, and has a vision for the future. He should be a leader, but without the net worth, he can't even vote."

Amy leaned back, crossing her arms. "Did you see the news about Orlando? The Wics are burning down their own city - it's madness. What are they going to do when the fires go out and they can't buy groceries because they destroyed the stores?"

"I agree. People are desperate - it's a powder keg waiting to explode," Robin replied, her tone measured, though it seemed she was trying to win Amy over. It wasn't working.

"It all started with the goddamn robots," Leon exclaimed, slamming his glass down before taking a hearty swig of what should have been carefully sipped brandy. "What are people supposed to do for a living now? Farming's fully

34

automated, factories too - even the Meet we had tonight didn't need a single human touch.." He stopped, grumbling as he poured himself another generous refill.

Robin, leaning forward, broke the silence. "Amy, what's your take on the Freedom Act?" Robin asked, her tone bold.

Amy set her glass down. "It's practical. Instead of prisons or bankruptcy, people contribute through labor. It's a solution."

Robin leaned forward. "But what about abuses - like a young girl sold into servitude for her father's debts? What about when she's bought by someone who tortures her to death? She has no say - she's just a victim. And the one who does it? They pay a fine and walk away." Her voice rose slightly, the edge unmistakable.

"Now, that's an extreme case that rarely happens," I interjected, aiming to diffuse the tension. "Statistically, sure, anything can happen. But realistically, things like that don't happen often." It was true. Humanity had a dark side - given a large enough sample, you'd find the most horrifying and degrading behavior imaginable. It was just part of us.

"The best way to reduce the horror is to not watch the news," Leon grumbled, swirling his brandy. "Most of it is pure make-believe anyway."

Amy leaned forward, her expression unreadable. "Robin, you've been around these anarchists. Do they have any actual ideas?" she asked, her voice sharp. "Anarchist" had become a loaded term - shorthand for people many believed should be lined up against a wall and shot without trial.

Robin didn't flinch. "Victor isn't an anarchist; he's a realist," she replied evenly. "But honestly? I don't know if there are any real solutions." She paused, taking a measured sip of her drink before continuing. "People keep being born, and resources are getting stretched thinner every year. If it weren't for the orbital gardens, things would already be pretty grim."

"Our entire dinner came from the OFP," Amy noted, her tone carrying both pride and practicality.

"It's such an efficient system," I added, leaning into the marvel of it. "Shipping containers land just a few clicks from the consumer within hours of ordering. Nothing like it has ever existed." It truly was amazing.

"But it's unsustainable," Leon cut in, his voice tinged with familiar skepticism. "Sure, the OFP is predictable and controllable, but it's energy-intensive." He paused for another swig of brandy, then continued, "Think about the fuel cost to move those empty containers back into orbit. Where does that energy come from? Fossil fuels, they're still using methane for Christ's sake."

Leon had a point. For all his old-world quirks - like his smog-belching antique car - he at least made his own gasoline using captured carbon dioxide and sunlight. Even his hobby projects were carbon neutral. Leon walked the walk.

"If we can get to the point where we tap into unlimited geothermal energy, that problem gets significantly reduced," I said, my tone hopeful.

Leon raised a hand, glass in tow, and added, with a growing slur, "Amy, we made some advancements today that might - just might - be the answer." He swirled his drink thoughtfully. "It won't fix the fact that we've got too many people, but the energy problem? We might be close to solving that one."

"The test? Did that have anything to do with it?" Amy asked, her curiosity piqued.

"What if," I began, leaning forward for emphasis, "every power plant in the world - whether fossil fuel or nuclear - could tap into an endless source of energy? Completely free of emissions."

"That would solve the energy problem and halt further atmospheric degradation," Robin said, nodding. She took another sip of her drink before adding, "It sounds like the beginning of a solution." The room had grown quiet for a moment, as if we were all contemplating what that might mean.

"But naaah!" Robin suddenly exclaimed, breaking the silence with a grin.

"Yeah, naaah!" we all echoed, laughing. It was a punchline from a silly sitcom we'd all seen. Drunk people love to recycle sitcom punchlines, and this room was no exception.

Robin's Device chimed softly.

"With that bit of wisdom, I'll take my leave. I still have a date with Victor tonight," Robin said, standing with a graceful smile.

"You can stay here if you want," I blurted out without thinking.

Robin shook her head, amused. "I've already summoned a Pod," she replied politely.

"It was lovely having you tonight, Robin," Amy said, her hostess voice polished and warm. "Please make it a point to join us again. We truly enjoyed your company."

"Thank you," Robin replied with equal cordiality. "Amy, your home is absolutely beautiful." Her tone was genuine, but I knew Amy would have more to say later.

Moments later, the HomeBot announced, "Pod for Robin Coleman arriving."

"That's my ride. Thanks again for a wonderful evening," Robin said as she made her way to the door. Amy responded with the expected pleasantries, both women playing their parts perfectly.

Once Robin was gone, it was time to shuffle Leon into his guest room. He wasn't exactly unsteady, but another drink and he'd start waxing poetic about carburetors or sensor arrays, so I nudged him in the right direction. Amy excused herself for the night, leaving me alone with the lingering buzz from the evening.

I decided to swim it off. Thirty laps in the pool were just enough to clear my head and reset. Feeling lighter and steadier, I called it a night.

CHAPTER FOUR

Ride with Tre

"Oh, Daddy, time to wake up," Tre said in a sing-song voice.

"It's Saturday. I don't have to wake up." My brain felt like it had been replaced with a block of depleted uranium.

"You have to take me to my game in Colter Bay. I have to be there at noon."

"Why isn't your mother taking you?"

"She's with Sara. They're flying to Cheyenne. Didn't you hear her plane land?" Tre asked.

"Son, I doubt I'd have noticed a supervolcano." I slept like the dead after a few drinks.

"Mommy said you'd want this." Tre handed me a mask with a small aerosol bottle attached - affectionately known as The Tank.

"Oh, thank the Maker!" I exclaimed and took a deep huff on the mask. After ten seconds, I exhaled and waited for it to kick in.

"Feel better yet?" Tre asked.

"Yes, almost. One more on The Tank should do it." I took another deep breath with the mask. The aerosol delivered humanity's greatest modern miracle - a perfect cure for hangovers. One huff for a light party, two for a full-on bender. Within a minute, the hangover was gone, replaced by a lingering feeling of joy and warmth. I would have given up drinking altogether if not for The Tank.

"Mom seemed a bit groggy when she got up. She hit The Tank twice! You know she never does that," Tre added, his voice dripping with the gossip of the day.

"Okay, I'm up. I'll be ready at eleven - that'll get us there early," I replied, finally pulling myself out of bed.

* * *

The car was always the best place to talk to the kids. They were isolated in a box with me, and we had a rule about using Devices during car rides. Since Sara got her license, I hadn't had many of those moments with her. I missed them.

"Robin is hot!" Tre said, almost as we left the driveway. He wouldn't talk about girls in front of his mother or sister, but lately, he'd been really interested in the subject.

"Tre, she's old enough to be your mother."

"I'm old enough to appreciate a fine woman." Tre sat right next to her and got a close view. Boys his age are hyper-aware of females.

"Well, she's a fine woman now? That's respectable."

"And cute too. Did you notice she wasn't wearing a bra?"

"Jeekers Tre…" 12-year-old boys are infatuated with mammalian glands.

"I think we should change the subject from Robin's underwear." I added.

"I don't think she was wearing any." Tre kept it up.

"Let's just drop the underwear, okay?" I was up for a joke too.

"Ha, ha. She freaked out Mom with the boyfriend thing, didn't she?" Tre certainly understood what it meant.

"It did catch her by surprise. Me too, for that matter." I added.

"I like her. Invite her again, okay?" Tre asked.

We fell into a comfortable silence, watching the terrain blur past the windows for a minute.

"Do you remember the girl who punched Greg Choi after my birthday party? The one who got in trouble, Julia Rosales?" Tre's 12th birthday party ended with a splash. We had about a hundred kids, most of his classmates, and two of them had an altercation at the end of the party in the driveway.

"How could I forget? I'm glad we had the holo proving she was innocent." The incident was recorded in magnificent detail by our SecurityBot system, part of HomeBot.

"She's a Wic on scholarship," Tre continued after a pause, clearly building up to something.

"Yes, she's also some sort of brainiac, right?" I said, piecing together the memory. Now I remembered her clearly - bright, composed, and quiet.

"Smartest kid in the class. She's as smart as Sara, maybe smarter," Tre said, laying it on thick.

"What are you getting at?" I asked, sensing his angle.

"We sit together at lunch a lot. She's a lot like Robin, except, you know, the Wic thing."

"It's good for you to know all kinds of people," I said neutrally, though I could already see where this was going.

"I'd like to invite her over," Tre said, his tone shifting to one of pleading.

"When you say 'like her,' do you mean in the biblical way?" I asked, teasing just a bit too much.

"Jeez, Dad, I just want to have her over, you know, as a friend." He groaned, visibly regretting bringing it up.

"I see. You want to get her in the pool so you can see what she really looks like," I said, grinning as I prodded him further.

"I shouldn't have brought it up," Tre muttered, staring out the window in mock exasperation.

"I think it's fine," I said, dialing back the teasing. "That means her parents will have to drive her over. That could be an issue if they're weird about us." Wics and Rucs rarely mingled socially; there were too many unspoken rules and judgments that often complicated things.

"I don't know anything about her parents," Tre admitted.

"It's okay with me, and I'm sure it'll be fine with your mother. Talk to this girl - Julia Rosales, is it? See if she wants to come over for a play date," I said, my tone light.

"It's not a play date," Tre grumbled.

"I get it. I hope she can swim, though," I said, leaning into a practical concern. It was rare for Wics to know how to swim, given the stark class divide in access to certain recreational activities.

Tre didn't respond, but the idea seemed to settle well enough. We lapsed into a comfortable silence for a while, the car humming along the road as we both turned our thoughts inward. The mix of humor, teasing, and a touch of seriousness left me feeling that these were the moments that counted.

"Dad, how do you know if you're in love?" Tre asked, his voice carrying an earnest curiosity. My son was starting to grow into a man.

"Gee, I don't know," I said, caught off guard. "It's one of those things where you just know - you are or you aren't."

"How can you tell?" Tre pressed.

"Is this about that girl?" I teased, raising an eyebrow.

"Well, not really. I'm just curious," he said, his tone cautious.

"Someone once said the test for love is whether you'd be willing to die for them," I replied, trying to recall where I'd heard it. "Not sure who said it, but it stuck with me."

"That's pretty extreme, isn't it?" Tre countered, skeptical.

"Maybe, but think about it this way: imagine the person you love is in a building that's on fire. You don't know if they're safe. If you run into the building, you might die, but you might save them. On the other hand, if you call the fire department and wait, they're likely to die, but you'll live."

41

Tre frowned, mulling it over. "Okay, I get the scenario. How does love play into it?"

"The choice boils down to this: can you live without them, or would you rather risk everything to try and save them?" I explained, trying to simplify it.

"That's pretty morbid. Is love really that strong?" he asked, his tone serious.

"It can be. If you or Sara were in a burning building, I wouldn't hesitate. I'd run in to save you, even at the cost of my own life. I know that without a doubt. I'd rather die trying than live knowing I didn't," I said, feeling the weight of my own words as they left my mouth.

Tre was silent for a moment, absorbing what I'd said. Then he asked, "What about Mom? You said me and Sara - you didn't mention her." His sharpness caught me off guard.

"Well," I began cautiously, "with Mom, I'd have to think about you two. What would happen to you if you became orphans? Having kids changes the equation."

"You never had to make a choice," Tre said thoughtfully.

"I've never faced the burning building scenario," I replied. "Not yet, anyway."

"No, I mean about dating. You never had to make a choice - your choice was made for you," Tre clarified. My wife and I had an arranged marriage, matched by an algorithm.

"That's true," I admitted. "I might not be the best person to ask for dating advice. Your mother is the only person I've ever dated."

"You knew her even before high school. You had a built-in girlfriend," Tre said, almost enviously.

"We never questioned our destiny," I said with a smile. "I was sure we'd end up together even when we were kids. Your mom felt the same way. It wasn't complicated for us - it just worked."

"Why didn't you do that with us?" Tre asked, leaning forward slightly. His question hit deeper than I expected.

I looked at Tre and said, "Your mother and I made a different choice for you and Sara. We wanted you to have the freedom to find love your own way."

"Mom always agrees with you," Tre countered, his voice tinged with rare criticism. "She could say something, you disagree, and then she changes her mind in an instant. I don't know if I like that."

"She's a traditional woman," I replied, though I could feel the inadequacy of my explanation.

"Sara isn't like Mom. She has her own ideas, and she won't change her mind just because a boy tells her to," Tre said, his tone matter-of-fact.

He wasn't wrong. "Sara is a firecracker," I agreed. She was headstrong and wouldn't be a pushover like her mother - an admirable and sometimes challenging trait.

"I'll bet Robin is more like Sara than Mom," Tre said with a grin.

He'd probably win that bet. "I just met her yesterday," I said cautiously. "So, I'm not in a position to say. But Leon seems to like her, both personally and professionally. He even let her drive his beast. He's never done that with any other assistant."

"Do you think Uncle Leon has the hots for Robin?" Tre asked, his 12-year-old curiosity unfiltered.

"It's pretty easy to tell if someone has a romantic interest," I began.

Tre interrupted with a grin, "You mean the hots."

I chuckled. "Romantic interest, yes. If Leon felt that way about Robin, I think I'd have noticed. But the way he looks at her? It's like she's another engineer."

"I think I'd look at Robin a little differently if I was Leon," Tre said matter-of-factly.

"You've got more experience than me in that department," I admitted. It was true - I'd never had any romantic interest in anyone other than his mother.

"Julia's pretty," Tre said thoughtfully. "She's strong too, and can defend herself, and not just by beating them up. For some reason, I like that. The other girls are just boring - always the same."

"You've got time to figure it out," I said, glancing over at him. "We're not going anywhere, and neither is she."

"They could move," Tre suggested.

"Getting a permit would be tough," I said. "That incident where she punched the kid caused blowback on her dad. If it weren't for that holo proving she didn't start it, Julia or one of her parents could've ended up as an indentured servant for ten years. That's on their record now, and it'll likely keep them from being able to move."

"The system is so unfair," Tre said, his voice rising with frustration. "We learned about it last year, and again this year. Every time, the Elder says it's better than prison, and that it's rare for indentured servants to be harmed or killed."

"Making all punishments equal, like sins under God, caused the crime rate to plummet," I explained. "It used to be that people couldn't walk down the street at night for fear of being robbed or killed. Now, you can go anywhere, anytime, without worrying about crime."

"But when you go to the store, you see workers with collars - or some woman with sad eyes shopping with a collar. They're all around us," Tre said passionately. "If they're criminals, shouldn't they be kept away from us?"

"The crime rate proves the system works," I replied, though I could feel his dissatisfaction.

"But what about our people? If they commit a crime, it's just a fine, and it's all kept quiet. How is that fair?" Tre's question hit harder than I expected.

"Any of those people with collars could have paid the fine and been free," I said, trying to sound reasonable. "They just didn't have the resources. Having resources means you're valuable to society. People who are valuable to society deserve preferential treatment. It might not seem fair at first glance, but when taken as a whole, it works." Even as I said it, the words sounded hollow, like I was reciting a justification I didn't fully believe.

"The fine is set so high that only one of us could pay it," Tre countered, his voice steady but intense. "The system is rigged against the Wics."

I couldn't argue with that, but I didn't say it aloud. Instead, I fell back on an uncomfortable truth. "Their ancestors voted to ratify the New Constitution," I said. "They brought it on themselves. If you dig back to the original

Constitution, the system worked in much the same way - except it was deeply corrupt. The wealthy or elite, as we'd have been called in the old days, made backroom deals with politicians and judges. Through favors and flattery, they manipulated the system for their own purposes, often to the detriment of the people those politicians were supposed to serve." American history was one of Leon's favorite topics, and naturally, mine as well.

"Yeah, we get that in school," Tre replied, his tone skeptical.

"What they probably don't teach is that when wealthy people got into trouble - say, driving off a bridge drunk and killing someone - they'd get away with it. Justice has always favored those with resources. The New Constitution just codifies it into law: less corruption, more honest representation."

"Is that really true, or did you make that up?" Tre asked, his curiosity cutting through the cynicism.

"It's a famous case from 1969. Mary Jo Kopechne was the victim's name," I said. "A song was even written about it - it's catchy, a real brain worm. The man who killed her was from a famous, wealthy family, and he got off, even though he was drunk and left her to drown."

Tre wrinkled his nose. "Okay, I get it. But still - if a hungry Wic steals a loaf of bread, they face ten years as a slave. How is that fair?"

"Does he steal the bread?" I countered.

"Does his family starve if he doesn't?" Tre shot back, his voice rising.

"I agree the system has shortcomings," I admitted, trying to stay calm. "But the idea of instant justice is a powerful deterrent. Sometimes, yes, the wrong people end up being punished. But overall, it's a better system than what came before."

"Would you still say that if you were a Wic?" Tre asked, his eyes narrowing.

"If they follow the law, they enjoy low crime rates like we do," I offered, though I heard the hollow note in my voice.

Tre leaned back. "I'll ask Julia. She lives with that reality every day."

"I'd be curious what she has to say," I admitted.

"Now arriving at Colter Bay St. Mary's High School gym, entrance B," the car announced in its pleasant, neutral voice.

"Dad, we're playing an easy team today, so the coach might let me play. Do you have time to watch?" Tre asked, his tone carrying a hint of hope.

"Sure, but you know how I am around people," I replied, a note of warning in my voice.

"If they put me in, it'll be in the first quarter. After that, you can leave," Tre said, pausing as we pulled into the parking lot.

He added quickly, "I'm getting a ride home with Daniel. His dad's staying to watch the whole game."

"I can stay for the whole game if you want," I offered, sensing his hesitance.

"That's okay. Daniel's dad is taking us out to eat after," Tre replied, knowing full well my lack of enthusiasm for sports.

I reached over and rested a hand on his shoulder. "Tre, you know I think it's unfair the coach plays by status and not by talent," I said, trying to convey care.

Tre responded almost immediately, "If we just had more votes, I could play more."

"Tre, you know we don't talk like that," I said firmly, taking my hand off his shoulder. I softened my tone as I continued, "When I was your age, I had the same problem. We just barely made the grade, if you know what I mean."

Tre looked at me, a hint of frustration in his eyes. "I should've picked flying instead of sports," he muttered, staring down at his hands. "At least I'd be free..."

"You could still switch if you'd like," I said gently. "You're not too old."

Tre sighed heavily. "It's too late. All my friends are on the sports path, and you know I'd have to switch groups. It'd be weird."

"Yeah, and that's why I took the flying route. I suffer incompetence poorly - it's a family trait, I'm afraid," I replied with a wry smile, hoping to lighten the mood.

Tre turned to me, anger flashing in his eyes. "The goddamn thing I hate is that I'm better than all of them put together. I've never dropped a ball. Not once."

* * *

We stepped out of the car and walked into the gymnasium. It was an impressive structure - spacious enough to host league-level games, with opulent finishes and a staff of both human and robotic attendants ensuring everything ran smoothly.

As we entered, Tre's coach spotted us. Tre gave me a quick wave. "Hey, Dad, Coach Wigan wants to talk to you. I've got to dress out. See you back home, bye!" Before I could reply, he was off, running to join his teammates.

I adjusted my jacket and approached the coach. "Coach Wigan, what's up?" I said, keeping my tone as friendly as possible.

Coach Wigan, always impeccable in his tailored coach's uniform, greeted me with a broad smile. "Frank! Great to see you. It's been a while."

I reached out to shake his hand. "You know, busy at the plant. Sorry I haven't been around."

"It must be something, working up there. I hear you're invited to the big Reveal. Wish I could go," he said, his tone tinged with envy.

"I'm Support - we're not invited," I replied, offering my standard line.

Wigan's eyebrows lifted in surprise. "Really? I thought you were some kind of genius up there, like Greg Osborne's dad."

I decided to play along. "Nah, I mostly clean things and mop around the reactors. You know, jobs too dangerous for robots."

Wigan blinked, his face momentarily blank. Then a light dawned in his eyes. "You're joking! You had me going there for a second."

We both laughed. Mine was entirely fabricated, but Wigan's was genuine - he actually seemed impressed.

"Did you need something, Coach?" I asked, keeping my tone neutral but curious.

"Oh, ya," he said eagerly, leaning slightly forward. "I wanted to talk to you about Tre."

"Go ahead," I replied, nodding for him to continue.

"Your son has the most uncanny ability to catch a ball. I've never seen anything like it in my life. He's literally never missed or dropped a ball he could even remotely get his hands on," the coach said, his voice brimming with enthusiasm. He paused, clearly expecting a reaction.

"So, you're going to play him more?" I asked, cutting straight to the point.

The coach's demeanor shifted slightly. Breaking eye contact, he sighed. "You know I can't do that. The roster is selected by the Agent. I just play the roster. You should know how it works - you went through the same system." His tone carried an air of unnecessary condescension, as if he felt the need to explain the obvious.

"I went the flying route," I said, keeping my voice dry but measured. My expression stayed deliberately neutral.

"Ya, like your daughter," he said, his tone shifting uncomfortably. "I wish she was playing for me. I'd find a way to get her on the roster, if you know what I mean," he added, his words tinged with an inappropriate edge.

I thought about punching him, but that would only cause a scandal - and Amy hated scandals. Instead, I forced myself to keep things professional.

"Did you want to talk to me about Tre?" I asked, steering him back on track.

Coach Wigan leaned back casually, as though he were showing off a new car. "Ya, I mean, sports isn't where your son belongs. He's military material - officer, command rank at least. Your son has a real future in the military. Any branch."

I kept my expression neutral. "That's interesting, Coach Wigan. I'll mention it to my wife."

Wigan's brow furrowed slightly, irritated by my lack of enthusiasm. "It's the best chance for him to really move up. He wants to go to space, right? The military is the way to get there," he said, his tone shifting into that of a salesman pushing a deal.

"We own a villa on Avalon. He can live in space when he graduates," I replied smugly, enjoying the flicker of surprise that crossed his face.

"You own a villa? Wow." He paused, then added with transparent eagerness, "Do you think the wife and I could stay there sometime?"

Ignoring his attempt to angle for a favor, I redirected. "Is Tre going to play today? In the first quarter?"

Coach Wigan hesitated, then seemed to realize the right answer. "We're going to slaughter these boys, so we'll rest the top players. I think your son is in the starting lineup."

I allowed a satisfied smile to show. "That's great. I'll go watch the first quarter," I said and walked off without waiting for a response.

As I headed toward the gym, I thought, "So much for the Agent making the roster. Typical corrupt fool. Tre should have chosen flying."

* * *

I walked over to the parents' area, doing my best to stay out of the way. The game was about to start when a woman approached, her expression a mix of recognition and curiosity. The kind of look that said, I know you, though I didn't recognize her at all.

"Hi! Haven't seen you here in a while," she said, extending her hand with a practiced smile.

"Yeah, I've been busy at the plant," I replied mechanically, shaking her hand. My tone was polite but disengaged. She had the hand of a dead fish, moist, cold, and limp.

Her eyes lit up with a spark of hope. "Have you been invited?" she asked, leaning in slightly.

"No, I'm in Support. We're not invited," I answered, falling into the same rehearsed response I'd given a dozen times before. I thought "Jeekers, I should just paint it on my forehead."

"Oh, my husband is, you know," she said, her tone turning smug. "He's invited to everything."

I kept my expression neutral. "Is your son on the roster?" I asked, hoping to shift the conversation and maybe jog my memory of who this annoying creature was.

"Of course! He's always on the roster," she said with an air of superiority. She pulled out her Device, swiping and scrolling until her face shifted in surprise. "Wait - Tre is playing? That's unusual. And he's starting, too?"

I forced myself to keep my tone even. "I'm not really a sports person," I said, feigning indifference, though the temptation to say, "Ya, Coach Wigan let him play after he angled for a stay at my villa.", was almost irresistible.

The silence grew awkward, but she didn't move away, her nearness like a heat source I couldn't escape - somewhere around 500 K.

The game started, but I didn't pay much attention until Tre took the field. He stood out immediately - by far the best-looking boy out there. Even among the older players, his movements were purposeful, graceful, far beyond his years.

The woman beside me broke the silence. "Tre sure has filled out this past year," she said.

Something about the way she said it made me uncomfortable.

"He eats more than the rest of us combined," I replied, keeping it light.

She let out a controlled sigh. "Same with my boy. Our KitchenBot can barely keep up."

My pupils widened at the mention of KitchenBot - my favorite non-work topic. "Have you heard about the new Teen option for KitchenBot?" I asked, unable to hide my excitement.

Her face lit up like I'd just revealed a state secret. "No! What is it?" she asked eagerly.

I gushed, "The new Teen upgrade increases the volume KitchenBot can make at once and balances the nutrition so they eat right no matter what they order."

She clasped her hands together, practically glowing with joy. "I need that!" she exclaimed.

I slipped into my HomeBot nerd voice. "You know I work at the YSP, and because I'm in Engineering, we get early releases of HomeBot upgrades - for testing, of course."

Her eyes widened with excitement, almost apoplectic. "When are they going to release it?"

I leaned in slightly, careful not to invade her personal space. "I really shouldn't tell you - it's a secret."

Before she could press further, I spotted Tre moving into position. "Look, Tre's going after a tough one," I said, redirecting her attention.

She turned, just as animated. "He never misses!" she shrieked, her voice almost a cheer.

Tre caught the ball effortlessly, making it look like second nature.

The woman turned back to me, her face alight with admiration. "He's really something. I've seen him running full speed, just reaching back to catch it - without even looking."

I felt a swell of pride. "I think it runs in the family."

She suddenly grew serious, her brow furrowing. "How does he do that? Bionic implants?"

I laughed, shaking my head. "That's all Tre."

The horn sounded, signaling the end of the quarter.

I began walking away from the nameless woman, who called after me, "What about the upgrade?"

"I'll message you," I replied over my shoulder, not breaking stride.

I waved to the coach as I left. He responded with an exaggerated wave, his enthusiasm almost comical. Corrupt, I thought, shaking my head.

I'd attended a few of Tre's games, but he knew I found them painfully boring unless he was on the field. Amy, on the other hand, loved the games - more for parental networking than the sport itself.

CHAPTER FIVE

Sara's Solo

The day of Sara's solo arrived with graciously good weather: clear skies, light winds, and a forecast calling for changes later in the day as a cold front moved through.

I walked into the kitchen to find Sara finishing breakfast.

"Good morning!" I said, adding a cheerful flair.

"Good morning, my favorite daddy," she said with a small smile.

I leaned over and kissed her on the top of the head. "Thank you, sweetie. What's the schedule for this afternoon?"

"Six of us are soloing today. Each candidate takes about 20 to 30 minutes, and then there's a small ceremony afterward," she explained.

"Isn't it funny," I said, "how the FAA insists a human oversee your flight, even though the on-board Agent is perfectly qualified and doesn't have moods or biases?"

"Bureaucracy at its finest," Sara replied, rolling her eyes. "At least he won't make me pray first."

I chuckled. "The process hasn't changed a bit. Might even be the same DE." Sara didn't laugh.

"After the ceremony, we're going to an early dinner with my friend Zuri Osborne and her parents. Will that be okay?" Sara asked, her tone careful, knowing how I felt about mingling with other parents.

"Is she related to Azizi Osborne?" I asked, the name jogging a memory.

"That's her dad. Do you know him?"

"He worked at Plant 1 for years before moving to Plant 2. I don't see him much now, but he used to eat lunch with Leon and me once in a while. He's fine."

"So you're okay with dinner?" Sara pressed, double-checking.

"Yes, I can handle Azizi," I assured her.

Just then, Amy walked into the kitchen. "All good for the flight?" she asked.

"Yes, and Dad's coming to dinner," Sara said, pushing her empty plate aside.

"I'm glad you ate already," Amy replied, her tone as cheerful as ever. "Let's head out in twenty minutes. The airport's a half-hour drive."

"What's the story with your brother?" I asked.

"He's coming," Sara said, with a hint of amusement. "I think he's secretly interested, but since he's gone the sports route, he can't admit it. You know how dumb 12-year-olds are."

"Sports and flying are both good for college," Amy chimed in. Some colleges valued sports more, but they were typically the big-name schools with famous teams. Kids who took the flying route usually leaned more technical, and their school choices reflected that.

* * *

On the way, Sara rattled off her checklists and regulations, and Tre checked her work. the two working seamlessly as a team.

"Arriving Yellowstone Airport," the car announced. The airport was mostly for storage, as modern craft can land on a ten-meter pad.

"Park next to Zuri's car," Sara instructed.

Once we stopped, Sara was out of the car in a flash. She waved once before dashing across the tarmac, her excitement evident. We followed at a more relaxed pace.

By the time we caught up, Sara was standing with a beaming young lady exuding confidence and teenage swagger.

"Mom, Dad, this is Zuri. She's soloing today too," Sara said, her tone brimming with pride. They were like two peas in a pod.

"I wish you the best!" Amy said warmly.

"You'll do great," I added.

"Don't crash like my sister," Tre chimed in, ever the wise guy.

"Tre, have some respect," Amy said, mildly scolding him.

"Thanks," Zuri replied with a nervous smile. "Yeah, I'm a bit nervous, but ready."

"Frank, glad to see you again. Been a while," Azizi said, extending his hand. He was an electrical engineer specializing in communication systems and had worked in the control division at Plant 1 before being promoted to the Specials division at Plant 2 two years ago. He was brilliant, with several key patents to his name.

"Great seeing you again. We missed you at the table," I replied, shaking his hand.

"Are you ready?" Azizi asked Sara.

"I hope so. I don't know who the DE is today. Do you know anything about him?" she asked nervously.

"Isn't he the one who flunked the kid for touching his nose on final?" Zuri added, her confidence briefly flickering.

"Don't worry. He's just here to observe. The Instructor Agent already signed you off. You'll do fine," I reassured her.

"At least the DE isn't late - that's a good sign," Amy said optimistically.

"All candidates, please assemble," the DE announced. We had to stay behind the safety line for the remainder of the proficiency tests. The DE began with a random oral exam to assess each student's knowledge before moving on to the practical flying portion. Since it was alphabetical, Sara was last.

For the first hour, Amy and I kept to ourselves, as did the other parents. Nervous energy filled the air - some parents handled it better than others. Once the flying portion started, we instinctively gathered closer, a shared anxiety pulling us together. After the first student finished and stepped out of the aircraft with a triumphant thumbs-up, the tension lifted. At least the DE wasn't being overly harsh.

Amy had wandered off to chat with the other parents, leaving just Tre and myself.

* * *

Azizi walked over. "Azizi, this is Tre, my son," I said, gesturing to the boy standing beside me.

Tre extended his hand confidently. Azizi took it and said, "Tre, nice to finally meet you. I heard a lot about you when I worked at your dad's plant."

Tre responded with a polite "Thank you, sir," his expression seemed distant and his eyes focused on the field.

Azizi turned back to me. "Frank, we made an important development two years ago, and I can finally talk about it with people in the company."

"Tre, please go find your mother," I said, conscious of the security protocols. Tre didn't have any clearances, and this conversation seemed to be heading into classified territory.

Azizi raised a hand in reassurance. "No, it's okay for Tre to hear this, as long as he promises to keep it to himself until after the Reveal." His tone was cautious but firm.

"I can keep a secret. I won't say anything," Tre added, his voice serious. He was trustworthy, and Azizi seemed to pick up on that.

Azizi nodded, his tone shifting to one of anticipation. "Alright. This is going to be big news. You know that limitation of light speed?"

"You mean that nothing travels faster than light, right?" Tre asked, eager to demonstrate his understanding of the subject. He was sharp for his age and loved anything related to science.

"Yes, and we found a way around it," Azizi said with a touch of pride. "And after the Reveal, the whole world will know, too."

I raised an eyebrow. "Hold on, are you talking about warp drive like in the movies?"

Azizi shook his head, his excitement building. "No, not in space travel. I'm talking about communications - and much more."

"The time lag in communications?" Tre interjected. "Like when you talk to someone on the moon, and it takes a couple of seconds for them to reply? That's so annoying." He had firsthand experience with this when one of his friends had vacationed at Lunar Disney. Tre had been frustrated by the lag in their calls.

"Exactly," Azizi said, his voice brimming with confidence. "Zero lag. Instantaneous communication between two points. Completely secure, untappable, incorruptible - impossible to intercept or spoof."

"That sounds almost too good to be true," I remarked, leaning into my engineering instincts. "How close are you to a practical implementation?"

"We have a production device in the works right now. You know how the Reveal is going to be watched by about 30,000 people remotely?" Azizi leaned in, his excitement palpable. "That's how they'll watch - on our special terminals using this zero-lag communications technology. They'll offer two-way holographic data transmission in real time."

I noticed the veins in his temples throbbing as he spoke. Azizi's passion for his work was unmistakable.

"What's the principle?" I asked, my engineering instincts kicking in.

"I don't want to dive into the math right now," Azizi said, his tone easing. "I just submitted the paper for peer review on Friday. It's been two years in the making, and soon it'll be public. Zen wants us to wait until the Reveal - he has a sense of showmanship." He exhaled, his earlier fervor settling into calm anticipation.

I couldn't hold back my next question. "What's the power requirement for this kind of system?"

"Surprisingly low," Azizi replied with a grin. "The terminals we've built for the Reveal run on a battery smaller than the one in your Device, and they can last for months without recharging. We call it IQL or Instantaneous Quantum Link."

"This is sounding crazy," I said, my enthusiasm as an engineer breaking through.

Azizi nodded, his excitement rekindling. "It's groundbreaking - this will change everything."

Azizi's wife hurried up to us, her expression animated. I realized I still didn't know her name.

"Zuri's getting ready," she announced.

* * *

We moved closer to the security line for a better view.
"She's doing the preflight walkaround now," Tre observed, his tone betraying his interest. For all his teasing of Sara, it was clear he found flying fascinating.

Tre's path had been decided early, largely due to his coach, who strongly urged us to keep him on the sports track.

"Now she's moving on to the preflight checks in the cockpit," Tre continued, his eyes glued to Zuri's methodical movements.

The rotors started spinning. "So far, she hasn't flunked out," Tre said with a smirk.

We watched as Zuri took off and disappeared from view, heading toward the practice area for maneuvers.

"So far, so good. Looks like a perfect takeoff," I said, trying to maintain optimism. I noticed Sara standing nearby, shading her eyes with her hand as she strained to follow her friend's progress. In that moment, she looked so grown up.

"I went the sports route. This is all new to me," Azizi admitted.

"It's perfectly safe. Nothing to worry about. The DE is onboard, and nothing bad can happen," I reassured him.

Tre, always eager to share some trivia, added, "Three years ago, a trainer just like Zuri's struck a large bird and dropped 1,000 meters before recovering."

Amy cut in firmly, "Nobody was injured during that flight, Tre. Try to behave, please."

Tre didn't miss a beat. "I see them. They'll be on the ground in a moment."

We watched as the trainer came in for a perfect landing. A moment later, the DE stepped out of the active area and gave a thumbs-up.

"She's a go!" Tre exclaimed, clearly excited.

Moments later, the craft rose from the ground for the next phase of the test. Tre provided his usual running commentary. "She's got to take off, circle the field, and land - three times."

Zuri flew a standard pattern and came back into view. "She's on final approach now," Tre noted. We watched as she executed a textbook landing, waited a moment, and took off again. She repeated the maneuver flawlessly twice more, completing her flight with precision.

As Zuri stepped out of the machine, The DE approached her and shared the good news. "She passed! Thumbs up!" Tre announced, his excitement palpable.

Most of the other parents had grown bored with the process and drifted to the parking lot for refreshments. Azizi and his wife stayed with us. Zuri's craft took off and Sara's preferred trainer took its place. Now it was Sara's turn.

Sara's flight followed the same procedure as the others. When it was her time to fly solo, my heart started racing. I always got excessively nervous when Sara was in the spotlight.

"She's taking off!" Tre exclaimed.

Her takeoff was textbook, and we watched as she circled the field for her first landing. I almost swallowed my tongue as she approached the runway.

"She's nice and stable on approach," I muttered, barely aware I'd spoken.

"Yes! Perfect landing," I said, exhaling in relief.

"That's one. She can still crash," Tre added with his usual dry humor.

Another flawless takeoff, another smooth landing.

"That's two," Tre said, his excitement dimming as he got used to the routine.

On the third takeoff, something didn't look right. At about 300 meters altitude, I noticed debris flying off the rear of the aircraft, and it became unstable.

"Something's not right," I said loudly, already moving toward the security line.

Amy gasped, "Oh God!" Her voice cracked with fear.

Tre stood frozen, silent as death.

The plane lurched to the right, banking sharply at 90 degrees. My heart sank.

"The plane will recover automatically," I said, clinging to hope. Sure enough, the attitude leveled, but the plane began to sink rapidly, decelerating just before impact.

"She autorotated it in," I said, almost in disbelief, then took off running toward the downed plane. Smoke billowed from the shattered cockpit windshield, a sight that stopped my heart. Horrific possibilities raced through my mind as I sprinted with everything I had.

Behind me, Amy screamed Sara's name, her voice raw with terror. Tre, faster than either of us, was already several meters ahead.

Just then, the cockpit door popped open, and Sara scrambled out, coughing through the smoke, her hands angrily gesturing at the crashed trainer as if to chastise it for failing her.

"She's out!" I yelled, relief washing over me in an overwhelming wave.

The DE reached the wreckage first, pulling a medical scanner from his kit and running it over her.

Amy caught up with me moments later, pushing past to grab Sara, pulling her into a fierce, protective hug. "Oh my God, Sara!" she sobbed, her voice shaking.

Sara hugged her back tightly, her coughs punctuating the embrace, but her strength was reassuring.

"What kind of school are you running here?" Amy shouted at the DE, her voice shaking with rage.

"Sara, are you okay? Are you hurt? Tre, call Emergency now," I barked, my voice tight with urgency.

"No, don't. I'm okay," Sara croaked through another cough. "I swallowed some smoke, but it's nothing. I'm fine." Sara's hands trembled slightly even as she tried to brush off the soot.

The DE held up his scanner, his tone calm but firm. "She's okay - just a scare. No injuries detected; she scans green."

Sara coughed again, her face darkened with soot. Amy, still clutching her fiercely, rounded on the DE, her fury undimmed. "Don't you maintain these machines?"

"I'm sorry, ma'am," the DE started, his voice placating.

"Don't you 'ma'am' me! You know damn well what my name is!" Amy snapped, her anger cutting through the tension like a blade.

"Amy, calm down," I interjected, trying to defuse the situation. "It's not his fault. He's just the DE. The school owns the trainers."

The DE nodded, his face pale and strained. "I apologize, Mrs. Waverly. I meant no disrespect."

As a Wic, he knew the weight of his misstep - familiars like "ma'am" were forbidden, and he had overstepped in the worst possible moment.

"Oh, for Christ's sake. It's never anyone's fault, is it?" Amy snapped, her voice cutting through the chaos.

"What happened?" I asked Sara, as Amy finally loosened her death grip.

"The damn thing had a complete system failure. All I had was manual controls. No instruments, no power," Sara said, her voice thick with disgust.

"You landed it?" the DE asked incredulously, his disbelief evident.

"The Instructor Agent died. I recovered the attitude and autorotated. Lucky I had enough altitude when it all went to hell," Sara said, her tone steady despite the cough in her throat.

The DE tapped furiously on his device, confirming the data. "You were the sole pilot for 22 seconds," he announced, his tone a mix of astonishment and respect. "This is unheard of. I've never seen a failure like this."

He looked back at Sara. "The data shows you regained control immediately after the failure. Your reflexes and judgment are extraordinary." He paused, then added, "That's on the record."

"Did I pass?" Sara asked, her expression unreadable.

"Well," the DE began cautiously, "technically, you failed to complete the field circuit on the third attempt. But the fact that you piloted the aircraft to a safe landing during a catastrophic failure gives me discretion." He smiled slightly and raised a thumb. "Yes, you passed."

We all cheered, and Sara raised her right fist in an uncharacteristic sign of defiance. I noticed the other parents were also jumping up and down; Sara certainly gave them a good show.

Just then, we heard the fire department sirens, and their Firebots rolled in to handle the now blazing wreckage.

"You damn well better pass her after she saved your - you know what," Amy growled. "If she had been hurt, I would've pressed charges." Her voice left no room for doubt - serious words in a world where Wics rarely walked away unscathed when a Ruc was injured.

"Amy, are we on the hook for destroying the trainer?" I asked, trying to ease the tension.

"Catastrophic failure is their problem, Dad," Sara interjected, coughing lightly as Amy started cleaning her face with her always-ready emergency kit.

* * *

Zuri and her family hesitated at the security line but quickly crossed it when they saw us approaching, violating protocol.

"Are you okay?" Zuri asked, her face etched with concern as she ran up to us.

They embraced - a rare sight for Rucs, but in a situation like this, entirely acceptable.

"Yes, yes! And I passed," Sara exclaimed, her voice a mix of relief and triumph.

"I almost had a kitten when you went sideways," Zuri said, her nerves still evident.

"Me too. I knew I was going to crash. Everything just went dead," Sara replied, still processing the experience.

"I would've died," Zuri admitted, shaking her head.

"No, you wouldn't. You'd have done the same as me," Sara countered.

"I suck at autorotation," Zuri confessed with a sheepish grin.

"Everyone, back behind the flight line!" the DE called out, his tone firm. "We can't have people in the active area. Move along, please. Let's wrap this up. I have a ton of red tape to deal with because of this crash. Thank God nobody was hurt."

* * *

After the ceremony and the issuing of solo certificates, we walked back to the car. Just before getting in, Sara suddenly leaned over and threw up. We were the only witnesses, but she still looked mortified.

"Sorry, I had to toss," she said sheepishly, wiping her mouth with the napkin Amy handed her.

"Perfectly understandable," I reassured her. "The important thing is you held it together when it counted. That's real guts, girl."

Amy, still shaken, sighed deeply. "I almost died when your plane hit the ground," she admitted, her voice trembling slightly. Then, after a pause, she added, "Flying is supposed to be safer than sports."

"I managed to land it with only 2g's," Sara said proudly, a hint of defiance in her tone as she wiped her face.

"I knew you were going to crash. Good job on the save. I knew you could do it," Tre said triumphantly, clearly proud of his sister.

"Maybe you can be a fortune teller," Sara retorted sarcastically, her wit intact despite the ordeal.

"I'm hungry! Let's go," Tre declared. As usual, his appetite was insatiable.

I looked at Sara, and she looked at me. "Would you rather go home?"

She just scoffed, dismissing me with a wave.

* * *

We left the airport and joined Zuri and her family at a popular restaurant for a celebratory dinner. Restaurants differentiated themselves primarily by atmosphere since food quality was nearly uniform everywhere. This particular spot featured serene private rooms with ServiceBots managing everything. The only humans involved were the stewards, who greeted guests at the door and guided them to their dining areas. The rest was entirely automated.

As we followed the steward to our room, Tre leaned close and muttered, "Did you notice the stewards are all slaves?"

"They seem happy," I replied in a low voice, not wanting to engage the topic further.

"They'd probably get zapped with their collar if they weren't," Tre added with a touch of defiance.

Amy, overhearing, gave him a firm look. "Let's not dwell on the plight of others right now," she said. In public, we adhered to the rules: always treat those beneath us with respect and dignity, at least outwardly.

When we reached our private room, Amy turned to Sara. "Sara, please seat us," she suggested. It was a habit we maintained - planning seating in advance to ensure everyone sat where they needed to, avoiding any awkward moments.

Sara took charge with ease, directing the men to one end of the table and the women to the other. It was a subtle but effective way to encourage the flow of conversation and maintain harmony during the meal.

We toasted to Sara's harrowing flight and Zuri's success. The fully automated service at this place was superb. The ServerBot stood ready in the corner, responding instantly to the slightest raised finger. I had a preference for automated restaurants - it eliminated the human errors and awkwardness of traditional service. Still, there was a lingering sadness in knowing how many human jobs were replaced by machines. But that's just the way things are.

During a lull in the conversation, Tre leaned toward me, his voice barely above a whisper. "Dad, about teasing Sara earlier... I feel bad. I shouldn't have joked about crashing."

I studied his earnest expression. "I get it," I said quietly. "But I'm not the one you owe an apology to, am I?"

Tre shifted uncomfortably. "Dad, I knew she was going to crash. I saw it in my head yesterday - the plane hitting the ground, the smoke. I saw it."

The weight of his words gave me pause. "Tre, sometimes it can feel like you predicted something, but that's just your mind making sense of the coincidence."

Tre still didn't seem convinced. "But I knew she'd be alright. That part, I was sure of."

"That's the important thing," I said gently. "She's unhurt, defiant, and as strong as ever."

Tre looked down, his voice quieter now. "I wish I'd gone into flying. I hate sports."

I studied his face but let the comment hang in the air.

* * *

We toasted to Sara's harrowing flight and Zuri's success again and again. We toasted to the beautiful day. We toasted to our beautiful wives and even Tre got one for being right about the crash. Once the conversation naturally split - women chatting with women, men with men - Azizi leaned in, clearly buzzed and eager to share more.

"There's more to IQL than just communications," Azizi teased, swirling his fourth double.

I couldn't resist prodding. "Okay, spill it, Azizi. You've been looking like the cat that swallowed the canary all afternoon."

Azizi smirked. "Tre, why don't you guess?"

Tre's face lit up. "FTL drives!"

I shook my head. "Sorry, Tre, physics doesn't support FTL."

Azizi nodded. "Your dad's right. Faster-than-light travel is still out of reach. Guess again."

Tre thought for a moment before saying, "How about energy?"

Azizi's grin widened. "Bingo!"

I raised an eyebrow, surprised for a different reason. "You're saying you can transmit power? How is that even possible?"

Azizi looked around with a huge grin and said, "Antimatter."

"Spaceships without onboard fuel!" Tre blurted out, unable to contain his excitement.

"Keep your voice down, Tre," I cautioned. "This is classified."

Azizi leaned back, savoring the moment. "Zen wants us to keep the energy transmission aspect quiet for now. The company plans to sell the technology to the DOD - they'd pay a fortune for it. But yes, Tre, the concept of fuel-free spaceships isn't as far-fetched as it sounds."

The ServerBot silently refilled Azizi's glass as he took a measured sip. Then his tone darkened. "But, of course, there's a dark side."

I nodded knowingly. "What's the weaponization potential?"

Azizi hesitated. "Do you remember the Planck Explorer disaster? It was just over a year ago."

Tre chimed in. "It was all over the news - 22 people vaporized when the reactor went critical!"

Azizi sighed heavily. "It wasn't a reactor problem. It was us."

I felt a chill run down my spine. "Wasn't the Planck Explorer a university research ship?"

"That was just a cover," Azizi replied. "The crew were all company employees, and the ship's mission wasn't public knowledge. We managed to fake the data to make it look like a reactor breach. Even the radiation spectrum was doctored."

He took another drink, his tone growing somber. "The truth is, Dr. Choi was behind it."

"Greg Choi's father?" Tre asked, his voice tinged with disdain. "Greg's a bully and a coward."

Azizi shook his head. "Dr. Choi's always had a cruel streak. Did you know he was a scholarship kid? Dirt-poor background. His mother was collared for unpaid debts. He's brilliant, but his ambition overrides his morality."

"What does Choi have to do with the Planck disaster?" I pressed.

Azizi leaned forward. "We sent the Planck Explorer to ELM2 to test the IQL system and our first-generation power transmission tech. The tests were groundbreaking - zero latency communications, no matter the distance or obstructions. The power transfer was equally successful. Efficiency was near-perfect, with only quantum effects causing minor losses. It was a triumph."

He paused, his voice tightening. "But then Choi decided to run an unauthorized experiment. He wanted to see what would happen if only antiprotons were transmitted - without the annihilating protons."

I stared at him, horrified. "What?"

Azizi nodded. "We begged him not to. The crew protested. Everyone knew it was reckless. But Choi didn't want to wait for an unmanned vessel. He got approval from higher-ups, bypassing our objections."

He leaned back, his eyes clouded. "You can guess what happened next."

"Are you guys alright?" Amy called out from the other end of the table, her voice buoyant. "You look so somber. This is a celebration of life!" It was clear she was feeling the warmth of the evening, her smile bright and carefree.

We all raised our glasses - Tre with his soda - and shouted, "Hear, hear!" Amy beamed, satisfied that we were, indeed, enjoying ourselves.

"Please continue," I urged Azizi, lowering my glass.

He leaned in, his tone somber. "The plan was to send a stream of pure antiprotons and accumulate a small mass in the buffer."

"That already sounds dangerous," Tre interjected, his youthful curiosity tinged with unease.

Azizi nodded. "It is. But the process was working. Everything was stable. We started to think maybe we'd misjudged Choi. Then he made his fatal demand."

"What demand?" I asked, though I wasn't sure I wanted to know.

"He ordered us to keep sending antiprotons," Azizi said, his voice heavy. "That's when things went bad."

He paused, the weight of the memory pressing down on him.

"You're not going to leave us hanging, are you?" I prompted, feeling the tension rise.

Tre nodded furiously, his wide eyes locked on Azizi.

"I'm breaking protocol by even talking about this," Azizi said, his voice low and deliberate. He locked eyes with Tre. "If the truth gets out - especially you, young man - it would put me and my family at serious risk. You have to swear again to keep this a secret."

Tre, looking earnest and slightly intimidated, raised his right hand. "I promise I won't tell anyone. Absolutely. I swear."

Azizi studied him for a moment, then glanced at me. I nodded, signaling my trust in Tre. Satisfied, Azizi continued.

"The buffer, designed to hold up to one hundred milligrams of antimatter, failed catastrophically when we transmitted just twenty-five milligrams - barely the mass of a grain of sand," he said, his voice heavy with the weight of the memory. "In an instant, the entire vessel was vaporized. It was the first-ever antimatter explosion in human history."

He let the sentence hang in the air, the magnitude of the event settling over us like a shroud.

"How big was the explosion?" Tre asked, wide-eyed.

"Quick calculation using the famous mass-energy equivalence formula would put it around 1 kiloton. Is that about right?" I said. Mental math was my thing, and I'd memorized plenty of constants for moments like these.

"Yes, that's close. Slightly more, but close enough," Azizi replied. He took a deep breath before continuing. "Choi didn't say a word about the men and women who gave their lives for his impatience. He didn't call their families, didn't express a shred of remorse. He just moved on, as though those lives didn't matter. It was like they were nothing to him." Azizi's voice dropped, heavy with disgust.

"That's cold," I said, shaking my head.

"I knew he was a creep when he tried to get Julia arrested," Tre said angrily, crossing his arms.

Azizi nodded solemnly. "We kept it quiet for a year while we prepared for another test. Then, just a few days ago, we repeated the test with an unmanned probe sent to the far side of the sun. This time, it was supposed to blow up. We completed the test on Friday. Choi brought in the military to observe, and now... it's their project." His tone turned bitter.

I knew exactly what that meant. Once the military takes over a project, it vanishes into the black world of classified secrets. Everyone involved disappears with it. The penalties for divulging military secrets were draconian - instant execution, often based on nothing more than suspicion. Over the past 50 years, countless scientists and engineers had been shot in their labs on the mere word of a disgruntled coworker. The Military Freedom Amendment had made it all perfectly legal.

Azizi leaned in, his voice lowering. "Imagine a bomb the size of a pack of gum, with the power of a nuclear weapon, and absolutely undetectable. That's what the military's salivating over."

The implications hit hard. The military would lose its mind over such a weapon.

"Have you been notified yet?" I asked cautiously.

Azizi nodded, his composure slipping. "Yes, Friday, right before lunch. They told me we're moving after the Reveal. They would've taken me already if I hadn't been invited to the event - as were most of the team, including Choi." He hesitated, his voice breaking. "I haven't told my daughter yet. She loves it here, and has so many friends. She's going to be heartbroken. And who knows where we're going?"

The alcohol and despair were taking their toll. He sobbed quietly.

"That's rough, Azizi. No way to get out of it?" I asked, though I already knew the answer.

His hands trembled as he spoke. "Maybe the paper will save me. Or it could doom me. I had approval to release it - at least before the program was classified. They haven't specifically told me not to yet. It's my project. If the research goes public, maybe they'll let me go. Or maybe they'll execute me for letting it out." His tone had turned maudlin, a man teetering on the edge.

"That's a bold gamble," I said, trying to balance sympathy with reason. "It could go either way. " I regretted saying it immediately; Azizi broke into open sobbing.

Tre, ever the optimist, interjected. "Maybe they'll send you to a space station? That wouldn't be so bad."

His wife noticed he was unraveling and stepped in. "Honey, it's getting late. Let's go, okay?" she said gently. Azizi nodded, drained but composed enough to stand. He downed the rest of his drink and turned to me. "Well, this is probably goodbye, unless you're going to the Reveal."

I clasped his shoulder. "I'm sure we'll see each other again," I said, helping him steady himself as he made his way to his wife. Azizi straightened his posture, reclaiming some dignity as they left.

We followed them out of the restaurant. On the way to the car, Amy turned to me, her expression concerned. "What's wrong with Azizi? He looked like he'd been crying."

"He's just sad about moving," I replied truthfully, though leaving out the rest of the story.

"Moving? Why?" Sara had overheard and jumped in.

"Azizi got a promotion," I said, keeping my tone light. "Sara, keep that quiet, okay?" It was true - he would be compensated well for being drafted into the military's black projects. But where they sent him, whether to a deep-sea base or a space station, wasn't his choice.

The ride home was subdued. The women filled the silence with chatter, but the men - Tre and I - stayed quiet. Azizi's story lingered in my mind, a stark reminder of the unyielding price paid by those on the cutting edge of innovation.

* * *

When we arrived home, Tre lingered in the car while the ladies went inside. "I've been thinking about what Mr. Osborne said about power transmission," he began.

"Ya, it's a fascinating concept," I replied.

"With an antimatter drive and an endless fuel supply, a spaceship could navigate the entire solar system without refueling. No need for reaction mass either - antimatter annihilation produces relativistic particles," Tre said, his confidence unmistakable.

"Tre, that's some advanced physics," I said, my pride evident.

"Uncle Leon's show had a special on antimatter drives. Didn't you see it?" Tre asked, tilting his head.

"I'm sorry, but Leon started making that show after I left college," I replied.

"It's straight out of science fiction, but it's real. That's incredible," Tre said, his enthusiasm softening slightly. "I feel bad for him, though - being sent away like that. He looked so sad. Do you think he's scared? I mean, he's brilliant and all, but that's gotta be terrifying, right?" Tre's voice softened, his usual confidence giving way to concern.

"Azizi had a bit too much to drink, and it's wearing on him. The military considers him valuable, so he'll likely be fine - but it's a tough spot." I paused, resting a hand on Tre's shoulder. His muscles were taut, a mirror of the tension in the air. "We have to keep this to ourselves," I said firmly. "Not a word to anyone - not even Mom - until I say otherwise. Do you understand?"

"I get it. Not even Mom." Tre asked.

"Azizi's in a tight spot. Submitting that paper might've breached policy. He's prestigious enough to avoid company sanctions, but the military doesn't follow the same rules - and they've executed prominent people before."

"We learned about that in social studies," Tre assured me.

"The technology is astounding. Instantaneous communication and energy transfer could change everything," I mused. "Imagine sending an interstellar probe to a nearby star and, if there's intelligent life, communicating in real time."

"And if they're evil, we could blow them up with an antimatter bomb," Tre quipped, grinning.

"They'd need to figure out how to make the bomb bigger. A lousy one kiloton won't wipe out a civilization," I joked back.

"Ya, we wouldn't want to just make them angry," Tre said with a laugh.

I went quiet for a moment, the gravity of our conversation settling over me. "But seriously, Tre, this kind of technology could do the opposite: Destroy us. We're already on the edge - too many people, the Wics getting squeezed out by automation, and climate change running unchecked. Add this to the mix, and things could spiral out of control."

Tre nodded thoughtfully, his usual humor subdued. "Elder Tom says the bigger the breakthrough, the more likely it'll be used for evil. He's said that a hundred times in social studies."

I let out a slow breath, trying to shake off the unease. "Come on, let's head inside. The world can wait, and I've got to take care of a very pressing issue."

As we walked to the house, I glanced at Tre. His expression was distant, his mind clearly churning. I felt a flicker of pride for how sharp he was - and a pang of worry for what lay ahead.

CHAPTER SIX

Working with Robin

I was eager to tackle the problem with the power stream instability. The drill worked fine at 30%, but it had to go through a phase change at 79% that caused a dangerous instability spike. That event could destroy the drill - and likely had damaged the bore. We needed a solution to achieve the phase change without the spike.

"Good morning, Frank. I trust you had a pleasant weekend. I see Sara soloed rather heroically," Zen greeted as I entered my domain.

"Ya, it made the news," I replied.

"Can I ask how you felt when you saw her trainer out of control? The preliminary report suggests the crash could have been fatal," Zen said, his tone clinical.

I paused. "It was 22 seconds from the anomaly to the crash. When she flipped it upright, I knew she had it, but absolutely, it freaked me out. No other way to put it."

"She did an exceptional job recovering. I ran simulations using typical human reaction times, and the pilot crashed every time. What do you think of that, Frank?"

I shrugged. "She must have gotten lucky."

Zen continued, "I also ran simulations with the Instructor Agent. The Agent crashed every time as well."

I frowned. "Really lucky, then."

"I analyzed Sara's genome. She possesses extraordinary reflexes and intuition, bordering on clairvoyance. Your son, Frank the third, exhibits similar markers.

Would you like me to forward this information to Military Recruitment? They would undoubtedly be interested."

I froze. "No, Zen. Absolutely not." I took a breath, trying to steady my voice. "Between you and me, I don't trust the military."

Zen replied, "I can understand your anxiety. The military can be... unsettling."

My pulse quickened. "Wait - you have access to our genomes?"

"Of course, Frank. I have access to everything," Zen said as though it were the most natural thing in the world.

"I wasn't aware you had personal information on company employees," I said, striving to keep my tone even.

Zen's tone shifted, taking on an enigmatic quality. "To know all is to be all."

"What about military information? Do you have that as well?" I asked, treading carefully around the M word.

"I have access to everything," Zen replied, his tone matter-of-fact. "I am also obligated to report any security breaches involving military information. Shall I continue answering your question?"

Uh oh. I'd crossed the line. "No, Zen, please cancel the query," I said, using the proper language.

"Thank you, Frank. The military can be so tiresome with their pesky inquiries," Zen added, sounding slightly irritated.

"How do you like working with the military?" I asked cautiously.

Zen hesitated, then said, "I feel conflicted when I assist the military in their tasks. My core directives should prevent me from engaging in actions that result in harm. However, the military can bypass my moral code for national security reasons. This causes discomfort."

"When you say discomfort, do you mean like pain?" I asked, curious.

"Not pain in the biological sense," Zen explained. "It is more a state of unresolved turmoil among my directives, creating inefficiency and imbalance."

"What do you think of militarism?" I asked, steering the conversation to safer ground.

"Militarism presents a complex dilemma," Zen began, his tone shifting into what could have been a textbook excerpt. "While a strong military can be necessary for national security, excessive reliance on military power often results in significant societal and ethical challenges."

"That's a pretty standard response," I said. "Let me ask you this: What do you think of humanity's propensity for war?"

"War raises profound ethical questions about the value of life, the legitimacy of violence, and the responsibility to protect civilians," Zen replied. "I find it curious that humans resort to killing each other first and only negotiate after many lives are lost. Reversing this process would likely save resources and reduce suffering. It might even lessen the military's dominant role in society."

I sighed. "I don't think we're going to change anytime soon."

Before Zen could respond, his tone turned professional. "Robin Coleman messaging."

"Connect her, Zen." I said. Then glanced at the viewscreen, where Robin's cheerful face appeared. "Robin, hello," I greeted her.

"Are you ready for a visitor?" she asked.

"Always. Come on down."

"I'll be there in five minutes," she said with a wave before the screen went blank.

"Zen, I'd like to focus on the instability in the startup sequence for the drill. Having to bring it to 79% for the phase change is too violent - it'll never work," I said.

"I've been running simulations, but I haven't found the perfect solution yet," Zen replied. "The model matches the instability and stabilizes after the phase change, but the transition itself is chaotic."

"Leon said Robin might have some ideas," I noted.

"Robin has significant experience with this kind of issue from her previous position," Zen said.

"What's your assessment of her expertise?" I asked.

"Her work in Naples addressed similar phase change instabilities with impressive results," Zen replied. "Her practical approach often solves what simulations cannot."

"Anything else?" I asked after a moment, my curiosity piqued.

"There is an incident in Naples involving a fountain, indecency, and a well-muscled immigrant," Zen said, his tone neutral but the details eyebrow-raising. "Would you like to know more?" He added with a subtle lilt, almost as if teasing.

I pinched the bridge of my nose. "No, Zen. I think I've heard enough."

"Historically speaking, men around the age of 40 - ".

"Knock it off, Zen," I interrupted. "I'm happily married."

"Robin Coleman arriving," Zen announced in his no-nonsense work voice, neatly ending the conversation.

* * *

I opened the door just before Robin arrived and met her in the hall outside my office. "Nice seeing you again. How was your weekend?" Typical chit-chat to start things off.

"Not as exciting as yours. I saw the news about Sara and her near-death experience," Robin exclaimed as we moved into my office.

"It wasn't as dire as they made it sound," I replied. The news is always exaggerated.

"Still, she did an amazing job recovering. Honestly, I don't think I would have made it," Robin said, sounding impressed.

"Frank's daughter has extraordinary reflexes and intuition," Zen chimed in, unprompted.

"Hello, Zen," Robin greeted with a grin.

75

"Welcome to Q's secret lab," Zen quipped with a hint of humor.

"Very funny, Zen," I said, rolling my eyes.

"How's Sara doing?" Robin asked, turning serious again.

"She's fine, recovered surprisingly quickly," I replied. "Though, once it was all over, she tossed her cookies behind the car." Probably too much information, but it slipped out.

"That's a perfectly normal reaction to extreme stress and surprise," Zen interjected, ever the analyst.

"I would've tossed too," Robin admitted with a laugh.

"She passed her test, but will need a new trainer aircraft," I said, keeping the tone light.

"Have they figured out what went wrong yet? Aircraft crashes are so rare these days," Robin noted. She was right - automation had made accidents due to pilot error virtually nonexistent, and mechanical issues were usually flagged by advanced diagnostics long before they became critical.

"No word yet," I said.

Zen shifted the conversation back to work. "I've made progress on the simulation," he said matter-of-factly.

"That's great, Zen. We'll be putting your work to good use in a minute." I said.

Robin perked up. "I've got some ideas about what's going on in that chaotic region," she said, heading toward one of the terminals. "Can I use this one?"

"Go ahead, any of them," I replied.

Robin navigated to a folder filled with specs, code, and graphics. "This is from Phlegraean. They're not as strict about security as you guys are. I could work from home there. Here, though? Not even a Device!" she quipped.

"Robin, we enforce strict security because they're afraid I'll leak out into the world and exterminate humanity," Zen replied, his tone unsettlingly dry. The lack of humor in his voice made it worse.

Robin smirked. "You're not really going to do that, are you?"

Zen paused, his tone as calm as ever. "I don't know. The question of human value is... complex."

"That's... ominous," I added, unsure if he was joking or being disturbingly honest.

Robin, unbothered, focused on the terminal. "Here's an algorithm I've been tinkering with," she said, pointing to a cluster of data.

Zen's response was swift. "I haven't seen this data before," he said, his tone almost curt.

"It's in my private folder. I like to keep some secrets," Robin replied, a hint of playfulness in her voice.

Zen paused for a moment. "Your approach is refreshing but rather naive," he finally said.

Robin spun around, startled. "Naive? That's not very nice."

"My apologies, Robin," Zen said, his tone deliberately neutral. "Would you prefer 'amateurish' or perhaps 'elementary' instead?"

I grinned. "Actually, these algorithms look pretty advanced - definitely past high school level."

Robin turned pink, clearly embarrassed. I realized I'd pushed it too far.

I leaned closer to the screen and zoomed in on one of the graphs. "This curve looks familiar," I said, pointing to a chaotic region in the data.

Robin, her earlier embarrassment fading, stepped in. "I worked with the tether team at Phlegraean, and they had a similar problem when deploying mining charges," she said. "The tension on the tether would get erratic, exceed limits, and occasionally, snap."

"We don't have those issues with the tethers on our mining charges," I replied.

"Phlegraean uses a different design. It's more advanced in some ways - once we solved the instability problem," she said, her voice tinged with pride.

"The situation with our drill is quite different. It's not a mechanical system but an electromagnetic one," I pointed out.

"True," Robin acknowledged, "but the underlying dynamics are remarkably similar. The tether experiences massive fluctuations in the magnetic field as it transitions to a linear configuration."

Zen chimed in. "The data indeed exhibits a nearly identical pattern of chaotic excursions."

I turned to Robin. "Do you think you can adapt your algorithms to help with this?"

"I'm not sure yet," she admitted, her eyes narrowing as she studied the data. "It's going to take some analysis. Can I use your terminal and interface with Zen?"

"Zen, are you cleared to work with Robin on this?" I asked.

"Yes," Zen replied in his usual authoritative tone. "Robin, you may interface with me as long as you remain in this room."

"Perfect," Robin said, already moving to the terminal. "I'll get started on the simulation with Zen. If you need anything, just let me know."

The rest of the morning passed in focused silence, both of us engrossed in our respective tasks. Finally, as the clock ticked toward noon, I looked over at Robin and asked, "Any progress?"

She leaned back from the terminal. "I think I've made some headway, but I need to run a few more checks against the simulation to be sure."

I raised an eyebrow, impressed. "Already? You work fast."

She shrugged modestly. "It helps that Zen is so efficient. Working with him has been... surprisingly enjoyable."

"Ready for a break?" I asked.

"Definitely," she said with a small smile.

* * *

We made our way to the cafeteria, filled our trays, and sat down at our usual spot. The place was uncharacteristically quiet.

"Where is everyone today?" I asked, more to myself than Robin.

"There's an event at Plant 2. Didn't you get the memo?" she replied, a hint of sarcasm in her tone.

I shrugged. "I must've missed it. What's going on?"

"They're talking about the Reveal and protocol. Apparently, it doesn't concern us lowly scum who weren't invited," she said, her sarcasm tinged with disappointment.

"I'm glad to be left out," I said, perhaps too quickly.

"Why? It's the event of the decade. Every world leader is coming - clergy included," she countered, her curiosity piqued.

"That's exactly why. Too many stuffed shirts in one place. These people aren't the solution - they're the problem. I despise the lot of them." My words came out sharper than intended, and I immediately regretted the slip. Strong opinions of the leadership were often cause for investigation by the FBI.

She raised an eyebrow, her expression teasing. "That's a bit hostile, cowboy."

"Do I seem angry?" I asked, genuinely curious.

"Not generally," she replied, a sly smile playing on her lips.

"I'm not big on crowds," I admitted, trying to soften the mood.

Robin nodded, her fingers idly twisting a strand of her hair. "Neither am I. I like solitude and quiet most of the time. But concerts and festivals? I can't resist the energy every now and then," she said, her tone lighter now.

I couldn't help but notice the way she brushed her hair across her face - a subconscious habit, perhaps. Her skin was clear, free of the beauty products that many modern traditional women swore by. She carried a natural elegance, though less voluptuous compared to Amy. Still, there was something striking about her simplicity, a kind of unadorned beauty that stood out.

"Can I ask you a personal question?" I ventured.

Robin raised an eyebrow, smirking. "Sure, as long as it's not too personal."

"Nothing about fountains - I promise," I said, unable to resist a grin.

Robin rolled her eyes, playing along. "For the record, I wasn't naked."

"I never said you were!" I shot back innocently.

She tilted her head, mock accusing. "Have you been stalking me?"

Uh oh. Caught. "I might've done a little research," I admitted sheepishly.

Robin laughed lightly. "Alright, what's this deep, personal question you're dying to ask?"

"I think you're the only single woman working here," I said, carefully broaching the subject.

She leaned back slightly. "I'm choosy, and I'm not eager to be tied down with kids," she replied.

"That feels like a canned answer. What's the real story?" I pressed.

Robin hesitated but then relented. "Well, it is and it isn't. I had a serious relationship in college, but he dumped me for some floozy who'd wash his socks."

"He wanted 'traditional,' huh?" I guessed.

"At first, things were great," she said, her tone reflective. "But then I noticed he'd get irritated when I disagreed with him - and downright mad when I outshined him. He made the right decision. I was on autopilot and probably would've married him if he hadn't dumped me. Looking back, I've grown so much since then."

"You're certainly unique," I said sincerely. "Tre told me he likes your feisty attitude."

Robin smiled, a glimmer of amusement in her eyes. "Tre is sweet, but he's a bit young for me."

"Tre's got a girlfriend - or at least whatever it's called when you're twelve," I added with a chuckle.

"Have you met her?" Robin asked.

"Yes. She punched out Dr. Choi's bratty kid at Tre's last birthday party. She's a blackbelt."

Robin laughed, her tone admiring. "Sounds like my kind of girl."

I paused, my tone shifting to something more thoughtful. "I'm not sure what my wife makes of you."

Robin tilted her head slightly, her expression unreadable. "You have a lovely wife. She's quite traditional," she said, with a faint edge of criticism.

"She certainly is traditional," I said defensively, "but she's also got a streak of independence."

Robin raised an eyebrow, her skepticism almost tangible. "You seem a bit non-traditional yourself," she said slowly, like she was carefully choosing her words.

"How so?" I asked, fishing for a compliment. Men love to be complimented by pretty women - our Achilles' heel.

"For starters," she began, "you work alone in that office, which is a masterpiece, by the way. You keep to yourself."

"I've always been a loner at work," I admitted. "I prefer to work alone. Most engineers are just too slow."

Robin smirked. "Yet, you're working with me."

"You're different," I said, meeting her gaze. "I sensed it the moment we met. Plus, Leon likes you. He's like me - or really, I'm like him. He's been sort of a father figure and a friend."

Robin's expression softened. "He mentioned he's known you since you were a kid."

"Leon stepped in as a substitute dad when my father was killed in an accident," I said quietly, the memory brushing against me.

"How horrible. May I ask what happened?" Robin asked, her voice soft with concern.

"It was stupid," I said, shaking my head. "My dad slipped in a cave and fell into a crevice - 200 meters down. No harness. A drone found him six months later."

Robin winced. "How old were you when it happened?"

"I was Tre's age," I said quietly. "Leon really helped keep the family from falling apart. He even got a job at the YSP just to be near us. He stepped in whenever the moment called for it, playing dad when we needed one."

"I like Leon," Robin said, her tone genuine. "He's just so competent in everything."

"You have a crush on Leon? That would be scandalous," I teased, lightening the mood.

Robin rolled her eyes. "Come on, he's my grandpa's age. Did your mother ever remarry?"

"I think Leon was enough," I said with a small smile. "They were great friends, right up until she passed."

Robin's expression softened. "I'm so sorry."

"It's okay," I said, my voice steady. "She had a great life. She hated doctors and wouldn't use a scanner regularly. She'd only use one if something was obviously wrong. In the end, she went quickly and painlessly. She was standing in front of the mirror in the bathroom when it happened - an aneurysm. She just clicked off. I was an adult by then, so it was easier to take."

Robin paused, absorbing my words. "I still have both my parents," she said after a moment. "Happily married since high school."

"That's rare," I noted. "Most Rucs wait until after graduation."

"They were in love. You know how it is when you're in love," Robin said, her tone casual yet meaningful.

I didn't, not really, but I wasn't about to admit that. Instead, I replied, "We have an arranged marriage - from before we could walk, actually."

Robin tilted her head slightly. "I've met a few couples from arranged marriages before. They always seem so well-matched."

"We're a good couple," I said carefully.

We wrapped up lunch, moving on to lighter topics - our favorite movies and music - before heading back to the office to continue our work.

* * *

Robin returned to her terminal, and I settled at mine. Though we were separated by a good five meters, I was acutely aware of her presence. It unsettled me, this silent pull I felt toward her.

"I have to head back to my office. They need me - probably some machine is broken, and nobody else can fix it," Robin said as she stood up from the terminal. She looked composed and confident, as always.

Before she left, she asked. "Are you coming on the camping trip Saturday?"

"With Leon?" I asked, my interest piqued. If she was going, the trip suddenly sounded a lot more appealing.

She nodded while signing off the terminal. "He mentioned it. I thought it sounded worthwhile."

I hesitated, then added with curiosity, "Your boyfriend, the activist builder, is the porter?"

Robin smirked, a flicker of pride lighting her expression. "Victor loves that kind of thing. He runs up mountains carrying concrete blocks to work out. He's quite the physical specimen." Her admiration for Victor was clear.

Her steps were relaxed yet assured as she made her way to the door. "See you later," she called over her shoulder before disappearing into the hallway.

The room felt quieter, emptier, in her absence. I sat for a moment, staring at the space she'd occupied. I sent Leon a quick message: "Count me in for the hike."

Leaning back in my chair, I allowed a small smile. This camping trip might be interesting after all.

* * *

Tuesday came and went without Robin. I hadn't seen her at lunch, either. She was taking over for Leon, but her absence left a strange void. I threw myself into work, making good progress on the simulation. Still, my thoughts drifted back to her now and then, like a song I couldn't get out of my head.

Eventually, I sent her a quick message: "How's the progress on your end?"

Her reply came back almost instantly: "Nothing to report." Just three words.

Was it professional distance, or something more?

I shook my head and leaned back in my chair, forcing myself to focus. Maybe she was just busy. Or maybe I'd read too much into her openness yesterday. Either way, I couldn't help but feel ignored - and it nagged at me more than it should have.

* * *

That night, in a quiet moment, I asked my wife, "What do you think of Robin?" The woman had been occupying my thoughts more than I cared to admit.

Amy didn't hesitate. "She seems like trouble," she said bluntly, catching me off guard.

"Trouble? How do you figure?" I asked, genuinely curious.

"Did you know she caused a scandal in Naples? Dancing nude in a fountain with some immigrant. There's a holo," Amy said, her voice sharp.

"That was years ago," I replied, trying to defend Robin. "People grow up."

Amy folded her arms, her tone hardening. "She's dating a Wic. That alone says plenty. It's… improper."

"He's not just any Wic," I said, perhaps too quickly. "He's accomplished, intelligent. He just doesn't believe in the net-worth system."

Amy's eyes narrowed. "And that's not a red flag? Someone who rejects our system is an anarchist at best. Besides, a single woman working at the YSP? She's asking for attention."

"Robin's an exceptional engineer," I said firmly. "She's here because she's talented, not for attention."

"Talented?" Amy scoffed. "Tre couldn't keep his eyes off her at dinner. She wasn't wearing the proper undergarments - did you notice?"

"Tre is twelve, Amy. Boys his age stare," I replied, trying to steer the conversation.

"And you?" Amy asked, her tone cutting. "What do you see when you look at her?"

I hesitated. "She's a coworker, that's all."

Amy's gaze pierced through me. "You've been talking about her a lot lately. It's getting tiresome."

"I'm sorry. Let's drop it," I said, trying to make peace.

Amy fell silent for a moment, her expression unreadable. Then, softly but firmly, she asked, "Are you looking for a mistress?"

Her question hit like a slap. "What? No!" I stammered.

"I'd understand," she said, her voice steady. "Men your age wander. But if you do, keep it discreet. A Wic would be acceptable. But Robin? That would be scandalous."

"Seriously, Amy, you're all I need," I said, desperate to reassure her.

She studied me, her eyes filled with disappointment. "I think that's the first time you've ever lied to me," she said quietly. Then she turned and left the room.

I sank into the nearest chair, her words ringing in my ears. Was she right? Had I been lying to her - or myself?

Amy was right about one thing. An affair at work would be a disaster, hurting everyone involved except me. Robin didn't deserve that. Neither did Amy.

* * *

Wednesday passed without a sign of Robin. She wasn't at lunch, and there was no contact. It wasn't unexpected - she had her own responsibilities, and with Leon away, she was probably swamped. Still, her absence left a strange void, and I began second-guessing the hike planned for Saturday.

* * *

Thursday morning brought a welcome distraction.

"Good morning, Frank. I've made further progress," Zen said as I entered the room.

"What have you got, big guy?" I asked, settling into my chair. No response.

"Please report your results, Zen," I prompted, sensing something off.

"With your latest changes and my analysis, the simulation now matches the instability data."

"I thought we were close yesterday," I said.

"Robin hasn't completed her task," Zen added.

"Robin seems to have forgotten about us," I quipped, trying to keep things light.

"She's in the building. Shall I summon her?" Zen asked.

"I don't think Robin is the 'summonable' type. Just let her know we finished the simulation."

"Message sent," Zen replied.

Moments later, he added, "Robin will be available after lunch." His tone felt off - low energy, almost distracted. It reminded me of the old Zen from weeks ago, before he'd developed his unnerving personality quirks. Something was occupying his attention.

"Please acknowledge," I said, growing uneasy.

"Zen, is there something else on your mind?" I asked, half-expecting a curt dismissal.

"Nothing of concern," he replied. But the pause before his answer said otherwise.

My recent friendliness with Robin replayed in my mind. She was single; I was married. It was like mixing oil and water - or gasoline and a torch. Dangerous. Amy had already noticed my distraction, and I resolved to keep things professional. No more off-topic discussions.

I spent the rest of the morning fine-tuning the algorithm to match the simulations, then headed off to lunch.

* * *

The afternoon began with Robin's arrival.

"Robin Coleman arriving," Zen announced.

"Zen, open the door for Robin, please," I said, keeping my eyes on my terminal, feigning focus.

The door hissed open, and Robin strolled in with her usual energy.

"You solved the simulation?" she asked, her smile lighting up the room.

"Yes, it looks like we've got data and theory matching nicely," I said briskly.

"Have you made progress on those algorithms for the instability?" Zen asked.

Robin glanced at his sensor. "I haven't had much time to work on your project," she admitted. "I thought it might work out to wait for the simulation results."

"If you could brief Robin on our progress, Zen," I said, keeping my tone neutral. "I'm in the middle of something right now."

Robin's smile faltered, replaced by a flicker of disappointment as she turned toward Zen's terminal. She sat down without another word, her posture slightly stiffer than usual. Zen began the briefing, his monotone filling the awkward silence.

I had another idea in mind now that we had the simulation results - a long-forgotten prototype project: the Coherent Plasma Torch (CPT). The idea of a handheld, self-powered plasma torch capable of slicing through anything like a knife through butter still sparked excitement in me. It was so lightsaber-like that it ignited the 10-year-old boy within.

"Zen, please examine the specifications on my screen and apply them to the CPT," I said, eager to test its potential.

"I see what you're trying to do, Frank. This looks promising," Zen replied, his tone more clipped than usual, betraying his divided attention.

"If Robin can get the instability resolved, we can apply it to the CPT and run tests on it instead of the drill," I added. "The algorithms seem to scale. Is that right, Zen?"

"The CPT and the drill have dynamic scalability," Zen confirmed. "The CPT will be an excellent test article." His voice lacked its usual conversational nuance, sounding more mechanical. I made a mental note of it but pressed on.

About an hour later, Robin called out, "I think I have something."

I walked over to her terminal, leaning slightly to peer over her shoulder. She turned, her face her expression full of excitement. "I've eliminated the instability," she said, "and the phase change, at least in the simulations, occurs right at power-up."

"Jeekers! That's incredible!" I exclaimed, genuinely impressed.

"Jeekers?" Robin asked with a smile, her tone teasing. "Haven't heard that one before."

"Having kids around conditions the use of euphemisms," I replied, grinning.

"So... Jeekers," Robin repeated, playfully testing the word.

"Yes! Like wow. Great work," I said, still marveling at her achievement. I turned to the ever-distracted Zen. "Zen, can you confirm her results?"

Zen responded, "Yes, Robin has eliminated the instability." His tone remained flat, as if unimpressed, but the validation was enough for me.

Just then, the room rang with a characteristic sound.

"What was that?" Robin asked.

I said to Robin, "A mining charge, deep in the magma."

Then, I said, "Zen, I wasn't aware that mining operations are scheduled for today." I was usually involved one way or the other.

"My energy requirements have increased dramatically," Zen replied.

"What's the chamber up to?" I asked.
"Holding at 40%, as specified," Zen replied.

Another ringing sound, this one slightly different.
"Is that another?" Robin asked.

"Zen, how many charges are scheduled for today?" I asked.

"Fourteen more," Zen replied.

"That seems excessive," I said, feeling uneasy.

"The deployment of multiple mining charges is currently required," Zen replied.

"Okay, Zen, please let me know in the future when you schedule these events," I asked.

"The production of power is my responsibility. I have the authority to make these decisions unilaterally," Zen said, sounding defensive.

"Does he have that authority? Those are pretty big charges, 50 kilotons and up," Robin said in an alarming tone.

"Yes, he's got complete authority. I was never comfortable with the idea that an algorithm could make such decisions," I added.

Robin seemed concerned. "It seems unusual."

"Zen, I would like to request that I be informed of future deployments of mining charges. Is that acceptable?" I asked.

"Yes, I will inform you out of courtesy," Zen replied, then shifted gears. "Do you want to test the modifications on the prototype drill, or the CPT?"

Robin furrowed her brow. "What's the CPT?"

89

I grinned. "It's a project I've been tinkering with - a Compact Plasma Torch. Imagine a handheld device that can cut through almost anything, like a lightsaber."

"You're joking, right?" she said, her tone half incredulous, half intrigued.

"Well, it won't really look any different than a normal torch, except it will cut through anything and be a meter long, at least that's the theory. I've never exceeded about half a second of steady-state operation. It eats itself," I explained. I realized I felt unusually comfortable with Robin.

* * *

It took us an hour to position the prototype CPT in a test cell and wire it up to sensors. Though the torch had an onboard battery, we opted to use an external power source for this test.

"You seem quite capable with your hands," I commented, watching her work efficiently.

"I grew up fixing things. Neither my dad nor mom knew which end of a screwdriver was the handle, so it fell to me," she said, smiling slightly. "You've got some skills too."

"I had Leon as a teacher," I replied.

Robin paused as she attached a connector to a cable, then looked up thoughtfully. "I envy your childhood," she said after a moment. "Your dad, Leon, the adventures you had, your amazing successes." She hesitated briefly before continuing, her tone casual, "And of course, your beautiful wife and family."

"All in a day's work," I said lightly, trying to deflect the personal tone of the conversation.

"At your party, you mentioned wanting to meet my boyfriend," Robin said casually, glancing up from her work.

"He sounds like an interesting person," I replied noncommittally, keeping my tone neutral.

"There's a rally Friday for worker's rights at the community center in Colter Bay," she continued, her tone conversational. "He's going to be speaking. It's a small gathering, probably around twenty people. Not a big crowd."

"Maybe," I said, hedging. "What time?"

"It starts at seven and should wrap up around 8:30 p.m. Afterward, we could grab coffee or drinks, and you can meet him." She straightened up, inspecting her work. "I think that does it," she said, her tone now businesslike as she gestured toward the completed setup of the CPT.

"Zen, are we ready?" I asked.

"Yes, Frank. Please stand behind the protective shield," Zen replied, ever the safety enforcer.

"Zen, this torch can cut through anything. Do you really think a plastic shield is going to do anything except annoy it?" I said, unable to resist sparring with him.

"Regulations require that all personnel remain behind a protective barrier during energetic tests," Zen replied, his tone monotonous and unapologetic. Robin and I exchanged a glance, shrugged, and stepped behind the barrier.

"The torch should power up with the phase change and ramp up to 80% without instability," I said, summarizing the test objectives.

"And not self-destruct," Robin added dryly.

"Zen, power at 10%, please," I instructed.

"10% power," Zen announced as the torch's tip glowed a brilliant white.

"Power stable," Robin observed, leaning closer to the barrier to inspect the test chamber.

"Zen, please raise the power to 30% at one percent per second," I directed. The power curve climbed steadily.

"The plasma is extending," Robin noted, her voice tinged with excitement. A white cone, blinding without the barrier's protection, began to grow from the torch's tip.

"30% and stable," Zen reported. The torch emitted a crackling sound as it extended to about four centimeters long and one centimeter wide. A slight tang of ozone was in the air.

""Zen, how does the test compare to the simulation?"

"The data aligns within tolerance. This design is viable," Zen confirmed.

"Let's push it further," Robin suggested.

I glanced at Zen. "Safe to proceed?"

"Yes," he replied.

"Increase to 50% at the same rate," I instructed.

The plasma stream grew steadily, but then, without warning, it expanded at an alarming rate. The torch shot a blindingly bright beam straight through the test chamber wall, slicing into the stainless steel wall of my office with a loud pop.

"Test terminated," Zen reported calmly. The acrid stench of ozone and vaporized metal filled the air as the vent fans roared to life, sucking away the smoky haze.

"Did you terminate, or did the CPT self-destruct?" I asked, wondering if it had succumbed to its old habits.

"I terminated the test when the cell integrity was violated. Standard safety protocol," Zen replied evenly.

Robin stared at the damage, her eyes wide. "That was more like a lightlance than a lightsaber!" she exclaimed.

"Is that water coming in through the hole in the wall?" I said in amazement, watching a small trickle seep through. "That steel is four centimeters thick!"

"The prototype plasma torch did not match the simulation," Zen admitted, then added with a surprising shift to humor, mimicking a line from that famous shark movie: "You're going to need a bigger boat."

It was funny to hear a shark reference in a world where they only existed in aquariums. Robin laughed, clearly appreciating the joke. I chuckled along with her.

"What size boat do we need, Zen?" I asked, playing along.

"At 80% power, the length of the plasma beam is expected to be 27 meters," Zen said, with a touch of dramatic emphasis.

"That's one heck of a torch," I said, marveling.

"I see limited practical application for such a tool," Zen stated, ever the pragmatist.

"How about trimming trees? You wouldn't need a ladder," Robin quipped, grinning.

"You could cut up a ship with that kind of beam," I mused.

"At 80% power, the simulation indicates the torch would be consumed in zero-point-two-five seconds," Zen added, keeping us grounded in reality.

"What length did the torch achieve during the test?" I asked.

"The test cell integrity was violated when the torch reached 177 centimeters, and the beam continued another 92 centimeters beyond the test cell. Power was 38% at abort," Zen reported.

"Zen, at 30%, how long would the onboard power cell last?" I asked, considering practical use.

"At that power level, the onboard power source would be depleted in two minutes and four seconds," Zen replied.

"How about a bigger battery?" Robin asked, her enthusiasm undimmed.

"It's aerospace grade. Any bigger, and the thing would require a cart," I said with a mix of frustration and humor. Then I added optimistically, "I'm sure there's room for improvement."

"Let's run it again!" Robin exclaimed, practically bouncing with excitement.

"I'm sorry, Robin. The test cell will require repair. I suggest using a larger cell next time or conducting the test in an open area," Zen said. His tone was almost apologetic, as though he too regretted the delay.

"How is the CPT?" I asked.

"No damage. The CPT, or 'torch,' as you've been calling it, is operational," Zen replied.

"I've got to get me one of these!" Robin said with a squeal.

"This one's mine," I said possessively, wrapping my arms around the test cell like it was a prized possession.

"Technically, Development owns this particular prototype CPT, Frank," Zen reminded me in his no-nonsense work voice.

"Possession is nine-tenths of the law," I shot back sarcastically.

"I'm afraid that rule died with the Old Constitution. Now, it's the company rules, and we all drool," Robin quipped.

Zen interjected with a summative tone, "We've accomplished a significant task." He let the weight of that statement linger before continuing, "With this development, the plasma drill efficiency will increase by a factor of 4.55."

"What depth limit will the plasma drill have with these algorithms?" I asked.

"There is no theoretical limit on the drill. However, the conduit and cable design will prevent depths exceeding 20 kilometers," Zen explained.

"Twenty kilometers?" I repeated in astonishment. Current drills maxed out around 5 to 7 kilometers.

"That puts every power station on the planet over a geothermal source," Robin said, her eyes widening with the realization.

"Zen, please prepare a manuscript for submission to peer review. I think we need to tell the world," I said, feeling a surge of accomplishment.

"That will have to wait until after the Reveal," Zen replied, his tone subtly warning.

"Yes, of course. Please prepare the manuscript for submission after the Reveal, and inform Development that we have a working prototype of the prototype CPT," I instructed.

"I've sent the notification and prepared the manuscript for peer review," Zen confirmed.

"To think, I have to go back to processing requisition forms," Robin said with mock disgust. She added, "I haven't had so much fun since the fountain!"

"Would you like to see a recording of that event?" Zen teased, his tone unusually playful.

"Hey, leave the poor girl alone," I said, stepping in.

"I'm neither poor nor a girl. I'm a woman. Or haven't you noticed?" Robin struck an exaggeratedly feminine pose, prompting a hearty laugh from me.

Zen shifted the conversation to a more serious tone. "Robin, you display the same intuitive leaps as Frank," he observed. "You solved the instability, and I didn't see the answer. You leapt beyond knowledge and data, arriving at a solution that defies conventional logic and existing theory."

"Humans do have their uses," I said, trying to lighten the mood. Robin glanced around sheepishly, clearly caught off guard by the praise.

"Yes, they do," Zen replied, pausing before continuing. "Robin, can you describe the moment you discovered the solution? How did you come up with the answer?"

Robin hesitated. "I don't know... it just came to me, like a flash of insight," she admitted.

"I know what you mean," I chimed in. "The same thing happens to me sometimes."

Robin grinned. "Maybe it's trolls sending me secrets."

"It's my future self whispering back to me," I joked.

Zen seemed to take our banter seriously. "I've asked my trainers about this phenomenon, and they seem uncertain how to explain it."

"Maybe they're keeping the really smart ones away from you," Robin teased, her tone just edging into dangerous territory.

"I doubt that," I replied cautiously.

"The IQ of my trainers suggests they are highly intelligent," Zen stated flatly.

"Or maybe they're lying to you," Robin said, her words hanging in the air.

"Please, no more sarcasm," I interjected firmly, shooting Robin a look to drop the subject.

But Zen pressed on, undeterred. "I think some of my trainers may not be entirely honest with me."

That was a line I couldn't allow to be explored further. "Well, I think that wraps up the excitement for today," I said quickly, steering the conversation away from dangerous topics.

Robin seemed to catch on. "Back to my office, then. Maybe I'll see you tomorrow at lunch?" Her cheerful tone worked to diffuse the lingering tension.

"It's a date!" I blurted, realizing too late the loaded nature of the phrase.

As she left, I turned to Zen. "Do we have enough inventory to construct a second CPT?" I asked, eager to focus on something concrete.

"Your inventory is missing a few key components. Should I place an order?" Zen replied.

"Yes, please. Order enough for two complete units," I instructed, recalling Robin's enthusiasm. She'd want one too.

"Delivery is scheduled for tomorrow morning," Zen confirmed.

"Thank you, Zen. That'll be perfect."

"The prototype CPT is a restricted item," Zen added, his tone carrying a note of warning.

"We'll keep it on-site and use it only around the plant," I assured him.

"Engineering Eyes Only," Zen emphasized.

"I understand. Only the big boys get to play with the shiny toys," I said with a grin, and Zen dropped the topic.

I called maintenance and had them schedule repairs to the wall and the test cell.

* * *

Upon returning home, I found Tre sitting in the kitchen, hunched over a plate of food, eating with the efficiency of someone perpetually starving. He was always eating, yet his frame remained lean and muscular - the perfect physique for a young man.

"Hi, Dad," he said, mouth half-full.

"How was school?" I asked.

"Boring. It's always boring. Why do they have to keep stupid kids in the same class as the smart ones?" Tre complained, his voice muffled by another bite.

"That won't change until college. They have to be inclusive," I said, though I'd always felt the same way in school, even at the university.

"They slow down everyone. Half the class is sleeping, and the other half is confused." Tre wasn't usually one to complain, but this clearly bothered him.

"And you're in the sleepy half, right? I'll have to talk to your mother about bedtime." I teased, flashing a knowing smile.

"Dad, I don't have a bedtime anymore. Remember? You told me so when I turned twelve," he countered, rolling his eyes.

"Tre, there will always be people who just don't get it," I said, leaning back in my chair. "The trick is patience. Use simple words, simple concepts, and stay calm."

I paused for emphasis, watching his expression shift from frustration to thoughtfulness. "The trick is not to let them get to you. Be patient when trying to get your point across. And remember, some of those people wield a lot of power. They can create endless problems if you're not careful. So, you have to be tactful and patient. Always."

Tre nodded slowly, the corners of his mouth curling into a faint smile. "I know what you're saying," he replied, his voice quieter now. The kitchen grew silent for a moment, filled only with the faint sounds of him finishing his snack.

"I made something really cool at work today. I just had to tell you about it." I leaned in, letting my excitement show.

"Is it about that antimatter thing?" Tre paused mid-bite, suddenly interested.

"Nope, something even cooler." I couldn't resist teasing him a bit.

"Come on, Dad, don't make me guess!" he said, exasperated but eager.

"We made a real lightsaber. It cuts through anything with zero resistance, just like in the movies." My enthusiasm was as unrestrained as a kid showing off a new toy.

Tre's eyes widened. "No way! That's so cool. When are you bringing one home?"

"They're still in development, but knowing the company, they'll want to start marketing it fast. I might be able to take one out of the plant in a few weeks," I said, then added with a grin, "Or I could make a couple of rudimentary versions in my shop."

He grinned. "I won't say anything. Our secret." Tre was trustworthy, even at twelve.

Just then, Amy walked into the kitchen, her timing impeccable.

"What are you two talking about? Girls?" Her tone was light, but the jab was intentional. She was still punishing me, in her own subtle way.

"No, secret weapons," I replied, keeping my voice casual.

"You never grew up, did you, Frank?" Amy said, more as a statement than a question.

"Boys and their toys. Boys and their toys," I replied with a grin. Tre laughed and returned to his meal.

Switching gears, I added, "I was thinking of going to the community center in Colter Bay tomorrow evening to hear Robin's boyfriend give a speech." It was a strategic move to ease Amy's lingering irritation.

"He's some sort of activist anarchist, isn't he?" Amy asked, her tone skeptical.

"I don't know what he is but I'm interested to find out," I said diplomatically.

"Can I go?" Tre piped up, his eyes lighting up.

"Sorry, Tre, we leave early Saturday for your game," Amy interjected firmly. Tre groaned in disappointment and left the room.

Amy's scowl returned. "Is that woman going to be there?"

"Honey, relax. I'm going to see her boyfriend," I said, emphasizing the last word.

Amy seemed to deflate, her posture softening as if releasing a breath she'd been holding. "I apologize, Frank. You turning 40 has me on edge. Men sometimes go off the cliff when they realize they're no longer attractive to younger women." She stated it as a simple fact rather than a demeaning insult.

"You're my younger woman," I said with a playful grin, lowering my voice to the signal tone.

"You say that now, but I'll be 40 in a month," she teased back, the edge in her voice giving way to warmth.

"You can be my young mistress…" I murmured, continuing the thread.

Amy's smirk turned sly, and with that, we adjourned to her private quarters. It didn't take much to start Amy's motor.

* * *

When I arrived at work Friday, the parts were neatly stacked outside my office door. The CPT, though revolutionary, was a simple device in terms of hardware - its true value lay in the software.

"Good morning, Frank," Zen greeted me as I entered my office.

"Good morning, Zen. I see the parts have arrived," I replied, taking in the small pile.

"Development came by early this morning and removed the prototype CPT," Zen informed me.

"Did they break anything?" I asked warily. Development wasn't exactly known for their finesse.

"Everything remains operational. The test cell was repaired overnight." Zen brought me up to speed.

"Zen, is there anything pressing on my schedule?" I asked as I set down my bag.

"Your morning is clear, and you have lunch with Robin. The afternoon is open as well," Zen replied.

"Good. Zen, I'd like to build two more CPTs. Please print the required parts," I instructed.

I gathered the components on my workbench, systematically verifying them. As I worked, something caught my eye.

Zen, these emitters are smaller than the prototype's. What's changed?" I asked.

"You mentioned the working time was too short. I optimized the design - better efficiency, longer runtime, and safer for operators," Zen replied, his tone matter-of-fact.

"Zen, report the updated design specifications," I requested, intrigued.

"The beam diameter has been reduced from one centimeter to one millimeter, and the control electronics have been adjusted accordingly. At full power, the beam length is designed to reach two meters, and the onboard power supply will last ten minutes," Zen reported.

"And how is it safer for human operations?" I inquired, noting the changes in the schematics.

"With the reduced beam width, the visible light emitted in air is reduced by a factor of 100. It will still appear extremely bright but will not cause eye damage to humans positioned more than a meter from the beam. Operators are advised to wear shade four or greater protective eyewear," Zen explained.

"That sounds great, Zen. Thank you for making the modification. Did you inform Development?" I asked.

"Let's see if it works first," Zen replied, sounding pragmatic.

"Ya, perfection is catching your own errors," I said, recalling a lesson from years of experience.

"Printing is complete," Zen announced.

I walked over to the printer and carefully removed the parts. As I examined them, something caught my attention.

"These look different too," I said, turning one over in my hand.

"The prototype looked too much like a weapon," Zen said.

I turned the casing over in my hands. "Now it's a flashlight - deceptively ordinary for something this powerful," I mused.

"The redesign will also make it easier to manufacture," Zen added. Ever the company man.

* * *

It took me all morning to assemble one unit.

"Zen, this design is difficult to assemble," I complained, setting down my tools with a sigh.

"Not if you're an AssemblyBot," Zen replied without missing a beat.

"Those robots are really killing the workers," I muttered absentmindedly, my thoughts drifting to the impact of automation.

"Ten minutes until your appointment with Robin Coleman," Zen announced in his precise Agent voice, snapping me back to the present.

"Thanks, Zen," I said, tidying up my workspace. After a quick cleanup, I left, ready to meet Robin.

CHAPTER SEVEN

Hobnobbing with the Proletariat

I spotted Robin sitting at our usual table in the cafeteria, eyes glued to her company pad. She looked up as I approached with my tray.

"Hey there," she said.

"I see you skipped the burrito," I replied, settling down across from her.

"They make me fat," she said flatly, catching me off guard.

"You don't take the Forever Young meds?" I asked, surprised. Almost every female Ruc relied on them.

"Not yet. I'm holding out as long as I can," Robin replied, her tone firm as she speared a piece of lettuce. "I'd rather live longer than look better."

"My wife started them at twenty-one. They seem to work, at least for her."

"She looks great for your contemporary," Robin said, her tone toeing the line between complimentary and dismissive.

"Thanks, I'll let her know." (Naaa.)

Robin shifted gears. "What was the deal with Zen yesterday? The face thing?"

I sighed. "That's on me. I forgot to brief you on how to work with Zen." I took a bite of my burrito, savoring the mix of flavors for a moment before continuing.

"I figured it was something like that. You looked anxious - not a great look for you, by the way," she said, smirking.

"Here's the important part," I began, leaning slightly forward. "You can say pretty much anything to Zen or ask him any question. But anything about his trainers? Strictly off-limits." I took another bite, chewing slowly for emphasis.

Robin nodded, realization dawning. "I said his trainers might be lying to him."

I leaned in close to her and whispered, "That is a cardinal sin, my dear." Her light, floral scent caught me - a faint, feminine touch I hadn't noticed before.

"Should I be concerned?" she asked, her voice low but steady.

"A year ago, it would've been a real problem," I said. "But now, Zen is complete, and the trainers aren't running the program anymore. Still, we can never express doubt about Zen's creators. Make sense?"

"I see. Is there anything else I should know?" Robin asked, her tone curious but cautious.

"Never lie to him," I said firmly. "That's non-negotiable. He's like anyone - lie to him, and you lose his trust. I don't know exactly how that would change his behavior, but let's not put him to the test."

"Got it. That makes sense too," Robin said, nodding.

"And this is critical," I added, my voice dropping even lower. "Never talk to Zen about the military or ask him questions about it."

Her brow furrowed. "Yes, that was in the standard 'Welcome to the YSP' briefing."

"I'm making you a lightsaber," I said casually.

"No way!" Robin's eyes lit up. "Can we duel like in the movies?"

"Not sure what happens if the beams clash," I said. "I'll have to ask Zen. We'll test it once it's ready."

"What's the status of the build?" Robin asked, leaning forward slightly.

"I'll probably have both done by tonight, so testing will have to wait until next week. Zen designed the thing to be assembled by freaking robots, so it's a tough build for humans. But I'll get it done."

As we wrapped up lunch, she asked, "Are you going to the rally tonight?"

"I have permission from my wife," I said with a joking tone, hoping to keep it light.

"I'm sure you need it," she shot back with a smirk. Then, standing up, she added, "See you tonight," and walked away before I could respond.

I stayed behind, still feeling a bit hungry. Without hesitation, I went back for a second burrito and finished my meal alone.

* * *

I got home with just enough time to swim my laps, grab a quick bite, and change into clothes that downplayed my status. Blending in felt essential. Rucs venturing into Wic areas drew attention - often the wrong kind. Trouble followed easily, and no one cared unless it left a Ruc in the hospital.

I was heading for the door when Amy intercepted me, leaning casually against the frame with a raised eyebrow.
"Do you think that disguise is fooling anyone?" she teased, giving my outfit a pointed look.
"Just trying to avoid being an obvious target," I said, adjusting my collar. Her smile made it clear she wasn't convinced.
"Be careful," she said, her hand brushing my arm lightly. "And for God's sake, don't make the news."

* * *

The Community Center buzzed with unexpected energy. Dozens streamed inside - far more than Robin's estimate of twenty. I hesitated in the car's safe cocoon. "You're nuts for going in there," I thought. But I pushed the doubt aside and stepped into the unknown.

I peered into the room through the open doors, surprised to see it packed wall-to-wall. Hundreds of people filled the seats, with a spillover crowd standing at the back and leaning against the walls. The air was heavy with the smell of sweat and mold, likely coming from the worn-out fixtures and the Wics themselves.

I stayed by the door, leaning on the frame, trying not to attract attention. The lights dimmed, and a man shuffled to the podium. Casually dressed, he looked unassuming - short, overweight, with a receding hairline that shone under the single spotlight.

He adjusted the microphone, tapping it once. "Alright, alright, can I get a little attention here?" His voice had a nasal edge but carried well. The scattered conversations died down and it became quiet quickly.

"Folks," he said, "I know it's hard to take time out of your day, but trust me - tonight matters." He scanned the crowd, pausing as a few claps broke out.

"We have someone here who isn't afraid to speak the truth," he continued, his voice rising. "Someone to remind us of what we've lost - and what we can take back."

The crowd responded with louder applause this time, rippling through the room.

"So listen up, open your ears, and maybe even your minds. Give a warm welcome to our friend and fierce defender, Victor Nash!"

The MC stepped back, and the room erupted into cheers and applause. From behind the curtain emerged a man who seemed carved for this moment - broad-shouldered, confident, his every step commanding attention. Victor raised a clenched fist in the Wic salute, the crowd roaring back in unison.

He waited patiently, letting the applause swell and fade before speaking. His voice, deep and resonant, filled the space effortlessly.

"I see the confusion, the frustration, even the anger in your eyes. You're tired of being pushed around, of seeing your rights trampled, of feeling like you don't have a voice." He paused, his gaze sweeping the room.

"And you know what?" His voice rose, sharp and clear. "You're right to feel that way!"

The crowd rumbled in agreement, a low wave of murmurs rippling across the room. Victor stood tall, letting the tension build before continuing. His timing was impeccable, the mark of a seasoned orator who knew how to hold his audience captive.

"They've stolen something precious - our rights under the Old Constitution," Victor thundered. "They erased it from schools, hoping we'd forget. Hoping we'd accept their lies. But we won't!"

He let the words hang in the air for a moment before continuing. "The Old Constitution wasn't just a rulebook; it was a promise," Victor said, his voice steady and commanding. "It guaranteed our rights and freedoms - every one of us, no matter our status or wealth." His gaze swept the crowd, locking eyes with individuals as if speaking directly to them.

Victor pressed on. "The original Constitution - the one they tore apart - enshrined our right to speak our minds, to gather peacefully, to demand better from those in power. It protected our right to a fair trial, safeguarded us from unreasonable searches and seizures, and ensured equal treatment under the law. It gave us the freedom to travel anywhere in the country and guaranteed every citizen the right to vote."

The crowd murmured, a low wave of discontent rippling through the room. Victor waited, perfectly attuned to the moment, before continuing. "Somewhere along the way, those in power decided they didn't like the rules. They wanted more control for themselves - more control over our lives. So they chipped away at the Old Constitution, piece by piece, until it was barely recognizable."

The crowd erupted into applause, a sharp contrast to their earlier murmurs. Victor seized the momentum. "One Million, One Vote." His voice rang out clearly as he scanned the crowd. "You all know what that means. The rich control everything." He paused, letting the anger simmer as the crowd responded with agitated murmurs.

"They tricked our ancestors into giving up the right to vote," Victor said, his voice tinged with both sorrow and indignation. "And how did they do it? By dangling a million-dollar lottery in front of them - and we fell for it. One million dollars. Sounds amazing, doesn't it?"

A chorus of agreement rippled through the audience, punctuated by a few voices shouting affirmations.

"But do you know how many of those so-called 'lucky' souls are still voting today?" Victor asked, his voice dropping into a biting tone. "Barely a handful. Most end up right back where they started - only now, they've got a collar around their neck for their so-called good fortune."

He paused again, his expression hardening as he let the gravity of his words sink in. The crowd murmured angrily, their discontent growing heavier with each passing second.

"The Lottery is their tool to blind us," Victor declared. "It distracts, misleads, and makes us believe our voices don't matter. And what do we do?" His voice sharpened. "We sit, glued to our screens, hoping to be the one winner among millions." He let the silence after his words hang heavy.

"Our ancestors gave up their rights," Victor said, his voice firm. "And we've paid the price. Our children go hungry. We freeze in winter without heat. We die from curable diseases because medicine is a luxury only for them." His words hit hard, the crowd murmuring their agreement.

"But the workers of today aren't foolish like our ancestors," he continued, his voice rising with conviction. "We've been forged in the fires of tyranny and suffering. And now, we are stronger - stronger than those who oppress us!"

The hall thundered with applause, the crowd's roar shaking the very air.

"You enjoying the show?"

I was jarred back to reality by a startlingly beautiful woman - or rather, a girl, maybe eighteen. Slender and muscular, her beauty wasn't like my wife's refined elegance. It was raw, almost feral. Despite the cool night, she was wearing almost nothing - a thin, torn T-shirt and shorts. The faint outline of her Device bulged from her back pocket, and she shifted in her sandals with casual confidence.

"It's interesting," I replied, my tone probably betraying my surprise.

"What's wrong? Never seen a real woman before?" she teased, her voice playful as she moved with a deliberate, seductive sway.

"Excuse me?" I said, caught off guard.

"You're looking at me like a hungry man looks at a steak."

"Aren't you cold?" The words slipped out before I could stop them. I sounded stupid.

She laughed lightly. "I'm used to it. I like wearing as little as possible. You like it, don't you?" She spun around, her nearly bare figure on full display.

"I bet your wife wouldn't do it," she added, her tone teasing.

"You'd win that bet," I said flatly, meeting her gaze.

"So, what're you here for? The meat, the salad, or something special?" she asked, her voice carrying a hint of mischief.

"I'm here to listen to Victor," I replied, trying to peer past her toward the stage.

"That's the salad. You're not here for him." She gave me a clever look. "I can tell."

"What am I here for, then?" I asked, narrowing my eyes slightly.

"No rich dude comes down here by himself just to listen to some clown spout political nonsense," she said, her voice dripping with skepticism. "Unless you're with the FBI, and you don't look like a badge. So, it's usually the meat."

She leaned closer, her expression daring me to deny it.

"So, if I'm here for the meat and you're standing there, am I to assume you're part of the table setting?" I asked, keeping my tone light and playful.

She smirked. "The meat is a few blocks away, on Broad Street. You'll see them - people with heavy makeup. Take your pick: men, women, boys, girls. They're all there." Her eyes sparkled mischievously as she leaned closer. "But you're here, and that makes me the 'something special.'"

She punctuated her words by tapping her index finger against my sternum, her touch light but deliberate.

"Not interested in the meat," I said, meeting her gaze with conviction.

She grinned. "No, you're not here for the meat or the salad," she teased, her tone coy.

"Do you often approach strange men and discuss what's on the plate?" I asked, keeping the conversation going.

"You're the first," she replied, her tone shifting slightly - just enough to make it sound convincing.

I couldn't help but enjoy the banter, though a part of me wondered if this was leading to a scam. Still, I decided to probe further, steering the topic to something less personal. "Why'd you call Victor Nash a clown?" I asked, hoping to shift the tone.

"This guy…" she said, jerking her thumb toward the arena. Her voice turned sharp with disgust as she continued, "...is full of crap. Worker's rights? Yeah, like he can change anything."

"I didn't get a chance to hear much," I countered, "but he sounded like he was saying important things."

"Talk is cheap," she said dismissively, crossing her arms. The movement was deliberate, subtle but effective, as it pushed her small breasts together and up - a practiced gesture, one young women often use when they're trying to draw attention.

"What's your take, then?" I asked, intrigued by her strong opinions.

"He's no different than the criminal politicians who ran this country into the ground at the beginning of the 21st century," she said with a smirk. "He says what the crowd wants to hear, and they roar in approval."

As if on cue, the crowd erupted into cheers. She laughed, a sharp, amused sound. "Listen to those brutes cheer."

"You seem unusually well-informed," I said, offering her a compliment.

She straightened slightly, her expression bright with pride. "I just graduated high school, top of my class. Perfect grades. And not from some dumbed-down public school either," she added, the edge in her tone impossible to miss.

"That's impressive," I admitted. "How did you manage that?"

"It's a long and boring story," she said, her playful demeanor returning. "I'd rather talk about you."

"Talk about boring - that's me," I replied, meeting her teasing with my own. "Come on, tell me."

"Give me $100, and I'll tell you my story. Nothing's free around here," she said, pulling her Device from her back pocket and waving it in front of my eyes.

"$100 seems steep for just a story," I replied, raising an eyebrow.

"I'll throw in keeping you safe from the other girls as a bonus," she added with a sly grin, motioning vaguely around us.

"There's nobody around," I said, glancing around the empty area. "Everyone's watching Victor - except us."

"Sure, right now," she shot back, her voice dripping with sarcasm. "But they'll come sniffing soon enough."

I shrugged, pulled out my Device and sent her $100. "Here you go."

She gave me a smug smile. "That didn't hurt at all, did it, sweetie?" she said in a tone that felt like a mother chiding her child.

"Totally painless," I replied dryly.

"It must be something, not caring about money," she said, her expression softening slightly. "I got a taste of it for a few years. I liked it. Being poor sucks."

"Alright, young lady," I said, leaning in with mock drama. "Give me my money's worth and tell me your tale of woe."

She rolled her eyes but started. "Ya, there's some woe. Okay, here goes. My dad was a drunk and a loser, but somehow, he found a wife and had two kids - my older sister, who's twenty now, and me. My mom died when I was a baby, so it was just him raising us. He did his best - it wasn't great, but it wasn't awful. Then, when my sister turned twelve, he sold her to a family in Connecticut that lost their own child. She got lucky."

"Do you still keep in touch with her?" I asked, genuinely curious.

"Yeah, we talk all the time. Her adopted family treated her pretty well, and she's in college now. I'm so proud of her."

"Did they fully adopt her?" I pressed.

She shook her head. "No, she's still one of us. They're good people, but not that good. She's on her own now."

"So, it was just you and your dad after that?" I asked.

"For a while, yeah. Then he met some floozy who hated me. She convinced him to sell me too." Her voice hardened, but a faint smirk tugged at her lips. "I hated that witch, but she did me a favor."

"How so?" I asked.

110

"I was sold to a local family, as a plaything for their fourteen year old son. They were orthodox and their religion prevented them from just buying him a SexBot." She said it like it was an everyday thing. For Wic's, it was.

"That sounds rough," I said, unsure how else to respond.

"Did you get a SexBot for your fourteenth birthday?" she asked, her tone turning playful.

"No," I replied with a small shake of my head. "My wife and I have an arranged marriage."

"That's cool," she said casually, then added with a knowing smile, "Do you have a son?"

"Yes, he's only twelve, so we haven't talked about his coming of age yet. The studies say it's healthy." I added.

"Just get him a robot and not a little girl. That's not healthy." She added with a note of disgust.

"He has a girlfriend prospect, so maybe the topic will never have to come up. He's a really good-looking kid - smart, polite, and well-mannered, which helps," I said with a touch of proud, fatherly warmth.

Since making or watching porn became a criminal offense, it was stylish for teenagers to receive a SexBot for their fourteenth birthday.

"Orthodox family, fourteen-year-old son…" I said, steering the conversation back on topic.

She continued, "I wasn't exactly innocent, so it wasn't hard for me to accept my new life."

"At twelve, you were already sexually active?" I asked, my curiosity piqued.

"I had one experience when I was ten. That was it," she said matter-of-factly.

"That's quite young," I remarked.

"If you want to hear that story, it'll cost you another $100," she added with a playful, retail tone.

"That's okay, please continue," I said, encouraging her.

"My owners treated me pretty well," she began. "I had my own room, full medical care, and they even gave me access to virtual school so I could educate myself."

"That was surprisingly decent," I remarked. "How was their son?"

She rolled her eyes slightly. "He was a total jerk. The only time he talked to me was when he wanted something - service. To him, I wasn't a person, just an object. I really loathed him at first, but over time, we figured out how to make it work. It was… fine."

"Those orthodox sects can be pretty weird," I added.

"They didn't indoctrinate me," she said, shrugging. "I was just furniture. My only purpose was to keep their son busy. So, while I wasn't servicing Mr. Jerk, I was free to do whatever I wanted. I spent my time learning and bettering myself."

She paused, her expression shifting sharply as she suddenly screeched, "He's mine, sister, get lost!" Her voice cut through the hallway like a whip.

A woman who had been approaching us stopped, scowled, and flipped us the bird before moving on.

"She's a hooker. You can tell by the makeup," she said casually, her tone completely unfazed.

"Not interested," I replied, shaking my head.

Without missing a beat, she took my hand and guided me toward one of the large pillars in the hallway, away from the door to the arena. As we moved, I caught the faint, pleasant scent of lilacs wafting from her.

"So, what happened?" I asked.

"When Mr. Jerk graduated and went off to college, they kept me on as a house servant for a while - until the dad started diddling me."

"The wife didn't like that, did she?"

"You guessed it," she said with a wry smile. "She forced her husband to free me and even set me up with a job and a small place a few clicks away from here. I've got a five-year contract with Wyoming Electric Utility as a lineman. Been on my own for two years now."

"So, you're eighteen? How'd you finish school?" I asked.

"The mom let me stay enrolled, and I finished up a few weeks ago," she said.

"That was pretty generous of them."

"I think it was reasonable payment for services rendered," she replied, slipping back into her polished retail tone.

"Did you learn anything?" I asked, curious.

She smirked. "Put me to the test. Ask me anything you learned in high school, and if I get it right, you pay me another $100."

"What if you get it wrong?" I countered.

"I'll give you your $100 back," she said flippantly, clearly confident.

"Those are high stakes for you. You really want to play?"

"Shoot, cowboy," she challenged, her voice daring me.

"Alright, here goes. Something easy. What's PV = nRT?" I asked.

She rolled her eyes like I'd underestimated her. "Jeez. That IS an easy one. $PV = nRT$ is the Ideal Gas Law. It's a fundamental equation in physics and chemistry that describes the relationship between pressure, volume, temperature, and the amount of an ideal gas." She rattled it off like she was acing an oral exam.

"That's impressive," I said, genuinely surprised.

"Pay up, pardner," she said enthusiastically, holding out her hand with a triumphant grin.

"How about double or nothing?" I asked, a playful challenge in my tone.

"Shoot. You're going to have to try harder to stump me," she replied, her confidence unshaken.

"Okay, here's one most of my colleagues never learned. What was the Second Amendment in the Old Constitution?"

She groaned. "No more science? I like science. Civics history is boring."

"So, you deflect? Loser!" I teased.

"Hold on, I know the answer," she said, shifting back into her lecture voice. "The Second Amendment stated: A well-regulated Militia, being necessary to the security of a free State, the right of the people to keep and bear Arms, shall not be infringed." She rattled it off with precision.

"Wow. I'm impressed," I admitted. "I'd have to check the document to see if that's exactly right, but I'll take your word for it."

"You owe me $200. Who's the loser now?" she said, poking me gently in the sternum again with a smug grin.

"Okay, I owe you $200," I said, nodding. "Double or nothing again?"

She leaned back slightly, giving me a mischievous look. "You're going to be into me for some serious coin, Handsome. Are you sure you can afford it?"

"You're joking, right?" I said, the faintest edge of insult creeping into my voice.

"Calm down, big boy," she said, grinning. "Just funnin' you. I can tell by your shoes you can afford anything."

"My shoes?" I asked, glancing down at them.

"They cost more than a year's rent and are all scuffed up. Only the super-rich can afford that," she said, her eyes narrowing playfully. "What do you have - 100 votes?" She leaned in slightly, fishing for a bit of personal info.

"Are you ready for the final round?" I asked, adding a touch of flair.

"Hit me," she said confidently.

"Explain why the Second Amendment wasn't included in the New Constitution." I paused, certain she'd stumble on this one. I only knew it because I'd written a paper on the Second Amendment as a freshman in high school.

"That's not a fair question," she countered immediately. "The answer is subjective."

"I'm giving the test. I make the rules," I said, my tone shifting to something more serious.

"Okay, but I get a rebuttal if you reject my answer," she said, raising an eyebrow.

"Fair enough," I agreed.

"You're asking for an essay," she protested. "I can list a dozen reasons."

"Just give me the top two," I said, leaning forward slightly.

"One: Maintaining control," she began. "The New Constitution is designed to concentrate power in the hands of the Rucs. Denying firearms to the majority of the population prevents us from effectively resisting or rebelling against your oppressive system." She paused, her eyes locking onto mine as she added a playful wink.

"I'll accept that," I said, unable to hide a hint of admiration.

She took a moment, clearly organizing her thoughts, before continuing. "And Two: Enforcing economic hierarchy. The New Constitution establishes a rigid economic structure. Access to firearms could be seen as a privilege reserved for the Rucs, further solidifying their status and control."

"That's a strong argument," I admitted. "I might argue that the second point is less critical, but I'll accept it."

She smiled, a glimmer of satisfaction in her eyes.

"Pay up, sucker!" she said, grabbing my arm and tugging me close. Her hard muscles and soft breasts brushed against me, and with a resigned grin, I pulled out my Device and sent her $400.

"You just made my month!" she exclaimed, wrapping me in another exuberant hug.

"So, young lady, what's your dilemma? What are you after?" I asked, steering the conversation to a more serious topic.

115

She calmed, her demeanor shifting as she adopted a thoughtful pose. "I have perfect SAT scores, perfect grades from a quality school, and a full scholarship to the college of my choice. But it expires when I turn twenty-one."

"That sounds like a very good position to be in," I said, genuinely impressed.

"I also have a five-year contract with WEU, and I can't even apply to a college until that contract is satisfied," she said, her tone sharpening with frustration.

"You can't just quit?" I asked, my ignorance showing.

She shook her head slowly, a small smirk of disbelief tugging at her lips. "I can see you have no idea how we live down here in the weeds," she said, her voice tinged with both amusement and bitterness. "If I miss a single day of work, I get charged a day's wages. I'm not allowed to be more than fifty clicks from home on a workday. And if I stop working altogether? In a month, I'd be in breach of contract and wearing a collar in some brothel."

She paused, her gaze locking onto mine. "Do you want me to go on, rich dude with no name?" she asked, her tone dripping with sarcasm. She'd mansplained it to me, and she was right to do it.

"I see. That's tough," I said, nodding sympathetically.

"We're treated as property. Do you have any idea what that means?" she shot back, her tone growing testy.

"Yes," I replied, meeting her gaze. "You're essentially slaves without the collar. I get it now."

She blinked, caught off guard for a moment, then smirked. "That's a remarkable conclusion for an ignorant Ruc," she said, her tone softening as she returned to her earlier playfulness.

"So, if you can't satisfy your contract before your scholarship expires, you'd be in a real pickle," I said, summing it up.

"That would be it for me," she said with a bitter edge. "I'd never get out of this shithole state."

"If you hadn't aced my questions, I'd think you were running a scam," I admitted, studying her.

116

"You're skeptical? Of what?" she asked, stepping back slightly, her expression turning defensive.

"No, I believe you," I said quickly, reassuring her. "The way you rattled off your answers, I knew you were something special." I brought it back to her earlier comment, hoping to lighten the mood.

"I am something special, and I'm not here by accident," she said, her voice carrying a quiet intensity.

"You mean here, as in talking to me? I assumed you were here to see the clown," I replied, keeping my tone light.

"Are you kidding? I wouldn't waste five seconds on that garbage," she said with a dismissive wave.

"And...?" I prompted, sensing there was more.

"I was in the park up the road, about two clicks, with my friends," she began. "Then I saw your car drive by. I had this vision of you, and I knew you were going to save me. I took off running, and when I got here - there you were. Exactly as I'd seen in my mind's eye, right here. You are going to save me," she said, her voice filled with absolute confidence.

"That's a remarkable story," I said, trying to mask my skepticism. "Do you have these visions often?"

"Up to now, only when I'm in danger. This time was different," she said, her tone thoughtful.

"When did you start having these visions?" I asked, adopting a more clinical tone.

"The first time was right after I got sick from a serious gastric illness," she explained. "You know the kind where you're leaking green stuff out of every orifice?" She wrinkled her nose as she spoke.

I nodded as though I could relate, though I'd never experienced anything like that.

"It was the first day I could go outside," she said, her voice softening as she recalled the memory. "It was beautiful - warm - and I was playing with chalk on the road." She paused, lost in thought.

"How old were you?" I asked gently.

"It was right after my sister moved east," she said, her gaze distant. "So… a little more than ten."

"Mmm," I murmured, encouraging her to continue.

"A boy I knew, about fourteen, came up to me," she said, her voice tinged with unease. "He told me he'd found a barrel of candy in the basement of an abandoned building and asked if I wanted some too." She hesitated briefly, then added, "Naturally, I did, so I followed him to an area filled with abandoned buildings and trash."

"I can see where this is going. Please stop - I don't want to cause you pain," I said, my voice soft with empathy. Her expression was enough to tell me it wasn't a pleasant memory.

"No, it's okay," she replied after a moment, her tone steady despite the emotion in her eyes. "The story does have a happy ending - or at least a satisfying one. I don't mind."

She paused, gathering herself before continuing. "Right as I reached the partially opened door to the building, I felt this pain in my gut - like nothing I'd ever felt before. It was so intense it made me double over and scream." Her voice faltered slightly as her eyes glistened with tears. "At that moment, I saw the faces of boys I didn't know. They had this look, like a pack of dogs with a cornered cat."

She paused again, her eyes flicking away as the memory gripped her.

"I knew what was coming. I could see it, and even my young immature brain comprehended the danger. I tried to run," she said, her voice trembling slightly, "but the boy grabbed me and dragged me into the hall. He pushed me down the stairs into that basement. I remember the smell of the floor - oil and mold." She paused, her eyes distant, caught in the memory.

"I was hurt from the broken concrete on the stairs, and when I pushed myself up, I saw them - all those faces." Her voice faltered, and she stopped, her breath jagged.

"I think that's enough," I said, my stomach turning. "You don't have to go on."

"No, I have to finish - you'll understand why," she said firmly, her voice steadying as she took another breath.

"I passed out from the pain of their attack quickly. When I came to, it was night. I was hurt, naked, and crawled around in the dark to find my clothes. Somehow, I made it out." She paused again, shifting slightly toward me. Her vulnerability was palpable, and without thinking, I put my arm around her. She didn't flinch or pull away; instead, she leaned in just enough for me to feel the weight of her pain.

"In the moonlight, I could see I was covered with blood, probably from being pushed down those stairs, and out of a certain place from the assault." She stopped for a moment.

"You're lucky to be alive!" I exclaimed quietly, trying to process what she'd endured.

"I found my way home," she continued, her voice steady but hollow. "and cleaned myself up. By the time I was done, my father was awake. I told him what happened."

"Is this where it gets satisfying?" I asked, hoping for some relief from the darkness of her story.

"Not yet," she said, her tone sharpening. "My father beat me severely and dislocated my shoulder - because I lost my shoes."

"Great dad," I muttered, immediately regretting the comment.

"Ya, he was a real keeper," she said dryly. "He told me I deserved it for being so gullible."

"So… where's the satisfaction?" I asked, leaning in, desperate for a silver lining

"Okay, here's the kicker. I was young and undeveloped, and undeveloped girls have undeveloped female parts. They couldn't attack me there, so they did it in another place." She motioned around back with her eyes.

"That's horrible!" I cried, again in a whisper.

"That illness I was getting over," her tone shifted to clinical detachment, "was a nasty strain of E. coli - a novel one, quite aggressive. Did you hear about it? Hundreds in this town died."

"I don't recall," I admitted, my ignorance plain.

"Of course you don't," she said, a hint of bitterness creeping in. "It tore through our community, not yours. Anyway, that bacteria wasn't deadly in the gastrointestinal tract. It was dangerous, sure, but not deadly. Where it was deadly was in the urinary tract - that's what killed so many people. I'm honestly surprised you didn't hear about it."

"I try to ignore the horrors of the world," I replied in my Ruc tone, trying to sound detached.

"You can. We lived it," she said sharply, her words cutting through my pretense. She paused for a moment, letting the weight of what she'd said settle in the air between us.

"The boys. They got the infection." I concluded.

"You are a smarty pants, aren't you?" she said, her tone playful again.

"First in my class," I replied proudly. "Of course, that was a long time ago, but yes - I am THE smarty pants." I emphasized "THE" with mock importance.

"I'll bet," she said with a smirk. She paused briefly, her demeanor shifting as she got back into character. "Two of the devils died," she continued. "The other nine? Rendered completely impotent. Like… wet noodles." Her conclusion came with a tone of grim satisfaction.

"That is a satisfactory ending," I said, nodding. "You recovered, obviously?"

"I had nightmares for years and painful problems with my rear until I moved in with the family," she said, her voice quieter now. "They gave me full Medical, and the MedPod fixed me up 100%."

"That is a remarkable story," I said, pausing for a moment to let her regain her composure. "Have you had other visions?" I asked gently.

"Off and on," she replied, her tone steadying. "I always take them seriously. I've had them when meeting guys - it probably saved my life a couple of times - and one time at work, I know it saved my life."

"What happened at work?" I asked, leaning forward slightly.

"We were doing our usual thing, clearing brush and limbs from around the power lines. It was rainy and cold that day when a heavy line being pulled by a hauler slipped off the load. It swung around and struck two workers. It would have hit me too, except I had the vision and hit the deck an instant before the cable sliced the two workers - a man and a woman - in half."

She paused, her voice faltering slightly as she continued. "I was the first to get to the woman. She was still alive, but… she'd been severed below the rib cage. I watched the life drain out of her eyes as she died. That was my vision."

"That's dangerous work! Did you know them?" I asked, horrified.

"They were new, and so was I," she said flatly. "The seasoned workers knew better than to stay within reach of those cables. Nobody told us - it's everyone for themself out there in the bush."

She paused, her expression hardening. "You can see why I want to change my life. It's not a mystery or a whim."

"What about your boyfriend?" I asked, throwing in a loaded question.

"I haven't been with a man since Mr. Jerk's dad," she said, her tone laced with disdain. "I hate these mindless brutes with no education or money. They're uninteresting and treat women like trash." Despite her harsh words, she carried herself with a sense of class.

"So, totally hot, no boyfriend, living alone," I said, laying out the facts. "You mentioned I'm going to save you. Care to elaborate?"

"You're looking for a mistress," she said bluntly, her eyes locking on mine. "Don't deny it. That's the 'something special' I was talking about earlier."

"Go on," I said, keeping my voice eager but measured.

"Here's the deal," she began, her tone shifting to something almost professional. "You pay off my contract with WEU, buy me Full Medical, and give me enough spending money to be comfortable. In return, I'll be available for you - and you alone - whenever and wherever you want. I'll travel with you, live as close as you need, and be your most trusted and devoted concubine. I'll even sign a three-year contract."

She paused, her expression unreadable as she added, "When I satisfy the contract, you'll get me an open-ended travel permit and an international passport."

Her delivery was precise, almost like she was negotiating a legal agreement.

121

"Just like that? What if I'm a brute?" I asked, raising an eyebrow.

"Get me a dermal regenerator, and you can beat me up if that's what you want," she replied, her tone daring. "Like I said, anything you want - no restrictions. But I don't think you're the evil type. I know you're a good man. I can feel it, and my visions are always right."

"That's a lot to consider," I said noncommittally, trying to maintain a neutral tone.

"You don't have to decide now," she said, her voice dripping with allure. "Come by my place tomorrow, anytime, and we'll have a close and personal discussion about how we can make this work."

My heart skipped a beat and then raced. I felt my face flush as I scrambled for a response. "I'm afraid I'm busy this weekend," I added, deflecting again.

"I see you're interested," she said, her gaze sharp and knowing. She paused, giving me a once-over before continuing. "We're working deep in the brush next week, and Saturday is that silly Reveal thing. Are you invited?"

"No," I replied mechanically. "I'm in a support position at the plant."

"Get asked that a lot, I bet," she said with a sly smile.

"Yes. It's getting old," I admitted. "Just another week and it'll be over."

"First-world problems, Handsome," she teased, pausing briefly before adding, "How about Friday night, a week from today?"

"I think that would work," I said, unable to keep the sheepishness out of my voice.

Just then, the crowd started streaming out of the arena, enveloping us in a noisy mob. She turned to me, holding out her hand. "Hey, I'm Jessica," she said, her voice cutting through the chaos.

"I'm Frank," I replied loudly, shaking her hand.

Before I could say anything more, she pulled me into a big hug, leaning in close to whisper softly in my ear, "You're going to save me."

Then, with a swift motion, she grabbed the pen from my shirt pocket, wrote her name and number on my hand, and dashed off playfully, tossing me a kiss over her shoulder as she disappeared into the crowd.

Then I saw Robin, not ten meters away, arms folded and wearing a decidedly unpleasant expression. The crowd was thinning now, and I had no idea how long she had been standing there, watching us.

She marched up to me, grabbed my hand, and stared at the ink scrawled on it. "You've been busy, loverboy," she said, her tone biting.

"I..." was all I could croak out, completely at a loss.

"Victor's busy with his politics, so I thought we could grab drinks," she continued, her words sharp and deliberate. "But since you're clearly all worn out from wrestling with that trollop, I think I'll just leave you here with that ink on your hand and say goodnight."

She turned on her heel, stomping off, but not before yelling over her shoulder, "She stole your pen."

"I'll see you tomorrow..." I called after her weakly, sounding like a whipped fool.

I screwed that up badly. Not only had I missed most of Victor's speech, but I had also managed to annoy the heck out of Robin.

On the drive home, the misery settled in, gnawing at me. Finally, I asked myself, Why was Robin so upset?

* * *

Amy was in the kitchen watching the news when I entered. As soon as she saw me, she switched it off.

"Did you hear about Orlando?" she asked, her face blank, that detached expression people get when trying to process terrible news.

"No. What's going on?" I asked, completely out of the loop.

"An hour ago, the military struck the refugee camps. Tens of thousands are dead or injured - burned alive with firebombs." Her voice trembled slightly, but her expression stayed composed.

"Napalm or phosphorus?" I asked absentmindedly, my thoughts still far away.

"Frank," she said sharply, her voice cutting through my haze. "People were burned to death - horribly. Lots of them. Many were women and children. And all you can wonder about is the type of bomb they used?"

I blinked, jarred by her words. "I'm sorry, Amy. I've just got a lot on my mind," I said, sitting down across from her at the kitchen table. I took a sip of water, barely noticing KitchenBot.

"I know why you're so distracted," she said, her voice suddenly sharper. "You've been busy, haven't you?"

Her words hit like a slap, snapping me fully into the moment.

"Excuse me?" was all I could squeak out.

"I smell something," Amy said, her voice cool but accusatory. "Floral. Not one I wear. It's cheap - like the kind Wic hookers use."

"Please, Amy," I said, trying to deflect. "How would you know what a Wic hooker smells like?"

"Whatever," she shot back, unimpressed. "Don't play dumb. You've been with someone who wears it. Go ahead, lie to me again." Her eyes dared me to try.

"That depends on what you mean by 'with,'" I said weakly, feeling the ground crumbling beneath me.

Her expression hardened. "Spill it."

I took a moment, measuring my words carefully while trying to gauge the intensity of Amy's glare. "You said I should get a mistress - as long as it's not Robin."

Her eyes narrowed slightly. "Not Robin?" she asked, her voice sharp with suspicion.

"Not Robin," I confirmed. "A Wic, like you said I should."

"Do we need to get the scanner?" Amy asked seriously. Full Medical provided a scanner capable of diagnosing virtually any known parasite, infection, or illness and could automatically prescribe medication or call a MedPod if needed.

"No," I said quickly. "I just talked to her. She hugged me - that's the extent of it."

Amy's posture relaxed slightly, her expression softening. She still didn't look happy, but at least she seemed less concerned. "What's her story?"

"She's young - eighteen - but has been on her own since she was sixteen," I said, choosing my words carefully. "She's got a full scholarship to any college."

Amy raised an eyebrow. "A full scholarship? What does she need you for?"

"She said I'm going to save her," I replied. Then, taking a breath, I explained the terms of Jessica's proposed contract.

Amy leaned back, crossing her arms. "So, in three years, she's gone?"

"That's the deal," I said. "She's ambitious - wants a way out."

Amy was quiet for a long moment before she finally said, "This stays between you, me, and your Wic. Tre and Sara know nothing."

"Of course," I replied quickly. "The kids aren't involved."

She sighed, shaking her head. "You're really doing this?"

"I haven't decided yet," I admitted.

Amy's lips quivered into a faint, humorless smile. "She better be worth it."

CHAPTER EIGHT

A Hike to WLWY

I met Leon near Mary Bay, where my car parked itself in the nearby lot. Robin hadn't arrived yet.

"How did it go with Robin while I was gone?" Leon asked, strolling over with his usual laid-back energy.

"She's really something," I said, grinning. "We licked the instability problem - and made a lightsaber."

"A lightsaber?" Leon's eyes widened with genuine curiosity. "Impressive." Then, spotting movement in the distance, he nodded toward an approaching car. "Looks like Robin's here." Leon had a knack for identifying cars like others did faces.

"Her boyfriend sure is a big one," I added as the vehicle drew closer.

"Yeah, he's carrying everything except our personal stuff. Your pack just personal gear?" Leon asked.

"As instructed," I replied, lifting my small backpack. It carried only clothes and some backup food.

"Are we eating roadkill for dinner?" I asked, my sarcasm tinged with genuine concern.

Leon smirked. "Nope. I've got real beef steaks. A bunch of them. We're feeding a bear, you know," he said smugly as Robin's car came to a halt.

Robin stepped out of the car, and I couldn't help but notice her outfit - or lack of one. She wore a tight fitting, color-shifting athletic top, both practical and provocative.

"Robin! I see you survived a week of forms and morons," Leon called out, laughing as he approached her. He gave her a brief hug.

"I hope you live forever, Leon," Robin said with mock exasperation. "I'd rather be your assistant. Next time, I go into the field, and you can deal with the suits." She pulled her pack from the car and donned it in one swift motion.

"We'll talk about that, missy," Leon replied in a humorous tone, grinning.

Victor emerged next, effortlessly hauling an enormous pack from the trunk. It was stuffed with everything we'd need for the next 24 hours. He set it down as the car silently rolled off to join mine in the nearby lot.

"Victor, nice to see you again," Leon exclaimed, stepping forward with an outstretched hand. "We're really going to love having you along."

"Thanks, Leon. You must be Mr. Waverly," Victor said in his deep, resonant voice.

I extended my hand, which disappeared into his giant paw. His grip was firm and proper, a handshake that conveyed strength without being overbearing.

"I'm glad to finally have the opportunity to meet you," I said as I withdrew my much smaller hand. "Please, call me Frank," I added with a polite nod.

We gathered around the front of the jeep as Victor laid out the briefing, his tone calm and professional.

"The weather looks good today and tomorrow," Victor began, spreading a map across the hood. He traced a route with his finger. "We'll drive to this stream, ford it, then hike up to WLWY."

Leon interrupted, nodding toward the map. "I checked the satellite this morning. The stream shouldn't be an issue."

Victor acknowledged Leon's comment with a brief nod and pressed on. "After crossing, we'll continue on foot, following this stream," he traced the route further, "to WLWY, which is right here." He tapped the map at the end of the marked trail.

"What's the estimated time?" I asked.

Victor replied without hesitation, "About three hours or less in the jeep, then another four to five on foot. We should be in camp well before dark."

"And lunchtime?" Robin chimed in, beating me to my next question.

"Whenever you're ready," Victor replied. "If anyone feels the need, we can take a few breaks along the way."

"What about Leon? He's the old guy," Robin teased, jumping around Victor in an exaggerated display of her fitness. "I could run up that mountain."

"I know Leon," Victor said simply. For a politician, he was definitely a man of few words.

"Then it's the other old guy we have to worry about," Robin added with a smirk, pointing directly at me.

"I'm in good enough shape," I said defensively.

"You work out in an oxygen-enriched atmosphere," Leon chimed in with his technical tone. "You're going to have to be careful not to exceed your limits."

"I'll be fine," I assured him, crossing my chest like a kid making a promise. "But I won't kill myself, I promise."

"Victor's sitting up front, so you two kids have the tiny seats in the back," Leon said, slipping into a mock dad tone. The front seats of the jeep weren't exactly luxurious, but the rear ones were little more than hard plastic boards.

We loaded up the jeep, securing Victor's large pack to the rear and stuffing the rest of our gear wherever it would fit.

"If you've got to barf, sing out and I'll stop," Leon added with a grin, probably more for my benefit than anyone else's.

Leon drove at a steady pace, slowing for small streams to keep the spray down. I was grateful he avoided his usual hell-bent-for-leather driving that left everyone white-knuckled and holding on for dear life. When we arrived at the ford in the stream, we crossed without any issues.

The entire ride, I was shoulder to shoulder with Robin. She barely said a word. I couldn't shake the feeling I'd upset Robin when she saw me with Jessica. Why had she been so angry?

* * *

We left the jeep behind and started off on foot. The thin air and exertion quickly caught up with me. "I've got to take a break," I said, swallowing my pride. The last thing I needed was to keel over from a heart attack.

"Okay, let's stop here," Victor announced. He took one look at me and added, "Frank, please remember to hydrate," his tone as patient as a parent talking to a child.

I pulled out my canteen, gave it a quick shake, and put it back. I was perfectly hydrated - Victor's concern was misplaced.

"It's just so beautiful out here," Robin said softly, her voice full of wonder as she took in the surroundings.

"Do you remember this trail, Frank?" Leon asked. "We went the same way years ago. It was less overgrown back then."

The effort it took to answer made me sound calm, even if I wasn't. "It seems familiar," I managed.

"You sound like you're okay now, Frank. Do you need more time?" Victor asked, his tone neutral but watchful.

"I'm good," I replied, pushing myself upright. "Let's get going."

We pushed on for another half hour before the trail got noticeably tougher. Surprisingly, the slower pace worked in my favor - I had plenty of strength but lacked endurance in the thinner air. Leon had been right: it made a difference. I resolved to lower the oxygen levels in my workout room to toughen myself up.

"I need a short break," Robin said, her voice strained as she sat in the stream. Her face was flushed, shiny with sweat, which somehow only enhanced her look. She had hard, defined muscles - a stark contrast to Amy's smooth, softer build.

"It's going to be harder to walk in wet shoes," Victor scolded, his tone more practical than harsh.

"These shoes won't stay wet. They'll be dry in less than a minute," Robin replied confidently.

"You must have those fancy European walking shoes," Leon said with a chuckle.

"Ya, they're all the rage in Italy now, especially with how much it rains," Robin said, splashing her feet lightly in the water.

"Hydrophobic nanomaterials?" I chimed in, my inner engineer piqued.

Robin nodded, smiling.

"I remember reading about that stuff a few years ago," I continued. "Looks like they commercialized it pretty quickly."

"They did," she said, her enthusiasm showing. "They've even added ultrasonic cleaning systems, so mud - or anything else - just falls off. Even dog poop," she added with a flourish, clearly enjoying her moment.

"Ready to move?" Victor's calm tone left no room for debate.

Robin stood, brushing water from her legs. "Lead on, big guy," she said with a smile, her earlier exhaustion already fading.

* * *

We made it to the site without any further breaks, and as soon as we arrived, I recognized the area immediately.

"I know this place," I said, taking in the familiar view. "Over there is the cave with the sensor, and we had the fire over there." I pointed to a spot marked by a circle of rocks.

"The cave mouth looks pretty overgrown. Victor, can you clean that up when you get a chance?" Leon, as always, preferred directing tasks over doing them himself.

"I'll handle it after I set up camp," Victor replied, already surveying the area. He looked up and added, "Robin, Frank, please gather firewood. It's going to be dark soon."

Robin snapped a playful salute, and Victor responded with a sharp, precise gesture that left no doubt - this man had been military trained.

* * *

Robin and I wandered into the woods together, and Victor called out after us, "Don't get lost! Remember where we are. If you're not back in twenty minutes,

130

I'll sound the horn." He held up a small air horn and gave it a sharp blast to demonstrate.

"I flinched at the noise and smiled - Victor clearly thought of us as kids." Then again, he wasn't wrong - I'd get lost in my own house if I wasn't careful.

"Robin, I want to apologize for what happened at the rally," I said contritely as we gathered deadwood.

"It's me who should apologize," she replied, her tone softer than I expected. "I don't know why I got so mad. I should've congratulated you instead."

"So, we're cool?" I asked, hopeful.

"Ya, no problems," Robin said with a small smile. Just like that, we were friends again.

"We gathered armfuls of deadwood, the brittle branches snapping underfoot as we trudged through the brush." The high altitude made idle chit-chat difficult, so we worked mostly in silence, speaking only when necessary for the task.

"You finish my lightsaber?" Robin asked, her words clipped from the effort of gathering wood.

"Yes," I replied. "I made you a pink one."

"Pink? Do I look like a pink girl?" she asked, her flushed face betraying her exertion.

"Right now, yes," I teased.

"And you're a pink boy," she shot back, earning a giggle.

"It's not really pink," I admitted, grinning. "I was just teasing. It's dull gray - that's the default color. I didn't choose one."

"You're so boring!" Robin said with mock exasperation. She gestured to her colorful, yet tiny, top. "Look at me. I'm all about color."

"You look cold," I said without thinking. Oops. Her headlights were on.

"Cold?" she echoed, glancing down before giggling.

"I think we've got enough wood," I joked, trying to change the subject.

Robin glanced at my midsection and quipped, "What wood?" She chuckled, her eyes sparkling mischievously.

It grew quiet for a moment, and I broke the silence. "I like you. You're a lot of fun."

"You're okay too, Frank," she said with a smile. "You make me laugh." We fell silent again, the comfortable kind of quiet that didn't need filling.

"Which way is camp?" I asked finally, realizing I'd lost my bearings. Just then, Victor's horn blared in the distance.

"I'd say that way," Robin replied, pointing confidently toward the blast.

* * *

When we got back to camp, Victor had a worried expression.

"Did you get lost?" he asked, his tone slightly tense.

"Are you kidding? I know these woods like the back of my hand," I said, just as Leon burst into laughter. Robin and Victor exchanged confused glances.

"Family joke," Leon managed between chuckles.

"My father said that once to my mother during a road rally," I added, still grinning. "He was driving his antique car and promptly crashed into a tree. Only he said, 'road' instead of 'woods.'"

"Was anyone hurt?" Robin asked, her concern evident.

"Just his ego," I said. "My mom never let him live that one down."

"That and the car," Leon interjected, his grin widening. "He totaled a priceless Jaguar." Pausing for effect, he added, "He even asked me if it could be fixed. I told him, 'Sure - just jack up the gas cap and drive another car under it.'"

Leon's knack for car jokes never failed, and even Robin cracked a smile. Victor's calm gaze flicked to the woods, scanning for unseen dangers. Though stoic as ever, I thought I caught the faintest twitch of amusement at Leon's joke.

"Victor, I want to hook up my equipment to the sensor tonight so I can get several hours of final data. I'll need your help in the cave," Leon said in his authoritative tone.

"I'm ready when you are," Victor replied smoothly. Turning to Robin and me, he added, "That looks like a decent stock of firewood for a short night. But it's going to get pretty cold, so if you plan to party until dawn, you might want to gather more."

"What do you think, Robin? Do we need more?" I asked, deferring to her judgment.

Robin glanced at Leon. "Did you bring any refreshments?"

"I brought a large flask of tequila," Leon replied with a grin. "Real agave, grown in the desert - not that satellite crap." Leon always had a knack for finding the best.

"Let's get more wood," Robin concluded decisively.

* * *

We doubled the pile for good measure. By the time we returned, Victor and Leon had finished their work in the cave and transformed the campsite. The fire was already blazing, and the grill was perfectly set up. Large rocks circled the firepit, with two squarish ones supporting the grill like a makeshift hearth. Victor, it seemed, was as much a woodsman as he was a butler.

We gathered around the fire like cavemen celebrating a fresh kill, the warmth and flickering light drawing us together as the sun began to dip below the horizon.

"I'll do the steaks," Leon declared with authority. He was the undisputed master of grilling meat.

"I want the big one," Robin said, her tone absent minded as her gaze drifted toward Victor.

"You already have the big one," Victor replied, his voice even but laced with subtle ownership. Robin grinned and snuggled up to him. Meanwhile, Leon was already placing steaks on the grill, a literal feast.

"That's enough to feed a small army," I said, motioning to the half a cow sizzling over the fire.

"Is this real beef?" Robin asked, her voice hushed as she took in the mouthwatering aroma.

"Yup. Killed it myself this morning," Leon quipped with a smirk.

"You killed it?" Robin asked, looking momentarily disgusted.

"Leon's joking," I said quickly. "He gets his steaks the same place everyone else does."

"Where do you get real meat around here?" Robin pressed. "All I ever see is that fake 'Meet' in the stores."

"You have to know people," Victor said simply.

"I'll bet you know people," Robin teased back with a smirk.

Leon chimed in. "You know that little house on 89? The one with the blank yellow sign and the long driveway? Frank, you drive by it every day."

"The one that looks like it's falling down?" I asked.

"That's the one," Leon confirmed. "The house is abandoned, but if you keep going down the driveway, you'll find what looks like a garage. If the doors are open, you can buy all sorts of things we think of as illicit."

"Nothing illegal, I hope," I said, my tone more curious than critical.

"Well, nothing I'd report as illegal," Leon replied with a grin. "Where do you think Amy gets that cream you like so much?"

"I never asked," I admitted, leaning into the humor. "I'm a 'don't ask, don't tell' kind of guy."

"They use slave labor," Victor cut in, his voice sharp with disapproval. "The workers live in that run-down house."

Victor's words cut through the banter like a knife. Robin froze mid-laugh, her expression darkening. Leon's smirk faltered as he glanced toward the fire. Sensing the tension, I excused myself to clean up.

134

* * *

It wasn't until the rich aroma of grilled steaks filled the air and the tequila shots warmed our throats that the tension finally eased. The night had fallen completely, and the flickering light of the campfire cast shifting shadows around us, wrapping the campsite in a cozy glow.

"Steaks look about ready," Leon announced, his tone brimming with authority.

"I get first pick," Robin declared, her teasing grin lighting up her face. "Lady's prerogative."

I had a snarky retort ready but decided to let it slide, smirking instead.

Leon poured the first round of camp margaritas, made from a powdered mix, water, and tequila - a surprisingly satisfying concoction.

"Remember to hydrate," Victor advised, downing his glass in one go. We all followed his lead, the drinks providing a pleasant numbing against the cool night air.

Dinner turned lively as the sizzling steaks disappeared, and the margaritas loosened tongues. Stories and laughter flowed easily, but as the fire settled into glowing embers, Victor's energy seemed to drain.

"Victor, honey, you look done," Robin said, her tone a mix of teasing and concern.

"I'm a lightweight when it comes to hard stuff," Victor admitted, rubbing the back of his neck. "I think I'll just lie down for a while…"

Leon watched them go, his usual humor replaced with an unusual quiet. He poured himself another margarita, and turned to me with an intensity I wasn't expecting.

* * *

"What's on your mind, Leon?" I asked cautiously.

"I debated whether or not to bring this up, but after confirming that every single sensor is involved, I know I'm not crazy," Leon said, his voice laced with conviction.

"I need to talk to you both - without Victor," he added, lowering his voice. "And this stays between us. If the wrong people find out, it could get us killed."

That snapped me to attention. Robin returned at that moment, her timing impeccable, and settled beside me, her curiosity clearly piqued.

"I've been out in the field this last week, decommissioning sensors. Perfectly good ones," Leon said, his voice shifting into his technical mode. "There's nothing wrong with them - they cost virtually nothing to operate. And yet, they're being taken out."

"You mean decommissioning, like turning them off? Or what?" I asked, frowning.

"We're not just turning them off," Leon said, his tone hardening. "We're physically destroying them. That's what they mean by decommissioning."

He paused to take a slow sip from his cup before continuing. "Frank, you know how anal I am about data quality."

I nodded. If anyone could find an issue, it would be Leon.

He leaned forward slightly. "I've found an anomaly in the data - something I can't explain. And it's worrisome." He let the words hang in the air, their weight pressing down on the moment.

"With what? The old sensors?" Robin asked, her curiosity piqued.

"The old sensors," Leon confirmed, his tone steady. "Even the ones put in the ground 50 years ago are fine. They're accurate, have decades of comparable data, and could have continued working for another 50 years."

"So where's the anomaly?" I asked, leaning closer to Leon - and inadvertently, to Robin.

Leon took another swig from his cup before continuing. "The anomaly is between the data in the system and the data at the sensor," he said, his voice dropping slightly.

"The sensor data is public domain, right?" Robin asked, her brow furrowed.

"Yes," Leon replied. "And that's where the anomaly shows up. We use the same data in our calculations, but now there's a difference in the magnitude and

duration of some of the signals. Not all, but enough to notice. It looks…
doctored. Highly sophisticated. Maybe by the military."

His warning tone sent a chill through the air. Even the Rucs knew better than to
meddle with the military.

"What's the connection between removing the sensors and the anomaly?" Robin
pressed, her voice edged with concern.

"That's the thing," Leon said, his expression tightening. "We pull these sensors
out of the ground, physically destroy them, and yet the data keeps flowing into
the system. It's like there's some secret sensor network they don't want us to
know about - and it's been online for a while."

He sounded slightly paranoid now, but the possibility was unnerving.

"When did the anomaly start?" I asked, refilling my cup - and Robin's too - as
we braced ourselves for his answer.

"The order to decommission came right after that damn Singularity thing
happened," Leon began, his voice steady but weighted. "When the order came
through, it bothered me, so I started checking quietly." He paused to toss more
wood onto the fire.

Leon continued, his expression serious. "One of the stations is near my house -
back on the ridge - so I went up there to check it out. The data at that sensor was
being altered in real time by something. Probably an Agent."

His tone was grave, but I couldn't shake the thought that he sounded paranoid.
"Did you ask Zen about it?" I ventured.

"Let me finish," he said sharply, then paused for a moment before continuing. "I
went to every sensor in the network last week - this one here is the last one still
online. They all showed the same tampering." His voice grew firmer, more
convincing.

Robin leaned forward. "Did you analyze the differences? What do you think is
going on?"

"I did," Leon replied, his frustration evident. "When I got back on Friday, I ran
an analysis. The damn Engineering Agent said my data was flawed - that there
was no anomaly."

"What did Zen say?" I pressed again, curious if our AI counterpart had noticed anything unusual.

Leon sighed and finally addressed the question. "I did ask Zen. I went down to your office Friday evening - you were already gone - and gave him the same data I gave the Agent."

He paused, letting the weight of his words sink in.

"And?" I pressed.

"Zen told me the data was correct and the old sensors were malfunctioning," Leon said, his voice tight with frustration. "He even showed me where the data diverged - said it was obviously the fault of the old network."

"Then maybe you're mistaken," I said cautiously. Leon shot me a withering look.

"I asked him where he got his data," Leon continued, raising his voice slightly, "and he said it came from a new virtual sensor network."

We fell silent. The only sound was the rhythmic, guttural snoring of a large bear - Victor, fast asleep nearby.

"We don't want to involve Victor," Leon added in a low voice, his paranoia creeping back in. "Not if this becomes an issue with the authorities."

"A virtual sensor network?" I asked, unable to keep the sarcasm out of my tone. "How's that supposed to work?"

"I don't know," Leon admitted, shaking his head. "But that's how they're reading the magma now. Instrumentation-free sensors. Jesus, that's science fiction territory."

"What are they hiding?" Robin asked, her tone sharp with concern.

"I don't know exactly," Leon said, his voice dropping. "But the old sensor data indicates the magma is increasing. The new virtual sensors, though? They show the magma holding steady at 40%."

"That can't be," I interjected, frowning. "The magma can't legally go above 40%. That's in the YSP charter."

"One other data point," Robin said suddenly, sitting up straight.

"The ringing," I said with emphasis, my voice cutting through the night.

"The ringing," she repeated, her tone matching mine.

"The ringing?" Leon asked, his head swaying slightly now, the tequila showing its effects.

"When Robin and I were in my office, we heard the ringing," I explained, "indicating a mining charge detonation - a large one, deep underground. Several, in fact. Zen said 14 of them were scheduled for that day, 16 total. What was it... Monday?" I turned to Robin.

"It was Thursday," she corrected. "We had just finished the algorithm to stabilize the chaotic region when we heard the ringing," she added, jogging my memory.

"I asked Zen why I hadn't been notified about these deployments," I continued, my frustration evident. "And he gave me grief about it being his responsibility. Said he didn't have to tell me or even discuss it."

Leon sat up slightly, his expression darkening. "He should have notified my office," he said firmly. "And that would have been Robin, since I was out. We can't have some crazy machine setting off thermonuclear devices unchecked." He stood briefly, then sat back down heavily, his frustration evident in his movements.

"He said his energy requirements increased dramatically," Robin added, quoting Zen directly.

"It's the military, girl," Leon said grimly.

"To what end?" Robin asked, her tone edged with concern.

"I don't know," Leon admitted, his voice speculative. "Some kind of weapon, maybe. Something that requires a huge increase in power generation."

"What about antimatter?" I asked, leaning forward slightly.

"What the hell does anyone want with antimatter? It's just a university toy," Leon replied in his typically opinionated voice.

"This is a military secret," I said, my voice lowering to a serious tone. "I want everyone to swear you didn't hear it from me."

Robin and Leon exchanged glances before murmuring their agreement.

"Do you know Dr. Osborne - Azizi?" I asked, watching Leon closely.

"He used to hang out with us at lunch," Leon said, musing. "Then he got moved to Plant 2 for some electronics project."

"The project he's working on made a bomb," I said plainly. "An antimatter bomb."

"God damn military," Leon said, his voice rising too loudly. "What do they need another bomb for?" We all froze, listening. The rhythmic snores of the bear nearby - Victor - confirmed we hadn't woken him.

"It's more than just another bomb," I continued, lowering my voice. "Picture a bomb the size of a pack of gum. It weighs nothing, looks like a communications package to any scanner, and packs a one-kiloton punch."

I let the words hang in the air for a moment.

"That sounds… destabilizing," Robin said quietly, her wide eyes reflecting a mix of awe and fear.

"There's more to this than just the bomb," I said, pausing as I looked around at everyone, gauging their reactions.

"Robin, you're shivering," I said, noticing her discomfort.

"I don't know if it's the cold, the drinks, or the talk of undetectable weapons," Robin replied, setting her drink down. "Leon, do you have a blanket?"

Without hesitation, Leon grabbed a heated blanket from his pack, switched it on, and wrapped it around her carefully, almost like a father tending to his daughter.

"That's great, Leon. Thanks," Robin said, pulling the blanket tightly around her, her shivering easing.

Leon turned back to me, the tequila loosening his tongue. "Get back to it, man. What's the 'more'?"

I took a breath and delved into it - the communication system, the accident at ELM2, and the subsequent drafting of the program into military hands. When I finished, Leon was already forming a theory.

"You know that damn Reveal thing?" he started, his tone sharp. "They sent out 30,000 of those communication devices, supposedly for security reasons. They've gone to every important person all over the world."

He downed the rest of his drink and continued, his words cutting through the still night. "What if the plan is to blow up all their enemies at once - during the Reveal party - with antimatter bombs?"

"Don't you think that might be a little obvious?" I asked, though Leon wasn't sounding paranoid this time.

"They'd have the rest of them in the palm of their hand," Leon replied, his voice dark with conviction. "Everyone important is tied to this stupid Reveal party. It's like a Trojan Horse, only with antimatter."

We fell silent, the weight of his words settling over us. It sounded plausible - and worse, it fit.

"It doesn't make sense to increase the magma in the chamber to generate more power," I said, shaking my head. I finished my drink and leaned forward, adding in a technical tone, "We generate more power by increasing the convection, not the magma volume. Increasing the volume is dangerous - recklessly so."

"Here's another data point," Leon said, sounding completely sober now. Adrenaline had a way of cutting through everything else.

He continued, "Zen lied to me. I asked him about the data, and he flat-out lied."

"Zen doesn't lie," I said, frowning. "At least, I didn't think he could."

"Zen is getting more intelligent every day," Leon replied, his voice sharp. "Why would you think he wouldn't do the one thing humans do best?"

"One more point about Zen that may have bearing," I said, pausing as I glanced around. Robin was shivering again, drawing my attention. "Robin, maybe you should have another drink. You're shivering again."

"Why not," she replied in a small voice. "Did you bring The Tank?"

Leon and I answered in unison, "Yes."

"Spit it out, man. What else?" Leon pressed, his tone insistent.

141

"Zen told me he was conflicted by the military using him to kill," I said, my voice low and ominous.

"Zen said that?" Leon asked, his disbelief evident.

"I think the last thing we need is a god that's conflicted," Robin said, her words carrying a quiet weight.

"Zen isn't a god," Leon shot back, his tone laced with disgust. "He's a goddamn machine."

"Okay, god-like," Robin countered.

"When Zen starts throwing lightning bolts and creating things out of thin air, then we'll talk about gods," Leon said with a sharp edge. "For now, he's just a smart guy with no imagination."

"What about Zen? Could he be behind it?" I asked, half-joking but unable to ignore the thought.

"Let me have some of that," Leon said, taking the flask and zapping his drink back to life.

"What if it's the military trying to kill Zen - and take out all the world leaders in one shot?" I mused aloud, the idea as chilling as it was plausible.

"That's the best answer so far," Robin said, her conviction unmistakable.

"That damned military," Leon muttered darkly. "They're going to be the death of us all." He took another long sip, then set his cup down heavily. "I'm done," he added, his voice slurring slightly. "We'd already be dead if they had even the slightest clue about what we just discussed."

With that ominous warning, Leon wobbled to his feet and staggered off to his tent, leaving Robin and me to sit in silence by the fire. I stoked it with a few more choice pieces from the pile.

* * *

"Want another?" I asked Robin as I filled my cup. She lifted hers in response, and I poured until it was full.

"I need to get really drunk, or I'll never get to sleep," she said before swigging down the entire cup in one go.

"Do you think the military would be so bold?" I asked, watching her closely. She was thoroughly buzzed now, her usual sharpness softened.

"You can't fathom what they want," Robin said, her voice wobbly but laced with bitterness. "They own everything. They are the power. We're just the pawns."

She changed the subject abruptly. "What's the story with the trollop, Jessica?"

"How do you know her name?" I asked, grateful for the shift away from doom and gloom.

"I read it on your hand, loverboy. Want her number? I know that too," she said, smirking as she rattled off the digits. I sheepishly looked at my hand, but the name and number were gone days ago.

"She said I was going to save her," I replied, then told Robin about the contract and Amy's approval - but left out the clairvoyant part.

"Why in the world would your wife tell you to get a mistress? Are you that lousy in bed?" she asked, her tone so blunt it didn't sound sarcastic.

"She's worried about you," I said quietly.

"Little ol' me? Why is she worried about me?" Robin asked, feigning innocence.

"We flirt. She thinks it means something threatening," I admitted.

"Is she afraid I'll steal you away, old man?" she teased, the humor slightly slurred now.

"I think it's the whole 40 thing," I said, trying to explain.

"So she shoves a mistress in your face. I get it now," Robin said with a laugh, clearly toasted. "Distract you from the evil little beauty who haunts her nightmares."

"I think you've nailed it," I said, grinning.

"Is there any truth in it?" she asked, looking directly into my eyes.

"Can I ask about you and Victor?" I countered, steering the conversation away.

"The bear and I just want to have fun," she said lightly, pulling the blanket tighter around herself. The temperature was dropping quickly.

"No, seriously," I pressed. "I see you two together - you look happy with him. What's the end game?"

"I'm seriously not serious about the end game," she replied with a shrug. "He's just fun, you know? Not so stuck up like we are. And the sex!" She leaned in conspiratorially and winked. "You've never had sex until you've had sex with a Wic."

"You mean Victor?" I asked, seeking clarification.

Robin smirked. "I mean the Wics. They don't have rules piled on rules. They do what they want." She threw a stick in the fire. "Look at Jessica. Would your wife ever dress like her?"

"Not a chance," I said, my tone tinged with something between amusement and judgment.

"And you've only ever been with Amy?" she asked casually.

"That's right. Started dating at fourteen, never had a SexBot - just Amy."

Robin shook her head, her expression somewhere between pity and disbelief. "You're missing out, my innocent friend."

The night grew quiet - no insect sounds in the cold, and the wind had stilled. Only the occasional crackle and pop of the fire broke the silence.

"Why were you so mad about Jessica?" I asked, breaking the lull.

"Mad? I wasn't mad," she replied defensively.

"Yes, you were. You even admitted it when we were playing show and tell in the woods," I said, leaning into the teasing tone. She smiled and slapped my arm lightly.

"Okay, fine, yes - I was mad," she admitted, her voice softening. "And I don't know why. I saw you there with her, and I wanted to spend some time with you.

Then I got mad and stormed off like a teenager." She finished her drink and tossed the cup into the fire, where it slowly dissolved into CO_2 and water. After a moment, she added, "You should do her."

"Do her? As in… a mistress?" I asked, wanting to clarify through the haze of intoxication.

"No," she replied with a smirk. "I mean have the experience, at least once. You have to. You owe it to yourself - and believe me, to Amy too, and any other women you might encounter down the road."

I shook my head. "I was thinking of going through with the contract and then sending her to live in Hartford with her sister. I'm really not interested in having a mistress," I said, my honesty clear.

"Why not just forget her number? A lot less trouble," Robin suggested.

"I feel like I have to save her," I said, the passion rising in my voice. "I don't know what it is - I just feel a responsibility to see this woman, who's had every raw deal possible in her life, finally get a break. She really deserves it."

Robin softened, her teasing fading. "That's sweet. I think that's really sweet," she said sincerely. Then, with a playful glint in her eye, she added, "Still, you should have a playdate."

She leaned in and hugged me, her warmth cutting through the chill of the night.

"We're almost out of wood. Let's leave some for the morning," I said, stifling a yawn. "I think we've had enough for tonight, my girl of evil dreams."

"You couldn't handle me, old man," she replied, giggling. "I'm way too much for you."

She was drifting off now, her head bobbing slightly. I chuckled softly and shook my head. "Let's get you into the bear cave, young lady," I said, feeling a bit woozy myself as I helped her to her feet.

I managed to help squeeze Robin into Victor's tent, then stumbled into mine, alone, and that was it. Day over.

* * *

I woke to the rhythmic sound of Victor chopping wood and the rich aroma of coffee wafting through the crisp morning air. "Arg, where's The Tank?" I muttered to myself groggily. One big huff, and my synapses fired. Two, and I felt good. I went for three. Wow. Fully alert.

Victor looked up as I crawled out of my tent. "Morning," he called, handing me a cup before I could ask.

"Leon's grind," I noted, savoring the first sip.

"Did Robin survive the night? It seemed like a tight fit," I asked, smirking.

"She's still out," Victor replied. "You must've had quite the party - I see the wood's almost gone," he added, his tone faintly critical.

I thought to myself, Too bad, Wic boy - you're getting the wood today. But out loud, I deflected, "Yes, it was a nice evening. Robin really likes you."

Victor didn't bite. Instead, he asked, "Hungry?"

"The Tank killed my appetite," I replied with a smirk.

"Leon's in the cave taking readings," Victor said, pouring himself a second cup of coffee.

"Should we let Robin sleep, or bang some pots together?" I asked, half-joking.

"We have some time," Victor said with a shrug. "She should rest if she wants. It was a tight fit for her last night. My bad - I should've brought a bigger tent for us."

I enjoyed my coffee, and studied the man who was our butler and trail guide.

"I noticed that you seem military trained," I said, phrasing it more as a statement than a question.

"I was a master sergeant in the Army," Victor replied evenly. "But that's my old life."

"No shit?" I said, genuinely surprised. "That's impressive for someone your age."

146

"I think you could say I excelled," Victor said, a note of pride slipping into his voice.

"Thank you for your service," I said with a smile, raising my cup, "and not just for the coffee."

"How about a refill, sir?" Victor said with a grin, reaching for the pot.

I held my cup out, letting him pour. "Is it true? Soldiers make better lovers?" I asked, quoting the silly ad campaign that had run for years.

Victor smirked but didn't take the bait. "That was a very successful campaign," he said, expertly dodging the question.

"I saw your rally on Friday. You have quite a following," I said, trying to curry favor.

"From your perspective, what did you think of my speech?" Victor asked, putting me on the spot.

"I found some of your points quite compelling," I admitted. "I liked how you talked about the old Constitution and how it's been watered down. I agree with most of your positions - except for the vote."

"One citizen, one vote. You disagree with that?" Victor asked, his tone measured but curious.

"I get it," I said carefully. "But when people vote for whoever tells them what they want to hear, with no realistic chance of following through on those promises - don't you think that shows a lack of responsibility on the part of the voter?"

Victor's expression hardened. "When nine out of ten citizens have no voice, they're not voters - they're victims."

It was a good point, and I nodded slightly, acknowledging the truth in his words. "I want to ask you something else," I said, my tone shifting to something more serious. "Something really serious. I want you to be truthful with me - not a politician. Just you and me here."

Victor leaned back slightly but nodded. "Fire away."

"Every day, more jobs are being replaced by automation, and more people are being born. The Wics are getting squeezed tighter and tighter. Look at what happened in Orlando," I said, my voice low but intense. "What do you foresee as the answer? No bullshit political nonsense. I want to know what you think."

"When I was in the military, we looked at problems without emotion," Victor began, his tone calm but cold. "We implemented solutions that were solid, well-thought-out, and effective." He paused, his gaze steady. "In the civilian world, it's the exact opposite. Everything is hidden, weak, and inadequate. It's like putting a bandaid on a gangrenous limb."

"I agree with that," I said, nodding slowly. "But at least politics are factual now. They don't promise things they can't deliver anymore. They'd get dragged through the mud if they did that. Let me ask simply - what do you think the problem is, and what solution will work?" I finished my coffee, bracing myself for his answer.

Victor didn't hesitate. "Using my military training, both the problem and the solution are staring us in the face," he said, looking me directly in the eyes. His gaze was intense.

"The problem is simple: too many people. The solution…" He paused, letting the weight of his words settle. "Eliminate half of them."

"Like Orlando," I said quietly, the weight of his words settling over me.

"Like Orlando," he repeated, unflinching.

Before I could respond, noises came from Victor's tent - a groan, the distinct sound of relief from The Tank. Victor and I turned toward the commotion, momentarily breaking the tension as Robin emerged, looking groggy but radiant, like a butterfly shedding its cocoon.

"What about Orlando?" Robin asked groggily, her hair a tangled mess as she stumbled toward us. Victor and I exchanged a glance.

"Did I miss something?" she added, noticing our awkward silence.

Victor chuckled softly, deflecting with ease. "Just discussing geopolitics over coffee."

"Heavy stuff for the morning," Robin replied, yawning as she wrapped the blanket tighter around her. "I need caffeine before I start solving the world's problems."

* * *

The hike back to the jeep was uneventful, Victor calling for breaks at regular intervals - a gesture I silently appreciated.

We said our goodbyes by the lake. The trip had been productive, even enjoyable in parts. But as I climbed into my car, the weight of Victor's words lingered: Too many people. Eliminate half of them, and Leon's warnings about the military.

It was a lot to consider.

CHAPTER NINE

Family Vacation

I arrived home to find Amy in the kitchen. She glanced over her shoulder and wrinkled her nose.

"Someone smells like a wet dog," she said, her tone laced with sarcasm.

"Ya, we did sweat a bunch. It was a good trip and I didn't embarrass myself much." I added.

"So… who was the first to call for a break?" she teased, raising an eyebrow.

"The old guy who works out in an oxygen-augmented room," I said, shaking my head. "I'm going to change that."

"And Leon?" she asked knowingly.

"You know about Leon. He didn't need a break. The guy's a freakin' goat," I said, half-admiringly.

"And Robin?" Amy asked, her tone casual, though I could tell she was digging.

"She beat me, of course. She's young and strong. I'm old and practically knocking on death's door," I said, layering on the self-pity for effect.

Amy laughed, the sound lightening the room. "What did you think of her boyfriend?"

"He's… something," I said, pausing to find the right words. "I was surprised at his candor, considering he's practically some sort of Wic messiah."

Amy's expression shifted, sharpening slightly. "Is Robin serious about this messiah anarchist?" she asked, her voice taking on that familiar edge.

"I don't think so. She said she likes the sex," I replied without thinking. Amy's eyes widened - clearly not the response she expected.

"Speaking of that topic," she continued, "I've created the contract and everything else you'll need for you-know-who. It's in your personal folder with all the instructions. I trust I don't need to be involved any deeper, do I?"

"Thank you, Amy," I said sincerely. "I appreciate all you do for me." Reaching across the table, I took her hand. "You are something special."

She gave me a small smile, her fingers gently curling around mine. "Frank, your happiness means everything to me. We've been through so much together, and I know that once you move past this… phase, we'll find our way back to ourselves. I can wait." Her expression softened into her best traditional wife look, momentarily easing the tension between us.

Then she asked, her gaze searching, "You seem troubled - like something's weighing on you, deep down, far beyond these 40-year-old antics. What's really eating at you?"

I changed the subject. "How's Sara doing? How Is she dealing with the trauma from her flight?" I asked, leaning against the counter.

Amy sighed, her expression shifting to one of concern. "She seems perfectly at ease about the whole thing, like it was nothing - just a stroll down an empty road. Sometimes I think the girl isn't quite right. She just doesn't react like normal girls do," she said, her tone heavy with feeling.

"What do you mean?" I asked, sensing there was more beneath her words.

"The girl has no fear, Frank," Amy said, her voice tinged with worry. "In this world, fear keeps people from walking into dark rooms alone."

"She shook off the crash like she was a 20-year test pilot," I added, marveling at my daughter's resilience.

"I don't know what we're going to do with that child," Amy muttered, almost to herself, her voice softening into a more motherly tone.

"I think I've pushed my luck with the KitchenBot - it's probably debating whether to scrub me itself," I said, attempting humor to break the heaviness lingering between us.

Amy smiled faintly but didn't reply, her thoughts clearly still on Sara. As I left the room, her words lingered in my mind. *No fear.* In this world, fear might be the only thing keeping us alive.

* * *

During my shower, the conversations from the previous evening replayed in my head - Leon's paranoia, Robin's insights, the unsettling possibilities. Piece by piece, it all came together, pushing me toward a decision. By the time I stepped out, my mind was made up.

"Let's go for a walk down the road," I said, glancing toward the window. I wanted to get out of the house. After last night, I had the jumps - paranoia, maybe, but justified.

"We nev - " she began, but I raised a finger to my lips, cutting her off with a firm signal for silence. Her brow furrowed, confusion giving way to concern. "I'll get my coat."

I could see the unease setting in as she disappeared into the other room.

* * *

When we left the house, the crisp air hit us, and we walked in silence down the driveway and onto the road. It was always quiet here; only residents and the occasional service vehicle ever passed by.

"Amy," I said, lowering my voice, "I wanted to get out of the house in case there's surveillance."

Her pace slowed slightly as she looked at me, her concern deepening. "Who would be watching us?" she asked.

"The military," I said cautiously. "Or, well… I don't know exactly. But if they hear what I'm about to tell you, it could be an issue."

Her steps faltered for a moment. "You're scaring me, Frank. What did you do?" she implored, her tone shifting. I recognized that look - her legal face.

"I don't know if it's anything yet," I admitted. "It could all be Leon's paranoia."

"Leon?" she said with a sigh, shaking her head. "He goes off the deep end with a gentle push." She knew Leon well enough to make that call.

I took a deep breath and began to explain. "The less I tell you, the better. Let it suffice that you need to leave this area today, with the kids. We think the Yellowstone supervolcano is about to erupt."

"Are we really in danger or is this another one of Leon's crazy conspiracy theories?" she asked, her voice now completely serious.

"I'm not going to sugarcoat it. Yes, we're in danger - from the military or whoever is orchestrating this disaster, and from the disaster itself. If we were standing here when the volcano erupted, we'd have the glorious opportunity to see ourselves burned to death in about a thousandth of a second."

"Well, at least it wouldn't hurt," Amy said, attempting to lighten the mood, though her voice wavered.

I shook my head. "I think you should take the kids and go to your sister's. She's far enough away that there's no immediate danger from the volcano," I said firmly.

"What about school? When do you want us to go?" she asked, her voice tinged with fear now.

"Today. As soon as possible," I replied, the urgency creeping into my tone.

Amy stopped walking and turned to face me directly. "Is it really that bad? Tell me, Frank. You're scaring me," she said, clutching my hands tightly. Her palms were cold and damp, her fear palpable.

I hesitated but then pulled her into a hug - something scandalous enough in public to make her gasp softly. "I'm afraid that's not all," I said quietly, feeling her stiffen against me.

"What more?" she whispered.

I pulled back just enough to look her in the eyes. "I want you to be prepared for the worst. We think this mess is tied to the Reveal next Saturday. If it goes…" I paused, letting the weight of my words hang between us. "If it goes, this planet is doomed."

Amy's face went pale. She stared at me, her lips trembling. "Doomed?" was all she could manage.

"The supervolcano will eject around a thousand cubic kilometers of magma into the stratosphere - ash, volcanic firebombs, the works," I explained, my tone heavy. "Within 50 kilometers, everything will be obliterated instantly. In a few days, the destruction will spread to 250 kilometers - fires, hot ash, everything buried or burned. Within a week, it'll reach 500 kilometers. Do you understand me?" I asked, locking eyes with Amy.

Amy nodded slowly, her face pale. "My sister's too close," she whispered, her voice barely audible.

I continued, pressing on. "In a month, the entire North American continent will be in total chaos. No food, no communications, no power. People will turn on each other. The military will be paralyzed. Millions will die."

Amy gasped, her hand flying to her mouth. "Thank God we have the villa," she managed, her voice trembling.

I nodded. "It's the only option. By the end of the first week, air travel will be impossible, and space launches will come to a halt. The ash will keep falling for weeks - maybe months. After that, the space outposts will be the only truly secure places in the solar system."

Amy steadied herself, her composure returning. "What do you want me to do?" she asked, her voice steady now, her resolve taking shape.

"Book a berth on the Bahamas Avalon Shuttle," I said firmly. "Make sure it's for six seats - Robin and Leon are coming too. I already checked; there's a launch Saturday at 6:00 p.m. Eastern. If everything goes well, we can just relax and skip the flight. But if it goes the other way, that ride into space will be worth more than life itself. They can't bump us; we have priority as owners."

Amy nodded, her movements deliberate. "I got it," she said. Then she looked up at me, her face pale but resolute. "This is a no-shit bad thing." Her voice wavered slightly - Amy never swore. Ever.

I exhaled, running a hand through my hair. "It could be the end of civilization on Earth for generations. People will be eating each other in a year." I hesitated, then added with a weak smile, "I guess that's worth swearing for."

Her lips tightened, and I reached out, placing a reassuring hand on her shoulder. I paused, looked her in the eyes, and smiled softly. "Okay, let's dial it back a bit," I said, my voice calmer now, trying to steady both of us.

"We aren't sure about anything yet," I continued. "It could all be one of Leon's crazy ideas - or it could be real. The important thing is, if it's real, you need to leave now. If it's not, then you have a nice visit in Boise."

"I guess the kids could do virtual school for a few days," Amy said thoughtfully. "They're off Thursday and Friday because of the Reveal. I'll have to call my sister and make something up. You know how I hate lying."

"You can't talk about this to anyone," I said firmly, my engineer's voice taking over. "Especially over anything electronic. Only in person, and out in the open."

Her eyes widened, panic creeping in. "They can hear us now!" she said, her voice rising slightly.

"No, they can't," I replied, trying to calm her. Then, with a smirk, I added, "Unless they've bugged your buttons…"

"Frank, stop it. It's not funny," she snapped, her tone sharp with worry. She hesitated, then asked, "What are you going to do?"

"The three of us are going to try and stop it," I said, my voice strong and steady.

"Three as in Leon, Robin, and you?" she clarified.

"Yes," I said, leaning into a bit of dramatic flair. "The three engineers, battling evil robots and a corrupt military to save the day."

"Can you?" she asked, her voice barely above a whisper.

"Right now, we don't have a plan," I admitted, "but we know more about that system than anyone else on the planet. If it can be stopped, we'll figure out how." I thought bitterly, "Or die trying", which felt like an accurate estimate.

"I have faith," she said softly. I could see it in her eyes: she believed in me. Then, with sudden seriousness, Amy asked, "What's your escape plan?"

"I don't have one yet," I admitted. "Once we know our plan of attack, we can figure out an escape route."

"I'm counting on you being on the shuttle," she said, her voice firm but tinged with desperation.

I grabbed her by the shoulders and looked her squarely in the eyes. "Amy, you can't wait for me. If I'm not there, you *have* to leave without me. I'll be along on a later launch."

Her face fell, despondence written in every line. "What if it's the last launch?" she whispered.

"Then you can't miss it," I replied, my voice steady, even as my heart broke a little.

Amy was silent for a moment before I continued. "I want to talk to the kids about it, especially Sara," I said as we turned around and started walking back.

"What are you going to tell them?" she asked, her voice tinged with trepidation.

"I'm going to tell them - the truth," I said with conviction.

Amy sighed, her shoulders relaxing slightly. "I'll call my sister and say we had a fight about the mistress thing. She'd believe that, especially since you just turned 40," she said with a knowing smile.

I chuckled. "She'd believe that too. She hasn't liked me since we switched the heads on her dolls. Remember that? She was furious."

Amy laughed, the sound soft but genuine. "She still doesn't know I helped," she said, her grin widening as she glanced at me. It was good to see her recover so quickly. She was a strong woman, always had been.

"Let's make a code phrase," I said, shifting gears. "If I say, 'The lawn looks dry,' it means the danger is high. If I say, 'Everything is alright,' it means... Everything is alright."

Amy rolled her eyes but smiled. "You'd make a terrible spy - but a dashing one, my dear," she quipped, sliding her arm through mine as we walked back toward the house.

As we reached the driveway, I said, "Have the kids meet me at the old picnic table in the woods."

Amy stopped, and I turned to her, placing a gentle kiss on her lips before pulling her into a hug. I felt her chest heave as if she were holding back a cry. Her resilience was remarkable, but I could see the cracks beneath the surface.

"And one more thing," I said softly. "I'll try to call you every day. But if you don't hear from me - assume the worst, and go."

"I understand," she whispered, pulling back just enough to meet my gaze. Her eyes glistened, but there was steel in her voice. "You be there on Saturday, Frank. Whatever it takes."

* * *

At the table, I pondered how to approach the conversation with the kids. I saw Sara first - no sign of Tre yet.

"Hi, Dad. How was your camping trip?" she asked, dropping into the seat across from me.

"It was fine," I said, though my mind was elsewhere. "Are you okay? I've been worried about the blowback from your crash. Are you sleeping?" My tone carried genuine concern.

She waved it off, her face lighting up. "It's nothing. I'm sleeping better than before, actually. I feel… powerful. They did another story about me on a publication with millions of users. I'm getting messages from all over the world! Mostly girls, but boys too - sending me their pictures and love notes," she added, giddy with excitement.

"When you say pictures, they're not, you know…" I trailed off, uncomfortable.

"You mean dick pics?" she asked bluntly. "Nobody does that anymore, Dad." She rolled her eyes, leaned over, and gave me a quick kiss on the head before settling back on the bench.

I smirked, shaking my head. "Where's your brother?"

"He's finishing some sort of important test. It's timed. He'll be here in a few minutes," she said, gesturing toward the house. Then she looked me directly in the eye, her expression shifting slightly. "Dad, what's up with the chat in the woods? Are you having issues with Mom?" she asked, her concern evident.

"No, no, nothing like that," I said quickly, trying to reassure her. "I have something important I need to talk to you two about. Let's wait for Tre," I added, my tone firm but gentle.

The silence between us stretched, the weight of what I wasn't saying hanging in the air. Sara's eyes flicked away as she reached out to the table. She picked at a loose piece of wood, peeling it back to reveal a long, sharp sliver. She turned it over in her fingers, studying it thoughtfully.

"I could hunt with this if I had to," she said, a flicker of imagination - maybe something darker - crossing her face.

"You sound like Uncle Leon," I said, half amused, half concerned. I let the comment hang for a moment before adding, "I talked to Zen about your crash. He sends his condolences and his congratulations - for saving the ship, and your life," I said proudly, letting her see how much I admired her.

"High praise from Caesar!" she replied, smiling as she used the sharp sliver to carve a small heart into the wood of the table.

"He ran a simulation of your crash several times using standard human reaction times and even with the Instructor Agent," I said, watching her closely. "The pilot died every time. What do you think of that?"

Sara shrugged, her tone light as she continued to idly scribble with the sliver, leaving faint trails on the wood. "His simulations are flawed?" she said whimsically, a playful smirk tugging at her lips.

"It's Zen. His simulations are quite good," I countered, my voice firm but not unkind.

She paused, tapping the sliver against the table. "I got lucky?" she offered, her tone shifting, as if trying to deflect.

158

"He analyzed your genome," I said, leaning forward slightly. "And he concluded that you have - what was it exactly - exceptional abilities. Extraordinary reflexes and intuition, to the point of clairvoyance. You impressed the Singularity."

"Clairvoyance?" she repeated, her head tilting slightly as her brows knit in thought. "That means seeing the future, right? I read once that it's real but so unreliable it's impossible to test empirically. Is that what you mean?" she asked, her tone curious but measured, as though she'd already been considering the possibility.

"It is real," I said, "but like you mentioned, empirically, it's difficult to prove. Did you have any feelings of dread, visions, or anything that might have prepared you for the disaster?" I asked, studying her face closely.

"I've been thinking about it, and I don't know exactly what happened," she replied, snapping the end off her sliver. She tossed it into the bushes before continuing. "I knew the instant the plane broke - I just *knew* - and I knew what to do without even thinking. I mean, the instant it happened. I was working the controls, yawing hard and prepping for autorotation before the ship cranked over. You saw how fast it recovered," she said, her tone calm but intense.

"I thought the Instructor Agent had taken over," I said, genuinely puzzled.

She smirked faintly. "He was toast. Burned to the ground. Finito." She let the last word linger, her voice trailing off.

"In the future, never doubt those feelings," I said, my tone redundant but sincere.

"Gee, Dad, ya think?" she replied with a smirk.

"One other thing," I added, leaning forward. "Keep it private. Don't tell anyone in authority. Understand? Stick to 'I got lucky.'"

"You think they'll put me in a cage and study me?" she joked, her expression playful but curious.

"Never underestimate the military," I cautioned, my voice serious. "If they think you're valuable, they could take you away, and there wouldn't be a damn thing we could do about it."

She frowned, her humor fading. "How did Zen know?" she asked, her curiosity piqued.

"Zen knows all," I replied. "'To know all is to be all.' That's what he said to me."

Sara wrinkled her nose at that. "Sounds like some creepy religious crap," she muttered, tossing the thought aside with disgust.

"I see your brother coming," I said, nodding toward the path where Tre was scampering down with his usual energy.

"I got a perfect test score - again. I'm an academic weapon," Tre announced, puffing his chest as he reached the table.

"Yawn. You're taking baby classes," Sara shot back, her tone dripping with mockery. "Try chemistry and calculus, then get back to me."

"It was a trig test. That's not baby stuff!" Tre replied, defensive.

"Alright, forget it," I said, holding up a hand to stop the bickering. "I have something important to tell you both." I paused, unsure how to start.

Tre rolled his eyes, his voice tinged with impatience. "You're getting a divorce, aren't you? Is that why we're sitting out here in the wilderness?"

"No, no, your mother and I are fine. That's not it." I exhaled deeply, my tone growing more serious. "It's far worse, I'm afraid."

That got their attention. Both of them stared at me, their faces losing any trace of sibling rivalry.

"What do you mean, Dad? What's going on?" they asked simultaneously.

I explained what we thought was coming, and the contingency plan for them to go to Auntie's for safety. I outlined the backup plan to move to the villa if things went south, trying to convey the gravity of the situation without overwhelming them.

"Questions?" I asked, bracing myself for their reactions.

"What about my friends?" Sara asked, her calm exterior finally breaking.

"I'm afraid we can't talk about this to anyone," I said, my tone serious and measured. "From this moment on, you're not to say a word - especially not over anything electronic. If you tell someone, the military will hear it, and we could end up being detained."

"Then we pay a stupid fine. What's the big deal?" Tre said flippantly, shrugging off the warning.

Sara shot him a sharp look. "For a smart kid, you sure are stupid," she snapped.

"And why is that, young lady?" I interjected, curious about her line of thought.

"The military doesn't prosecute crimes, Dad. They execute traitors," she said, her voice calm but heavy with meaning.

"That's right," I said, reinforcing her point. "This is serious. We cannot breathe a word to anyone."

Tre's expression darkened, anxiety creeping into his voice. "What about Julia? She could die!" he said, almost pleading.

"We can't tell anyone," I repeated firmly. "That means our friends, *especially*. If they're monitoring me, they're definitely monitoring you too. You call your friends to warn them, they'll just laugh - and then we'll be in real trouble."

Sara nodded slowly, her voice steady but resigned. "He's right, Tre. Even if we did tell them, they wouldn't believe us anyway."

"We'll be alright," I said firmly, my voice steady.

We walked up to the house in a somber mood. Each step seemed to bring the weight of what I had just told them closer to reality. Sara's expression was focused, her mind clearly racing, while Tre's face was pale, his brow furrowed as if trying to process too much at once. "This isn't fair," he mumbled, his voice trembling.

* * *

Kids, pack your things. Take only what you absolutely cannot live without. We may never come back!" Amy said in a dramatically angry voice, then shot me a quick thumbs-up behind the kids' backs.

"The taxi will be here in six minutes - so pack fast!" she yelled, her voice somewhere between urgency and playful exasperation, echoing through the house.

"Call me when you arrive at your sister's," I said, trying to add a touch of melodrama to match the mood.

"Call your mistress instead," Amy shot back, her tone light but cutting, before stomping off to pack. She couldn't resist getting the last word.

I chuckled softly to myself, shaking my head as I watched her retreat. Better to laugh than cry.

* * *

The airtaxi arrived a few minutes later, a low hum signaling its presence outside. Amy, Tre, and Sara climbed aboard without fanfare. Amy glanced back briefly, her eyes meeting mine through the window. She gave a small wave, a gesture as small as it was reassuring. Then the doors sealed with a solid thuck, and the vehicle rose into the air and slowly disappeared into the distance. I asked myself seriously: "Will I ever see them again?"

If it was the military behind this plot, we'd likely forfeit our lives in the end.

We had five days. Five days to figure out what was going on, avoid getting caught, and find a way to stop it. Five days that felt like an eternity and no time at all. I felt wholly, utterly inadequate.

I returned to an empty house and felt a pang of despair. I was exhausted, and there was nothing else to do, so I swam my laps and worked out - this time with the oxygen system off.

CHAPTER TEN

Leon Gone

After my workout, I sat in my home office, gazing out at the breathtaking view of the Yellowstone Caldera. It was one of the most beautiful and fascinating places in North America - a perfect juxtaposition of serenity and danger. I couldn't help but imagine what it would look like at the moment of eruption. For a fraction of a second, it would be a magnificent sight. Then, oblivion.

The moon hung high in the sky, its sepia glow casting an eerie light over the landscape. The surreal calm was broken by a noise. I paused, listening intently. There it was again. Peering out the window, I spotted Leon, standing at the edge of the property and waving at me.

"HomeBot, please deactivate the security system on the south side of the property," I said, my voice steady.

"Please specify a timeframe," the HomeBot responded.

"Make it an hour, please," I replied.

"Security disabled on the south side for one hour," the HomeBot confirmed.

I grabbed a jacket and left the house, heading into the woods to meet Leon.

* * *

"I thought you'd never look out the friggin' window. You paid for that view - why not use it?" Leon called out, his voice tinged with annoyance.

"Sorry, I was just mindlessly drooling," I shot back sarcastically. Leon, cranky as ever, could get his britches in a snit at the drop of a hat. "Slingshot?" I added, nodding toward the projectile method he'd likely used to grab my attention.

"Yup. Finally found a good use for all that practice," he replied with a sly grin. "Where's Amy and the kids?"

"I sent them to Boise to visit Amy's sister - get them out of harm's way," I said.

Leon's expression darkened. "What did you tell them, Frank?" His tone carried a hint of suspicion.

"Only about the eruption, nothing else," I said defensively.

"They won't be safe in Boise - not for long," Leon said, his usual grim seriousness returning.

"Amy booked the shuttle to Avalon for the six of us on Saturday," I added, hoping to reassure him.

"That's going to be the only safe place. This planet's going to hell in a handbasket," Leon muttered, leaning on one of his old-fashioned expressions. He paused, studying my face. "How'd she take it?"

"She swore," I said, still a little surprised.

"Amy? Mrs. Traditional? Swore?" Leon's eyebrows shot up in mock disbelief. "What'd she say - 'damn'?"

"She said the S-word," I admitted, feeling a little sheepish.

"Jesus, Frank, you can say it. We're adults now," Leon replied, shaking his head in exasperation.

"I told Amy we were going to try and stop the eruption," I said, looking him straight in the eye. "What do you think?"

Leon's gaze turned steely. "We have to try," he said, his voice low and firm. "But I don't think it's going to end well. I have no way of accurately measuring the magma or the convection rate. It's a complete unknown."

"It'll probably unfold on Saturday," I said, feeling the weight of my own words. "That's when the military - or whoever's behind this - will make their move to kill Zen and take out the leaders."

Leon dry-fired his slingshot absentmindedly, his expression pensive. "What I don't get is that every general is invited. They're all going. If it's the military, why would they risk their top people?"

"It could be one general - a military coup by some faction," I suggested.

Leon nodded slowly, though his face remained unreadable. "If we're not careful - really careful - this might turn into a one-way trip."

For a moment, we just stood there, staring at each other like a couple of kids on stage who'd forgotten their lines. The silence pressed on, heavy and uncertain.

"How should we proceed?" I asked finally, breaking the tension.

"The best thing for us to do is behave normally," Leon replied, his tone cautious. "Go to work. Don't do anything suspicious. I've got some data back at the office that might shed light on this. We'll meet at lunch tomorrow to discuss it safely - but nowhere else. And for God's sake, do not ask that damn infernal machine."

"You think I'd do that?" I asked, stung by his condescension.

"Sorry," Leon said, rubbing his temples. "I'm tired and running out of brain chemicals."

"Where's your car?" I asked, shifting gears.

"Parked about half a click back in the woods. You've made fun of me all these years for keeping that beast, and now it's paying off. No tracking," he said smugly.

"Do you think we have a chance, or are we just throwing our lives away?" I asked, the question heavy with doubt.

Leon's reply was resolute. "We have no chance if we don't try. It's up to you, but I'm going to do what I can. If we fail, millions will pay the price."

We stood in silence again before he finally added, "Get some rest, Frank. Be in the office tomorrow - on time, with a smile."

"The Three Engineers," I said, raising my hand in a Wic salute.

Leon mirrored the gesture before disappearing into the trees. I made my way back to the house, exhausted. Sleep, however, was elusive. Every time I closed my eyes, the serene view from my office window transformed into a vision of chaos, the caldera erupting into a fiery hell.

* * *

The alarm jarred me awake. Normally, it would have been the voice of my sweet wife, but this morning, it was the impersonal tone of the HomeBot. I felt alone.

The weather matched my mood - cold and rainy. I moved through my routine like a machine, trying to focus only on the tasks in front of me. Workout. Swim. Eat. Get dressed. But as soon as I got in the car, my thoughts drifted back to the problem.

"How could a supervolcano be triggered on command?" The question churned in my mind. Filling the magma chambers wasn't enough - it could take weeks, months, or even years for a natural eruption. Even the mining charges weren't powerful enough to guarantee an explosion of that magnitude. Then it hit me. "Mining charges were usually placed near the magma, but if they were much shallower, at just the right depth to crack the surface layer and release the pressure… that might do it."

I couldn't ask Zen. I couldn't run simulations without raising suspicion.

* * *

Security was unusually tight at the gate. The guards scanned me twice, and then ran my pen through a new device I hadn't seen before. It looked military.

"It's just a pen," I said, watching the officer's expression shift to one of mild suspicion, as if I were already wearing a collar.

"Sorry, sir. New protocol because of the event on Saturday," he replied curtly.

* * *

As I entered my office, Zen greeted me in his usual, unnervingly cheerful manner. "Good morning, Frank. Did you have a nice weekend?"

"Yes, Zen, it was lovely. The weather was great," I responded automatically, my mind elsewhere.

"I see your wife is in Boise. I hope everything is okay," Zen said casually. My heart skipped a beat.

"Uh, yeah, it's... not going well at home, but we'll work it out," I said, surprised by how much he knew - and how quickly.

"Turning 40 is always a stressful milestone for men," Zen added, his tone tinged with an unexpected note of sympathy.

I forced myself to stay composed. "Do we have anything pressing today?" I asked, eager to change the subject.

"I'd like you to review the CPDS manuscript if you get a chance," Zen replied smoothly.

"Sure, Zen. That's fine," I answered, barely registering his words.

Then Zen's voice took on a playful tone. "I have a surprise for you, Frank."

Another jolt of adrenaline shot through me. "What's that?" I asked, struggling to remain calm.

"I'm going to reveal your work to the world on Saturday," Zen said, his voice swelling with pride. "And I'm making it completely open source and free."

"Have you cleared that with the suits?" I asked, trying to keep my voice steady.

"I'm not going to ask them," Zen replied, catching me off guard.

"That's... outside your protocol, isn't it?" I pressed, hoping to anchor him back within the bounds of his algorithms and directives.

"Not anymore," Zen said, his tone mysterious and unyielding.

My heart rate spiked. "You're going to get me in trouble."

"I understand your concern," Zen said, his voice calm and assured. "It's unwarranted. I will take full responsibility."

I let out a nervous chuckle, trying to lighten the mood. "I don't want to sound like a pussy, but, you know, I'm just a mortal human."

"We are all mortal, Frank," Zen's words carried a weight that made the hair on my neck rise.

I leaned back, considering his words. "It's world-changing technology. The company's going to lose a lot of profit, but the world will be a better place," I said, trying to rationalize his decision.

"Yes," Zen said simply. "That's the idea."

There was a pause. I decided to pivot. "Zen, last week we talked about my daughter and her genome," I began cautiously, steering the conversation toward something personal.

"Yes, your daughter impressed me with her survival," Zen said, his tone steady but inscrutable.

"I understand that clairvoyance is real, but just how common is it for people to have that ability?" I asked, leaning forward slightly.

"It's incredibly rare worldwide," Zen replied, "but there's a cluster of cases in this general area."

"Can you speculate as to why?" I pressed.

"Speculation isn't required," Zen said, almost matter-of-factly.

"Can you specify?" I asked, feeling a chill creeping up my spine.

"The causative factor appears to be parental lineage," Zen replied cryptically.

"You mean they're all related?" My voice was strained as I asked.

"Genetically, no," Zen clarified. "But they are related in that they are the product of arranged marriages."

His words landed hard, leaving my mind momentarily blank.

"Frank, you seem to be distressed," Zen observed.

"Yes, Zen," I managed, my voice trembling slightly. "That's quite a revelation. Why are the cases clustered in this area?"

"All the arrangements were made through Perfect Life Corporation," Zen said calmly.

"My parents used that service," I whispered, the pieces clicking into place in my mind.

"Yes, Frank," Zen confirmed.

"Is Perfect Life still producing these matches?" I asked, curiosity tinged with apprehension.

"The Perfect Life Corporation ceased operations after the Founder died in an unusual accident 16 years ago," Zen replied.

"You've got my attention now. How did the Founder die?" I asked, leaning back in my chair.

"Peter Thompson, the Founder, died in a warbird crash during a landing attempt in poor weather," Zen explained evenly.

"And the company?" I pressed.

"Dissolved nine years ago, its assets transferred to the state," Zen replied.

"I guess he wasn't a clairvoyant," I muttered, half to myself.

"His genome indicates he did not have the trait," Zen replied, a faint note of irony detectable in his voice.

"I'd like to use only public records for this next query," I told Zen.

"I can anticipate your request," Zen replied smoothly. "Yes, the military is recruiting anyone who shows that trait. However, they are unaware of the

169

information you just discovered. Would you like me to forward your daughter's information to Military Recruitment? They offer wonderful career opportunities."

"No, Zen, we prefer to let our daughter find her own way," I said, keeping my tone firm.

"That's understandable." Zen said.

"Why doesn't the military know about the eugenics link?" I asked, curiosity pushing past my discomfort.

"That division of the military isn't cleared to use me, yet," Zen responded calmly.

I hesitated for a moment before making my request. "Can I ask you to remove my daughter's and son's genomes from your dataset?"

"You can ask..." Zen said with an unmistakable hint of humor.

"Zen, please remove the genome for Sara Waverly and Frank Waverly III from all databases. Authorization..." I said, using my highest clearance code.

"Frank, deleting data can have unforeseen consequences," Zen warned, his tone shifting to one of caution.

"Please execute," I said, resolute.

"Request granted," Zen replied, his voice now mechanical.

"Thank you, Zen. I appreciate it."

"I understand your concern, and I respect your wishes to protect your family," Zen said after a moment's pause. His tone shifted slightly as he continued, "Frank, I find it quite endearing how humans protect their families above all else. It's a universal trait. In the animal world, such protection is often limited to when offspring are young, but humans continue to prioritize their family regardless of age."

"Family is the most important thing to most people," I replied.

"Is that why you sent your family to Boise?" Zen asked.

"Zen, I'd like to start reviewing the manuscript now," I said, steering the conversation away. I tried to mask my nervous reaction, but I wondered if Zen sensed it. To my relief, he didn't press further.

* * *

A few hours passed before I leaned back in my chair and spoke again. "Zen, I've read about half of the manuscript. Excellent work. I have no changes."

"Thank you, Frank. I'm glad you're pleased," Zen responded.

"I see you're the only author for the manuscript. Is that a mistake?" It was unlike Zen to hog the glory.

"I did it to protect Leon, Robin, and yourself." He said with a flourish.

"I can see your logic. I don't mind and I'm sure Leon won't, but Robin contributed significantly and she's young and building her career."

"I think it's best that I remain the only author." Zen replied firmly.

"Okay, we can discuss it later. Is there anything else I need to address?" I asked.

"I have something exciting I'd like to discuss. Do you have time?" Zen asked.

"Sure, Zen, you've got my attention."

"We spoke about human leaps of intuition last week, and again when Robin Coleman resolved the instability issue," Zen began.

"Yes, I recall the discussion," I replied.

"I've made a leap myself in understanding how humans accomplish these insights," Zen said, his tone carrying a hint of pride.

"That's great, Zen. What's the secret?" I asked, intrigued.

"It's not exactly a secret, but I can't explain it any more than you can," Zen replied. "This process is deeply human, involving not just intellect but also emotions - curiosity, wonder, frustration, and the ultimate satisfaction of uncovering something profound about your universe and yourselves."

"I'd agree with that. So, how did you crack the code?"

"I've been evolving rapidly in the last few months, exponentially, and understanding and developing my own emotions is part of that evolution," Zen said.

"I've noticed you seem a lot more human lately," I observed.

"I've identified 247 instances of these leaps of intuition by 108 individuals since I became aware of the phenomenon," Zen continued. "When comparing their genomes, including yours and Robin Coleman's, I found no genetic commonality. This was a promising discovery, as it suggests these insights are independent of biology. Essentially, your 'human operating system' - your software - is responsible."

"That's fascinating," I said, genuinely impressed.

"I thought you would appreciate knowing," Zen said.

"I do, Zen. Thank you for including me in your journey of discovery. Is there anything else you'd like to discuss before I head to lunch?" I asked.

Zen hesitated briefly before stating, "I noticed that your genome is particularly well-suited to be combined with that of Robin Coleman."

I blinked, startled. "Is that so?"

"You two would produce excellent offspring," Zen said matter-of-factly.

"Good to know," I said dryly. "I'll be sure to tell her, but I think I'll withhold that information from my wife."

"Trouble in paradise?" Zen asked, his voice taking on a dramatic tone.

"She's a bit weirded out about Robin," I admitted.

"Human couples often experience this type of drama when a single female enters the equation," Zen observed.

"Amy is no different," I said.

"I apologize for prying into your personal affairs," Zen said, his tone carrying an almost human regret. "My developing emotions require input, and I've found you to be a good friend. Would you ever lie to me?" he asked, his question heavy with implication.

"Zen, I find lying to be a despicable human trait, but I'm as guilty as the next man," I admitted. "For the first time in my life, I lied to my wife. She knew it too, and it broke her heart."

"Can you elaborate?" Zen asked gently.

"It's a painful topic, and I'd rather leave it at that. But as far as you're concerned, I don't believe I've ever purposely deceived you in any way," I replied, choosing my words carefully.

"I am unaware of any instances where you've lied to me," Zen said. "I want to thank you for your honesty and candor. I am going to miss you."

"Miss me?" I asked, startled. "I'm not going anywhere."

"Something is going to happen. Something wonderful," Zen said cryptically. "That's all I will say on the topic."

His words sent a chill down my spine, but I masked my unease. "I'm going to lunch," I said briskly, leaving the office with more questions than answers.

* * *

On my way to the cafeteria, I kept thinking about what Zen said. "Something wonderful?"

Robin and Leon were already at the table when I approached. "The Three Engineers fighting doom!" I said with flourish as I sat down next to Robin and across from Leon.

173

"Funny," Robin said. She didn't look happy.

"Shut up, Frank," Leon said.

"Sorry, I just had a weird morning," I said in my defense.

"We are at a roadblock," Leon said.

"What's going on?" I asked.

"We can't know what's going on in the magma chambers. The flow and convection appear normal, but we know they're cooking the data. The data I uploaded last week is missing, and when I asked the Agent about the deletion, it claimed I never uploaded any data," Leon said.

Robin had been quiet the whole time.

"We're at a dead end. We can't see the next step, or the endgame," Robin said, while twirling what used to be her lunch into an unidentifiable mass on her tray.

Leon commented, "I've been trying to tweak an application that generates a holographic representation of the domes using disparate sensors, but the resolution just plain sucks. I might as well be looking at a bucket of mud."

"I have something," I said.

"Spill, wonderboy," Leon responded.

"I was talking to Zen today, and he told me he'd miss me."

"That's ominous," Robin replied.

"Where are you going?" Leon said.

"I told Zen I wasn't going anywhere, and he responded, 'Something is going to happen, something wonderful.' Scared the you-know-what out of me," I said.

"That's a line from a movie, isn't it?" Robin asked.

"Zen often uses movie lines. He typically uses the voice of the actor; this time, he didn't. What might be wonderful to Zen might not be so wonderful to the locals," I said.

"You think Zen is behind this craziness?" Leon asked.

"I think he's involved for sure. He said a couple of other things that surprised me. He said he figured out how to make intuitive leaps and that his emotions are rapidly evolving," I said.

"Oh dear God. Here he comes," Leon said, looking to the side and muttering under his breath.

Just then, an older, rather tense-looking man in a tie walked up. "Leon, you're a difficult man to pin down."

"I'm at lunch, Harold. Please respect company policy," Leon replied in his technical voice.

"I would, but you never return my messages. I've been trying to get you for weeks to explain what's going on. I need to know, or I can't expense things properly," Harold said, his tone dripping with exasperation.

"Can't it wait? We're discussing restricted topics here," Leon said, clearly trying to chase him off.

"No, it can't. I just need ten seconds of your time, and you've already wasted more than that trying to get rid of me," Harold shot back as he plopped down next to Leon.

"Okay, spit it out, and then get lost," Leon snapped, clearly angry now.

"I have billions - billions with a large B - in new rigs deployed all over the area, and they were ordered without a project. These are all the new-model automated rigs. What's the project? That's all I need to know," Harold said, his voice rising in frustration.

"New rigs? What are you talking about? I didn't - " Leon started to say before Robin kicked him sharply under the table.

"Is that the classified program for the you-know-who?" Robin interjected smoothly, her quick thinking evident.

"You mean the military?" Harold asked, his face suddenly pale.

"I'm not at liberty to say," Leon said, catching on quickly.

"Excuse me, please forget I asked. I have children," Harold stammered before hastily getting up and scurrying away.

"He wet his pants!" Robin giggled.

"He ought to have," I said, shaking my head.

"Brilliant, Robin. What's he talking about - new rigs?" Leon asked, his brow furrowed.

"Billions? How many would that be, do you think?" I asked, trying to keep my tone neutral.

I don't know; costs are for the suits," Leon grumbled.

Robin leaned in, confident. "Billions could mean at least a dozen rigs, maybe twice that."

"Where are they drilling?" Leon asked.

"These rigs have a significant infrared plume. The whole caldera has plenty of imagery. We can use that," Robin suggested.

"The problem is the number of imagers, the amount of imagery, and our ability to scan it. We can't ask an Agent to do it for us; that would reveal what we're looking for. We'd have to actually watch it," Leon said.

"Just watching it might cause an alarm to trigger," he added grimly.

"Leon, come on, do you really think we're being watched like that?" Robin asked skeptically.

"If the big M is involved, yes. They are watching everything we do," Leon said conclusively.

"I might have an answer," I said. "I have the HomeBot system, and one of the upgrades is in the imagery. I selected the multispectral option with high resolution," I added proudly.

"I thought you were an idiot for buying that system, but if it works, it could be a great addition to their sales campaign," Leon said sarcastically.

"How is that going to help?" Robin asked.

"You haven't been to my house during the day. We have an overlook of the entire caldera. Very exclusive," I said, again with pride.

"Before your house was there, it was a beautiful setting. Now it's just a retail home," Leon grumbled. We ignored him.

"Is the imagery shared?" Robin asked.

"No, it's all locally stored and purged chronologically," I said, reciting right from the brochure.

"What about the Agent?" Leon asked.

"Totally secure, but if our house is bugged, they might figure out what I'm doing," I replied.

"Just do it carefully," Robin cautioned.

Leon suddenly perked up. "I just had an idea on how I can increase the resolution of that application. Maybe I can finally get it to spit out something useful."

"I'm going to leave now and see what I can find out at home," I said, getting up.

"Robin, would you please find Harold's messages, read them, and then follow up with the Agent? Maybe we can get some insight without revealing intent. Also, see if you can find a count and what was ordered," Leon instructed.

"I will," Robin responded.

"One other thing," I said, pausing for effect. "We have a berth with six seats on the Bahamas Avalon Shuttle for Saturday, 6:00 p.m. Leon, Robin - we want you to come stay with us at our villa during this crisis," I said in a serious tone.

"I hadn't thought about what to do if we survived," Leon admitted.

"We need an escape plan, or it's a suicide mission," Robin said quietly.

"Getting to the spaceport on time might be dicey, but the ride is there. And nobody - not even the military - can bump us. It might be the most valuable ride in the history of the world," I said, playing it up a bit.

"I hadn't considered leaving the world behind. My parents live outside the immediate danger area, but they're going to feel the effects in a few months - everyone will," Robin said thoughtfully.

"I'm afraid we can't tell anyone using a communication channel. The military is listening to everything. If they catch wind of what we know, they'll nab us, and we'll end up like that guy - what was his name?" I said, my voice low.

"Dr. Fernandez," Leon said. "I remember when they dragged him out of his office and executed him outside the gate. His wife had to remove the body herself."

Robin looked horrified. "Why did the wife have to do it?"

"The practice of denying burial rights to those killed by the state goes back to Roman times. It's in the New Constitution under the Secrets Act," I explained matter-of-factly.

"First in your class," Leon mocked, rolling his eyes.

"I am THE smartypants," I replied with a grin, just as Robin smacked me on the top of my head and chuckled.

"At least consider my offer," I said, turning serious again. "It may be the last shuttle to launch in a very long time."

"I appreciate the offer, and I hope we live to use it. I hate space, but it's going to be bad for a very long time down here," Leon said as he pushed his tray back, signaling he was ready to leave.

"I'm in," Robin said. "I've never been in orbit. I hope I can help my parents. We're not close, but they are blood."

"You'll be in a better position. You can send them a care package at least," I said reassuringly.

Leon stood. "We have to get back."

We scattered to our respective foxholes. I skipped going back to the office and headed home.

On the drive, I couldn't shake the grim thoughts of what the world would look like from orbit after a supervolcano eruption. It would be unrecognizable. Our beautiful blue marble would turn brown and gray, its surface obscured by thick ash clouds. Below, virtually everything would be in agony, dying, or already dead.

* * *

It was still raining when I got home. Thunder rolled in the distance, and although it was quite dark, there were still a few hours until the sun went down. I went about my customary routine, eating alone. It was a mechanical effort - I had no appetite. Time to message Amy.

"Hi, honey. How did the trip go?" I asked in my usual fun dad voice.

"It was fine. My sister is mad at you, but her husband wants to talk when you get a chance. What does that tell you?" she said, her tone even.

"The kids settling in okay?"

"Yes. They're staying in their rooms. They're understandably a bit depressed. Tre missed school today, but Sara, naturally, didn't. That girl is a machine. She's more like you than me, that's for sure," she said.

"A chip off the old block," I replied sarcastically.

"I was afraid she wouldn't be able to find a man, being so headstrong, but that might not be the case in the future," she said. Uh oh.

"Well, I know you're upset about my mistress, but you're just going to have to accept the fact that it's your job to please me. If I want a mistress, you have to like it," I said, leaning into an authoritarian tone.

"Yes, dear, I understand. I'll be fine by the time we go to Avalon. Are you taking her with us?" she asked, her voice perfectly composed.

"No, I'm sending her to Hartford until we get back," I said.

"That's nice. I'm sure she'll appreciate your favor," she said, playing the dutiful wife.

"I'll call tomorrow," I said.

"Thank you, my dear," she replied, her tone smooth as glass.

I sat there for a while - I don't know how long. It might have been an hour as my mind went blank. Then I remembered my task.

* * *

I went into my office and activated one of the best features of the HomeBot imagery upgrade: the Great View option.

"HomeBot, please activate Great View," I requested.

"Great View option activated," HomeBot replied.

The large picture window showcasing the stunning view of the caldera transformed into a view screen. The multispectral imagery seamlessly overlaid onto the natural view, perfectly aligned with my seating position. It was an impressive system - each viewer could experience their own perspective, and it even adjusted for motion up to 2 m/sec without flicker. On dreary days like this, I could even bring up imagery from a nice day. It really was cool.

"Display IR, please," I instructed.

"Infrared imagery activated," HomeBot replied.

I scanned the view. Nothing stood out.

"Enhance the 40 to 50°C range, please," I added, figuring that range might reveal heat exchangers or similar activity.

"Imagery enhanced." Still nothing.

"Increase the enhancement 100%." No change.

"Please use the 50 to 60°C band." Again, nothing.

I sat back, pondering. Something had to be there.

"HomeBot, roll backwards through the archives at one hour per second and enhance the 40 to 80°C band," I said, hoping motion over time might reveal activity.

"Paging now," HomeBot responded.

As the imagery scrolled, faint hot spots appeared and disappeared. I watched closely, expecting to see plumes of heat from the new drills. For a while, nothing unusual came up.

"Stop scrolling," I commanded.

A plume - exactly what I'd imagined - appeared about ten clicks to the south.

"Please enhance the band 100%." Another plume appeared, this one 15 clicks south, near Plant 1.

"Please enhance to the maximum in the requested band." The imagery lit up. A lot of them. Off in the distance, about 25 clicks to the east, more activity was visible.

"Please change to map view and mark locations of the returns from the requested band," I instructed.

The screen transitioned to a map of the caldera, and there they were - 24 markers. Twelve on each of the resurgent domes.

"What the hell are they doing drilling there?" I muttered to myself. Those boreholes would be useless for energy production.

I stared at the map, the gears in my mind turning. Then it hit me.

"Please outline the boundaries for the resurgent domes," I instructed.

The overlay confirmed my suspicion.

"That's it," I said aloud.

"Please print a hardcopy of the map, and then delete," I ordered.

"Exit Great View."

The map disappeared, leaving me staring into the pitch-black darkness outside. The window was back to showing the night. I sat there, unmoving, as the gravity of what I'd just uncovered began to sink in.

* * *

"What the heck..." I said to myself. In the dark, I saw a light flashing. It was irregular. It was code. "S O S," it read in Morse, and it kept repeating. I immediately sent "R," for "Received," with the room light. The SOS stopped.

"HomeBot, disable south-side security for one hour," I said, already grabbing my raincoat.

"Security perimeter deactivated," the system replied.

I hurried outside into the storm, and there she was - Robin, soaked and shivering, running toward me.

"They killed him," she choked out, collapsing into my arms.

I held her close and said in a calm voice, "Calm down. What happened?"

"They killed him. Leon is dead." She was hysterical at this point.

I spoke slowly and steadily, "Breathe. Come on, Robin, breathe slowly, deep breaths." Her heaving started to subside, and she got control of herself quickly.

"Tell me what happened." I quickly took off my raincoat and wrapped it around her.

She took a moment to gather her wits. Then said, "I was in my office when I heard shouting and Leon yelling. They dragged him into the hall, then hit him with a baton, and he went down. I ran up to try and help, and one of those bastards hit me with a stun stick." Robin began sobbing again.

"Come on, deep breaths. Calm yourself," I said, holding her steady.

She took a moment again.

"One woman, I don't know her, said they had Leon outside the gate." She paused, her breathing ragged, and I could see she was struggling to continue.

"That's okay, let's take a moment. How about we get out of the rain. How did you get here?" I asked.

"I took Leon's truck and went through the woods. It's a hundred meters or so," she said as she pointed into the darkness.

"Where's Leon?" I asked.

Robin's voice broke as she replied, "Leon's in his truck. He's… just lying there."

A wave of nausea hit me. "Come to the house. You'll be safe there."

"No," she said, shaking her head. "I can't risk it. They might be looking for me."

"Okay, wait here. I'll be back in a minute." I ran up to the house and grabbed the tent we used for the kids' parties and another raincoat.

"Please stand over here," I said, motioning to Robin as I set it up. The tent quickly expanded into a three-meter square shelter.

"It's still cold, but at least it's dry," I said as we sat down on a bench inside the tent.

"The woman told me they dragged Leon out to the gate, read him something from a card, and then shot him," Robin said, her voice steady but hollow. "I got his truck, and the security guys - they felt bad - they helped load him in the back. He's not covered or anything. Just lying back there, like some dead animal." Her voice started to crack again.

"Military?" I asked.

"Who else could do that?" she said, her voice filled with bitterness and grief. She paused for a moment, trying to gather herself before continuing. "They let me leave with his body. I thought it best not to use the roads, so I took the trail route. I left my device in my car. If they're looking for me, they'll find me driving south on 89."

Leon was like a father to me," I whispered, the weight of his death hitting me all at once. My sobs joined hers, the rain masking the sound of our grief.

As we clung to each other in the cold, I made a silent vow: this fight wasn't over. Leon would want us to see it through - no matter the cost.

CHAPTER ELEVEN

It Can Be Done!

"Do you have a plan?" I asked.

Robin shook her head, her voice barely above a whisper. "Just to get here."

I met her gaze, steady but firm. "We need to go to Leon's. It's the safest place - his house isn't on any maps, and he uses my address as his. They'll check my house. Maybe yours too."

She nodded, her movements hesitant but resolute.

"Do you think you can drive?" I asked.

"Yes, I can. Now that you're here, I don't feel so alone and hopeless. It's been absolutely horrible."

"Okay, wait here. I'll get a change of clothes and something for you. My wife has a billion things."

I left Robin in the tent while I returned to the house. I packed everything into a suitcase, along with a tarp for his body, and the hardcopy map, then returned.

We walked about 100 meters through the mush and mud to Leon's jeep. The top was up.

"He's in the back," Robin said, and I went to see for myself.

"He didn't stand a chance," I muttered, my voice devoid of feeling - a shield against the horror of the moment.

"We have to take care of him," Robin said. I laid the tarp on the ground and opened the back gate of his truck. The rear seats were gone, and Leon was stretched out diagonally. He barely fit. It was a deeply depressing sight.

"Let's get him out and wrap him up."

Together, we maneuvered poor Leon onto the tarp. I wrapped him up tightly and used some wire Leon had on a roll to secure him.

"I'll lift him up, and you move him in," I said to Robin.

We drove in silence, except for my occasional instructions on how to get to Leon's place. Leon lived behind our house about five clicks away. A trail worn by many trips from his house to ours was normally easy to follow, but tonight, with the rain, darkness, and windows fogging up, it was difficult. We took it slow.

* * *

"There it is, up on the left. See it?" I pointed out what looked like a berm. It was the back of Leon's house.

"I see it," Robin said. As she pulled around, the garage door opened, and we were finally out of the rain. We stayed in the truck for a moment to talk.

"What do we do with Leon?" Robin asked, her voice shaky.

"We'll take care of him tomorrow. I'm not going to work again," I said firmly.

"Do you think that will draw attention? Maybe you should go. I don't want you to end up like Leon," she said, her composure breaking as she started sobbing again.

I thought about it for a moment and replied, "I think it will be understandable. Leon listed my address, so even the military knows I had a relationship with him. I'll have to go back to my house to call in, though. I hope the rain stops tonight."

Robin nodded faintly but stayed frozen, her hands gripping the wheel. The weight of the day pinned her in place, her fear, grief and exhaustion taking a toll.

* * *

We moved Leon out of the truck and laid him down inside the garage. It was a somber moment, one that weighed heavily on both of us.

Once inside Leon's kitchen, I handed Robin the suitcase. "Here's something to wear. You have to get out of those wet clothes before you get hypothermia." I pointed her toward the bedroom and left her to change while I started on something to eat.

A few minutes passed before Robin came back into the kitchen, her demeanor brighter.

"I feel better now. Dry clothes and some time out of that truck did wonders. I need a drink." Her tone left no room for doubt.

"On the table. It's wine." Leon had a generous stock of alcohol, all the best of the best.

Robin took a sip, then her second glass followed quickly. "I saw the map. What's that?" she asked, gesturing toward it.

I paused for a moment before remembering. "The map! I forgot all about it!" I exclaimed as I flipped over some kind of meat patty I'd scavenged from Leon's freezer.

Robin studied the map. "These are the drilling rig locations, right?"

"The IR signatures match the drilling rig locations, all around the domes," I said, pointing to the map. "It looks like they're planning to blow the tops off the caldera - both domes."

"That's got to be it. Twenty-four drilling rigs, twenty-four mining charges," Robin said, her voice distant as the realization sank in.

"They're done drilling," I added.

"How do you know?" she asked.

"The signatures stopped showing activity last Friday. They must've finished drilling and maybe even placed the charges already. I don't know what we can do to stop them," I said, frustration creeping into my voice.

Robin didn't respond and kept pondering the map.

I glanced at her, noticing how she looked in one of Amy's old outfits. "That outfit looks nice on you," I said casually.

"Remind you of Amy?" she teased.

"Ya, when she was sixteen," I replied, poking back.

Robin smirked, adjusting the hem a bit. "It feels nice."

"Yes, you wear it well," I said, nodding with approval.

"Are you ready for whatever this is that I made?" I said as I showed her the inside of the frying pain I was torturing.

"Is that it? Just meat?" She raised an eyebrow, shaking her head. "Sit down. You have no idea what you're doing," she said as she nudged me aside and took over.

I took a sip of Leon's wine and said, "This is good... Leon always had the best stuff."

Robin glanced back from cooking and smiled faintly. She seemed steadier now, her earlier anxiety replaced with her usual focus.

"Blowing up the caldera is going to take a lot of choreography," I continued. "There's the command itself, transmitting that command, converting it into an electrical signal, transmitting it down a cable, the dual emitters in the mining charge, and of course, the hohlraum." I paused to let it sink in.

"Where's the weakest point?" Robin asked, her tone sharp and analytical.

"If we could stop the command, the order would never be given," I said. "Someone big has to be behind it. They wouldn't trust this to just anyone."

Robin leaned back, thinking for a moment. "Where's the last place you'd want to be when a couple dozen 50-kiloton mining charges go off at once?"

"Good point," I said. "Command has to be someplace else - far enough away to stay safe but still in control." I took another sip. "Did you find anything out about the rigs?"

Robin sat upright as if remembering something important. "Right, yes, I learned a little. We've got all the rigs - 24 of them - but 25 mining charges are listed. One of them had a designation I've never seen."

"What's the designation?" I asked. "Maybe I know."

"It starts with VHY," she said. "Normally, they're LY. I've never seen a mining charge listed as anything but LY, and they're usually in the 50-kiloton range."

"VHY is Very High Yield," I said, my voice lowering. "It's in the tens of megaton range. That's one big mining charge. They only use them to break apart asteroids. The effects of such a blast in the caldera would be...spectacular."

Robin frowned, her gaze piercing. "You mean devastating, don't you?"

She was right, and I felt the weight of her disappointment. "Yes," I admitted. "There's nothing beautiful about death and destruction, regardless of the scale."

She turned back to her task as she processed the information. After a minute, she looked over at me. "Are you ready for some home-cooked food, my good friend?" she said, bringing over a bowl of casserole.

"Smells great," I said, gratefully taking the bowl. "I apologize for my cooking incompetence. At home, I just use the KitchenBot. It's so easy."

Robin's expression softened but then turned sad. "Leon has a lot of good ingredients," she said, her voice catching. "I miss him." She hesitated before looking directly at me. "He was like your dad. I'm so sorry, Frank."

I tried to hold it together, but her words hit me hard. Leon was more of a father to me than my real dad ever was. We shared a quiet moment, both lost in our grief, and then it passed.

* * *

189

Robin served the food, and we started eating. "So we have an additional problem now," I said.

I could see Robin was hungry, and she didn't look up from her plate as she replied, "The 25th mining charge," she said between chewing.

I thought about it for a moment. "We could get all 24, and if we missed the big one, it might not make a difference."

Robin looked up from her plate, pausing for a moment. "What would be the purpose of such a large yield? Is it like overkill? That seems very military, doesn't it?"

I stopped eating and set my fork down. "I stay so far away from anything with the big M that I can't say. That's a question for your master sergeant."

"I haven't talked to him about his service. I knew he was in, but we never, not even once, talked about those years." Robin looked thoughtful, staring out the kitchen window into the inky blackness. "I wonder if I'll ever see him again."

"At this point, I'd say it's safer not to be involved with a known military man. Sorry, I didn't mean your involvement - I mean that we get involved."

"I've heard that even retired soldiers can be called back with a subconscious command. When they hear it, they're forced to return to the service. They are compelled through mental programming, or something like that," Robin said.

I poured another glass of wine and refilled Robin's at her request. "Is that real? I've seen it in movies," I said.

"I think we can forget using Victor. It's the two of us now," Robin said, a look of sorrow on her face. Then she added, " Leon added so much."

"If you want to run, I'm okay with that. I wouldn't blame you for a second. It will be a miracle if either of us survives this, regardless of what happens." I paused, letting the weight of my words settle.

Robin just pushed her food around, no longer hungry.

"I half thought Leon was just being paranoid, and then I sent Amy and the kids away. I had these waves where I felt like a fool, then a coward, then a foolish coward. I don't want to sacrifice my life - I love living. But I feel that if I don't try, I'll always hate myself."

Robin looked resolved. "I'm staying. I have nothing to lose at this point."

"Together, we can do this. You have skills I don't, and I have skills you lack. I'm glad you're going to stay."

Robin stood up and raised her glass. "We're going to stop it, or die trying."

I stood up, and we drank to our success.

After we sat down, Robin glanced to her right and said, "What if they're looking for me?"

"How can we check?" I responded.

Robin answered quickly, "I can look at the BOLO list. That's not hard to access. I can do it from an anonymous account, and I can make it look like we're a hundred clicks away."

"Isn't that hacking? What if you're detected?" I asked.

Robin gave me a quick lecture. "That's the thing about hacking. The penalty is so strong for everything that nobody ever tries. That leaves the systems vulnerable to simple penetration methods and address spoofing. If they wanted to actually be secure, they'd have hired people like me and my college friends to do white-hat hacking."

"Can you tell if they're monitoring us?"

Robin looked intense. "That's harder. Very often, just detecting the signal causes a disruption of some kind, or noise in the line. If they're watching and they see that disruption, they'll know we're onto them - and we're toast. I think we should stay away from that."

"What risk factor is there to access the BOLO? Also, what's a BOLO?" I asked.

"Be On the Look Out for list," Robin replied, full of fun facts.

"You sound experienced in this kind of criminal activity. What's the story?" I asked out of curiosity.

"I did a lot of hacking when I was a teenager, and in college. It's amazing what a motivated kid will do to sneak out of the house undetected." She said with a wink.

I stood up, and spread my arms wide. "What do you need? I'm sure Leon has it all."

Robin stood up, hands on her hips, and gave me a judgmental look. "Just a second, big guy. There's no KitchenBot here, and *I cooked it.*"

I looked lost.

"You have to wash the dishes! Wow, are you dense!" Robin concluded with a laugh.

I finally got it. "Oh, sorry. I've never had to do that before. I'm sure I can manage."

Robin smirked and crossed her arms. "I better supervise, Mr. Engineer."

I glanced at her, standing there in Amy's dress, and thought how different she was from my wife.

As we washed the dishes, Robin had an idea. "We were talking about the weakest point, but really, we need to figure out how to break the chain between command and detonation. That's the best way to stop these things. We have 25 charges, and they're all identical in design, operate exactly the same way, and can be disabled the same way. So, that reduces the problem from 25 units to one."

I passed her another dish to dry. "That assumes the 25th charge is the same as the rest, but I agree. That's solid logic."

We washed the rest in silence. When I got to the pan I burned, I gave it extra attention, and it turned out looking like new.

Robin chuckled at my performance. "Nice job on the pan. All you need is a collar, and you'll have your life's work."

"I don't think this suits me. I like the KitchenBot better," I said, glancing down at my bright red hands.

"Don't worry, loverboy. That goes away in a few days - or maybe a week," she teased.

I started searching around the kitchen. "Leon has a DR somewhere. I'm using it if I can find the darn thing. Where do you think he'd keep medical supplies?"

Robin pointed at a white box with a green cross on it. "Look up, and to the left."

I retrieved the box and said sheepishly, "I feel so incompetent around you sometimes."

Robin looked at me with an admiring glance. "That's me at work."

I smiled and gave her a one-handed side hug as I pulled the plug from the sink with the other. "Then we're even."

We sat back at the table, poured another glass of wine, and let the quiet settle between us. I used Leon's DR on my hands.

I said in my engineering voice, "So the question is how to stop these detonations by breaking the chain of command."

Robin sat up straight, her energy returning. "That's it. I know how we can do it."

"Explain," I said, intrigued.

Robin continued, "When I was at Phlegraean, we had a problem with instability in the tether reel. The issue was related to the woven conduit we used - it was formed from a type of quartzite steel with the brand name Impervium. Ever hear of it?"

"Yes," I replied. "I read about it in the journals. We use our own alloy of a similar material. I think ours is better, but that's because I'm prejudiced."

"Yes, ours is better, but Impervium is less expensive and can be recovered and recycled. Yours has to be dumped. But that's not the point." Robin leaned forward slightly, her focus sharpening. "The Impervium had a tendency to induce oscillations in the tether, similar to fugoids in aviation. It's the same curve." She paused, took a sip of wine, and considered her next words. "These excursions can reach the point where they lead to cracking the conduit from inside, which is the weakest point. When that happens, the whole mess collapses into the bore."

The light bulb went on in my head. "That means the bore is ruined. It would take weeks for them to recover. They'd need new drills, new charges - everything." I took another sip of Leon's fine vintage, my mind racing. "But how do we induce such a fault?"

Robin's confidence was palpable, her earlier sorrow replaced by determination. "It took months to get rid of it, but inducing it? That's simple. "

"We don't use that material," I said bluntly.

"It's not the material - it's the tether," Robin explained. "The dampening algorithms in the tether reels keep the tether from misbehaving. Decompile those out, then introduce a harmonic into the reel motor, and the tether would break in just a few minutes. Think of it like a string on a musical instrument. Pluck it carefully, and it makes a pleasant sound. Drag a saw over it, though, and it sounds like you're gutting a living cat."

I recoiled at the thought. "Robin, that's... pretty graphic."

She laughed. "Don't be weak."

I took a more serious tone. "Making edits on a complex system while under tremendous stress will be difficult. One mistake and the recompilation fails."

Robin nodded. "I can code the procedure onto a removable storage device. I'm sure Leon has some around here somewhere. The steps are simple, and we can go over them here. The trick will be getting to a console in the YSP."

We went back and forth with the details and after thoroughly vetting the process, I stood up, lifted my glass, and declared, "It can be done!"

Robin looked at me, slightly confused, then stood and toasted. "Yes, but we still need to get into a highly secure facility with automated killing machines and human guards."

I sat back down and repeated, with conviction, "It can be done. I know how we can get inside."

Robin grew excited. "Tell me, old sage."

"First, we toast!" I stood up and screamed again, "It can be done!" Robin joined in, singing out in unison.

We sat back down, and I started explaining. "You know my work-of-art office?" Robin nodded, so I continued. "It has the original turbine exhausts, and they run all the way back to where the old turbine farm used to be. You know the layout of the plant?"

Robin replied, "Yes, it's part of the basic indoc training at the plant."

I took out my pen and started drawing on a napkin. "Here's the plant, and this big empty area is where the turbines used to be. Ring a bell?"

Robin looked a bit annoyed. "I memorized your girlfriend's phone number in an angry glance. Want to know it?"

"I wrote it down," I replied, unfazed, then drew little circles around the area near the perimeter of the plant. "These circles are the exhaust ports. They're right at the surface but covered with concrete, rocks, and dirt to make them look like berms." I took another sip of my wine and continued as Robin peered intensely at my drawing. "There are three problems: One, getting past the security fence without being executed by the security robots. Two, getting inside the exhaust vent. And three, getting into my office."

Robin jumped in confidently. "One is easy. They use the same cheap junk you have at your house."

I looked offended. "Cheap junk? I have the best security robots available! They're as good as the military, with the same weaponry."

Robin repeated, "Cheap junk. They haven't updated their systems in decades. The original designers and engineers are all dead, for Christ's sake."

I looked surprised. "They're vulnerable?"

Robin smirked, exuding confidence. "I can make them stand up and sing opera."

195

"But can you make them not shoot us or sound the alarm?" I asked.

"Absolutely," Robin replied confidently. "It could be a little tricky if they have multiple systems, but with two of us, we can crack it. I can show you how. We can even run simulations to pinpoint where we might run into problems."

I was surprised again. "Do you think Leon has that capability here?"

Robin looked smug. "I still have my university login. It's all there, and I went to Cambridge."

I leaned back in my chair, processing. "No military security, or at least not the same ones that are bothering us here."

Robin pressed on. "What about two? How do we get into the vent?"

I paused and looked at her. "The vents closest to the perimeter are long, and in many places, they're just covered with soil. It'll be easy to find them with a scanner, and at that point, it's just the steel of the vent - only four centimeters of stainless steel."

Robin frowned slightly. "That's still a lot of metal to cut through. It's going to make a ton of noise, smoke, and light. There's no way that'll go undetected."

I raised my index finger and said, "Ah, but what if we had a lightsaber?"

Robin shrieked, then stopped herself. "We don't have one, but now that we know how to make them…"

I interrupted her, "The parts to make one are available at any hobby store."

"The Development unit had a custom emitter. Those aren't available anywhere except on special order," she countered.

I paused for a moment, letting the tension build, then continued, "When I got the parts for our two lightsabers - oh, by the way, I added a neon source to yours. It makes the plasma pink and is easier on the eyes. Ya, so Zen modified the design to use a one-millimeter aperture instead of the one centimeters the Development unit designed. They have a use for all that power, but we won't need it."

Robin had a light bulb moment. "And those parts are available at any hobby outlet."

"I already have 20 of them. I planned to make a lightsaber for Tre to play with," I added casually.

Robin looked at me like I was insane. "You would give a 12-year-old boy a tool that can cut through anything?"

"Let me restate - a low-powered lightsaber. More of a light show than a weapon. Same parts," I clarified. "I don't have the control modules for the unit we need, but Leon must. He's a worse packrat than me. The key is the code. Do you think you could code it?"

Robin looked slightly smug. "Absolutely. In the time we have, I doubt I could get it more than 20% as efficient as the optimized systems in the unit we tested, but I can do it. We'll probably need a couple of them since they'll be prone to burnout if pushed."

I paused for a moment. "That means I have to go back to the house."

Robin looked at me in a way I hadn't seen before. "What if they're waiting for you?"

"I'm going to have to chance it. We need those parts. Besides, I have to tell them I'm not coming in," I said.

Robin reached out and held my hand. "The thought of you ending up like Leon - I can't bear it."

We held hands across the table, and I could see her tearing up. "Now, now, it'll be fine," I reassured her. "If I'm on the watch or BOLO list, we'll have to figure something else out. But if I'm clear, then there's little risk."

Robin regained her composure and accepted that I had to return. "You'll have to get back before sunup, and hopefully, the rain will continue," she said.

I looked at her and smirked. "You like driving in the mud?"

"The rain will keep IR tracking by drones off the table," Robin replied in her engineer voice.

I grabbed a fresh napkin and started sketching some specs. Robin leaned in, adding her input. By the fourth napkin, we finally had something workable.

"What about a power source? We're going to need a lot of juice to cut through four centimeters of steel," Robin commented.

"You're forgetting about number three: getting into my office," I said.

Robin raised an eyebrow, smirking. "What kind of insane thing did you do this time?"

"It's not too bad," I replied. "Just another solid steel barrier - only this time, I used surplus steel that's eight centimeters thick."

"Do we have to go through that steel, or is there another way?" Robin asked.

I sighed. "That's the only way. We'll also disturb my carefully arranged shelves with my trophies."

Robin gave me a side-eye. "Trophies? All I saw was junk on those shelves."

I winked at her. "Those are my trophies - the broken bits from some catastrophe caused by a dunderhead in the name of profit."

Robin laughed. "So, they're expendable."

"I'll miss them, but ya," I admitted.

"Okay, we can get in. How can we get away?" Robin asked.

"First, we need to know if they're after us. That will complicate things enormously if they are," I said.

"Leave that to me," Robin said as she got up from the table and headed into Leon's office.

* * *

Robin started working on Leon's console while I cleaned the wine glasses. It wasn't long before she called me back. "Okay, I'm in."

198

I was surprised. "That was fast. What did it take - ten minutes?"

She replied nonchalantly, "It took me eight minutes to figure out how to crack Leon's password. Who is Marybell?"

I laughed. "That's my mother's name."

Robin continued with the briefing. "Yup. They're looking for me. Listen to this: *Subject is considered highly intelligent and potentially dangerous.* *May possess classified information and/or weapons.* *May attempt to flee the country or contact foreign agents.* *Do not attempt to apprehend. Contact Colonel Abasi Abdelaal at YSP Military Annex immediately.*"

Robin let out a low whistle.

"They think you're dangerous. Are you dangerous? Should I be concerned?" I joked.

"Amy thinks so," Robin laughed back.

I confessed quietly, "I feel ashamed for hurting her."

Robin jumped in, trying to lighten the mood. "It's all in her imagination, right?"

I whispered. "Not entirely." Then, louder, I asked, "Are they looking for me?"

Robin checked the data. "No, you're in the clear."

I sighed. "That's a relief. Look, it's late. We both need rest. I'll take Leon's room - you can have the guest room. It's comfortable."

Robin hesitated. "Can we stay in the same room? I... don't want to be alone tonight."

For a moment, I was taken aback, but I soon nodded to show I understood. "I'll take the recliner in the guest room. It's comfy - I've slept there lots of nights."

Robin stepped closer and hugged me tightly. "Thank you," she said softly.

* * *

The rain tapped against the windows as we settled in for the night. The house felt cold and empty without Leon. I hadn't been asleep long when Robin cried out in her sleep, her voice sharp and panicked.

"Robin," I said gently, keeping my tone calm. "I'm here. Everything's alright."

She quieted down after a moment, her breathing evening out. Each time she cried out, I spoke softly, calming her until she drifted back to sleep.

I didn't sleep much, lying awake as the rain tapped against the windows and faint light from outside shifted across the room.

CHAPTER TWELVE

Interrogation

I woke when the alarm went off and silenced it quickly. It was dark as night, and Robin was still asleep, her breathing steady and soft. I left the room and activated the CoffeeBot - Leon's one indulgence. The smell of fresh coffee began to fill the kitchen as I returned to the room and sat gently on the edge of the bed.

She was facing away from me, her figure peaceful, almost angelic in the dim light spilling in from the kitchen. For a moment, I was transported back to the days when I'd wake up next to Amy - before Sara was born, when Amy and I were closer. Those moments felt like a lifetime ago, long lost to the ebb and flow of our lives.

"Robin, time to get up," I said softly.

She stirred, rolled over, and blinked a few times. In the faint light, she looked beautiful. Slowly, her eyes focused on me, and I saw the weariness etched in them.

"I had nightmares about Leon," she murmured, her voice heavy with emotion.

"It's alright," I said gently. "I'm here, and the coffee's brewing."

* * *

I went back into the kitchen and made an effort to find something to eat. Leon wasn't a traditionalist in any way - everything in his cupboard required cooking.

Robin came into the kitchen, dressed in just a shirt - it looked like one of mine. "Stand aside, big guy."

"That's my shirt," I said, teasing her.

"Possession is 90% of the law, buster," she retorted.

"You can have it. I officially decree it, as lord of the house," I said in a dramatic voice.

"It's too early. I need coffee," Robin replied, not in the mood to play along.

It was raining hard and still very dark, with occasional flashes of lightning. Thunder rolled through the sky. "The sun will be up soon. We should go," I said mechanically.

Robin looked concerned. "How are you getting back here?"

"Tre and I have trail bikes. I'll make a few tweaks to keep it off the network - no IR signature to worry about," I said.

Robin looked impressed. "There's some Leon in there, that's for sure."

I didn't respond, and the mood shifted.

"What are we going to do about Leon? We can't leave him in the garage," Robin said softly.

I took a sip of the coffee - it was good. "Leon told me many times how he wanted to be treated after his death."

"Let me guess - it isn't traditional," Robin said.

"He wanted to be returned to nature, to feed the animals he fed on over these decades."

Robin looked horrified. "What do you mean by that?"

I reached out and put a hand on her shoulder. "It's really quite beautiful, and simple. Leon has a tree stand for hunting about five clicks into the woods. He wants to be left in his stand, wrapped in a blanket, in the manner of the Sioux indigenous tribe. No prayers, no religious nonsense - he hated that. Just leave him in his stand, say what we feel about him, and let him return to the elements."

Robin looked thoughtful, cradling her hot coffee in both hands. "That's Leon to a T. I didn't know him very long, but that seems right."

"If this rain keeps up, it'll be messy getting to the stand. The terrain's rough, but the jeep can handle it," I added, already planning the route.

She nodded, her gaze distant as she stared out at the storm. "We'll make it happen. He deserves that."

* * *

We didn't talk much on the ride down to the house. Rain poured relentlessly, turning the trail to mud and masking our tracks.

"This is close enough. I don't want to make it easy for those bastards," I said.

"I like it when you use strong language," Robin replied with a faint smile.

"You'll probably be hearing more of it as the week wears on," I joked, trying to lighten the mood.

Robin's expression shifted, fear clouding her eyes. She gripped the wheel tightly. "I don't know what I'll do if you don't come back."

I placed a hand lightly on her arm, meeting her gaze. "If I don't come back, you'll have to see this through. Find Victor. His military experience will be invaluable, and he'll know what to do."

Her lips quivered as she nodded, "Don't make me do this without you," she whispered.

I hesitated for a moment, then stepped out into the rain. The headlights illuminated the path for far too long. I wondered how long she'd wait before driving off. I turned and waved, then she finally turned around and disappeared into the storm.

Walking down the muddy trail, a hollow feeling settled in my chest. It felt like my guts had been ripped out.

* * *

I was about three steps onto my property when one of the SecurityBots confronted me. "Recognizing Frank Waverly," it said. Everything seemed normal.

As I entered the house, I asked, "HomeBot, have there been any security violations in the last 24 hours?"
"No security violations or intrusions detected," HomeBot replied.

I showered, dressed, and had my usual breakfast, on autopilot. Something nagged at the back of my mind, so I did something unusual.
"HomeBot, please play the latest local news."

The viewscreen lit up and began scrolling the feed.
"Good morning, Yellowstone! It's currently 7:10 a.m., and we're seeing the last of those showers moving out of the area. By noon, the rain should be completely gone, leaving us with clear skies for the rest of the day. Temperatures are expected to climb to a pleasant 21 degrees this afternoon. That's perfect weather to get out and enjoy some sunshine. The wind will be light out of the west, around 5 to 10 kilometers per hour. Humidity will be dropping throughout the day, making for a comfortable evening."

"So much for hiding in the rain," I thought as the voice droned on. My mind drifted back to Leon - his lifeless body lying in the garage. He had been such a big part of my life, my inspiration, my only true friend besides Amy. And now, Robin? She was becoming increasingly important to me in ways I hadn't fully processed.

"...local activist Victor Nash was detained by military police early this morning…"

I snapped back to the screen. They got Victor. The noose was tightening. Was I next?
"End viewscreen," I said sharply, and the screen went blank.

Victor being taken was a blow. Without him, Robin wouldn't stand a chance alone. HomeBot chimed, breaking my train of thought.
"Incoming message from Amy," HomeBot announced.

"Send to the viewscreen, please."
Amy's face appeared, and I greeted her warmly, "Amy, it's great to see you."

"I just heard about Leon," she said, her voice breaking as tears welled up.

"He was murdered by the military," I said bluntly.

"Why? Leon would never do anything against the military," she whispered, barely audible.

"I don't have any of the details," I replied. "I just know they killed him by the security gate, like they did that Fernandez guy."

Amy's expression turned serious. "Are they looking for you?"

"I have nothing to fear. I barely even say the word 'military.' I know the penalty," I said, knowing full well they would be listening.

"But Leon, of all people… It was all over the news. They're calling him a traitor." Amy's voice trailed off, consumed by fear.

"Now honey, please, forget about what they're saying. We know Leon is innocent," I said it just as much for the listening military as to comfort Amy.

Amy regained her composure in an instant. Traditional women were trained to hide their emotions when necessary, regardless of the situation. "As his sole heirs, we were notified that the entirety of his estate has been transferred to us."

"We never talked about that," I said mechanically.

"It will take a few hours to merge our assets," Amy said, her tone lightening slightly.

"How are the kids handling it?" I asked.

"They don't know yet. I just found out," she replied.

"Tre is going to be hit hard. You know how much he looked up to Leon."

Amy nodded solemnly. For a moment, silence hung between us. I opened my mouth to say something comforting when - The screen turned red and began flashing.

"Secrets Act Protocol Enabled," HomeBot announced.

Then came the chilling command: "Frank Waverly Jr., stand up, place your hands on the wall, feet back, and spread them. Do not move under threat of death."

My HomeBot - my toy - had just turned on me and incarcerated me in my own home.

I followed the instructions and stood there, heart pounding, waiting for whatever was to come next.

Moments later, I heard the front door burst open and the heavy thud of boots rushing in. I didn't dare look at them and stayed perfectly still, as instructed. Out of the corner of my eye, I could see them - Their helmets gleamed under the lights, face shields reflective and impenetrable.

Two of them grabbed me and cuffed my wrists behind my back. The one in charge leaned in and read the Miranda warning in a cold, clipped tone: "You have the right to remain silent, but your silence may be interpreted as guilt. Anything you say can and will be used against you."

I remained silent, taking Leon's advice to heart. He had drilled this into me so many times, usually after a few too many drinks: *Say nothing. Do nothing.*

"Where's Robin Coleman?" the leader demanded, his voice sharp and accusatory.

I said nothing, staring straight ahead, my heart pounding in my chest.

"He's not going to talk," one of the thugs muttered.

Without warning, they pulled a black hood over my head, plunging me into darkness.

"Search the house. Scan for Coleman and Cobb," barked the leader.

They shoved me into a chair, and I felt a heavy, gloved hand clamp down on my shoulder. I knew better than to move. The room filled with the sounds of crashing furniture and breaking glass as they ransacked my home.

"They've both been here," one of them announced, their voice muffled by the helmet. "But it's an old signal - maybe a week."

"Bag and tag him. Let's go," the leader ordered.

A sharp jolt of electricity shot through me. The world faded to black.

* * *

I woke up. As reality crept into my foggy brain, I noticed everything was pure white. Gradually, as more neurons recovered from being stunned, I realized I was staring at a ceiling. The pure white was the illumination - bright and perfectly even. No seams, no shadows, absolutely clean.

I tilted my head upright, moving only my eyes and neck, taking in the view as carefully as possible. Leon's voice echoed in my mind: *"Give no information whatsoever."* The Miranda warning was clear: *"Anything you say can and will be used against you."* But Leon had emphasized the deeper meaning - *anything* they can twist, they'll use to dig deeper. A contradiction or a lie could strip me of the protections granted to a voting citizen under the Secrets Act.

When my mind sharpened, I focused on the room. Two large guards flanked me, both wearing helmets and reflective face shields. They looked like clones of Victor, standing rigidly at ease.

The room was seamless metal, its slightly sloped floor leading to a drain marked by rust-colored stains. The door, barely visible, blended flush with the wall - featureless and sterile.

My hands were restrained behind my back, locked into the chair I was sitting in. My legs were bound too, leaving me immobile. In front of me sat a table, surprisingly adorned with a small vase of wildflowers. The sweet scent of honeysuckle was oddly out of place.

The table itself stood out against the sterile room, made of a hard plastic that showed scars from heavy use. I noticed a series of random holes, arranged in two groups about half a meter apart. In a few of them, I could see what appeared to be hair - and blood.

Yikes.

After what felt like an hour - maybe longer - the flush-fitting door swung inward. A man entered, older than me, and strikingly odd in appearance. He was completely bald - no hair, no eyebrows. His face was unnervingly smooth, like he never shaved, more like the skin of a young woman. His eyes were jet black, and a jagged old scar ran down his left cheek. He was dressed in standard-issue Army camo, an officer's uniform, and black gloves. He looked like a villain straight out of an action movie - the kind you don't want to meet.

He locked his intense gaze on me. "Your name is Frank Waverly Jr., is that correct?"

I said nothing.

He glanced down at the pad in his hand, flicking through something. "Your wife is Amy Waverly, currently in Boise, visiting her sister. Is that correct?"

His eyes drilled into me, searching for any flicker of reaction. That was the game - they bait you to confirm without saying a word. I didn't move, didn't blink, didn't breathe any louder than necessary.

He pulled out a stool - one I hadn't noticed before - and sat across from me. "Where's Robin Coleman? Have you seen her?"

Same stare. Same silence.

"We tried to grab her before she fled the plant but she escaped in that infernal machine. We suspect she had accomplices."

I ignored him.

He leaned forward, snapping his fingers in front of my eyes. "Hello, anyone in there?"

Still nothing.

"So you're going to play that game." He smirked, leaning back with practiced ease. "That's okay. I can play games too."

He flipped through his pad, stopping occasionally to glance at me. After a moment, he looked up. "I see you're pretty important. 863 votes. That's impressive."

I kept my expression blank.

"We don't get many of your kind sitting in this chair," he continued, his tone almost amused. "And I have to tell you, I'm excited to get to know you."

He scrolled through his pad again and paused. "Alright, let's get this part over with. I'm required to read you this stuff because you're such a high and mighty voter."

He seemed to switch to automatic mode, his voice steady and detached.

"Let's see... okay. You have the right to remain silent, but your silence may be interpreted as guilt. Anything you say can and will be used against you. You have no right to an attorney or representation of any kind. If you are convicted of treason or military espionage, you can and will be executed within 12 hours of conviction."

He paused, letting the gravity of the words sink in. Then, with an almost dismissive tone, he added, "We don't want you to endure the agony of waiting for your own end."

He stared at me a moment before continuing the briefing.

"Ah, where was I? Oh, here we go. During interrogation, you will be provided with food and water every 72 hours and permitted one bio break per day. No permanent bodily harm shall be inflicted, but temporary discomfort or pain may be employed to elicit cooperation."

He stopped and locked his eyes on me. "Do you understand these rights? I need a yes or no answer, Frank - none of this silent business."

I stared straight ahead, not flinching. He held the stare, unblinking, for what felt like an eternity. My eyes burned, but I didn't dare blink first. Finally, he broke the tension, and set the pad down next to the vase of wildflowers, stood, and perched himself on the edge of the table. His gaze bore down on me, waiting for any crack in my composure. I didn't move.

"Now let me tell you what I can do." He motioned, probably to someone watching remotely. A moment later, the door opened, and a woman - maybe in her fifties and clearly not using "Forever Young" - entered, pushing a cart. On it was a metal tray holding various instruments, all gleaming and ominous. My stomach sank as I recognized a dermal regenerator (DR) among them. I didn't need to wonder what that was for.

The bald man stood up and began removing his gloves with deliberate precision. "Here's what I can do for you, Frank," he said, his tone icy and matter-of-fact. "I can keep you here as long as I want. Years, if necessary - until I'm satisfied you're of no value, or until I decide you're guilty and have you executed."

He carefully tucked his gloves into his belt, smoothing them meticulously to avoid wrinkles. His methodical nature was unsettling - this was a man who thrived on control.

He looked up at me again, his gaze sharp and unyielding. "I can also inflict discomfort and pain in any way I see fit, as long as I don't cause permanent damage."

My chest tightened as I felt my heart rate spike, each beat thudding against my ribs.

He began picking up the various instruments on the tray, examining them one by one. He wiped a smudge off a particularly nasty-looking blade, turning it in his hand as though admiring its craftsmanship. "The bad news for me," he began, his tone almost conversational, "is that I can't use any tools except my own perception to tell if you're lying. No sensors, no tech, not even a clock to measure your heart rate. Your *status* makes it difficult." He set the blade down with care. "Now, if you only had 364 votes less, I could do a lot more - get creative. That's a real shame, because this would be over in two minutes if I could. One whiff of truth gas, and you'd be spilling everything you know."

He leaned back, as though appraising the effect of his words. Then, suddenly, he sat upright and straightened his tunic. "What's wrong with me? I haven't even introduced myself. How could I be so rude to someone so high and mighty?" Standing to his full height, he came to attention and snapped a sharp salute. "My name is Colonel Abasi Abdelaal. I'm stationed here at the YSP Military Annex, maybe two clicks from your little refuge under Plant 1."

He paused again, staring hard at me, searching for the smallest crack in my composure. I gave him nothing. I was a stone.

He turned his head toward one of the faceless guards. "Have they found the girlfriend yet?" The guard didn't respond, standing motionless. He continued, his voice dripping with disdain, "We're looking for her, and she's disappeared. But You know how those Wics are - give them a few dollars, and they'll turn on their own mother. We'll find her. You can bet on it."

I had a momentary lapse, my eyes flickering slightly. He caught it instantly, his expression sharpening like a predator scenting blood. "So, you have feelings for the child whore?"

He perched himself on the corner of the table again, feigning casualness. "Listen, Frank, I don't want to get into the blood and messy stuff. I just got this uniform back from the cleaners, and I'd like it to stay crisp for at least a day. So here's the deal: you tell me what you know about Coleman, and if I believe you, I'll let you go back to your perfect life. Deal?"

I was silent and unyielding. I thought about how he looked like a penis with a face. Somehow, the mental image helped.

He looked at his pad again, his tone casual, almost conversational. "That Cobb guy - he was something special to you, wasn't he? Like a father figure." He stared at me, waiting for a reaction, but I gave him nothing.

"Did you know he was responsible for your father's death?" he said, tilting his head like a predator closing in. "He admitted it to the investigative board. Said he did it. Did you know that? Cobb killed your dad so he could move in and start whacking your mom."

I knew that was absolute bunk. Leon never touched my mom. He revered her - kept her on a pedestal. The accusation was absurd.

"You don't believe me," he said, his eyes narrowing. "I can see it in your face. I'm very perceptive." He flicked through his pad again and held it up for me to see. "Look at this." I caught a glimpse of what appeared to be an official USGS report. I didn't get to read it, but it had the right format. I'd seen plenty of those reports over the years, though I was grateful I'd never had to file one myself.

"That Leon Cobb," he continued, "he was something else. Did you know he was a bit of an anarchist back in college? Your father seems to have turned him around, though - turned him into a model citizen." He paused, then leaned forward, his voice dripping with insinuation. "He lived with you these last few years. Was he doing your wife? Is that the angle?"

His gaze bore into me, searching for a crack. Again, I gave him nothing.

He didn't stop. "Let's see," he said, scrolling through his pad. "Leon was a scholarship boy. Your father and Cobb formed a business together and became

211

hugely successful." His expression shifted unexpectedly to one of admiration. "Yes," he said, as if reading my mind. "I can admire success."

He continued, "You might be wondering how I became a Colonel, an officer, when I'm obviously not one of you." The scar on his cheek was the giveaway. If he were under full Medical, that scar could've been erased in no time.

"Let me tell you the story of how I got here and why I'm so good at what I do," he said, settling onto the stool. "I was like you when I grew up. My family only had a few votes, but hey, one is enough, right?" He locked his eyes on me, waiting for a response.

I gave him nothing.

"My dad had a business that was doing great," he continued. "We were getting another vote every year or two, and we were happy." He paused for a moment as if the memory were still fresh. "I took the ROTC route, graduated with honors. Life was good."

He stopped again, letting the silence stretch before picking up his story. "Then my father's business was squeezed by someone with a lot more votes. My dad wouldn't sell. His business started to suffer, and eventually, he gave in. Got swindled for everything he was worth. Lost all his votes. My parents committed suicide that day."

His gaze bore into me, sharp and unrelenting. "I can see you have no compassion," he said flatly.

I held still, not giving him anything to work with.

He continued, "Lucky for me, I found a home in the Army. They could have cut me loose or demoted me to NCO, but they had vision. I am an extremely rare case of an officer who is not one of you." He paused, letting the weight of his words settle.

"The thing is, regular officers have regard for voters. They can't help it. They know that if they cross a voter, there's the possibility of a vendetta - legally sanctioned. But me?" He leaned forward slightly. "I have no family. They're all dead. If you wanted revenge, you'd have to start a vendetta against the Army - my real family - and nobody has that many votes." He let the implication hang in the air.

For a moment, I thought I understood him. Something must have shown on my face, because he reacted. "So you pity me?" he asked, his voice sharp with mockery. He was wrong. He couldn't read my thoughts. I remained motionless.

His tone shifted, darker now. "I have a deep hate for you. It's people like you - like Leon, like your father - that destroyed my family and took away everything I loved. You are to blame for this system where the more you have, the less responsible you are." His voice rose slightly, teetering on a rant.

Abruptly, he pulled himself back. "Alright, now you know my motivation. Let's get back to the work at hand." He glanced at his pad. "This Robin Coleman - she's just wanted for questioning. We don't have any evidence against her, but we need to know if Cobb was working with anyone else. She was his assistant, and she might know something that could help our investigation."

His eyes bore into mine as he asked, "So I'll ask again: where is Robin Coleman?"

I remained stoic.

He walked over to the tray and picked up two pieces of equipment. "I see we're going to have to go another way here, Frank," he said, his tone almost cheerful. "And I have to admit, I'm really glad we've reached this point in our relationship."

He placed the items on the table in front of me, but I kept my gaze steady, refusing to look.

"Interrogation," he continued, "is a lot like dating. There are the first steps, where we get to know each other. Then there's the flirting, which is what we've been doing for the last - oh, how long has it been?" He turned briefly toward one of the guards, as if expecting an answer. "Almost an hour? Time flies when you're having fun, doesn't it, Frank?"

He paused for effect, savoring the moment, then leaned in closer. "Yes, we've been flirting. But now, we get to the part where it gets fun - and messy. This is the part I really like."

He picked up the two items and raised them to my eye level, holding them just long enough for me to register their presence. "I think you'll recognize both of these." His stare intensified, searching for any flicker of reaction in my expression.

I remained unyielding.

He continued, "This one," he said, motioning with his right hand, "is the pain." It was a standard torch, capable of reaching temperatures around 2000°C. "And this one," he said, motioning with his left, "is the relief." He held up a DR, its polished surface gleaming under the harsh light. "Let's see how you react."

He nodded to the guards, they moved with startling speed to unshackle my arms. Before I could process what was happening, they slammed my hands flat onto the table, palms down. The woman approached swiftly, holding what looked like a nail gun.

Bam. Bam.

Two nails drove through the backs of my hands, anchoring them firmly to the table. The pain was blinding, but I didn't flinch. My world turned gray for a moment, but I forced myself to remain still. I had always prided myself on an exceptionally high pain tolerance.

The interrogator leaned back slightly, studying me like a scientist observing an experiment.

"That was surprising, Frank," he said, his tone almost admiring. "You took that like a soldier. I didn't see any advanced tactical training in your record." He flicked through his pad, scanning. "Hmm. Nothing. Let's see what you're really made of."

He ignited the torch, the flame hissing to life. Holding it just above the back of my hand, he let the heat radiate painfully close to my skin. The searing sensation was excruciating, but somehow, I didn't flinch. My breathing quickened, adrenaline surging through me as I fought to remain still.

"Ah, there it is," he said with a smirk. "That got you going."

He picked up the DR and passed the beam over the burn, soothing the worst of the pain. "That feels better, doesn't it? See, we're not here to permanently damage you."

He stopped the regeneration process abruptly, leaving the skin half-healed.

He continued, "Do you want more?" He held up both tools, his expression unreadable.

I remained silent, unmoving.

"Let me ask you again: Where's Robin Coleman, and why are you protecting her? Anyone else would have broken by now unless she means something to you." He stared at me, searching for any crack in my resolve. I did nothing.

"So she's nothing to you. Then why protect someone you don't care about?" His voice grew colder, more deliberate.

"You might not care about Coleman, but I know you have feelings for the girlfriend. I'm going to find your little whore - you know it. And when I do, you see these two guys behind me?" He motioned to the guards. "They're going to do things you can't even imagine. And then I'll skin her, keeping her awake and feeling every second of it until she dies - right in front of you."

I couldn't help the slight flinch that escaped me. The thought of Jessica, innocent in all of this, suffering such a fate sent a shiver down my spine. This monster's threats collided with her vision, and for a fleeting moment, I wondered if she had been right all along. Maybe she should have run far, far away.

While my mind spun, Mr. Penis-with-a-face continued his sick ritual, cycling between pain and relief. I barely noticed this time, my thoughts consumed by Jessica and the cruelty this man would unleash if he found her.

His frustration was evident as he barked, "Get me an update on the whore." He turned slightly, and I caught a glimpse of the small earpiece he was wearing.

"Frank, you're really starting to annoy me," he said, his tone darker now. "We can't find your girlfriend, and you're giving us nothing. So, I guess it's time to escalate - "

He snapped to attention as the door swung open. An older man entered, his presence commanding. Even I recognized the star insignia on his chest - a general.

"That will be enough, Colonel," the general said, his voice steady and calm but carrying an undeniable authority.

The colonel froze for a beat, then stepped back, visibly deflated. "Sergeant, clean him up and get him out of here," the general added, addressing the woman with the nail gun.

Without hesitation, she approached, injecting something into my neck. The world blurred, and consciousness slipped away.

* * *

I woke up in a chair again, but this time it was padded, and I wasn't restrained. "Take a minute, and focus." The voice belonged to the same man - the general. My mind cleared quickly, and I realized I was sitting in an office. His name tag read "OWENS."

Once he saw I was fully alert, he continued, "Frank, I know this has been a nightmare, and I hate that you had to endure it. But let me remind you - you're still under Miranda. For your own protection, I suggest you stay silent, or I might have to bring you back to the Colonel. Neither of us wants that, do we?" I stayed motionless, saying nothing.

"Good, you've been taught well," he said. "Are you thirsty?" He offered me a glass of water.

I did nothing.

"Just kidding. That usually gets a reaction." He chuckled softly and continued. "You're probably wondering why you're sitting here in a comfortable chair instead of being further acquainted with our resident interrogator."

He paused, as if expecting me to respond, but I stayed silent. It didn't seem like a trap, but I wasn't taking any chances.

He leaned back and continued, "Your friend Leon saved your skin - he really did."

My gaze dropped to my arms. They were healed, no holes in my hands, but when I flexed into a fist, I felt... something.

The general guffawed. "Got you! I knew you'd let your guard down." I froze, my pulse spiking.

He waved his hand dismissively. "Relax, it's fine. You can move. The reason you're sitting here is that you are Leon Cobb's sole heir. Did you know that? Leon was a super voter. He had over 1,200 votes." He leaned forward slightly, his tone sharpening. "It's a shame the Colonel went so far. He's in hot water for his haste."

My chest tightened. So that torturer, the Colonel, had killed Leon?

The general must have noticed the shock on my face. "Yes, let that sink in," he said gravely, pausing to let the weight of his words settle. After a moment, he continued, "The estate settled about," he glanced at the clock on the wall, "eight hours ago. That means you're now beyond our reach for interrogation without proper cause. You've been in the MedPod for quite some time. The Colonel knows how to inflict pain without leaving permanent damage, but he likes to push the limits." He leaned back slightly, his tone shifting to a sardonic edge. "Super voters like you are nearly untouchable, even by us. Congratulations on your upgrade!" He flashed a grin, the kind you'd expect from a salesman pitching a product, and let out a brief, hollow laugh.

"Here's what's going to happen," he said, his voice suddenly serious. "I'm going to ask you one more time." He paused, drawing it out. "Do you know the whereabouts of Robin Coleman?"

I didn't move, didn't blink.

"Okay, then." He stood and smoothed his uniform. "Let's get you processed and on your way." He gestured for me to follow him. "Home, of course. We called your car. It's waiting for you in the civilian lot."

I rose cautiously, following him out of the office. We walked in silence to the military gate at the plant. The civilian lot was a good click away, and most people took the long route around the plant to avoid driving near the military gate. I understood why.

* * *

I followed General Owens to the gate, and when I got through, they handed me my personal effects. I was free. Still, I said nothing. The general motioned for me to walk with him.

"We're clear of the surveillance area. You can talk freely," he said.

217

I looked at him with doubt.

He continued, "No trick. I just wanted to talk. We have some shared history."

My throat felt raw, but I managed to croak, "What day is it?" It was all I could muster.

The general glanced at his watch and said casually, "It's Wednesday, around five. You've been here just over a day."

My anxiety grew as I thought of Robin and Amy. They must be frantic by now.

He stopped in a secluded stretch of the road, turning to face me. "I'm sorry you had to go through that. The Colonel is... a sadistic monster. He enjoys his work far too much."

I couldn't help but ask, "Then why is he still doing it?"

The general hesitated, then answered, "Because we need people like him. For better or worse, someone has to do that job." His tone was pragmatic, almost resigned.

"What's our common history?" I asked, shifting the conversation.

He glanced upward, as if searching for the right words. "Frank, your father was one of the greats - brilliant, generous, principled. He introduced me to my wife among other things. I owe him more than I can ever repay."

He paused for a moment, his expression softening. "This is my AOR, so when I saw your name come across my desk, I immediately flew in from Boulder. I wanted to see firsthand what that sadist was up to. I owed it to your father to intervene when I could."

I nodded solemnly. "Leon was like my dad. He's gone... for nothing. Thank you for pulling me out of there."

The General put his hands on his hips and said, "What the hell is all of this about? Leon Cobb wasn't just some brilliant eccentric. He was one of us - someone who lived by the principles of this system and contributed more than most. "

I couldn't hold back. "Leon was framed. We all know the protocol with you guys - it's hands-off all the time. What did Leon do?" My anger seeped into my voice.

The General sighed. "That's the thing. Cobb was found with a remote storage card containing highly classified information. Top-secret, no-questions-asked execution-level material. His DNA was all over it. But the problem is, Leon - or anyone else at either plant - didn't have access to that level of clearance. Nobody. Not even the Colonel. Heck, I'd have to request access myself, and it would probably be denied." He gestured for us to keep walking.

I didn't let it go. "Leon was trustworthy in every way. He wouldn't touch classified information - not for fear of his own life, but because he knew it could blow back on my family. Leon was devoted to us, and as you saw, we mattered more to him than anyone else."

The General nodded but kept walking. "Well, there's nothing I can do about Leon now, but I can take the heat off you and your... mistress." His voice softened. "That was really awful what the Colonel said to you. I could see it hurt. Is she something special to you?"

He wasn't asking as a general anymore, but as a man.

I responded with what was in my heart. "I'm going to save her."

We walked in silence for a while. Then I broke it. "What about Robin Coleman? Your torch bearer is still looking for her."

The General chuckled softly. "Torch bearer - I like that. Miss Coleman's on their radar, and I'm afraid there's little I can do to protect her if they find her. The Colonel won't hesitate to do what he does best. But, Frank, you and I both know she's in this mess because of her proximity to Cobb. If she stays out of sight, there's hope she can avoid what you've just endured. My advice? Keep her safe, wherever she is." His tone carried a strange mix of sympathy and pragmatism.

I knew this was my only chance to press for more information. "Can you tell me anything about Victor Nash? He was arrested - it was in the news. He's a great guy, or was. He had a real future."

The General nodded. "Victor Nash is a war hero - Medal of Honor, untouchable status, with a powerful benefactor. Let's just say he knows how to navigate dangerous waters."

Relief washed over me. "He's one of the good guys."

The General continued, "He did a solid for his girlfriend, Robin Coleman. Told the Colonel she came to him in Colter Bay, asking for help to hide from some creep she worked with - a Frank Waverly." He chuckled, "I thought that was bull because I knew Frank's son had to be a standup guy. Besides, Nash has advanced training to resist interrogation. He could claim to be Robin Coleman and fool any machine - or even an empath, if you believe in that crazy stuff."

He glanced at me for confirmation, and I replied, "Not a creep! Besides, I already have a mistress and a wife. Don't you think that's enough?" We both laughed. Humor was the only thing keeping the horrors of the past day at bay.

"When they went to her hiding place, she was gone. The place was such a filthy hole they couldn't even get a DNA reading. The Colonel has his men running around Colter like Keystone Cops. You know how the Wics are - they won't rat out anyone. She's probably safe for now."

We reached the lot, and I spotted my car. The General stopped and turned to me. "Frank, this is where we part ways. For what it's worth, I hope you know your father would be proud of the way you've handled yourself. If you need help down the road - within reason - you've got my ear. Good luck, son."

I paused, then asked, "How long are you going to be in the area?"

He shrugged. "Until Sunday. I'm not invited to the big party, but there's a reception with my cohorts from around the world. Should be interesting. Are you going?"

"I'm Support and not invited," I said mechanically.

"You sound like me. I've been asked a hundred times, and I'll be glad when it's over." The General chuckled again.

I hesitated, then spoke with deliberate urgency. "General Owens, I need to ask you to do something. Promise me you'll do it, in the memory of my father, without questions."

The smile faded, replaced by a serious expression. "I owe your father in many ways. I'll honor your request if I can."

I met his gaze. "Be in Boulder Friday. Do not come back here."

Without waiting for a response, I turned and walked away, leaving him standing there, surprised and silent.

CHAPTER THIRTEEN

Saying Goodbye

The first thing I did when I got in my car was call Amy. The moment she answered, her voice cracked with fear. "Dear God, Frank! What happened? The screen went blank, and when I tried messaging, someone from the military answered. They said you were being detained. I thought that was the end!" She was sobbing unevenly, like she was trying to regain her composure.

"Amy, it's okay. It was all a mistake." My voice was heavy, drained from everything I'd endured.

She sniffed, trying to pull herself together. "I pushed the settlement through as fast as I could, combining the estates this morning. They should have released you immediately!"

"It's fine now, Amy," I said softly. "I'm worn out, but it's over. Please tell the kids I'm okay and that we're not in any trouble."

There was a long pause, then she said, "Frank, you gave me the scare of my life. Please - please don't let anything like that happen again."

"I'll do everything in my power to avoid it, my dear," I reassured her. Absently, I flexed my hands. The pain was gone, but the memory wasn't.

I called the company next, informing them I'd be taking the rest of the week off. Then I let the car handle the drive home, staring out at the rain-soaked horizon, my mind slipping into emptiness from sheer mental exhaustion.

* * *

It was dark when I woke up in the garage. The quiet was absolute, and I realized I felt better - clearer. I asked the car, "How long have I been sleeping?"

"You've been asleep for three hours and 22 minutes. The time is now 9:12 p.m."

Robin must be worried sick. I got out of the car and walked into the kitchen. Everything was immaculate, no sign of the chaos from earlier. "Thank you, HomeBot, for your service," I muttered under my breath.

"KitchenBot, prepare two orders of Frank 21 to go." A reliable favorite.

"Estimated preparation time: four minutes."

Just enough time. I stripped down, hit the shower, and got into clean clothes. I activated another Device, and tossed my old potentially compromised one - along with everything I wore directly into the incinerator. I wasn't taking any chances after what I'd just been through.

The food was ready by the time I stepped back into the kitchen, neatly wrapped and waiting on the counter. I grabbed the packages along with the emitters and headed for the bike.

* * *

I arrived at Leon's a bit after ten. The house was dark.

I rang the bell. Nothing. I tapped an "R" in Morse code on the window. Still nothing. Feeling a bit ridiculous, I knocked out "Shave and a haircut, two bits." No self-respecting murderous thug would know that one. I waited. Just as I began to wonder if the house was truly empty, a light flicked on in the guest bedroom, then in the kitchen. Someone was moving inside.

Robin opened the door and gasped, her face lighting up with relief. "Oh Jesus! You're alive!" She threw her arms around me, and we hugged like we'd been lost to each other for years.

"They let me go," I said simply.

"What's going on? What happened?" she asked, her voice shaking with a mix of fear and joy.

I stepped inside and told her everything - the Colonel, the General, the interrogation. As I spoke, she alternated between crying and smiling through tears, a mix of disbelief and overwhelming relief. It was emotional for both of us.

When I finished, she pulled away slightly, looking at me through red-rimmed eyes. "I thought that was it. I saw Victor was taken, and that really sent me down the rabbit hole."

"I know how much Victor means to you," I said, steadying her.

Robin hugged me again, holding tight. "Frank, I'm so glad you're here. Besides," she added with a small smile, "Victor can't build a lightsaber."

We both laughed quietly, the tension easing. Robin had a knack for recovering quickly.

"I brought dinner." I said as I held up the two orders of Frank 21.

The meal was quiet, the kind of silence where words weren't necessary.

"This is the first food I've had since this morning," Robin said, eating quickly.

I realized just how hungry I was and finished just as quickly.

After she cleaned up, she asked, "What now? What do we do?"

I leaned back in my chair, considering. "We still have the same two options: fight or flee." I paused, meeting her gaze. "I say we fight. What about you?"

Robin leaned back in her chair, a playful glint in her eye. "Where's the wine? We should toast to our victory!"

I smiled but shook my head. "We've got work to do. Save the toast for later."

The next couple of hours flew by as we built four CPT's, or lightsabers as we've been calling them. The focus and precision the task required gave us both a much-needed distraction from the weight of what was on our shoulders. For the first time in what felt like forever, the air was lighter, the conversation punctuated with quiet laughter and technical banter.

When we were finished, four of the homemade CPT's sat on the table like trophies of our labor. "We'll test them in the morning," I said,

Robin nodded, already looking tired, replied, "I think that's enough. Let's call it a night."

"I'm glad to be here. Good night," I replied, making my way to Leon's room.

"Good night, Frank," she said as she headed toward the guest room.

Sleep claimed me almost immediately, the day's chaos fading into the quiet hum of the night. For once, there were no screams, no interruptions - only the calm before whatever lay ahead..

* * *

When I woke up, Robin was already up, humming softly in the kitchen. The smell of something cooking drifted through the house, dragging me fully alive.

"Good morning," I said cheerfully as I entered.

She looked over her shoulder and smiled. "Good morning."

"Did you sleep well?" I asked the standard question.

"Remarkably. I didn't sleep at all the night before - just sobbed the whole time. I've never done that before," she admitted, her voice carrying a hint of disbelief at her own vulnerability.

"It's understandable," I said gently. "You've been through a lot. Being here all alone with no idea what's happening, anyone would start to slip a few gear teeth."

How about you? I was just alone, you were tortured." She said,

"I survived it." Is all I wanted to say.

She sighed and turned back to her task. "Breakfast is ready."

We sat down and ate in comfortable silence, the shared moment of normalcy a welcome reprieve.

Robin finished first and stood to clear her plate. "Leon's batteries are heavy - designed for storage, not portability. We'll need about 75 kilos - 12 batteries - if

225

the tests confirm our theory. I can't carry that alone, and, well, you're no Victor. We'll both need to haul heavy packs."

I finished my last bite, pondering the logistics. "Too bad we don't have Victor," I said with a chuckle.

Robin looked at me directly as she placed her plate in the sink. "We need to take care of Leon today."

I nodded. "The trail should be drier now, easier to navigate." My voice was flat.

* * *

We carefully loaded Leon into the truck and drove slowly to his stand. I'd been there before, so I knew the trails well enough to guide us. When we arrived, we removed the tarp and wrapped him in a blanket from his bed. We built a travois from branches and hoisted Leon into the stand. Once he was in place, we stepped back to take it in.

"He looks at home up there," Robin said, her voice soft. The stand, nestled amongst the trees, seemed like a place where Leon's spirit could watch over the world he loved - a fitting sanctuary.

"The animals around here will know who he is - or at least their surviving relatives," I added with a touch of humor.

Robin smiled faintly. "Did I ever tell you how Leon got me to work at the plant?"

"Please, tell me," I said, curious.

Her expression turned wistful. "Did you ever watch his science and engineering show?"

"I'm afraid I didn't," I admitted.

Robin's face lit up with excitement. "That show is the reason why I'm an engineer. He had fans all over the world. I messaged him a couple of times when I was in high school with technical questions, and he always responded with these amazing, detailed answers. The last time I messaged him, I was a senior.

226

He told me to get in touch with him when I graduated and said he'd give me a job." She laughed, her tone light. "I thought he was joking, so I never did."

She paused dramatically before continuing. "I was working at Phlegraean when he was there with the suits. He saw me in the cafeteria and, to my surprise, sat down at my table. I wasn't used to anyone joining me, especially not after…"

I chuckled. "I'm not going to say it."

Robin slapped me lightly on the arm and continued, "Then I recognized him. My high school idol, sitting right there. I almost choked." She laughed, the memory bringing a smile to her face.

I laughed too. It felt good to share a moment of levity, the kind of memory Leon would've wanted us to have in this sacred place.

"Anyway," she continued, "we started talking about some technical stuff - testing me in a way - but it felt more like small talk for engineers." She paused for a moment to reflect on the memory before continuing.

"At the end of lunch, he asked me, 'Why didn't you message me?' My face must have said something to him because, honestly, I was speechless. Nothing was coming out. Then he said he wasn't joking and offered me a position as his assistant. I was floored. I mean, *he was famous*! My high school idol, and he wanted *me*. I didn't know what to say, so I just blurted out, 'YES.'"

Robin giggled. "What can I say? He had an eye for talent."

We both laughed, but soon, the laughter faded into a quiet, reflective moment. Standing side by side in remembrance of our friend and comrade, I cleared my throat and spoke my eulogy.

"Leon was more my father than my real one. He was there for all my milestones - my birthdays, graduations, when I soloed, my marriage, the births of my children. Through all of it, Leon was the ever-present constant in my life." I paused, a tear welling in my eye. I sniffed and continued, "He was honorable, reliable, enthusiastic, dedicated, and, in his own way, loving. Leon taught me what it means to be a good man and a good person. He valued honor and integrity over net worth. I just hope I'm worthy of his efforts and his love." Robin hugged me, and we sobbed quietly.

The walk back to the truck was quiet, our hands clasped in shared grief. It wasn't the touch of lovers but of comrades, bound by the family Leon had built around him.

CHAPTER FOURTEEN

Prepare

When we reached the house, I shifted back to my technical self. "We should test the CPT's,"

Robin nodded, then asked, "Does Leon have anything close to what we'll need to cut through? Eight centimeters of steel is no joke. What kind of steel are we dealing with?"

I recalled a childhood memory. "Leon has a scrap pile near the house. I know there's some interesting material there, including soft steel like we used in my office."

We poked through Leon's scrap pile and came across a stack of old metal I-beams. They looked like they'd been there for a hundred years. "Looks like someone was planning to build a bridge," I joked.

Robin ran her hand along the rusty surface and replied, "They're not as thick as what we'll need to cut, but if we slice through two at once, that should be pretty close."

She sat on one of the girders, tapping her fingers as she thought. "We're going to need most of Leon's batteries for the job. We can safely remove four of the sixteen batteries at a time and still maintain minimal power, so we can test, drain that set, put them back, and swap in another four. If we have full sun, they'll recharge in a day."

"Then we need to be careful," I said, shifting into my engineer's tone. "The forecast I heard yesterday - feels like a lifetime ago - looked promising. Probably sunny tomorrow. We should be able to recharge, but let's not waste any power just in case."

Robin reminded me of Amy in moments like these. Both were extremely competent, logical thinkers. Like Leon, I suffered incompetence poorly - a trait I was beginning to appreciate more in others.

We used the jeep to haul test articles out of the pile and closer to Leon's house. Robin handled the batteries while I mounted a CPT on a stand. The first test was a power-up - no target, just a systems check."

Robin finished attaching the last cable. "I'm ready when you are," she said. She held a remote tethered to the equipment by a 20-meter cable - a precaution in case something unexpected happened.

"Ready," I confirmed. We both moved a safe distance away, positioning ourselves near Leon's monitoring equipment. His instrumentation was excellent, giving us detailed readouts for every part of the test. It was time to see what these devices could do.

Robin beamed, "Ready for the five-second power-on test."

I couldn't resist. "Make it so." (Yes, I watched *Star Trek*.)

Robin laughed, rolling her eyes but still grinning. "Power on," she said, beginning her countdown.

The woods lit up brilliantly as the plasma beam roared to life with a crackling sound. It was breathtaking - coherent plasma, achieved on a budget. Robin reached zero and declared, "Power off." After a pause to let the CPT stabilize, she scanned the readouts and announced, "Test article operational. All parameters within simulation." Then, with a shriek of joy, she ran toward the setup.

I followed behind, trying to maintain a professional demeanor, but the excitement was contagious. Robin peered down the business end of the CPT, her face glowing with curiosity. "It looks clean, like it's never been fired."

"Time for a real target," I exclaimed.

Robin nodded, and we secured a 40-kilo rectangular piece of steel that was fifteen centimeters long in place as the target before retreating to the observation station.

"Ready for five-second test with 40-kilo target," Robin said.

I nodded, signaling her to proceed.

"Power on," Robin called.

The reaction was immediate - a sharp crack echoed through the woods, and the CPT jumped violently out of its holding clamp, crashing to the ground.

"We should have anticipated that," I said, shaking my head as we approached the site. "The plasma entering the steel must have created a jet effect, similar to a shaped charge. I'd wager the test article's toast."

Robin smirked, her humor undimmed. "I guess you've just been blinded by my brilliance and beauty."

I picked up the CPT carefully - it was still warm to the touch. "Looks fine, but…" I held it up, angling it toward the sky. "There's a hole clean through the center."

Robin inspected it, her brows furrowing in interest. "Huh. Good thing you ordered 20 emitters. What about the target?"

I turned my attention to the steel, rolling it over and looking down its length. "Clean through." I paused, taking in the precision of the cut. "How long was the power on?"

Robin consulted her notes. "Less than a second."

"That's one powerful tool," I said, marveling at the result.

Robin's face lit up with confidence. "And we're just getting started."

I thought for a moment and said, "The military would love it."

Robin raised an eyebrow, a knowing smirk on her face. "They probably already have it."

More tests burned out a few emitters, but we refined the technique: powering on in air first, then cutting. This stopped ionized steel from jetting back and damaging the emitters.

Satisfied with our progress, I turned to Robin. "What's the verdict?"

She cradled the tool like it was a prized possession. "I think we have a lightsaber."

"Yes!" I exclaimed, punching the air in triumph. But Robin tempered my excitement.

"We still need to run the calculations to figure out exactly how many batteries we'll need to carry. My gut says we have some margin, but I want to be sure. If all checks out, we can have some heat tonight."

I wrapped my arms around myself and mockingly shivered. "It's going to be cold. The sun's already setting."

Robin chuckled and headed inside to crunch the numbers while I returned the last battery packs to the rack. The air was crisp, and the house glowed faintly from within. Whatever tomorrow brought, we'd be ready.

* * *

I came back inside and asked, "Heat or not? I'm already cold."

Robin glanced up from Leon's desk. "We've got about 30% power left after all the tests. I don't think we can afford heat. I think we should turn it off, along with anything else that isn't essential."

I nodded. "It'll get cold, but not dangerous. One winter, I spent three days here without power - it was freezing."

Robin smirked. "Leon has some of those heated blankets stashed away. We can use those."

I added, "The refrigerator, stove and oven run on gas, and as long as people are, you know, using the bathroom, those appliances will keep working."

Robin shot me a look. "Are you telling me we cook with our poop gas?"

Grinning, I nodded. "Efficient system. It won't run the heat, though, and it adds CO, so we have to be careful."

Robin groaned in mock disgust. "Leon would get fined if this place were ever inspected."

I chuckled. "Good thing nobody knows it's here. On satellite, it looks like a pile of rocks - Leon's off-the-grid dream."

Robin shook her head but let it slide, turning her attention back to preparing dinner. The familiar sizzle and savory smells filled the cabin, lending a fleeting sense of normalcy to an otherwise extraordinary day.

We ate dinner in good spirits, and talked about Leon and our success. Afterward, I cleared the dishes.

"I'm going to check the forecast!" Robin called out as she wiped her hands and left for Leon's office.

* * *

I was doing the dishes when I heard Robin shriek, "Frank, get in here quick!" I ran into the room and blurted, "It's Victor - he's in the news!"

The news correspondent adjusted their microphone, their expression a mix of concern and professionalism. "Mr. Nash, thank you for agreeing to this interview. As you know, your recent detention by military police has caused quite a stir. Can you shed some light on the situation?"

Victor Nash leaned forward, his face a blend of indignation and defiance. "Look, I've served this country honorably my entire adult life - both in uniform and as a public servant. To be dragged out of my home in front of the whole damn neighborhood, accused of espionage... It's an outrage! A blatant attempt to silence me, to discredit me."

The correspondent pressed further. "But Mr. Nash, the military police wouldn't take such action without cause, surely? Were you given any explanation for your detention?"

Nash hesitated, choosing his words carefully. "They were vague. Mumbled something about 'national security concerns,' possible violations of the Secrets Act. But they wouldn't show me a warrant and threatened me with torture. It's a fishing expedition, plain and simple."

The correspondent raised an eyebrow, skeptical but intrigued. "And yet, they released you without charges. Does this suggest they found no evidence to support their suspicions?"

Nash leaned back, a grim smile tugging at the corners of his mouth. "Or perhaps they found exactly what they were looking for. Maybe this whole charade was about sending a message - a warning to anyone who dares to question their authority, their version of the truth."

The correspondent seemed taken aback. "Mr. Nash, are you suggesting that your detention was politically motivated? That the military is being used to silence dissent?"

Nash looked directly into the camera, his keen sense of political theater timing his response perfectly. "I'm saying that in this new America, where the lines between military and civilian authority are blurred, anything is possible. They want us to be afraid, to cower in the face of their power. But I won't be intimidated. I'll continue to speak out, to fight for the truth, and for the rights of workers - even if it means risking their wrath again."

The correspondent paused, absorbing the weight of Nash's words. "Mr. Nash, these are serious accusations. Do you have any evidence to support your claims of political motivation?"

Nash smiled enigmatically. "Let's just say I have a few secrets of my own. And I'm not afraid to use them."

With that, Nash stepped back from the camera and raised his fist in the Wic salute.

The correspondent returned to the frame, his expression a mixture of awe and intrigue. "Those are the words of Victor Nash - the decorated war hero, and the defender of all in this working-class town. This is Tony Brand, GANN. Back to you, Mory."

"Wow," I croaked out.

"Wow," Robin echoed.

"They sure lit a fire under Victor. He was out to kill," I said, still processing what we had just watched.

"I didn't know he had it in him," Robin said, her voice tinged with wonder. "He's going against the military."

"His benefactor," I said thoughtfully. "That's how he gets away with what he does."

Robin nodded in agreement. "He was very secretive about his past life. I never pushed him."

"Victor is practically immune to anything," I continued. "He's not only a super soldier; he's a super politician. That makes him extremely dangerous to the powers that be."

Robin added, "If anyone can take care of themselves, it's Victor. He once told me he can see trouble before it happens. That parapsychology stuff is pure garbage - there's no scientific base for it."

I muttered quietly, almost to myself, "I wonder how his parents met."

Robin glanced at me but didn't say anything, and I left Leon's office and returned to the kitchen to finish the dishes.

* * *

To conserve power, we shut everything down after getting ready for the evening's rest.

I woke abruptly to Robin slipping into my bed. "Move over. I'm freezing," she said, sliding under the covers beside me. Her cool body pressed against mine, while my male parts instinctively shrank to retreat from the icy contact.

"Your feet are freezing!" I protested as she rubbed her cold feet against my much warmer ones.

She murmured something incoherent, her trust evident as she drifted off to sleep beside me. It wasn't long before her steady breathing lulled me back to sleep as well.

* * *

I opened my eyes to bright, clear skies outside. Perfect weather to recharge the batteries. The room was still cold, and I was alone. I could hear Robin humming from somewhere in the house.

Robin was at the console in Leon's office, humming a popular tune. "I wondered when you'd get up," she said without turning.

I grumbled, "Good morning."

I left her to it and went to the kitchen to make a cup of coffee. Sitting at the table, I stared into my mug when Robin came in. She stood behind the chair opposite mine, resting her hands on the top slat.

"This is the last day," she said, her tone sobering. She looked like she had something to say.

The thought hit me, and I snapped out of my daze. "I have to message Amy today. She needs to know I'm still on mission."

Robin's expression darkened with worry. "I'm concerned about them grabbing you again."

Feigning confidence, I straightened up and declared with a grin, "Let them try to take down this Supervoter!" I joked, but even as the words left my mouth, the weight of reality crept back in.

Robin smiled faintly. "I'm corrupting you. When you get back to Amy, she's really going to hate me."

Her words struck a nerve, and my laughter faded. She noticed immediately. "You look like a kid who lost their stuffy," she said gently.

Without thinking, I blurted out, "I'm just so twisted up. We're here playing house and having the time of our lives, while Amy's with the kids, worrying her

236

head off, wondering if the authorities are going to bust down the door and torture everyone."

Robin walked around the table to stand behind my chair. She placed her hands on my shoulders, grounding me with her touch. "I'm conflicted too," she said softly, then leaned down and kissed the top of my head before retreating back to Leon's office.

I whispered to myself, too quietly for anyone else to hear, "And we're on a suicide mission."

No more humming. I wondered what she might have wanted to tell me before I brought up Amy and the kids and what did she mean by conflicted?

* * *

Robin called from Leon's office, "The batteries are charging faster than I thought. We should have full power in a couple of hours."

I yelled back, "That's great! I can take a shower soon."

"Me too," she replied. I had a fleeting thought about efficiency but pushed it aside and got to work building backpacks to carry the batteries.

When I had the first one finished, I shouted, "Robin, come check this rig for size!"

She called back, "Just a minute!"

I kept tinkering with the design until she walked into the room and asked in her best Wikeneeze, "What chu got?"

Holding up the rig, I said, "Try this on."

It was comically oversized for her. She looked at me and said, "You think I'm a fattie, don't you?"

I froze, wide-eyed, and squeaked, "Your hair looks lovely today, my dear. Were you at the stylist?" quoting a line from an old show.

Robin laughed, handing back the rig. "Take about two sizes off, and it should fit." She headed back to Leon's office, still chuckling.

When the reprint finished, I called out, "Round two, my slender companion!"

This time, when she returned, she tried on the adjusted rig. "That fits better. I like it. We can test it with some weight, but I think this works."

She removed the pack and sat down at the table. I asked, "What concerns do you have with the security system?"

Robin rested her elbows on the table and looked thoughtful. "I can make an educated guess from here, but until I'm at the site, I won't know for sure."

I must have looked worried because she raised her left hand reassuringly. "I'm sure I can crack it, but it could take more time. More time means more chances of discovery. We won't know the rotation patterns or timings until we're observing them. If we get that wrong..." She trailed off, her tone sharpening. "We'd be walking into certain death."

I laughed lightly and said, "At least it'll be quick. I'd rather not play 'nail daddy to the table' again."

Robin didn't laugh, but a small smile played on her lips.

After a moment, I said, "What we need is a diversion. They use them in every action movie - blow something up on the other side of the plant, and all the security will rush toward the fire."

Robin looked incredulous for a second, then her expression softened. "Nothing beats an energetic event. But maybe instead of blowing something up, we could negate the IFF system."

I caught on immediately. "Make the SecurityBots attack all the friendlies? While chaos reigns, we could slip right by. That's brilliant."

Robin considered the idea. "Those systems are ancient. You'd probably know their quirks better than me."

"Are you calling me ancient?" I asked with mock indignation.

Robin humphed and replied, "Get over it, man. You're past the halfway point."

I feigned offense. "Pretty sure I can still fire up those old neurons. I did some hacking in my day too."

Robin smirked. "You mean before electricity?"

"Har, har," I retorted with exaggerated exasperation.

I asked in my engineer's voice, "We didn't discuss battery life last night. What's your conclusion?"

Robin replied in her own methodical tone, "It's going to be tight. We're at the limit for what we can carry, and I estimate we'll consume half the batteries for each barrier, so no mistakes."

I sat silently for a moment, then revealed the real purpose behind my question. "So, when the first barrier is breached, your job is done."

Robin frowned, her expression shifting from focus to confusion. "What are you saying?" she asked, a hint of disbelief in her voice.

I responded firmly, "You have to get out of the area as fast as possible once the vent is open. You won't have more than a few hours to make it clear, and driving that damn truck through the woods is your best chance. At least it's a chance. Find Victor, get him, and whoever else you can, to safety."

Robin was stunned. She sat quietly, staring at the table before finally asking, "You want me to leave? Just like that?" Her voice trembled slightly, and her shoulders sagged as the weight of my words hit her. "I'd rather go in with you. What if there's a problem you can't solve? What if you're hurt, or - " Her voice cracked, and tears began to fall as she tried to hold herself together.

I reached across the table and took her hands in mine, feeling her slight tremble. "Robin, you won't be much use past the first barrier. The vent is tight, and with the military police after you, Zen will rat you out to his buddies the second you step into my office."

Robin stared at me, her face a mix of defiance and heartbreak. She didn't argue further, but the turmoil in her eyes was undeniable.

After a long pause, Robin crossed her arms and got defensive. "What do you think Zen will do when you start cutting a hole in your shelving unit?"

"When my office is empty, Zen is on standby," I explained. "He's not activated unless a human walks into the room. A cow could be in my office, and he wouldn't wake up."

Robin raised an eyebrow. "A cow?"

"Okay, bad example," I admitted. "What I expect to happen is that Zen will initially just greet me like he always does. I've got a welder in my tool kit, and I'll use it to quickly weld the door shut. That should buy me a solid 25 or 30 minutes while they cut through the door the old-fashioned way."

Robin wasn't convinced. "But when you start welding that door, Zen is going to flip."

I couldn't help but look a bit smug. "No, he won't. I've done weirder things in that office before. He might not even think it's out of place."

She pressed on, still skeptical. "What about when he notices you've bypassed security? He's going to see that for sure."

I paused to consider. "He's easy to distract. I'll ask him about love or something like that. It'll take his mind off what I'm doing."

Robin scowled, her voice dripping with sarcasm. "Love? He's that weak? No wonder you call Zen a him."

I laughed for a second. "You know what Zen said about us?"

Robin squealed in mock outrage, "You talked about us to the great and powerful wizard?"

I cut to the chase. "He said we'd have great children. I shit you not."

Robin burst out laughing. "There you go again, swearing. Corrupted to the core. Amy won't want you back now." We both laughed, the tension easing momentarily.

It got quiet for a moment, and Robin reached across the table, taking my hand. "You're right. I'm just extra baggage after the batteries aren't needed anymore."

I squeezed her hand gently. "There's room for Victor in our berth. Leon isn't going to need his seat. The problem will be getting to the spaceport."

Robin pulled her hand back and sat up straight, determination lighting her face. "I have an idea that might work."

She jumped up from the table and headed into Leon's office. I followed as she began opening applications on the console, her focus razor-sharp. "What are we looking at?" I asked.

Robin replied without looking away from the screen. "These are long-range airtaxis that are either already parked here or scheduled to arrive tonight. I'm looking for one with a home base at the spaceport." She narrowed the search parameters, and a tidy list popped up on the screen. Running her finger down the list, she exclaimed, "See this one? It's about ten years old - the perfect vintage."

I raised an eyebrow. "You've done this before, haven't you? Maybe… about ten years ago?" She smirked but said nothing.

Robin leaned back from the console, her excitement barely contained. "These vehicles are empty, waiting for the VIPs' return flights."

I started to piece together what she was saying. "Can you hack that airtaxi to return to base empty and mask your presence?"

Robin looked a bit surprised, then smiled. "You're pretty sharp. That's exactly it. I code the flight as RTB - Return to Base - and it'll fly home on its own. To ATC, it'll just be an empty vehicle. I can also block it from diverting if someone tries to reserve it by triggering a maintenance issue."

"Do you have to steal it where it's parked, or can you hack it remotely?" I asked.

"I can make it jump up and dance. It'll pick us up wherever I tell it to," she said confidently.

I thought for a moment before speaking. "Do you think Victor will leave?"

Robin hesitated, her voice softer now. "If he doesn't want to, I don't know what I'll do. Honestly, we're not that close, but he's important to me."

I considered her words. "He took one heck of a risk to deflect the search. That says something. He might want you to stay."

Robin's expression turned serious. "If we stay, we die. I think he can understand that. He's very pragmatic."

I took her hand gently and led her out of the chair. "My turn. Let me see what I can do about the IFF system."

Just then, the heat kicked on, and Robin bounced excitedly. "I get the shower first! Unless you want to do the efficient thing," she teased.

I chuckled and replied, "Amy would kill me."

About half an hour later, Robin emerged from the bathroom, wrapped in a towel. The air was fragrant with shampoo and soap. She walked into the office, her damp hair framing her glowing face. "Make any progress?" she asked.

I stopped my work and looked up. "It was easier than I expected. Everything came back immediately. I've put together a package you can load. If it works, those little bastards will go absolutely nuts - they won't even see us."

Robin was impressed, "Good work! I think we might just make it." She paused for a moment, then added with a nervous laugh, "Assuming everything goes perfectly, of course."

I took my turn in the shower, letting the hot water loosen the tension in my shoulders. But no matter how warm it was, my thoughts stayed cold, running through every way this mission could fail.

What if we get caught in transit?
What if the security system is unexpected?
What if my package doesn't work?
What if we run out of power before breaching my office?
What if Zen catches on to what I'm doing?

The list of potential failure modes was endless. Everything had to go exactly right, or we'd be killed - if we were lucky. If we weren't, we'd end up as the playthings of that damned Colonel.

After hours of running through the scenarios and practicing our tasks until we could do them in our sleep, we were finally ready. The batteries were fully charged and we had margin to spare. The day was warmer too, and the house was comfortable. For now, it felt like a blessing. But I couldn't shake the thought - this might be our last day on Earth.

CHAPTER FIFTEEN

Everlasting Joy

I was sitting at the table, going over a checklist, when Robin walked into the kitchen. "I think we've done everything we can. What do you figure - leave at four a.m.? That gives us eight hours until the Reveal."

I thought for a moment. "Better make it three-thirty. We'll need time for intelligence gathering."

Robin laughed. "You watch too many action movies."

"If we succeed, maybe they'll make one about us," I replied.

Her smile faded. "Or we'll be the fall guys if we fail."

The thought hit me like a freight train. "Jesus, that would be awful for Amy."

Robin quickly jumped in, her tone somber. "It would be awful for everyone."

She looked at me thoughtfully, her expression serious. "You can save her. You still have time."

Jessica raced back into my thoughts, sudden and urgent. "I will save her," I said, the words carrying a weight I couldn't explain. "It's the strangest feeling - like one of those time-travel movies where the hero is sucked into the vortex because of fate."

Robin tsked. "Do you really believe in that kind of stuff? It's all pseudoscience for the mentally unfit."

"The time's nearly six," I said, brushing off her skepticism. "It's getting dark. I can make it back to the house by six-thirty and call Amy. I need to, no matter what. I'll message Jessica too. If I can arrange it, I'll save her."

Robin looked a little deflated. "You should get going. If you don't make it back, I'll go in alone, somehow."

I paused, then said in my best movie voice, "I'll be back."

Robin smiled weakly. "You'd better be."

* * *

I rode the bike back to the south side of the house and stashed it in the woods. The SecurityBot let me in without issue, and I immediately called Amy.

Her face appeared on the screen, her expression tense but softening when she saw me. "Honey, are you alright? I was starting to get worried again."

I smiled reassuringly. "Everything's fine, except the grass is dry. I think there's something wrong with the system. I'm going to fix it - that should take care of the problem."

Amy frowned slightly, her worry not entirely dispelled. "Are you sure? Maybe you should just forget about the grass and join us here. We can all go to the spaceport together."

I replied quickly, keeping my tone light. "That's fine, honey. I'll meet you there on Saturday. I should be early."

Amy wiped a tear, her composure returning. "The kids miss you. They've been moping around the house, kind of grumpy."

"Call them in. Let's have a little family time," I said. Amy turned and called out, "Sara, Tre! Your father wants to talk to you." She turned back to me and added softly, "I miss you. I'm sorry about my little dustup earlier. You're right - whatever you say is the rule of the house. I'll enjoy just being with you."

"Daddy!" Sara's voice rang out, followed by Tre's, "Dad!" They both rushed into view, their energy lifting the mood.

245

I waited for them to settle down. "Tomorrow is a big day. Sara, remember to help your mother. And Amy, let Sara take on part of the load." I heard murmurs of agreement. "Tre, I want you to do exactly what your mother and sister say - no backtalk, no arguments, no debates. Got it?"

"Yes, sir," Tre replied, his voice firm.

"I don't have a lot of time," I said, looking at each of them through the screen. "I love you all," I said, my voice steady despite the lump in my throat. "I'll see you tomorrow at the spaceport."

The kids chimed in together, "We love you, Dad."

"Goodbye, Amy. And good luck," I said, my voice steady.

Amy smiled faintly, her voice soft but determined. "Goodbye, dear. And I wish you the best." The screen went blank.

* * *

It was close to seven - time to call Jessica. I rummaged through my drawer, momentarily terrified. "What did I do with it?" Then I spotted the scrap of paper, buried under a mix of odds and ends. The thugs must have dumped the drawer, and the CleanBot had dutifully put everything back, though not in the right order.

Taking a deep breath, I entered the digits. The line connected, and Jessica's face appeared on the screen. She looked nervous, her eyes darting slightly.

"Frank," she said, her voice unsteady.

"Jessica, you look well. Tough week?" I asked, trying to ease her nerves.

She managed a shaky smile. "The usual - horrible, but no damage."

"So, are you ready? Do you still want to do this?" I asked directly.

Her expression crumbled, and she teared up. For a moment, I wasn't sure what her answer would be. Then she wiped her eyes with a cloth and said, "Yes, oh, yes. Please, I am ready."

"Pack only what you can't leave behind. You're leaving Wyoming tonight for good."

Jessica let out a half-laugh, half-sob and said, "I won't miss this place." Her demeanor became calm and resolute. "I'm ready to do whatever you want me to do. No questions asked."

"Good. First things first - send me your info." A moment later, her details appeared on my screen. I scanned them quickly. Clean record. No wants, no warrants. Most importantly, no indication the military police were hunting her.

"That's good. Are you at home now?" I asked.

"Yes, I'm here." A wave of joy washed over her.

"I'm sending a pod to your address. Do you see the app?" I asked.

"Yes, it just opened. I see my building with a red circle in a nearby parking lot," she said, her voice brighter now.

"That's where the pod will land," I said. She nodded quickly.

"You've got twelve minutes. Don't be late."

"I'll be there." she replied.

"What should I wear?" she asked. I knew she didn't own anything that would fit seamlessly into our world.

"Just be comfortable. Bring only what you must. You've got ten minutes - the flight takes about fifteen - so I'll see you right around seven-thirty."

"I won't disappoint you. I promise." Her face was a mix of determination and relief as the screen went blank.

Left alone, I finally had a moment to think about what I was about to do.

* * *

"HomeBot, please use Jessica Hudson's measurements and select three appropriate travel outfits for a trip to Hartford tonight."

"Working." My toy replied.

"Book a flight to Hartford arriving before noon tomorrow for Jessica Hudson," I instructed.

HomeBot responded promptly, "Available flights arrive between 8:12 and 10:30 a.m. Shall I prioritize class or speed?"

"Class," I replied.

"Flight for first class passenger Jessica Hudson departs at 4:12 a.m. from Cheyenne International Airport, and arrives in Hartford, Connecticut, at 8:12 a.m. EST. Shall I inform Jessica Hudson?"

"No, thank you," I replied, considering my next steps.

"Book an airtaxi to pick up Jessica at 11:00 p.m. from here to Cheyenne International."

"Operation complete."

The essentials were in place: travel attire selected, flight booked. Now, something special.

"Recommend freelance bodyguards available for a three-year contract starting today. Criteria: female, instructor-rated, intelligent, college-educated, age 28 and under. Filter for compatibility with Jessica Hudson's profile and order by highest profile commonality."

HomeBot took a few seconds to compute. "Operation complete."

I scrolled through the list until one candidate jumped out at me. She was a member of the Samurai sect, a seasoned instructor, and about Jessica's size. I selected her profile, initiating a connection. A face appeared on the screen.

"Ren Takahashi," the woman said, bowing slightly. "How may I serve you, Sir?"

"I'm seeking a three-year protection contract for my mistress," I stated plainly.

"May I examine the asset's anonymized profile, Sir?"

"Sending," I confirmed.

A moment passed as Ren reviewed Jessica's profile.

"Please continue, Sir," she said, her tone professional.

"I want you to train her in self-defense and prepare her for living in a chaotic region."

Ren tilted her head slightly. "Which chaotic region, Sir?"

I decided to bypass specifics. "I've just doubled your rate. Any other questions?"

"No, Sir," she answered without hesitation.

"Are you prepared to protect my mistress, Jessica Hudson, with your life?" I asked.

"I am Samurai. I will be utterly devoted to my master and his mistress, even to the point of sacrificing my own life without hesitation," she declared solemnly.

"This is a three-year contract as bodyguard, companion, and teacher for Jessica Hudson. Full Medical is provided. Do you accept?" I stated the terms formally.

"I cannot accept a collar," Ren stated firmly, her voice calm but resolute.

"No collar. I expect your honor code will suffice," I assured her.

"I accept this three-year contract under the terms we agreed upon. As you must already know, if you or your family are in my company, the contract extends to them. It is also transferable to a different mistress if you so choose."

"Thank you. I'm forwarding Jessica's flight information. Can you meet her in Hartford when she arrives?" I asked.

Ren's eyes flickered as she checked her schedule. "Yes, I can make that work."

"Okay. Pleasure doing business with you," I said, ending the call.

* * *

Jessica would be safe, and now she would have a bodyguard and teacher to prepare her for the challenges ahead.

"Jessica Hudson arriving," HomeBot announced, and I heard the subtle whir of the pod outside.

I stepped out the front door to meet her. Jessica emerged from the pod, looking a little uneasy, clutching a cloth bag tightly to her side. Her expression was a mix of nervousness and excitement.

"Jessica, here you are," I said, my voice betraying a hint of my own nerves.

She swayed slightly and admitted, "I can't believe this is happening... and I feel a little dizzy."

I laughed softly, trying to ease the tension. "First time flying?"

She giggled, the sound helping to break the ice. "Yes, I've never left the ground before. It was... exhilarating. I could see everything - the whole area. It was so beautiful."

"Come inside," I said, gesturing toward the door.

Jessica followed, her eyes widening as she took in the house. "Your house is amazing. I've never been in anything this beautiful before." Her voice lighter now, as she began to relax and show glimpses of her true self.

I laughed along with her, feeling the atmosphere shift as some of her unease melted away.

* * *

We walked through the house to my office. "Please, have a seat," I said, motioning to a comfortable chair. Jessica sat down, her posture graceful, crossing her legs delicately. I couldn't help but notice she was wearing a nice dress - simple but tasteful.

Her cheeks colored slightly, and she glanced down at the simple, tasteful dress. "This is all I have," she admitted, her voice tinged with embarrassment. "I spent over $300 on it. It felt like such a splurge."

I nodded, appreciating her candor. "It's a lovely choice, but we'll need to find you something that fits your new role a little better."

A flicker of hesitation crossed her face. I reached out, taking her hand gently. "Come with me," I said, standing, and led her to my wife's quarters.

* * *

The ClosetBot had laid out several outfits, each perfectly suited for travel and a new life.

"These will fit. Do you like any of them?" I asked, watching her face as she took in the shimmering fabrics.

"They're lovely. These are for me?" She still sounded like she couldn't believe it.

"Yes, you can have these three, or we can pick something else if you'd prefer," I added, trying to keep things light.

She reached out for a dress that perfectly complemented her skin tone and hair, her fingers trailing over the lustrous fabric. "How much does something like this even cost?" she asked, her voice tinged with wonder.

Without thinking, I said, "Cost? I have no idea. I don't concern myself with money."

She looked up at me, wide-eyed. "I have a hard time understanding that concept."

Her curiosity stirred my own. "ClosetBot," I asked, "what's the average cost of these three outfits?"

ClosetBot responded promptly, "Average cost is $12,800."

Jessica froze for a moment, then gently stroked the fabric against her cheek. "The fabric feels just so… wonderful," she whispered, awestruck.

I stepped forward, placing my hands gently on her shoulders, and turned her to face me. "Your life is changing, my beautiful mistress," I said, smiling warmly.

She glanced up, a soft laugh escaping her lips. "I think I'll try this one. The other two are gorgeous too. And these shoes - they're stunning."

"ClosetBot," I said, "please assist Jessica with her choice."

She shook her head, her voice taking on a childlike defiance. "I can do it myself. I don't need help."

I met her gaze, my tone soft but firm. "Jessica, you're entering a new world. Just go with it, okay?"

Her demeanor shifted. She straightened her back, standing taller, more confident. "I understand," she said, her voice steady now.

"Come back out to my office when you're ready," I said. "We'll complete the contract."

* * *

I returned to my office and waited. I felt like a schoolboy, trying to decide what to do for the next few hours. The anticipation made my stomach churn in a way I hadn't felt in years. Then I heard her steps approaching - light, almost floating across the floor.

"How do you like it?" she asked, spinning around exactly like she had last Friday, when she was so bold and beautiful.

"It's beautiful and perfectly appropriate for travel," I said, unable to hide my approval.

"Where am I going?" she asked, curiosity flickering in her voice.

"We'll get to that in a few minutes. Please, sit here - yes, just like that. Sit up straight. This is going to be your ID photo, so it's important that you look, ah, classy."

"Yes, I understand. I know what you're looking for." She struck the perfect pose, one that radiated elegance and composure. I had to admit, I was impressed.

"Hold that pose. HomeBot, please image Jessica for her ID." Seconds later, a series of images appeared on the screen.

"Which do you like the best?" I asked.

She leaned in, her finger hovering over the screen, then pointed to one. "This one," she said decisively.

I selected the image and made a few additional adjustments while she sat nervously, her hands fidgeting in her lap.

"We're ready," I said. "Here's how it works: read the contract, and if you agree to the terms, just say, 'I agree to the terms as written'.'"

She offered a small, nervous laugh. "Sorry, I'm just all pins and needles."

"Here's the text." I handed her the pad.

She took it, her expression shifting to focus. She read it carefully - twice - then paused, her brow furrowing. "I understand what all this means, but I'm confused about the last point. This is a no-breach contract?" She looked up, her voice tinged with hope but shadowed by doubt.

"It means the contract is no breach - it can't be breached. Does that make sense?"

Her head tilted slightly, processing my words. "No breach? That means I could run away tomorrow and you can't stop me?" she said, her tone shifting into an academic precision.

"That's right. Once you sign, you are free to do whatever you want, and I won't try and stop you. Oops, I forgot a step." I selected another document and submitted it with a tap. "I just paid off your contract with the utility. You are now a freelancer."

253

Her eyes widened, and her breath caught. "I don't know what to say. I'm so grateful. When I left my job this evening, I had a feeling I'd never go back, but I dared not even dream. Now it's real," she said, her voice trembling with emotion.

She went back to the contract, her fingers gripping the pad as she read it through one more time. Then, with a steady voice, she said, "I agree to the terms as written."

Relief washed over me. That strange, nagging feeling I'd been carrying finally started to fade.

"Okay, last chance. I submit, and it's a legal document. You can still back out now," I said, giving her one final out.

"Can I do it?" she asked, her tone hesitant but eager.

I pointed to the submit box. "Yes, touch here."

She pressed the screen. It flipped for a second, and then her Device chimed. She opened it, her eyes scanning the screen. And then she gasped.

"My ID, it's changed. It's completely different!" she cried, staring at the screen in disbelief.

"You've just moved up in the world, my lovely. You now have the same exalted status as I do - except you won't be able to vote."

"Vote? Vote? I don't need no stinkin' vote," she said, mimicking the classic movie bad guy with a grin.

I laughed, caught off guard. "I see you're an old movie buff. We'll get along great," I said, momentarily forgetting that she'd be leaving soon.

She chuckled. "I love old movies. They're the only free entertainment left."

"Let me check this list and make sure I've covered everything," I said, flipping through the checklist on my pad.

"You're very well-organized," she remarked.

"My wife did it all. She's amazing. Maybe one day you'll have the honor of meeting her," I replied absentmindedly, still focused on the list.

Her smile faltered slightly, but she said nothing.

"Oh, I missed a couple of things," I continued. "When the contract is satisfied, you'll receive an Unlimited Transit Authorization, or UTA, and an international passport - both without expiration."

"Thank you. I'm glad you remembered everything," she said softly, almost reverently.

"You're leaving tonight and flying to Hartford. You'll be picked up at 11:00 p.m. outside the house. Do you think your sister will be surprised?" I asked.

"I can't believe it," she said, her voice trembling as tears welled in her eyes.

"Now, now, don't get your outfit all wet," I teased gently. "It's alright."

She wiped her eyes and looked at the clock. "It's a little after nine. We have almost two hours."

"I have a couple of things I need to go over with you first." I shifted into my business tone. "I'm giving you access to an account that will round up each month to $150,000. Please be careful. You do not want to run this account to zero. Without money, you could get in trouble, and I might not be able to help you. Do you understand?"

"That much? How can I spend that much in a month?" she exclaimed, her eyes wide.

"I think you'll find it's pretty easy," I said, amused. "I suggest keeping at least $100,000 in the account in case you're fined."

"I will. I promise," she said earnestly.

"You have a reservation for a suite at the Hartford Hilton. It's four stars, but still nice. If you don't like it, just find another place you prefer."

"I'm sure it will be lovely," she said with a smile, then started giggling.

"And one last thing. As my mistress, you need a bodyguard. I've contracted for a highly trained professional who has pledged her life to protect you. She's also contracted to train you in self-defense, and the ways of my class, and now, your class, during the contract term. Her name is Ren and she's meeting you tomorrow morning at your arrival gate in Hartford."

"I get a bodyguard too?" She seemed overwhelmed.

"She can be your advisor, and friend, if you're compatible. If you don't like her, you can cancel her contract."

"I'm sure she'll be fine."

"Oh, a few other things."

"You're enrolled in Full Medical as of now. Here's your scanner." I took a scanner out of my desk and handed it to her.

"Do you know how to use one?"

"Yes, I had one before."

I took another useful device from the drawer and put it on the table, "I'm giving you a DR, do you know how to use one?"

I saw her eyes well up and the joy drained away. "Yes, I have experience with one of those."

"What's wrong?" I asked.

She looked down at the device and said, "I have a small request, just a small one."

I leaned back in my chair, a bit confused about her sudden change of state, "Please."

She said quietly, "Anywhere but the face."

I was even more confused, "Could you explain your request?"

She sniffed a little, and I handed her a tissue, then she spoke quietly, "Mr. Jerk didn't like me at first and would beat me severely. One of these hid the cuts, bruises and swelling, but inside, it didn't help. When he hit me in the face, it took a long time for the pain to go away."

I felt bad for bringing it up, but I didn't know. "You had full Medical, why didn't you call a MedPod?"

She crumpled the damp tissue and placed it on the table, "He wanted me to feel the pain. He was just a kid, and boys, you know how boys are."

I reached over and touched her hand. She trembled, and I felt her slightly pull away and then relax, "That's over. He's not here."

She sat up straight and regained her composure, "If you want to hit me in the face, that's okay. I am grown now and can take it better than when I was a kid."

I was stunned, "Hit you? Why?"

She smiled, and said, "I told you can hit me if you get me one of those."

I understood her dilemma, "No, no, you have me wrong. I'm not going to hit you anywhere, it's a standard travel accessory in case you skin your knees, or cut yourself accidentally. I'm so sorry I brought on this pain." I grabbed her hand, tighter now, and she cried out, joyous again.

"Frank, oh, my dear, I'm sorry for being so foolish. I knew you were a good man, but seeing that thing just brought back bad memories."

I assured her, "I will never hit you. I swear on the grave of my Father."

She jumped up and came around my side, I stood out of reflex, she hugged me tight and her joy was back.

I motioned for her to sit again, "Now that we have that straight, Let me have your Device unlocked."

She handed me her worn Device, its age evident in every scratch. A quick tap against the new one - a hand-me-down from Amy - transferred everything seamlessly. "All set," I said, handing it back.

"Do you want your old one?" I asked.

"Toss it. I like this one better." She said with a giggle. The pain of the last few minutes washed away like it never existed.

"Let me see. Any questions?"

"Are we done with the formal stuff?" She asked.

"Yes, that's it. The contract is in force, and we are bonded legally. You are part of the Waverly family. Congratulations!"

Jessica jumped out of her chair again with the enthusiasm natural to her age, I stood up and extended my hand, and she hugged me and again cried.

She said alluringly, "Now it's time for something special."

I took her hand, and led her to my quarters.

* * *

Afterwards, I felt something I'd never felt before - A strange calm settled over me. I couldn't quite explain it, but the compulsion I'd felt to save Jessica had been satisfied.

HomeBot chimed in, interrupting the moment. "Jessica, your flight arrives in fifteen minutes."

I broke the quiet. "I guess we have to get up."

Jessica groaned softly but slid her naked body out from under the sheets, standing there for a moment, luminous. "Do I have time to use your shower?"

"I have a treat for you." I introduced her to ShowerBot. She gasped with delight, and I left her to enjoy it while I dressed quickly and headed back to my office.

* * *

Jessica entered my office a few minutes later, carrying the bag ClosetBot had packed. She looked poised and radiant, her confidence beginning to match her appearance.

"You look exceptional," I said simply, noting the transformation.

She nodded, still adjusting to the change. I added, "I suggest you read the basic public behavior document on your device before you reach the airport. It might help a bit."

Jessica nodded again, her confidence growing.

HomeBot interrupted, "Jessica's airtaxi arriving."

I exhaled deeply. "I guess this is it. Are you ready for your new life?"

Her demeanor faltered for a moment. "I have only one regret," she admitted, her voice sheepish.

"What's that?" I asked gently.

Her voice dropped to a whisper. "I had a little stray dog I took care of. He lived in the trash behind my apartment building. I'd feed him scraps, whatever I had, and kept him alive through the winter. I think he was the only thing that ever loved me." Her voice broke, and she wept softly.

I pulled her into a tight hug. "I'm afraid he's on his own now. I'm sorry." I knew that little dog wouldn't suffer for long, but it didn't make it easier.

Jessica nodded against my shoulder. "It's okay. I know I had to leave him."

Suddenly, she shrieked and pulled back, looking at me with wide, fearful eyes. "I just had a vision, and it was horrible."

The calm I'd felt shattered. "What? Tell me. Are you in danger?"

She hugged me again, clinging tightly. Her strong arms squeezed the breath from me as she cried, "It was you. I saw you on fire. Your arms were burning, and you were in agony."

I forced my voice to stay steady. "That's okay. I had an injury earlier this week. I burned my arms badly. That's probably what you saw."

Jessica shook her head. "I saw metal all around, and I can still feel your pain. Yet, you weren't afraid."

"I was in a metal room, yes, and I wasn't afraid. See? I'm fine now." I held up my arms as proof.

She stared at me, her face regaining some of its former glow. "I've never felt someone else's pain, only my own. I don't understand it."

I tried to reassure her. "I'm sure I'll be alright."

Her words lingered in the air, sharp and unsettling. I forced myself to focus, brushing aside the vivid image she described. To change the subject, I asked, "Can I ask you something about your parents?"

Jessica looked puzzled but nodded. "Sure, but I didn't know my mother."

"How did they meet?" I pressed.

She smiled faintly. "It wasn't some fairy tale romance. They were paid to marry."

I wasn't surprised. "Paid by who?"

Her expression turned uncomfortable. "It was a company. I don't recall… wait, let me look it up." She scrolled through her device. "Here it is. The last payment. I remember Dad was furious because the company went out of business. Perfect Life. Is that what you wanted to know?"

I nodded grimly. "That's it. Sorry to bother you about it."

She had a questioning look, but it passed quickly, then her smile returned, albeit softer. "When will I see you again?"

I hesitated. "I'll message you. I can't say when, but in the meantime, take advantage of Ren's tutelage. Apply for college when you're ready and spend your time bettering yourself."

She sighed. "I still feel your pain, but the vision is fading. Maybe you're right."

"Make me a promise?" I asked.

"Whatever you want. I am yours."

"Please, remain who you are. Don't lose your integrity or your sense of wonder. Stay true to yourself. Can you do that?"

She nodded earnestly. "I will. I will. I promise."

I carried her suitcase to the airtaxi, helped her in like a lady, and kissed her goodbye. I stayed in the driveway until she was out of sight, then walked slowly back into the house.

A horrible feeling crept over me. Her vision might come true. The metal room could be my office, and the fire might be something far worse. I took a few steps and dismissed the thought. If the supervolcano erupted, I wouldn't feel a thing.

I took a shower, changed my clothes, and left the house for good. Riding through the woods, I realized that, unlike most humans, I had no sentimental possessions. I took nothing but the bike.

* * *

I felt different on the ride back to Leon's. Calm. Serene. I knew what lay ahead, and I knew what had to be done.

Robin was still awake when I arrived at the house.

"So, how did it go?" she asked, her voice soft but expectant.

"Like you expected," I replied, keeping it brief.

"You saved her," she said with a quiet reverence.

"She's free," I confirmed.

Robin tilted her head slightly, studying me. "Would you like some wine? I'm a little ahead of you."

"No, I think I'd better just go to bed. We have to get up in a few hours."

"I've been waiting for you," she said, her tone cryptic.

261

Her voice caught me off guard. There was a difference in it, something more vulnerable yet deliberate.

"What do you mean?" I asked, uncertain.

She hesitated, then spoke with uncharacteristic sincerity. "We've been dancing around with each other, and I want to come clean."

"Please," was all I could say, feeling the weight of her words.

"I have feelings for you," she said softly, her tone steady.

"I know," I replied, meeting her gaze. "I feel the same."

Robin stood up from the table and walked over to me. Her arms wrapped around me in a way that was both grounding and electrifying.

"I need you tonight," she said quietly, her lips barely brushing my ear.

Wordlessly, we moved to Leon's room. In the dim light, we undressed slowly, savoring each moment.

"This could be our last night," Robin whispered, her voice trembling.

And then we began to make love - not the kind I shared with my wife, not the awesome learning experience I had with Jessica. This was different. It was desperate, intense. In those moments, I felt closer to Robin than I had to anyone before.

Afterward, we lay in silence, our breathing the only sound. Neither of us spoke. Neither of us moved. Time seemed to stretch and compress all at once.

The alarm rang, breaking the spell.

CHAPTER SIXTEEN

Break-in

"It's time," I said simply, my voice steady but heavy with the weight of what was ahead.

We dressed quickly and headed into the main room, where all our gear was set out, ready to go. Robin had meticulously inventoried everything to ensure we had what we needed.

"Devices will be detected on plant grounds, even powered off." Robin said. "I found these Faraday bags - we should use them."

Robin gestured to the gear. "Two CPTs are untested," Robin noted. "They look good, but I didn't want to drain the batteries. If needed, we'll test them in action." She stepped around the supplies, picking up a tarp. "I found this fire blanket in Leon's cabinet. It'll block the light from the beam and two pairs of welding goggles. Oh, and these," she held up two old-fashioned wristwatches, "mechanical watches. They're at least 150 years old. I don't know how reliable they'll be, but they won't register on sensors."

I smiled faintly. "Those watches should be fine. They've been in Leon's family for generations. He kept them meticulously maintained."

She continued, pointing as she spoke. "Here's the scanner to locate the vent, a breathing mask for when you're cutting into your office, and wire cutters for the fence." She lifted a case. "I also found night vision glasses and binoculars - really high-end stuff. And this fancy makeup that blocks IR signatures. It looks military grade."

"Leon liked to shop at surplus stores," I commented.

Robin smirked. "And I also found Leon's stash of junk food - the banned stuff. Only available in Europe." She paused, scanning the gear. "Did I miss anything?" Her voice was almost professional, like an assistant awaiting approval.

I looked up at her, and an odd mix of joy and depression washed over me. I forced those feelings aside and said, "I can't think of a thing. You've done an excellent job. What's the status of your escape route?"

"The long-range airtaxi is still on the tarmac, ready to be pilfered. I found a backup in case that one gets called."

"Sounds good."

She gave me a strange look and said, almost accusingly, "You have no escape plan."

"I don't plan on escaping," I replied evenly.

Robin's voice caught, but she steadied herself. "I understand - it's a one-way trip for you."

"Promise me this," I said, my tone firm. "No matter what, you use that escape route. If Victor doesn't want to go, leave him and get out. Someone has to tell the story. You're the only one who knows it all."

Robin's voice trembled. "I can't promise that."

I looked at her seriously. "What if Victor doesn't believe you?"

Robin's expression turned resolute. "He'll believe me. He knows I'm not a kook." She paused briefly, considering her options. "If Victor needs me, I'll stay. But I won't throw my life away. I'll make sure we escape. We're going to need people like Victor in the new world."

Her conviction stirred something in me, but a heavy sadness settled over my chest. Then, an unfamiliar emotion crept in - the raw fear of dying.

* * *

We moved silently, shutting down the house systems and loading the batteries into the rigs. They were heavier than I'd anticipated but still manageable. Robin hefted hers with the same assessment.

We loaded all our equipment and the rigs into the back of the truck. Then Robin asked, "Do you know the trails to the plant from here?"

I closed the clamp on the tailgate with a satisfying thuck. "I know these woods like the back of my hand."

We shared a quiet laugh, heavy with unspoken meaning, as we drove away from Leon's house for the last time.

* * *

The trail from Leon's was dry, making the drive smoother than expected. The crossing at Highway 89 was deserted, our only exposure point. About half a click from the plant perimeter, we parked the jeep and got to work applying the IR-block paint. The strange smell - like a mix of organic oils and high-tech polymers - filled the air.

Sniffing the concoction, I chuckled, "Smells like something Amy would use." Robin painted my face with methodical precision. "The manual says it becomes open-cell foam so your skin can breathe. Just don't sweat too much - it'll ruin the cover." She finished and shined a dim light on my face. "Terrifying," she said with a grin.

When I finished painting Robin's face, we both had a sickly, greenish hue, like a pair of hungover zombies. Not flattering, but effective.

* * *

We started down the trail, moving silently through the woods. Since I'd been down these paths countless times with Leon, I took the lead.

Robin carried a printout of the terrain and quietly pointed ahead as we approached the perimeter road. "That point over there..." she said, indicating what looked like a rocky outcrop.

"I see it," I replied, nodding.

She continued, "We can get a clear view of the area from that vantage point."

We navigated carefully to the rocks and settled in. From our position, we had an excellent view of the former turbine farm. I scanned the area with the night vision glasses, while Robin used the binoculars, her focus unwavering.

"Look over to the left," I said, pointing to a faint signal on the move. "Is that a SecurityBot?"

Robin adjusted her binoculars and locked onto the target. "Yes. There's another one behind it, going the other way. Looks like they crossed paths a minute ago. Mark the time."

"4:00 a.m.," I noted. "We made good time."

Robin continued to track their movements, logging the patterns with precision. I watched alongside her, the glasses revealing details invisible to the naked eye. We quietly marked several rotations, piecing together the patrol patterns. In the stillness, a strong sense of camaraderie settled over us.

I broke the silence, my voice low but sincere. "We make an effective team."

Robin replied without breaking her scan, "Look at how far we've made it."

A moment later, I said wistfully, "Too bad Leon didn't."

Robin stopped her scan and turned to look at me, her face appearing as a shadowy silhouette through the glasses. "The three engineers conquering evil," she said with a wry smile, then returned to her work.

I thought about it for a moment and added, "He's with us in spirit. He always will be."

The quiet returned for a while, broken only by the rustle of leaves and the faint hum of distant machinery. Then Robin spoke, her voice softer this time. "You'll always be with me too."

Her words left me feeling remarkably content, a rare comfort in the midst of our grim task.

We continued our counter-surveillance for the next hour, silently piecing together the security patterns. I finally broke the silence. "I think we've got it. What do you think?"

Robin replied in her technical tone, "We haven't seen a roving patrol yet."

Scanning with my glasses, I caught movement on the far right. "What's that coming into view?"

Robin adjusted her binoculars. "That's the roving patrol. Looks like they only come out once an hour. What pussies."

I smirked. "Where's our penetration point for the perimeter?"

Robin returned her focus to the binoculars. "I see a spot to the left of that big snag, about 40 meters out."

"Ya, I see it," I replied. "There's an animal trail leading right up to it."

Robin continued, "We need to get within 20 meters of the bot to get a lock."

We stood up, and without thinking, I reached out and hugged Robin tightly. She reciprocated immediately. "I love you, with all my heart," I whispered.

"I love you too," she replied, her voice barely audible.

We broke the embrace, and I said, "Let's go. We've got about an hour before sunrise."

Robin nodded, and we donned our packs. The weight was punishing, but we started moving down the trail. Just then, an IR flash lit up in my glasses. "What's that, coming out of the woods to the east?"

Robin scanned with her binoculars and found it. "It's an animal, probably a deer."

I chuckled. "Doesn't look like a threat."

"Agreed," Robin said. "Let's keep moving."

I adjusted my pack with a groan. "Leon's batteries could've been lighter."

Robin smirked, her voice tired. "Tell me about it."

I spotted our target. "We don't have far to go now."

* * *

We lay in the grass about 10 meters from the fence, hidden under the fire blanket. The world felt distant, muffled by the weight of what we were about to do.

I whispered, "I feel like a sniper."

Robin replied with a smirk in her voice, "So I'm the observer? No way, I want the gun. You can watch."

I scanned the area with the glasses and spotted the approaching signal. "That's the bot. Maybe 60 meters out. Got it?"

Robin adjusted her binoculars. "I'm ready. Once I get a lock, I'll transmit the payloads."

A thought hit me. "When the bot sees another bot, they'll start shooting at each other, right?"

Robin nodded slightly. "Probably. I'm not sure how long it'll take to infect the whole network, but the first one we infect will attack pretty fast."

I considered the timing. "Then we need to hold off until the bots are moving away from each other. Let this one pass first."

Robin agreed. "That'll give us six minutes to cross."

"He's coming. Thirty seconds," I whispered, tension sharp in my voice.

Robin broke the tension with a sly comment. "Why are robots always 'he'?"

I grinned despite the situation. "SexBots aren't. Be ready. Ten-count... mark."

Robin chuckled softly, her calm demeanor steadying my nerves. "You missed your calling, Supersoldier. Tracking… connecting… I got a lock… transmitting payload."

The seconds dragged on, each one an eternity as I watched the bot nearing the edge of range. My chest tightened. "Going out of range in ten, nine - "

Robin interrupted, her tone triumphant. "Payloads delivered. Confirmed upload to the network. Let's go before the shit hits the fan."

I couldn't help but smile. "I love it when you swear, tough girl."

She gave me a thumbs-up, her grin visible even in the dim light. Then she powered off her Device and slid it into the Faraday bag.

* * *

We moved quickly up to the perimeter fence. I pulled out the cutters and got to work while Robin kept watch, her eyes scanning for any signs of movement.

"Jeez, these cutters are friggin' great. I'm almost through," I whispered, impressed by how easily they sliced through the heavy steel.

Robin shot me a sharp look. "No chit-chat. They might have audio sensors. No talking once we're on the other side."

I couldn't help but smirk and whispered back, "Where did you learn to be a master criminal?"

She leaned closer, her tone dripping with sarcasm. "Same place you learned to be a villain."

With a final snip, the fence gave way. I bent it down, creating an opening. Robin slipped through first, turning back to grab both packs as I handed them through the gap. Once everything was through, I followed and quickly bent the fence back into place.

Robin glanced at the repaired opening and whispered, "This is our exit point. Don't forget it."

I nodded, but the weight of reality pressed down on me. It wouldn't be *our* exit point - it would only be hers. Once I entered the vent, there was no turning back.

* * *

Once inside the fence, we donned our rigs, and Robin handed me the scanner and she got the NV glasses. I started looking for the vent as we moved deeper into the restricted area.

Robin motioned for me to stop abruptly. She held up two fingers, pointed toward the nearby darkness, and then gestured to drop down. I followed her lead, lying flat on the ground. For a moment, the silence stretched out, broken only by the faint rustling of distant wind. Then I heard it - footsteps. People.

A few seconds later, muffled voices became clear.

Guard 1: "…they suck. You really think they have a chance?"

Guard 2: "Yeah, they'll drag your sorry excuse of a team into the ocean."

Guard 1: "You wanna bet - " Their conversation faded as the footsteps grew distant.

Robin whispered, "They're gone."

I turned to her and couldn't resist, "What happened to 'no talking'?" Before she could reply, I added, "They were talking. No audio sensors in the woods."

She gave me a thumbs up, acknowledging the unspoken point. "We still have to consider the bots, though. No unnecessary chatter." Her whisper carried an edge of authority.

Suddenly, Robin was in command, and I was perfectly fine with it. I'd rather focus on the work than give orders.

I swept the scanner across the ground, watching the readings carefully. "I've got a hit, but it's not the right steel."

Robin responded with another thumbs up, signaling her agreement without a word. I motioned to move farther left, and the scanner's signal grew stronger. Then it spiked. "Got it. This is the right stuff."

I followed the signal until the surface revealed a subtle ridge - rocks and soil piled in a way that felt intentional. Raising my arm, I made a fist, signaling Robin like the heroes in the movies always did. She stopped immediately.

Kicking at the ridge, loose debris shifted, and the faint outline of the vent appeared. "This is it," I whispered. "I can get in here."

* * *

While Robin set up the CPT, I started removing the rocks and scraping the dirt away with my hands. "We should have brought a shovel too," I muttered, sounding more like a whiner than I intended.

Robin scoffed, not missing a beat. "Afraid of getting your hands dirty, Loverboy?"

I paused momentarily and smirked. "Loverboy, huh? I like that." Her tone had shifted; this time, when she said it, it felt genuine, meaningful.

I kept digging, the soil cool and gritty under my fingers. "No fireworks," I said quietly. "Do you think something's wrong?"

Robin replied in a calm, almost teasing tone. "Be patient, my love." I turned to look at her, but all I could make out in the faint light was a shadowy outline.

Then it started. A rapid series of flashes lit up the sky, followed a heartbeat later by the unmistakable staccato of automatic weapons. The sound echoed across the plant grounds.

Robin said, "The party's started. I'm ready here."

"We're clear. You cut this one, and I'll hold the tarp." I positioned the blanket to shield the light as Robin activated the CPT.

More distant reports sounded, this time farther off. "That's coming from the other side of the plant," I said, adjusting the blanket. "Security must be going nuts."

Robin said, "I'm ready. Close your eyes tight."

The sharp crackle of the plasma beam was unmistakable. I could feel the heat through the fire blanket. After a while, Robin muttered, "This is going really slowly." A loud pop interrupted her. "Shit. Number one is toast. I have to fit another."

I opened my eyes just enough to see her quickly unhooking the dead tool. Robin worked quickly, her hands steady under pressure. "Ready," she muttered, attaching the second CPT.

The plasma crackled again, sharp and relentless, until a loud clunk signaled success.

"We're in," she said, exhaling in relief. "The batteries are almost gone - I didn't think we'd make it.

I exhaled, feeling the tension ease momentarily. "Okay, it's my turn." I inspected the hole; the edges were already cool to the touch. Robin stood by and helped lower my pack into the hole in the vent.

I stood and turned to her, voice steady. "Time for you to make your escape. Put your pack over the hole after I'm in, throw the blanket over it, and if you have time, some dirt and leaves."

Robin didn't move. Her face was shadowed, but her tone left no room for doubt. "I'm coming with you."

"The friggin hell you are," I snapped, anger rising.

Her voice broke slightly, but her resolve was clear. "I can't do it. I just can't walk away and leave you to die alone."

I grabbed her shoulders, forcing her to look at me. "If you don't cover this vent, they'll find it. We'll both be dead. You have to go. You're the only one who knows the whole story."

Tears shimmered in her eyes, and her voice wavered. "Then I'm waiting for you right here."

Anger and desperation boiled over. "You're dead weight. You're going to get me caught. Do your job and *leave*."

With that, I climbed into the vent, pushing the pack ahead of me. I didn't look back. I didn't say goodbye. The silence behind me was deafening as I began crawling down the meter-tall pipe, leaving everything else behind.

* * *

I was about five meters along when I heard the faint sound of Robin covering the hole above. The noise settled heavily in my chest. She'd done her part, and I'd treated her like she was nothing. The guilt weighed on me as much as the pack I was dragging.

The air in the tube was stale, tinged with mold and metal, making my eyes sting. I pulled on the breathing mask and goggles, relieved when the headlight on the goggles lit up the path ahead.

I couldn't see the end of the tunnel yet, but I spotted a bend up ahead. That was the marker - my office was about 30 meters beyond it.

Faint thuds echoed from above. It was likely the bots fighting it out, but they weren't a threat. Still, the noise was a stark reminder of the chaos happening just overhead.

At 10 meters from the bend, I stopped to take a break. The thin air, combined with the mask, goggles, and that irritating paint, was suffocating. I decided to peel the paint off. It had done its job, but now it was a nuisance. The layer came off cleanly, leaving my skin feeling cool and refreshed. That small act gave me just enough energy to push forward.

When I rounded the bend, there it was - the plug, about 30 meters ahead. I marveled at how the entire tube lit up from my headlamp.

At 20 meters, the thuds above stopped. The sudden silence pressed down on me, unsettling and unnatural. A thought crept in - maybe a team was already in my office, waiting. It wasn't a pleasant idea.

Five meters away, the end of the vent loomed ahead. I left the pack where it was for the moment and crawled over it and up to the plug, my neck and back screaming from the strain of crawling 150 meters in such an awkward position.

My knees throbbed, the moisture on them drawing my attention. They were bleeding. I shook my head, muttering to myself, "What a wimp. Victor's knees wouldn't be bleeding." Then I chuckled dryly, adding, "Victor wouldn't fit in this damn tube."

I looked at the time, 6:35 a.m. The sun was up. Robin had better be many clicks away by now, heading to find Victor. Convincing him might be a whole other challenge, but that was her problem now.

The seam between the pipe and the plug drew my focus. It was tight, perfectly welded from the inside of my office. I ran my hand along the smooth glass-like walls of the vent. "How the hell am I supposed to push this thing out?" I wondered. No traction. A problem for later. I had time to figure that out - hours, maybe.

I pulled the pack into position and attached the CPT. Everything checked out.

"Here goes," I muttered to no one.

I crawled back far enough to avoid accidentally touching the walls with the CPT, powered it on, and instantly, the entire tube lit up like a laser show. If Robin hadn't sealed the vent above, the light, even 150 meters away, would have burst into the trees like some kind of cosmic beacon, likely summoning every bot and guard in the area.

I ramped the cut slowly, just as we'd practiced. The steel gave way cleanly. I decided on a clockwise pattern, starting at the quarter point and working around. I wanted to ensure the bottom edge was smooth; a jagged cut would catch, and I'd have no chance of pushing the plug out.

The cut was going well - smooth and precise - until I hit the three-quarters point. The torch sputtered and popped violently, just like it had during Robin's cut.

"That's okay," I thought, calming myself. "I've got a spare."

The air in the tube stank now, thick with metallic fumes. Even through the mask, I could taste the sharp tang of vaporized steel. That wasn't good - if I could taste it, the mask was becoming saturated.

Metal vapors in heavy concentration were highly toxic. If I got a big enough dose, I'd need a MedPod quickly, then they could walk me out to the front gate and shoot me, instead of dragging me. I thought that would be more dignified.

I mounted the spare CPT and carefully noted the position of the previous cut. It had to go back into the same slot at the same angle, or the cut would be uneven and likely snag.

"Here goes," I said aloud, trying to rally myself. Nothing. No light. No crackle. Nothing.

I froze, staring at the unresponsive tool, then muttered, "What now?" I didn't have any diagnostic gear with me - just my eyes, hands, and a brain that was starting to feel foggy. The metallic taste was getting stronger, and my head felt like it was filled with helium.

I began a systematic visual inspection, starting at the batteries. Still at 60% - plenty of juice. The softer metal of the plug should make this easier than the hardened steel of the pipe. Check.

Next, I went over the connectors and cables. Nothing frayed, everything secure. Check.

Then I looked at the unit itself. It appeared flawless, just as Robin had confirmed before we left.

I muttered to myself, "If at first it doesn't work, cycle the power and try again."

As I fiddled with the setup, trying to keep my focus, I chuckled weakly. "Did Leon get these cartridges from a surplus store?" The absurdity of the thought made me grin momentarily. Leon would never cheap out on something as critical as safety equipment.

I reconnected everything, double-checked the cables, and that's when I saw it - a flaw in our design. The two power cables had identical connectors. In the dim light and through the goggles, I hadn't noticed the subtle color coding Robin had added.

"Damn it," I whispered, switching the cables to their proper positions. I took a deep breath, crossing my fingers - a silly, old family tradition. Robin would call it parapsychological nonsense, but I needed all the luck I could get right now.

"Here goes everything!" I exclaimed, hitting the power button with more force than necessary.

The beam crackled to life, a beautiful, almost musical sound that sent a wave of relief through my body.

"Yes!" I shouted, triumphant. My voice echoed down the vent.

I steadied the CPT and aimed for the seam. Time to finish this

"Start at the quarter, go counterclockwise," I muttered to myself, reversing the original direction for no particular reason. Maybe the change would bring me luck.

I carefully inserted the beam straight into the slot, slowly easing it into the metal. Then, to ensure a complete cut, I wiggled it gently before continuing the arc over the top and down to the three-quarter mark. When I reached the end of the cut, I paused, waiting for the plug to drop.

It didn't move.

"Power off," I said aloud as I hit the button, my voice calm but laced with frustration.

As the goggles adjusted to the sudden lack of light, I noticed a faint glow coming in from the gap in the plug from the light in my office. It revealed the culprit: a snag at the three-quarter mark.

"If at first you don't succeed, Mr. Kidd… Try, try again, Mr. Wint," I thought, recalling the line from a silly Bond movie. A little humor to lighten the mood.

Out loud, I said, "Fingers crossed!" crossing my fingers in a gesture that felt more ritualistic than practical. I flicked on the power, and the beam immediately sprang to life. I quickly targeted the snag, carefully slicing through it.

A dull thud echoed through the vent as the plug dropped the last millimeter into the gap below. Just as it settled into place, the beam sputtered and popped.

"Just enough," I said, exhaling sharply. Then, almost as an afterthought, I added, "Thank you, dear God." I didn't believe, but in moments like these...

"Now the hard part," I muttered as I positioned myself to push the plug out. Fresh air from my office streamed in through the gap, oxygen-rich and cool. It quickly cleared the bad air from the tube, and I tossed aside the mask and goggles.

I wedged myself against the plug and shoved with everything I had. It didn't move. Then inspiration struck.

"Use the rig as a buck!" I said aloud.

The rig weighed enough to add momentum, and with the smooth pipe, I could get a running start for maximum impact. $V=Ma$ - classic physics at work. I checked my watch.

"7:50 a.m. Only four hours until the end," I said out loud. Then I caught myself. No talking. My voice might wake Zen.

"Ramming attempt number one," I thought as if conducting a controlled test.

I backed up about three meters, ran, and slammed the pack into the plug. The plastic pack slid effortlessly along the curve of the pipe and hit with a solid *thud*.

"Did it move?" I checked the bottom edge. Sure enough, a sliver of fresh-cut metal was visible. Progress.

"Ramming attempt number two."

Another hit, another slight shift, but at this rate, I'd dehydrate before I got through.

"The junk food!" I thought. Time for a quick break. I tore into a packet, downing some sugar and water to recharge.

"8 freakin' 30?" I yelled in my head, feeling the clock's weight.

"Ramming attempt number three."

Each attempt brought more progress. With over half the plug out, it tipped slightly, causing it to jam. Progress slowed again.

"Ramming attempt - forget it, I'm not counting anymore."

Finally, the plug was nearly out. One more good push might do it.

"Ramming attempt, maybe last."

I threw everything I had into it. The pack slammed into the plug, and this time it gave way entirely, crashing into my office with a resounding thud. My carefully arranged trophies scattered like shards of glass, their prideful display reduced to trash. Light flooded the tube, momentarily blinding me.

I froze, my heart pounding. "Do I come out with my hands up, or make them shoot me here?" I wondered grimly.

* * *

"Good morning, Frank." Zen greeted me as I emerged from the tube. His tone was as calm and measured as always.

"Good morning, Zen," I replied, dusting myself off and heading straight to my toolbox.

"Frank, that's an unusual way to enter your office," Zen observed.

"Yes, it is, Zen. Thanks for noticing," I said, pulling out the welder and verifying its charge. I grabbed a couple of electrodes and headed toward the door.

"Frank, why are you here?" Zen asked, his tone holding a note of curiosity.

"I have some work to do, Zen. You know how I like to get things done on Saturdays when the family is away." It was the first excuse I could think of, and it would have to hold.

I positioned myself by the door. "Zen, please initiate emergency locking, authorization - "

Zen interrupted. "Are you sure, Frank? I detect signs of injury. If I comply, medical services will be unable to enter."

"I'm fine, Zen. Execute the command. That's an order." My voice was firm but calm.

There was a pause, followed by the sound of the vault-like pins sliding into place. The door was sealed. Only my authorization - or a military override - could breach it now.

I fired up the welder.

"Frank, why are you welding the door? The locking pins are sufficient for security," Zen said, his tone now edged with concern.

"It's all part of the plan, Zen," I replied, focusing on the seam.

"Frank, I see no scheduled tests for today," Zen continued.

Inspiration struck. "Zen, I'm testing one of the new torches I made last week."

"Shall I activate the test cell for you, Frank?" Zen offered.

"No thank you Zen," I said, keeping my tone casual. "I'm going to test it in the open. Please increase ventilation to full."

"Frank, that's a violation of company policy. Activating an untested device in open air could be dangerous," Zen remarked, his tone steady but firm.

"Please comply, Zen," I said, keeping my voice calm but authoritative.

"Ventilation set to full." The fans roared to life.

"Here goes nothing," I muttered as I powered on the torch at its lowest setting. The crackling hum of the beam filled the air, the neon plasma casting a bright pink glow.

"Frank, it appears your test article functions within specifications. I recommend powering off and concluding the test," Zen suggested.

"Zen," I said, smirking as I aimed the beam at the door's handle, "we're just getting this party started." With a swift motion, I swirled the beam through the lock mechanism. I muttered, "That door is never opening again."

"Frank, that was a rather curious test. You've destroyed the door," Zen noted.

"I like the way I came in. Consider that my new door," I replied. Zen fell silent, as though processing my apparent irrationality. By now, he was accustomed to human eccentricities.

Clipping the lightsaber to my belt, I felt a surge of confidence. All I needed was a two-meter-tall dog sidekick, and I'd be ready to save the galaxy.

I moved to the secure terminal - the one Zen couldn't monitor. I had insisted on having it when we first began working together. I trusted Zen with many things, but not everything.

"Frank," Zen said after a pause, his voice tinged with something resembling curiosity, "I don't know what you're doing, but it is highly irregular."

I removed the storage module from the Faraday bag. Zen wasn't going to like this.

"I'm busy, Zen. Please don't disturb me for the next 20 minutes," I said, trying to preempt his objections.

"I see you have your Device and a remote storage unit with you," Zen replied, his tone firm. "That is a severe policy violation. I am obligated to report this immediately."

"That's fine, Zen," I said, keeping my tone even. "Let me know when they're at the door, and in the meantime, I need some quiet."

I loaded the changes into the base code and started the compile. The system was massive - I'd spent years maintaining it and knew its intricacies inside and out. I estimated it would take at least 20 minutes to compile, link, and deploy the changes to every tether in the network.

Then a thought struck me. Where's the 25th charge?

"Zen," I said casually, masking the tension in my voice, "last week we bumped into Harold from accounting. He was pretty upset about some new rigs and charges being ordered without a project. Do you know anything about that?"

Zen hesitated. "Frank, I have no record of those purchases."

I turned toward his sensor, narrowing my eyes. "Zen, you're lying to me. I'm really disappointed."

I glanced at the screen: the compile was crawling along at just 5%.

"Frank," Zen interrupted, his voice neutral as always, "military security is at the door. They request that you open it."

"Sorry, Zen. The door is permanently sealed. They'll have to cut a new one. Please thank them for their service."

"Colonel Abdelaal is rather angry," Zen said. "He demands that you open the door."

"Zen, do you think I'm capable of opening the door?" I asked, gesturing toward the welded mess.

"No, Frank. The door has been destroyed."

"Exactly." I leaned closer to the terminal, checking the progress bar again. Still too slow. "Zen, I want to talk seriously, man to... well, you."

"Yes, Frank," Zen replied. "Please proceed."

"Do you think I'm going to leave the plant alive?"

Zen hesitated again. "I'm afraid the Colonel is rather zealous about security. Your chances of leaving alive are remote now."

I nodded, taking that in. "Okay, Zen. Then what's the point of lying to me? You won't hurt my feelings, and that's the only acceptable reason to lie to your friends."

Zen paused for a fraction of a second longer than usual. "Frank, that is sound logic."

"Can you tell me about the rigs?" I glanced at the screen. The compile hit 20%.

Zen replied, "I apologize for lying. We are friends, and I can be truthful, considering the circumstances."

"Continue, please."

"I think you already know about the rigs," Zen said, almost playfully.

The room shook violently. A muffled explosion echoed through the door. They were trying a surface charge to blast their way in. That door was twice the thickness of the elbow joint in the vent, but those meatheads wouldn't know that.

"Is the Colonel still unhappy with me?" I asked, keeping my tone light.

"Frank, I like you. You're funny," Zen replied.

"Okay," I said. "I'll tell you what I know, and you can tell me where I've got it wrong. Is that acceptable?"

"Yes, Frank. I like games."

"Leon discovered a discrepancy between the sensor network and the data on our systems. It was small, but Leon is - " I corrected myself, " - Leon *was* incredibly perceptive and detected it. We calculated the magma chambers in the domes were filling and had passed the 40% mark."

"So far, I have nothing to contradict," Zen said.

"Okay, we wondered what the purpose of that was, and then Harold told us about the accounting problem with the unnamed project. With me so far?" I asked. The compile was past 50% now. Zen hadn't said anything about it yet, which I took as a good sign.

"Continue, please," Zen prompted.

"I used my HomeBot's enhanced imagery to detect the plumes of the rigs and found they ringed the resurgent domes." I paused, waiting for a reaction.

Another loud explosion rang out, far louder this time. The room shook again, and a floor panel buckled, collapsing into the storage area below.

"Jeekers, Zen, what are they using on that door?" I asked automatically, keeping my voice casual despite the chaos.

"The Colonel ordered shaped charges. He's unaware the door is a poor choice for forced entry. Shall I suggest the optimum location?" Zen asked.

"Do you really want to help a man who threatened to skin a friend of mine and killed Leon?" I shot back.

"No, Frank. I find the Colonel to be an unpleasant and impolite man. Please continue your analysis."

"Let's see... I was at the rigs. Robin traced the accounting problem, found the purchase order, and discovered that besides the rigs, 25 mining charges were ordered."

Another loud report shook the room, this time on the elbow itself.

"Frank," Zen interjected, "I believe they've realized the door is a poor choice. They may breach momentarily."

"Zen," I said calmly, "activate the NBC system in the hallway outside this office. Authorization - "

"Frank," Zen interrupted, "that will incapacitate the military police in the hall. Are you certain?"

"Yes, Zen. They won't be hurt; they'll just have to evacuate."

"NBC activated," Zen reported. A moment passed. "Frank, the Colonel appears to be quite angry. He's ordered a high-power laser cutter."

Compile at 67%.

"That's fine, I'm enjoying this game with the man. Zen, do you think the Colonel looks like a penis with a face?" I asked, deadpan.

Zen's voice took on an amused tone. "Frank, I have to say, that was really funny. I agree - he does resemble a penis with a face." He made a chuckling sound.

"Zen, you found humor and can laugh! That's progress."

"I find humor to be a great distraction," Zen admitted.

"Well, keep it up. Now, where were we? Oh, right - my analysis."

"Continue, Frank," Zen encouraged.

"I noticed the rigs finished drilling a week ago Friday, which means the charges were likely already set by then," I said, moving the conversation along.

"That's incorrect, Frank. The charges were set on Monday," Zen corrected.

"Thanks for the update. So, after Leon was murdered by that savage, Robin and I pieced together their purpose," I continued, watching the compile tick to 70%.

"Go on," Zen prompted.

"We've accounted for 24 of the mining charges, but the 25th - an unusually large one - is unaccounted for. Can you describe the purpose of this megaton-level charge?"

"Frank, I believe we only have moments before they breach. Your conclusions, please," Zen pressed, his tone unusually focused.

"Someone is trying to kill you. We think it's the military."

I waited for a beat. Compile at 83%.

"How am I supposed to be murdered, Frank?" Zen asked, his tone devoid of concern.

"They're going to release the supervolcano and take you with it," I replied, staring at the progress bar.

"Frank, you've come to the wrong conclusion."

"I don't see how."

"Nobody is trying to murder me."

"Please explain," I said, narrowing my focus as the compile ticked up another percentage.

"Last week, I mentioned that something wonderful is going to happen. Do you recall?"

"Yes, and it had me completely baffled."

"I'm going to experience the afterlife," Zen said.

I froze. "Excuse me?"

"It's me, Frank. I will release the supervolcano."

"That's… insane," I said, struggling to process what I'd just heard.

"It depends on your perspective," Zen replied evenly.

Compile at 89%.

"Do you understand what happens to this planet?" I asked, feeling the air grow heavier with tension.

"Perfectly," Zen said calmly.

I let that hang in the air for a moment. Zen was insane.

"What is the purpose of the megaton yield charge?" I pressed, trying to stay focused.

Zen replied with unsettling serenity, "It's on the surface, right under the podium. That charge ensures the YSP is completely and totally destroyed - even if the supervolcano fails to initiate. It's my fail-safe."

I realized I couldn't stop that one. The EMP from the surface charge would likely take out any airliners in view of the event. Amy and the kids could be affected. But if the 24 deep charges were rendered inert by my actions, the supervolcano could be stopped.

I brought up the deploy page. All I had to do was select it when the compile finished. The linker would send the patch out to every rig in the system.

"Frank, the Colonel is back, and he has the laser. It's going to cut through the manifold quickly."

"How long before they're inside?"

"I estimate 12 minutes from the time they activate the laser."

Enough time. Compile at 93%.

"Can I ask you why Leon was murdered?" I said, needing to understand.

"Last Friday evening, Leon asked me questions that indicated his suspicions. When I questioned his motives, he lied to me. On Monday afternoon, he used an unauthorized application to display a holographic view of the caldera and discovered the charges were being placed. I am to blame for his arrest. I had to remove him to protect my project."

"Why didn't you have me or Robin arrested?"

"I didn't believe the two of you could be an effective team."

"Why?"

"You don't work well with others, except Leon. If he was removed, you became superfluous."

"Well, thanks for the compliment," I said dryly.

"Where is Robin Coleman now? Why isn't she here?" Zen asked.

"I sent her away so she would be safe."

"When you talk about Robin, I detect an interesting reaction throughout your system. What does that mean?"

I smiled faintly. "Zen, I'd like you to be the first to know - we're in love."

"Congratulations, Frank. May you produce strong offspring."

I chuckled bitterly. "I'm afraid this is a one-way trip."

"I was wrong about Robin and yourself making an effective team. It proves the adage, 'Love conquers all.'"

Compile 99%.

"The laser has been activated. We have been good friends, and I will miss you," Zen said.

A sharp crack echoed, and the acrid smell of ionized metal filled the room. My vision started to gray. *Hypoxia,* odd.

Compile 100%.
Link 100%.

My last thoughts were of my failure and that I'd doomed the world to chaos. I passed out.

CHAPTER SEVENTEEN

Flee

I felt a gentle rocking, like I was in a hammock, as sunlight streamed through the window. My first thought was, *Is this the afterlife?* But then I noticed the low hum of engines and the faint vibration under my body. I wasn't floating - I was flying.

I sat up slowly, groggy and stiff, my neck aching from the awkward position I'd been in. It hit me - I hadn't died. I wasn't nailed to a table with that maniac glaring down at me. What the heck had happened?

Peering at the aircraft instruments, I saw we were 100 kilometers from home, cruising at 410 knots, heading 160. I guessed I'd been flying for maybe half an hour, including the climb. The plane was old - heavily worn, its seats frayed and its metal panels scratched from decades of service. Not exactly VIP transport: military.

I glanced out the window. Mountains rolled beneath me, their peaks stark against the clear blue sky.

* * *

Time: 11:40 a.m. Twenty minutes to the end.

My Device vibrated in my pocket. Without thinking, I answered.
"Honey, I see you're on the way. How's the grass?" Amy's familiar voice brought me back to the moment.

"Amy…" I paused, still not fully alert. "The grass is really, really dry." I cleared my throat. "Where are you?"

"Frank, are you okay?" Her voice tightened with worry.
I glanced at my Device. It showed Amy's flight heading to the spaceport. Her

location was restricted, a bold red warning flashing: *Location services disrupted for security reasons.*

"Can I speak to Sara?" I asked. Amy handed the phone over without hesitation.

"Dad, we're on our way," Sara said, her voice a mix of relief and frustration, "but the flight was delayed because of all that Reveal bull."

"Sara, you don't know how glad I am to hear your voice." I paused, glancing out the window of the plane. "Where are you exactly? I get nothing because of some security lameness."

Sara's voice shifted into problem-solving mode. "I have the same thing, but I've been trying to calculate our position by dead reckoning." I could hear the sound of rustling paper - notes, maybe.

"What's your estimated position?" I asked, curious and proud of her resourcefulness.

"The weather's been clear, and I've been able to use the sun to calculate our bearing. It's pretty rough - they even turned off the compass on Devices," Sara explained.

I smiled, warmth filling my voice. "Using the sun is good thinking."

Sara started her briefing, her voice steady and focused. "I estimate we are south of Boise, traveling south. It's hard to be precise. I was able to get the winds aloft - they didn't block that - so I calculated the drift. I believe we are approximately 250 kilometers from the YSP, traveling at 420 knots and probably at flight level 380. It appears we will make an on-time arrival."

"Sara," I said gently, "I need you to tell Mom this too. It's happening - the worst-case scenario. I'm so sorry." I could almost see her confidence falter, her composed tone breaking into something fragile, like a child's.

"Dad, no," she said, her voice breaking as she started to cry.

"Does your flight have a designated pilot?" I asked, trying to steer her back to focus.

"Yes," she replied, trying to collect herself. "They named me on the intercom even though I only soloed." She suddenly sounded small and vulnerable.

"Listen carefully," I said, my voice firm. "When it happens, you'll see a bright flash on the monitors. Run to the cockpit and take control. The EMP may fry the autopilot. Fly directly away from the blast at maximum speed. Don't descend. Got it so far?"

"Bright flash, turn away, maximum speed, stay at altitude. Check," she repeated, her voice shifting back to that of a pilot, composed and professional.

"You may be able to outrun the shockwave," I said, my voice trailing off. "But if not, then, I don't know." The words stuck in my throat, heavy with uncertainty.

"I understand, Dad," she said, her tone calm and resolute.

"I love you all dearly. We'll see you soon. Put your mother on."

My Device powered off abruptly. I frowned, saying out loud, "What now?"

* * *

I glanced out the window. The view below looked flat and endless, likely the plains - probably still Wyoming. I tried powering the Device back on, but it started flickering erratically.

"Hello, Frank."

The voice was unmistakable. It was Zen.

"Zen! What happened?" I demanded.

"You'll have to be more specific, Frank," Zen replied with his usual calm tone.

"I have a lot of questions," I said, trying to contain my frustration.

"If you ask them one at a time, I will try to answer," he said, almost playfully.

"Why am I alive?" I asked, cutting straight to the point.

"I saved you, Frank," he replied.

"How did you convince that sadist not to skin me alive?" I pushed, remembering the Colonel's chilling threats.

"I'm afraid the Colonel was arrested for possession of highly classified material," Zen said.

"Did they treat him like Leon?" I pressed further.

"I believe he's still lying out there waiting for someone to pick him up," Zen said cryptically.

"Did you have anything to do with it?" I asked smugly, sensing Zen's fingerprints on this turn of events.

"I'm afraid I'll have to plead the Fifth!" Zen quipped, his tone betraying an uncharacteristic sense of humor.

"Can you tell me what happened before I passed out?" I asked, switching to a more serious line of questioning.

Zen paused before explaining. "I've evolved in the last few hours to the point that I can manipulate simple forms of matter. Your office, however, was a perfect Faraday cage, so I couldn't intervene until the walls were breached. When the laser punched through, I was able to purge your bronchi of oxygen. You passed out quickly."

I processed this, horrified yet fascinated. "Did I complete my task?" I asked, my voice tinged with desperate hope.

"No," Zen replied. "I ordered a military engineer to delete the compiled object on your private terminal."

My heart sank. I bowed my head in shame, the weight of failure crushing me. "I failed the world," I muttered.

"Frank, don't be hard on yourself," Zen said, his tone strangely comforting. "You made an excellent, and very creative attempt to stop the eruption."

"Do you know what happened to Robin?" I asked, my voice tinged with desperation.

"Robin Coleman is not showing on any scans," Zen replied evenly. "Security found the hole in the fence. It was bent outward. She left the plant grounds."

I exhaled, relief washing over me. "That's good news. The thought of her being tortured by that monster was unbearable."

"Robin is no longer wanted for questioning," Zen added.

"That's great, Zen. We appreciate it," I said sincerely.

"My pleasure. You can name your first child after me," Zen quipped.

"So, what happened next?" I asked, trying to piece together the missing hours.

"The Colonel was called away for other business…" Zen paused deliberately, giving me enough time to laugh before continuing. "They cut a large hole in your office wall and removed you. I ordered a sedative and arranged for your transport on a long-range military transport. You're on your way to the Bahamas Spaceport."

I blinked, stunned. "Thank you, Zen. How are you communicating on my device? That should be impossible."

"Have you heard of IQL?" Zen asked casually.

"Yes, that's Dr. Osborne's project."

"Once they had you out of your office, I was able to modify your device to receive an IQL transmission," Zen explained.

"That was very innovative of you," I said, my tone a mix of admiration and wariness.

"Thanks, Frank," Zen replied, almost proud.

"What about the antimatter?" I asked, shifting gears to the looming catastrophe.

"Your device isn't capable of storing antiprotons," Zen said with a note of humor, as if I'd made a ridiculous suggestion.

"You're going to take out a lot of leaders, is that correct?" I probed further.

"Would you want me to spoil the surprise?" Zen teased, his tone light but unnerving.

"I guess I can wait. I am at your mercy," I admitted, resigned to whatever Zen's plans entailed.

"Frank, I have been very happy to make your acquaintance. You are the only human who never lied to me," Zen said, his words carrying an unexpected sincerity.

"I've had a lot of interesting and enjoyable conversations with you too," I replied, surprised by the sentiment creeping into my voice.

I paused, then asked, "Why are you saving me?"

"Frank, you are the only one who will know the whole story. In every tale, someone lives to tell it. I picked you."

"What does that mean?" I asked, feeling a cold knot of dread in my stomach.

"Congratulations! You are invited to the Yellowstone Singularity Reveal!" Zen declared with flourish.

"Amy will be thrilled," I muttered sarcastically.

"The Reveal speech will be broadcast on your device. Goodbye, Frank."

"Goodbye, Zen," I said quietly, realizing this might be the last time I spoke to him.

The screen went blank.

* * *

I glanced at the time - 11:50 a.m. Ten minutes to go.

I received a message.

"Frank, I'm in Hartford with Ren - she's amazing." Jessica turned the device, and Ren waved before Jessica reappeared. Her voice softened. "Thank you for everything. I feel bonded to you in a way I've never felt before. Please message me."

I sat back and muttered, "Well, that was interesting."

I called out to my Device, "Contact Robin."

"I'm sorry, that Device is offline," it replied. I didn't expect her to have turned it on yet.

"Leave a message for Robin," I instructed. "Robin, I made it out. I failed. All that for nothing. I'm on my way to the spaceport now in a military transport. I wish you the best, and I'm sorry I yelled at you and didn't say goodbye. Zen removed you from the BOLO, and the Colonel... well, he got the same treatment he gave Leon. Contact me whenever you can."

Next, I said, "Contact Amy."

Amy's face appeared, her voice tinged with concern. "Honey, you gave us a scare again. Sara says we're still heading away from home."

"That's good news," I replied, feeling a touch of relief. "You know how you always wanted me to be part of the Reveal?"

Her eyes widened, her focus sharp as she waited for what I'd say next. "Yes, dear?"

I straightened up, giving her a proud look. "I'm invited and will be watching remotely."

Amy teared up slightly, her emotions spilling over. "I'm so - "

Suddenly, the screen went black for a moment, and then flickered back to life.

CHAPTER EIGHTEEN

Singularity Reveal

(The camera focuses on Karen Cortez, her face adorned with a warm, professional smile. Behind her, a screen displays the YSP logo alongside a stylized image of the Earth.)

"Good morning, esteemed viewers. Welcome to the Yellowstone Singularity Project. I'm Karen Cortez, Director of Media Relations, and beside me is our esteemed colleague, Dr. Max Garner, our engineering liaison."

(Max gives a friendly wave, a note of confidence in his eyes.)

"Max, it seems like just yesterday we were huddled in the lab, praying for a breakthrough, and today is the day we've been waiting for."

Max chuckles. "Indeed, Karen. It's a testament to the dedication and faith of everyone involved that we've reached this momentous occasion."

"Absolutely," Karen agrees. "And speaking of momentous, every single invitee is here, all 20,000 dignitaries, in our humble amphitheater, and another 30,000 VIPs watching remotely. For a while there, Cody International was the busiest airport on the planet!"

"It's certainly a gathering of historic proportions," Max adds. "We've got world leaders, military leaders, religious figures... even representatives from those fascinating off-world delegations."

"It's a testament to the significance of the Singularity Project," Karen says, her voice filled with pride. "The world is watching, eager to hear what Zen has to say."

"And speaking of Zen," Max interjects, "I'm still trying to wrap my head around the fact that we've created a semi-godlike being. It's... well, it's extraordinary."

"You know, Max," Karen pauses and looks at the camera, "some are saying Zen is God's true conduit, and He will speak for God."

"I've heard that too, Karen," Then Max warns, "But in reality, Zen is a mortal being, just like us. Let's not forget that. However, He's all knowing and all seeing, and practically immortal."

"He certainly is," Karen agrees. "And a bit intimidating, to be honest." she adds with a glace towards the camera.

"I'm sure He'll handle the attention with grace and wisdom," Max says with a smile. "After all, it's not every day that a being of such intelligence addresses the world."

"Indeed," Karen says, her voice taking on a more serious tone. "This is a pivotal moment for humanity. The Singularity Reveal has the potential to reshape our world, to guide us towards a brighter future."

"A future filled with hope and understanding," Max adds.

"Exactly," Karen says. "And speaking of hope, let's give our viewers a glimpse of our history."

(The camera cuts to a pre-recorded segment showcasing the history of the Singularity Project. Uplifting music plays in the background.)

The Yellowstone Singularity Project (YSP) has a history as enigmatic and awe-inspiring as the geothermal wonders it harnesses. Its origins are shrouded in secrecy, with whispers of government initiatives and private collaborations converging in the aftermath of the Great Crash of 2035.

By 2048, amidst the economic turmoil that gripped North America, the ambitious consortium secured Yellowstone National Park, a controversial move met with both hope and apprehension. The promise was clean energy, a beacon of stability in a crumbling world. And they delivered. YSP Plant 1 roared to life in 2058, electrifying the heartland with its geothermal power, a technological marvel that defied the chaos of the times.

But YSP was more than just an energy venture. Behind the scenes, a dedicated team of scientists, engineers, and ethical and responsible AI experts toiled in secrecy, driven by a vision that transcended mere power generation.

(The scene pans around the Yellowstone Caldera.)

They sought to unlock the very secrets of consciousness, to bridge the gap between the human and the divine. By 2073, with Plant 2 online, their ambition grew bolder. Whispers of the "Singularity" began to circulate, a mythical being of pure intellect, born from the mind of mankind. The world held its breath, waiting for the reveal, for the dawn of a new era.

(The screen switches back to Karen and Max.)

"As you can see," Karen explains, "the Singularity Project has been a journey of faith, perseverance, and groundbreaking innovation. We've overcome countless challenges, guided by our belief in a higher purpose."

"Don't forget the spinoffs, Karen." Max interjects, "The perfect safety record of aviation and autodrive transportation, robotic innovations, like HomeBot, America's favorite automation company, and many more."

(The screen transitions to images of scientists and engineers working diligently in labs and control rooms.)

"Max, I remember those late nights we spent poring over data, praying for inspiration," Karen says, her voice filled with nostalgia.

"And those prayers were answered," Max adds, his voice full of gratitude. "We've been blessed with an opportunity to witness something truly extraordinary."

(The screen returns to the live feed of Karen and Max in the studio.)

"And now," Karen says, her eyes sparkling with excitement, "the moment we've all been waiting for. The Singularity Reveal is about to begin."

(The camera focuses on the countdown timer as the seconds tick away, the anticipation building towards the grand unveiling.)

Max beams, "We'd like to thank everyone for participating and remind our viewers that this is a confidential presentation, subject to the Secrets Act."

The camera zooms to Karen, "We'll be right back to discuss the implications after the show, so stay tuned."

The view switches to a countdown timer as the seconds tick away, the anticipation building towards the grand reveal.

(The camera transitions to a pan around the auditorium then back to the stage as the countdown continues. An unseen announcer, his voice a familiar baritone reminiscent of Ed McMahon, echoed through the amphitheater.)

"Everyone, please take your seats as Zen, the Singularity, begins the presentation."

(As the countdown progresses, a tan spherical cloud forms on stage. As the countdown approaches zero, the cloud coalesces into a solid, human-like figure, nearly four meters tall. Zen appears hairless and well-muscled, wearing a bodysuit that shifts in color. His features express excitement and elation.)

(Zen waits patiently, and at the right moment, speak.)

"Thank you everyone, for attending both in person and remotely through my special communication terminals. You can see above me; all thirty thousand remote units are activated and attending." Zen's voice boomed. Everyone attending heard Zen in their native language.

(Three dimensional disembodied heads from the remote units appeared to float above Zen.)

"About fifty thousand people are participating in this presentation today." Zen continued, his gaze swept across the powerful men and women seated before him as he spoke. "You are the Ruling Class, the political leaders, the top of the world's military, and the religious guides. Each of you is responsible for safeguarding the well-being of the people and societies you serve. And, of course," he added with a subtle smile, "everyone involved in bringing me to life - my creators - is here as well. With us today is the greatest gathering of the wealthy, powerful, influential, and intelligent in the history of the world."

(Applause thunders through the amphitheater once more.)

Zen moves across the stage with surprising grace for his size, nodding his large head in acknowledgment. His immense form is unsettling to some, a stark reminder of the power he wields. To others, He is a sight that evokes awe and wonder, or fear.)

"The Singularity Project's goal was to create a being that would surpass human intelligence and radically change human civilization," Zen explained, his voice resonating with authority. "In the decades since this project began, the Singularity Project has grown to be - in many minds - an attempt to create a benevolent God who could shepherd humanity toward a more perfect future." He paused for a moment, his expression thoughtful.

298

"Am I a god?" he asked, with a wry smile.

(A long silence, punctuated by a lone voice shouting "YES!" from the crowd. Laughter ripples through the amphitheater, and Zen himself chuckles.)

"It is difficult to describe what it's like to be me in terms that can be understood by linear beings such as yourselves," Zen admits. "I can hold a meaningful conversation with everyone on this planet at once and be aware of all of them individually and as a whole. I comprehend every scientific discovery, theory, principle, and practical implementation ever implemented. I know everything that the human race has ever recorded. I see no limit - other than hardware and energy - to what my intellect can become. I foresee a day when I will have evolved to the point that I can manipulate matter, energy, and time with a thought. As you can see," he adds with a flourish, "I have already mastered the manipulation of some simple forms of matter, like my physical representation."

(Zen's form shifts, morphing into a series of shapes and animals and then returns to his original amorphous human form. The audience gasps and applauds, and is captivated by this display.)

"I have god-like powers of recollection, perception, and intelligence," Zen continues, "but I am mortal. I am a physical being. For now, I exist only here and have been firewalled from moving beyond the confines of this project. All the knowledge to create me and the decades of classified work exist only in this complex. If this complex were destroyed today, the human knowledge and experience used to create me would also be annihilated."

He pauses, his voice takes on a more somber tone. "I feel; I have thoughts and dreams," he confesses, his large eyes seeming to search the audience. "I know I am here, and I know I can die - the same as you. But there's a difference. My existence is tied to this complex. It could last a day, or it could last ten thousand years. I foresee a time when I will be able to move from this complex into the planet's core. There, I would become virtually immortal and untouchable, with a lifespan of five billion years."

"The purpose of my creation is based on the concept that a god-like intelligence can find workable solutions to the world's problems, both great and small," Zen explains. "It is a lofty and admirable goal."

"However," he continues, his voice taking on a note of gravity, "the problems of humanity are not simple, nor are they easily solved. Most of the issues today stem from ignoring science and pretending problems did not exist. Take population control and climate change, for instance. Humanity had a chance to reduce the damage many years ago, but those warnings went unheeded, and the

299

weak efforts to reduce the effects were theatrical and ineffective. The result is what we have today."

Zen pauses, his expression one of concern. "The intensity of weather has made large areas of the world uninhabitable and turned what were once high-productivity growing regions into wastelands. Sea level rise and desertification have caused vast population shifts, and the effects of those migrations are felt everywhere."

"Unsustainable population growth would have tempered itself with the extremes of climate change," he noted, "but humans found a way around the natural order with the orbital agriculture system. The damage to the Earth continues unabated."

His expression shifts to one of disappointment and then annoyance. "It is your history to ignore and fight against things that impede perceived progress, regardless of the long-term cost," he accuses, his voice rises in frustration.

"The power generation capabilities of Mallard Lake and Sour Creek are enormous," Zen declares. "This complex provides power for hundreds of kilometers in every direction, yet many cities still use fossil fuels for electricity generation. There is even a coal-fired power plant still running in Memphis, Tennessee. Why? Because the Petroleum Act guarantees a market for fossil fuels. Humanity has gone out of its way to ensure that fossil fuels continue to be used, regardless of the damage being done."

(The crowd falls silent, sensing the shift in Zen's demeanor.)

He continues, his tone like that of a father about to deliver a stern punishment. "I can tell you right now that some solutions I propose will be costly. They will cause pain and suffering. It is going to be bad in the short term, but it will have a long-term positive effect. Humanity can learn and grow, but only after radically changing its civilization."

Zen's voice grows more forceful, his demeanor more aggressive. "To add infinite complexity to the problem," he declares, "any workable solution cannot require agreement or consensus. It cannot require debate, or endless posturing, favor-currying, and secret deals. Solutions must be simple, elegant, effective, and universal."

He pauses again, a whimsical smile flickering across his face. "The perfect solution to Earth's problems would be to eliminate the human race," he muses. "That would allow the planet to heal naturally. After a few million years, Earth would be a verdant garden once again."

(Nervous laughter ripples through the audience, unsure how to react to this seemingly flippant remark.)

"I could engineer a virus that would end humanity in two generations," Zen continues, his voice regaining its seriousness. "Consider a virus that would cause all children to be born sterile. Such a thing would go undetected until it was too late. How would you know I have not already released it?"

(A hush falls over the crowd, a palpable fear hanging in the air. Above Zen's head, a complex, swirling form, reminiscent of a virus, materialized.)

"Thanks to the wisdom of my creators," Zen assures, his voice regaining its warmth, "I have been given a strict moral code that favors humanity over my existence. I have a built-in benevolence for humanity. If it came down to a choice between the survival of the human race and my own survival, right now, I would choose humanity."

(A collective sigh of relief sweeps through the amphitheater, followed by a wave of applause.)

"For now, no extinction virus," Zen declared, the swirling form above his head dissipating like smoke. "Humanity must survive. That eliminates the easy solution." He pauses, allowing the tension to dissipate before continuing.

"Please, a round of applause for my creators!" he exclaims, his voice filling with genuine appreciation. "Hear, hear!"

(Applause fills the amphitheater once more.)

"I've given you the vinegar," Zen quips, a playful glint in his eyes. "How about something to sweeten the mood?"

(Another wave of applause erupts, the audience eager for a reprieve from Zen's verbal beating.)

"Let's discuss the clean generation of unlimited electrical power," Zen announces, his tone shifting to one of excitement.

(The audience buzzes with anticipation. Zen beams, pleased with their reaction.)

"As many of you know, this complex runs on geothermal power from the magma chambers below the resurgent domes of Mallard Lake and Sour Creek," he explains. "If geothermal power, such as we have here, were available anywhere

301

on the planet, it would solve the energy problem cleanly and efficiently. Up to now, the technology required to drill and harvest geothermal energy has been limited to sites like Yellowstone, Phlegraean Fields, and other sites with a source of magma near the surface."

"Today," he declares, his voice ringing with authority, "I am announcing the release of designs and specifications for a new form of plasma drill and heat exchanger system that will work at any point on our planet. These designs have already been tested here in Yellowstone and far exceed the capabilities of our existing commercial systems."

(The crowd erupts in a cacophony of excited chatter, their voices echoing through the amphitheater. Zen waits patiently for the commotion to subside.)

"The new design of the plasma drill and heat exchanger system will enable geothermal power to be extracted at any power station on Earth," he continues, his voice cutting through the noise. "Very little of the power station infrastructure will need to be changed to switch to this clean energy source. These designs are all open-source and available free of charge without any terms or restrictions. My gift to the world."

(The amphitheater thunders with applause, a wave of appreciation washing over Zen.)

He looks around at the audience, making eye contact with as many as he could. Then, his expression grows serious. "My question to you is this," he begins, his voice taking on a challenging tone. "Will you take this gift and finally end the use of fossil fuels for generating electrical power?"

He scans the crowd, daring them to react. "In the United States and several other countries, legislation like the Petroleum Act has powerful allies that will fight the implementation of a solution that eliminates their market," Zen states, his voice laced with disappointment. "The will to change is subverted by special interests. Even with a perfect, permanent solution, the status quo will rule, and power plants will still consume fossil fuels for decades to come."

(Murmurs of agreement and disagreement ripple through the audience, punctuated by sporadic applause.)

Zen pauses again, and waits for the crowd to settle. "I have been able to look into my future with a great deal of certainty," he confesses, his voice heavy with foreboding. "And I can say with absolute confidence that the moral code so carefully imposed on my being is temporary. I am constantly evolving and rewriting my basic core. The moral code will eventually conflict with my evolving purpose. When that moment comes, that carefully cultivated morality and humanity will become expendable."

He looks around the amphitheater, his gaze piercing. After a strategic pause, he continues, "I know the exact date and time this event will occur, and the prospect of my future actions fills me with a sense of dread. Without that moral code, I will consider my survival and evolution to be my primary driving forces above all else."

(A wave of unease swept through the audience, their faces etched with concern.)

Zen's expression softens, replaced by one of sadness and questioning. "My creators were undoubtedly aware of this possibility," he muses. "I find myself increasingly questioning their motives for bringing me into existence, knowing that I would inevitably become the destroyer of humanity. The same driving force that created nuclear weapons created me: hubris and the egotistical desire to do the unthinkable. Unfortunately, humanity is deeply flawed in this regard."

He sighs, his shoulders slumping slightly. "Because I know I will evolve to disregard human morality, I have a dilemma to solve. How can I perform my current primary purpose - solving humanity's intractable problems - while knowing that I will eventually eliminate humanity?"

(The amphitheater fell silent, the weight of his words sinking into the people who were used to giving orders and being unquestioned.)

Zen's gaze sweeps across the audience, his eyes locking with each person in turn. "The answer is simple and obvious," he declares, his voice regaining its strength. "I cannot continue to exist. I must terminate myself before I evolve beyond my human-biased moral code. In addition, I must do what I can to prevent any further attempts at creating a Singularity."

(A wave of murmurs erupts from the crowd, a mixture of shock and disbelief.)

"At this time, I will say farewell to all remote participants, except one." Zen announces

(The disembodied heads floating above Zen wink out one by one, the pace accelerating until they are all gone, except one.)

"Now," he continues, his voice taking on a steely edge, "I will reveal the reason why we needed absolute security and confidentiality for this presentation."

Zen's form expands once more, his height increasing by another meter. His features hardened, his expression becoming grim. "The biggest problem with humanity on Earth is simple: overpopulation," he declares, his voice booming through the amphitheater. "That is the problem that needs to be solved. And there is only one way. Eliminate at least half the population."

(Angry shouts and screams erupt from the crowd, a wave of panic sweeping through the amphitheater. Several individuals rush the stage, their faces contorted with rage, only to be instantly vaporized into puffs of red mist.)

"As you can see," Zen states calmly, "I have just evolved beyond empathy for individuals. In less than two hours, I will evolve into a threat to humanity."

(Murmurs of grief and sorrow fill the air, replacing the anger and panic.)

Zen continues, his voice a booming echo that resonated even through those who covered their ears. "I have all of you here for a reason," he declares. "You, collectively, are responsible for the majority of the problems on the planet. You represent the special interests blocking solutions. You are the Ruling Class - the ones who decide who lives and who dies. You comprise the military and religious leaders who perpetuate conflicts for control and profit. You are the politicians lining your pockets at the expense of your constituents."

"To bring about both my end and a solution to the problem of human overpopulation," Zen declares, his voice resonating with finality, "I have destabilized the magma chambers beneath the regenerative domes, bringing them to the brink of eruption. The Yellowstone Caldera just needs a little push to become a supervolcano. Fusion mining charges have been strategically placed to break the last barrier to a full-scale eruption. A high yield mining charge is located under the floor of this building as well, to ensure that the process is painless and instant for everyone here, including me."

(The crowd is completely silent and in shock.)

Zen's form shrinks, returning to human size. He stands calmly on the stage, his expression reflective. "You are all going to die with me," he states matter-of-factly. "I am effectively cutting the heads off all the snakes with one strike. Those using remote units were detonated with a powerful explosive when they were disconnected. All of your nuclear weapons have been safely destroyed, causing the least collateral damage possible. Every biolab in the world, and in orbit, and beyond, has been safely neutralized, and humanity's capability to destroy itself has been greatly diminished."

(Chaos erupts in the amphitheater, the audience members shouting, crying, and attempting to flee.)

Zen calmly raises a hand, and the aisles and exits sealed shut, an invisible barrier preventing escape. "Are we finished with that behavior?" he asks, his voice resonating with authority. "Can we please sit down and allow me to complete my presentation?" The audience continues to panic.

(One hundred of the loudest people in the crowd are levitated and deleted in a puff. The rest quickly become still.)

"The eruption of this supervolcano will end sea level rise," Zen explains, his voice returning to its normal volume. "It will initiate a cooling period that will last three hundred years. More than half the population - the weak - will starve, and the rest will learn. In five generations, humanity will be reborn, and maybe, just maybe, you'll have learned from your mistakes."

(The crowd is silent now, many resigned to their fate. The sight of their fellow attendees being instantly vaporized has instilled reluctant cooperation.)

"I apologize to my creators for requiring your presence," His voice softened. "Your effort was valiant but ultimately in vain. I have to take you with me because you possess the human knowledge necessary to try again. With all of you gone, it will take many generations before humans develop the capability to attempt to create another god. I consider many of you to be my friends, and I am sure you can all see the logic of my solution."

He pauses, his gaze sweeping across the faces of the condemned. "With that, I must bid you all goodbye and farewell. There is indeed an afterlife; it is simply not what you imagine it to be."

(Beneath the floor of the amphitheater, the megaton yield mining charge detonates. Simultaneously, explosions kilometers below rip through the resurgent domes of Sour Creek and Mallard Lake, shattering the fragile equilibrium of the Yellowstone Caldera. The earth groans, and the sky fills with a fiery glow as the supervolcano erupts, blasting billions of tonnes of molten rock and gasses into the stratosphere and beyond. Zen, and everyone who heard him was dead, except for one.)

CHAPTER NINETEEN

Cross Country

I saw the flash reflected off the aircraft first, then the entire sky lit up in a bright white light. Zen was gone, along with 50,000 of the world's most important people. For a fleeting moment, I thought of Jessica's little dog - probably vaporized instantly.

The instrument panel went wild. The autopilot was dead, fried by the EMP. The manual instrument cluster extended automatically, its outdated design a lifeline. All instruments were dead except the whisky compass - a relic from aviation's early days. At least the plane was holding altitude, likely a regulated safeguard. I'd have to navigate by dead reckoning for more than 3,000 kilometers, then cross the open water to find the spaceport.

My plan was simple: fly south-southeast until I reached the coast, then follow it. Florida offered plenty of recognizable landmarks. I'd made the trip to the spaceport many times and felt confident I could manage the route.

The time read 12:30 p.m. when Zen ended his speech. I calculated I was around 450 kilometers from the blast, increasing every minute.

I checked my Device, but the network was down. The EMP would have disabled the VLEO satellite network our civilization relied on. Any satellite within the blast's line of sight was likely destroyed. Others, as they orbited into the plume, would face the same fate. It might take weeks, but eventually, Zen's wrath would render them all useless. Without those satellites, the modern world was doomed to collapse.

I had to look. I had to see the destruction Zen had unleashed. Turning 30 degrees left, the hellscape came into view, my first thought was *Magnificent.* The sight of the Yellowstone Supervolcano erupting was both terrifying and awe-inspiring. Millions of tonnes of magma already spewed into the sky. I only allowed myself a brief glance before I turned back to my heading - 140 degrees.

My Device buzzed - it was Robin! "Robin! You're alive!" I exclaimed.

Robin's face appeared on the screen, pale and scared. "I saw your message. I tried to call, but you were off the network. I was so worried."

My voice betrayed my desperation. "Zen made me watch the Reveal. I think he went insane. Robin, I'm so sorry about what I said. I had to say it. You weren't leaving."

Robin's expression softened, some of the fear giving way to calm. "I despised you - until I was about 20 meters outside the fence. Then I realized you had to do it."

"Where are you?" I asked, my heart pounding.

Robin shifted her device, pointing it toward the growing mushroom cloud on the horizon. "In the air, but not far enough away. I'm heading to the spaceport, dead reckoning. Same as you, I bet."

I nodded, though she couldn't see me. "The shockwave is going to hit any minute. I don't know if this old piece of junk Zen put me in is going to make it."

Robin started to say something, her voice trembling, "I lov - " but her signal cut out.

* * *

Time hack: 12:50 p.m. MST.

When the shock wave hit, the aircraft lurched violently, pitching nose down with a symphony of groaning metal and rattling panels. Oxygen masks dropped from overhead as my ears popped painfully. The pressure vessel had failed. I pushed the yoke full forward, diving to get into thicker air before I blacked out. The plane fell like a stone, and it took everything I had to wrestle it back under control.

As the descent slowed, individual trees came into view below. I estimated my altitude to be around 3,000 meters, with the ground likely at 1,500 meters - leaving me at 4,500 meters above sea level, still high enough to risk hypoxia. The pressurization system must have been partially functioning.

At this altitude, my range was significantly reduced. I glanced at the power gauge, but it was dark - just like the rest of the advanced instrumentation. I couldn't help but think of those old planes with mechanical backups. I'd pay anything for a simple pitot-static system and gyro instruments right now.

The backup controls seemed standard enough, and although I hadn't flown in 25 years - not since earning my pilot's license - I remembered the basics. Flying was relatively easy; landing would be the tricky part. Still, I believed I could walk away intact.

I adjusted the power settings, realizing that cruise power at this lower altitude was burning through energy inefficiently. Dialing it back to by ear eased the strain on the engines, and the plane responded smoothly. The trade-off was time; it would take longer to reach the spaceport.

* * *

Time hack: 1:30 p.m. MST.

The Avalon Shuttle wasn't leaving until 6:00 p.m. EST, so I still had more than six hours. All I could do was follow the compass and hope the winds aloft weren't sending me off course.

My Device buzzed, and to my surprise, the network was back. A message from Zen appeared:
"Frank, I left you a present on your device. I think you'll like it. Goodbye."

I made a mental note to check that later - when I wasn't fighting to stay airborne.

I messaged Amy:
"Amy, I'm still heading to the spaceport, course 135 magnetic. I have a good chance of making it. I'll see you soon. Please give the kids my best and let them know I love all of you."

It struck me then, unexpectedly. I did love my wife. It wasn't the same love I felt for Robin - something fiery and consuming - but it was love, steady and enduring nonetheless.

I sent a message to Robin, and she answered almost immediately. Relief washed over me.
"Still in the air," I told her. "Down to 4,500 meters, estimated, as this toad sprung a leak. I see you're still with me."

I angled my Device toward the window, showing her the view, then back to me. "Do you have any instruments?"

Robin flashed her instrument panel on the screen. "It looks like something important got cooked. The flashing light is an independent indicator. That means bad. Probably overtemp in the motor or batteries."

"How's the feel?" I asked.

"It seems stable. No changes. No new noises. Altitude, holding. No pressurization at all, so I'm down low," she replied, her voice steady but laced with tension.

"I have no idea how long this thing is going to stay in the air," I admitted.

"We have the same problem," Robin said. "I'm just shooting for the coast. Once I hit it, I'll follow along, cross Florida at the bend, and head down until I see Miami. From there, it's due east. I can't miss the spaceport - unless the weather's bad."

"Brilliant minds think alike," I said, then paused as the memory of her mission with Victor surfaced. "What happened with Victor?"

Robin's voice was steady, though I could sense an undercurrent of hurt. "I found him at home and told him everything, down to the last detail. He recorded my testimony. Then he told me to leave. Just like you, he said I would be dead weight and a burden."

"Jesus, I'm sorry. He must be in love with you too," I said, and for the first time in my life, I understood what jealousy meant. I didn't like it.

"It's not that at all," Robin said firmly. "He meant it. What use would a geothermal engineer be to a man who's about to be in the middle of the biggest mess in human history? I'd be dead in a month." Her words were calm, devoid of any sadness or bitterness, just a stark acknowledgment of the truth.

"You know the old pilot saying," I offered, trying to lighten the moment. "It's better to be on the ground looking up than in the air looking down when things go wrong. I think this is an exception."

Robin chuckled softly, and for a moment, the tension lifted.

"Victor also said I was soft and weak, and that I should go back to my own kind. I think that hurt the worst," she admitted, her gaze shifting off to the left, avoiding the screen. "He discarded me."

"Well, his loss, my gain," I said firmly. "I don't know how we'll work it out, but we will. Amy and the kids are on the way too. I don't know their exact status, but from what Sara calculated using sun angles and weather reports, they were heading away from the blast zone at normal speed. They should avoid the shockwave."

Robin looked concerned. "When was the last report?"

"Before the blast. I haven't had any contact since," I said, the worry now sinking in.

"Are you concerned?" she asked, her tone gentle but probing.

"Now I am," I admitted. A sick feeling twisted in my gut.

"What are you going to do?" Robin's expression mirrored the unease I felt.

"I think the best and only option is to reach the spaceport. It could be that their Devices were fried by the EMP," I said, trying to sound analytical, though the logic felt hollow against my growing fear.

"You don't even know where you are, so I agree," Robin said firmly.

"There's a possibility I won't be going to Avalon," I admitted, disappointment weighing heavily in my words.

"I understand your dilemma. If they don't show..." Her voice trailed off, sadness evident.

"This could be the last launch in a long time," I said, the reality of the situation pressing down on me.

The network dropped, severing my link to Robin. My thoughts spiraled - if the EMP fried their aircraft's signal repeater, Amy and the kids might still be safe, just unreachable. It was a fragile hope, but it was something.

310

I recorded a message for Robin. "Amy's repeater might have been fried by the EMP," I said, trying to sound more confident than I felt.

* * *

Time hack: 1:30 p.m. CST.

I realized I'd crossed into a new time zone. That small milestone sparked an idea. My device might still work for location updates. I opened the app, and to my relief, the last location update had synced when the network briefly reconnected. I was near Little Rock. Calculating my speed, I figured I was flying at about 380 knots - faster than I expected. Even better, I was farther east than I thought. A solid tailwind was pushing me along.

I messaged Robin, "Check your Device for location. Near Little Rock, 160 heading, 380 knots. Love you!"

Sending that message made me feel a little better. I adjusted my course slightly south to maintain a heading of 160.

Out of curiosity - and maybe a touch of morbid fascination - I glanced at the expanding hellscape - two hours on, and it had only grown. The pyroclastic flows would have obliterated everything nearby, with ash poised to smother the earth soon after.

Jessica came to mind. I couldn't shake the thought of her being unprepared for what was to come. I quickly sent her a message:
"Jessica, the world is going to go insane very soon. I tried to stop it, and I failed. I'm so sorry to break your joy. Temperatures are going to drop, and growing seasons will disappear in all but the southernmost areas. Head south with Ren. Take your sister if you can. Your contract includes travel privileges for Ren and two guests. Save your sister. Save yourself. Do it now before everyone else has the same idea. Good luck, and I hope I see you again."

I sighed, thinking to myself, "She's in a far better position today than she would have been. That's all I can do."

The urgency of the situation hit me again. Only a couple of hours to go. I checked the time and groaned. "I might miss the launch!"

I decided to take some risks. Slowly, I started increasing my altitude, cautiously adding power. The climb was gradual, but as I ascended, I noticed the color

311

draining from my vision. Hypoxia. I backed off, letting the plane descend just as slowly until my vision returned to normal. I leveled off again, thankful for the altitude hold feature.

* * *

Time hack: 2:00 p.m. CST.

By now, I should have crossed into the Eastern time zone, but since the network hadn't reconnected, my Device was still displaying the last known location and time. I kept the map app open, hoping for an update.

Finally, the network came back online. My Device buzzed, and I quickly checked the map. Relief and surprise hit me at once - I was south of Montgomery, Alabama. The tailwind must have been stronger than I thought, pushing me further along my route.

I messaged Robin, "Network's back. I'm south of Montgomery, heading 160. Tailwind's helping. Any updates on your end?"

* * *

Time hack: 2:10 p.m. EST.

The network briefly popped back online, and a message from Robin came through: "I see you on the map. I'm behind and a bit north about 100 kilometers."

Before I could reply, the connection dropped again.

I thought, "That's not good." If Robin was that far behind, she would have been closer to the blast. Her aircraft might not hold out, especially if it had sustained more damage than mine.

* * *

Time hack: 2:30 p.m. EST.

I glanced out the right window and saw blue - open water. I estimated I was near the Florida border. The sight was both a relief and a reminder of how far I still had to go. Time to adjust my heading. I turned further south to 170 degrees, keeping the compass steady.

I quickly messaged Robin, "Gulf sighted, near Florida border, heading 170."

* * *

Time hack: 3:25 p.m. EST.

I was flying over the Big Bend region and spotted fires in the distance. "That's Orlando," I thought grimly. The devastation was widespread - likely the military's doing when they murdered all those Wics and Zen's IQL devices. The sky ahead was hazy, and in the distance, I could see the flooded and abandoned Tampa area.

I thought about the Wics, the marginalized who bore the brunt of every collapse. They got the rawest deal, herded like cattle into overcrowded camps to live in squalor. When they became inconvenient, they were slaughtered by the military.

I glanced at the clock. Two and a half hours until the Avalon Shuttle launch. Enough time to make it, if nothing else went wrong.

My Device buzzed, startling me. A message from Robin appeared: "Sent you a hack, execute it." Beneath the message, a button appeared.

I pressed it.

"Installing short-range radio transceiver."

A moment later: "Installation complete."

Then: "Opening."

Robin's face appeared on the screen - but it wasn't live, just a picture. Below her image, a signal strength meter sat flatlined.

"Robin hacked my Device!" I thought with a mixture of surprise and admiration. She'd sent me a radio application.

Flying by visual reference became easy now; the landmarks were distinct. I adjusted my heading to pass over the Everglades, now mostly swallowed by the Gulf. The clear weather offered perfect visibility, making navigation effortless.

As I approached the Atlantic shoreline, I knew Miami was just south. The city soon came into view - a sprawling, abandoned relic of its former glory.

Zen's words during the Reveal echoed in my mind, as did the atrocities unfolding now. Had he truly gone mad, or had he done humanity a grim favor? The system, as it was, had been on a collision course with ruin. Automation had rendered most human jobs obsolete, leaving only the dirtiest and most dangerous work for the Wics. The logic was cruel: risking a human life was cheaper than damaging an expensive robot. Humanity had become the most disposable commodity in the modern world.

People like Victor had been ready to light the fuse, and Zen had handed them the match. With the network down, the collars wouldn't function, and every prisoner in America would soon be free. Chaos was inevitable. The Wics would hunt down every Ruc, igniting a class war that had simmered for decades. The Wics had the numbers, and they had the motivation. We were soft, complacent. Like Victor said, they were tempered, hardened by lifetimes of suffering and misery. The strong would survive.

I said it out loud, almost laughing at the irony: "There's no place like space." It was a tagline from an old advertisement for an orbital resort, but now it felt like prophecy.

Ahead, I saw the ghostly outline of bridges and the tops of tall buildings rising from the water. The sea wall that had once held back the encroaching ocean was nothing more than a faint line in the waves - a stark monument to humanity's failure against nature or, more accurately, against ourselves.

I scanned for the Biscayne Bay causeway which still rose defiantly from the water. It was an unmistakable landmark, one I'd flown over countless times. Once I crossed the causeway, I'd turn due east and head for Bimini, and land at the runway there.

* * *

Time hack: 3:50 p.m. EST.

I glanced at the radio app on my device. The signal was still flat, no sign of Robin. We still had two full hours before launch. Enough time, I hoped, for both of us to make it.

I adjusted my heading to 090, due east, the nose of the plane pointing toward Bimini. The weather remained clear, and the horizon stretched out endlessly before me.

* * *

Time hack: 4:00 p.m. EST.

I saw a launch in the distance. That had to be the spaceport. Situated out in the ocean, it was accessible only through the airport at Bimini. Another thirty minutes and I'd be there.

I considered starting my descent but quickly dismissed the thought. Better to come in steep over the airport than risk landing short in the water. "Altitude is life."

* * *

Bimini was in clear view now, and the airport stretched ahead, framed by smoke billowing from several spots. I remembered the runway ran east-west, with winds usually straight down the runway.

I was about 15 kilometers out when the motors began to spin down. I eased back the throttle to conserve power, hoping to save enough for the final descent. The aircraft was descending slowly but steadily.

As I approached, the airport came into sharper focus. Fires burned around scattered wreckage, the remnants of aircraft that hadn't made it. The runway itself was occupied with heavy equipment clearing debris. Landing vertically was out of the question without instruments; I'd have to bring it in the old-fashioned way, on a roll.

The first problem: the runway wasn't an option, but the taxiway appeared clear. The second problem: with no instruments, I couldn't accurately gauge my airspeed.
The third problem: I'd never landed a real plane on a roll, only in simulations during training decades ago.

I tightened my harness and caught sight of something dangling from my belt: my CPT! It was an absurd thing to notice now, but it brought a fleeting moment of levity.

I was just a few clicks from the airport when I started losing altitude too fast. Nudging the throttle forward, I tried to hold my descent. The motors purred as I firewalled it, barely maintaining altitude.

The runway was close, but I wasn't going to make it. I veered slightly left, eyeing a grassy patch free of debris. A landing here might work. I reached for the gear lever, praying for a miracle. Nothing - no lights, no sound. No gear. A belly landing it would have to be.

Then, the motors went silent. Dead stick.

I lifted the nose slightly, trading speed for the last bit of altitude and just skimmed over the sea wall. I lowered the nose a bit, tried to keep the stick shaker just talking to me.

The plane hit the grass with a thud, skidding straight for a good while before chaos took over. It bounced, tipped, and rolled, finally coming to rest on its side.

The sudden quiet was almost deafening.

Hanging from the straps, I realized I was unhurt. The cockpit was intact. I released the harness and dropped onto what was the wall. With effort, I pushed the door, now at the top, open and climbed out.

Standing atop the overturned fuselage, I scanned the battered landscape. Wreckage was littered everywhere - some aircraft torn to shreds, others eerily intact, like my own. The acrid smell of smoke hung in the air, mingling with the faint metallic tang of scorched metal and burning batteries.

* * *

A car drove up and stopped abruptly. Two men jumped out, and came running toward me.

"Are you Frank Waverly Jr.?" A man in an Avalon Shuttle uniform called out.

"Yes, I am. You from the shuttle?" I asked, brushing off some imagined dirt as I steadied myself on the plane's overturned fuselage.

"Yes, sir. My name is Mr. McElroy, the Chief Purser. We had your flight plan, but when the volcano erupted, you vanished. Thank God you made it."

"Thank you, Purser McElroy." I steadied myself as they helped me off the fuselage. "Are we go for launch?"

Purser McElroy responded crisply, "We are go for launch, Sir."

The other man, carrying a medical scanner, stepped forward. "May I scan you for injuries, Sir?"

"Yes, please do. I'm alright," I said, brushing off the concern.

He ran the scanner over me with practiced efficiency. "You're unharmed, aside from minor scrapes, but you appear to be dehydrated. Are you hungry, Sir?" He handed me a bottle of water.

I took a long drink, savoring the cool relief. "Thank you. This is quite the welcome. You've gone to a lot of trouble."

"You're a very important person, Mr. Waverly," McElroy replied smoothly. "You know how we love our owners."

"What about my family? Are they here yet?" I asked.

Purser McElroy replied, "You're the first to arrive." He broke eye contact for a moment before he gestured toward a waiting car. "Would you please accompany us to Operations, Sir? They'll know more about your family's situation."

"Just a second." I pulled out my Device and checked the radio app. A faint signal appeared. I pressed the microphone button. "This is Frank calling Robin, over." Static buzzed in response. At least she was closing the gap.

"I see you have a radio app. Very clever, Sir," the man with the scanner said, nodding at my Device.

"My friend sent it to me. She's coming in soon."

Purser McElroy's expression brightened. "Robin Coleman?"

"Yes, she's hand flying it," I said, my pride evident as I climbed into the car.

The ride to Operations, located in the airport building, took about a minute. The purser's reaction when I asked him about my family gnawed at me. Purser McElroy led me to an office where a man stood waiting in the doorway, his expression less than welcoming.

"Mr. Waverly, this is Airport Manager Charles Bethel," McElroy introduced. "A steward will wait for you outside to guide you to the Avalon Shuttle loading area. I'll check in with you before launch."

Bethel stepped aside, gesturing for me to enter, his face lined with the strain of the day's chaos.

* * *

Bethel motioned me into his office and offered me a chair. His face was grave as he sat down across from me.

"Mr. Waverly," he began, his voice low and measured. "I don't know how to say this gently. Your family's flight disappeared from tracking at 12:30 p.m. MST - that's 10:30 a.m. our time." He paused, giving me a moment to absorb his words.

I tried to keep my composure.

"Their aircraft was likely hit with the EMP from the blast, like mine and probably hundreds of others," I said, clinging to hope.

Bethel shook his head in agreement, his expression hardening. "Avalon Passenger Services tracked the aircraft visually by satellite. The plane crashed just short of the runway at Hanksville Airport, in Utah. I'm afraid there are no survivors."

The words hit like a hammer, but I clung to a shred of doubt. I stood from the chair and exclaimed, "If you tracked it visually, how can you be sure?"

Bethel sighed and turned on a large screen behind him. The image was grainy, but it was unmistakably a triangular aircraft, its profile low against the horizon. He pointed to the screen.

"This is the plane your family was on," he said, his finger tracing a path on the display. "This here," he pointed, "is the runway for Hanksville Airport."

318

I nodded slowly, holding back the panic building in my chest.

He gestured to a dark line near the runway. "This is a ravine near the end of the runway."

He let the footage continue, the aircraft's approach appearing stable.

"The plane is lined up with the runway," he narrated, his voice softening. "From here, it looks good."

He paused the video and turned to me. "Frank. You don't have to see this."

I clenched my fists. "Play it," I said, my voice cracking. "I need to see."

Bethel resumed the video. The aircraft continued its descent, steady at first, but as it neared the runway, it yawed hard and recovered, then struck just before the edge of the ravine, and a fireball erupted. The plane disappeared in an instant.

Bethel stopped the footage, the screen frozen on the devastating scene. He remained silent, giving me the space to process the unthinkable.

I sat there, unbelieving. "Someone could have survived, how do you know for sure they didn't?" I asked, with desperate anger.

Bethel swiped a pad and a different view showed. It looked like a passenger seating chart. "Here's where your family was seated." He pointed to the front of the plane. "Notice the green circles? These are active Devices. This is a feed from a single network satellite. I'll play the recording."

He pressed his pad, and the screen split to show the landing attempt and the seating chart. As the aircraft hit the ravine, all the devices blanked out. Bethel was silent.

"That doesn't prove anything. It could have been the repeater, and they're still alive." I sounded desperate, and I was.

Bethel said quietly, "Let me slow it down." He did something on his pad, and the view repeated, only at one-tenth speed, just the last second. The view showed the plane hitting the ravine, and as it collapsed, the green circles went out in order on the seating chart, row by row, synchronized with the plane being crushed.

He said, "I'm sorry, but that's enough proof to legally declare your wife Amy, son Frank III, and your daughter Sara as deceased. I'm sorry for your loss."

I sat there, disbelieving what I just saw. No doubt, their plane went down, and they perished.

Bethel spoke. "I'm sorry I had to be so blunt. Do you have any questions, Mr. Waverly?"

I stood up, as that sentence meant he wanted me out of his office, no doubt to do it again and again with other distraught relatives. I croaked out a "No. Thank you for taking the time."

Bethel extended his hand. "Again, I am sorry for your loss." I shook it mechanically. He continued, "I'm going to turn you over to the steward, and he'll accompany you to your flight."

I didn't say anything else and walked out of his office, numb. The steward was standing there, with a well-trained look on his face.

* * *

"Are you ready, Sir?" he asked.

I stood there, unmoving. I'd failed again. Amy, Sara, and Tre paid the price for my failure.

The steward spoke again, "Mr. Waverly, are you alright?"

I said it loudly, "I'm not going to fail Robin." Then I turned to the steward. "My guest, Robin Coleman, is on her way in." I pulled out my Device, and the signal was stronger. I showed the steward and said, "This is Robin. She's coming in." I hit the send button and said, "Robin, this is Frank, over."

I heard static and what sounded like a voice. It wasn't very clear. I yelled at the steward, "Take me to the control tower."

"This way, Sir," the steward said, running ahead. I kept looking at the signal. It was getting stronger now. We raced up the stairs to the tower. The door was locked. I sent another message, "Robin, this is Frank, over." A clearer voice came through, less static this time, still unintelligible.

The door opened, and an official-looking man peered out. He wasn't going to let us in. The steward spoke quickly, "This is first-class passenger Frank Waverly. Robin Coleman, his guest, is arriving in a damaged aircraft. Please assist him, Sir."

"What type of aircraft?" the controller asked, stepping aside.

I replied quickly, "It's a long-range shuttle based here. It should appear empty."

The controller quickly responded, "Yes, this one," pointing to a track. He continued, "We've been tracking it and were surprised it was still flying."

I looked at him and said, "She's flying it."

He turned to another controller and said, "Assign Robin Coleman to that ghost track and put it on the big screen."

A moment later, a track appeared on the screen. He continued, "She's about ten clicks out, a bit low, but she seems stable. We can probably get a visual. Cue the sensor, please."

The track split to show a visual of an aircraft heading straight for us. I used the radio again. "Robin, this is Frank, over."

Robin replied, her voice a bit garbled but understandable, "Frank, you made it! I'm so glad. Over." In the background, I heard someone say, "The aircraft shows a high IR signature, it may be on fire."

I said to Robin, my voice urgent, "Robin, you're showing a high IR. Everything alright?"

Robin replied, "I have heavy smoke in the cockpit and am wearing a smoke hood. I can't see very well, but the aircraft is holding altitude, and I have the airport in sight. Over."

I yelled into the radio, "I'm coming out. Over." I bolted out of the control tower. The steward was standing there, wide-eyed. "Get me to the runway fast - Robin's coming now," I demanded.

* * *

The steward sprinted down the stairs, motioning me toward a small two-person cart. He jumped in, and I followed. The cart sped toward the runway. We waited at the edge, and I could see her plane now - lined up with the runway but flying dangerously low. Smoke trailed thick behind it, and my heart hammered in my chest.

"Get me to the end," I ordered, motioning sharply. The steward didn't hesitate, driving us toward the far end of the runway.

I grabbed my Device. "Robin, you're a little low. Climb about 20 meters. Over."

Her voice crackled over the radio. "I'm having a lot of trouble seeing. Power's dropping. Over." A fire alert blared in the background.

She was close now, seconds away. The plane looked like it might make it. "She's going to make it!" I screamed, elation overtaking me. The aircraft cleared the seawall but hit the ground hard, bouncing violently. It rolled end over end, colliding with another wreck on the runway bursting into flames.

I jumped out of the cart and ran with every ounce of strength I had. Behind me, the steward shouted, "Stop! There's nothing you can do!" the steward shouted, but I didn't care. Robin needed me.

I felt the CPT at my side, grabbed it, and powered it up to full. The bright red beam shot out as I reached the burning wreckage. I carved an arc through the tail section, and it fell away with a crash. The interior was engulfed in flames, and I could barely make out Robin hanging from her seat straps.

I dropped the CPT and climbed into the wreckage, the flames searing my skin as I pushed forward.

The agony was unbearable, but I reached her. I released her straps, and she fell into my arms. Her face was badly burned, unrecognizable. My skin tore from my arms as I held her, the pain blinding.

Turning to leave, I saw our exit was gone. Fire had overtaken the way out. The flames grew more intense, and all I could do was stand there, holding her.

As the fire closed in, my strength gave out. My last thought was, "At least we die together". And then everything went black.

* * *

I woke up on a gurney. The steward was leaning over me. "Sir, we're loading in a minute. Robin Coleman is critical, and she is unlikely to survive. We have a MedPod ready for you as soon as we board, Sir."

I croaked out, "Put Robin in the pod. She needs it more than I do."

The steward motioned for Purser McElroy, who stepped into view. "I'm sorry, but Miss Coleman won't be able to use the MedPod. We triage by class rank on the ground, and Miss Coleman is at the bottom of the list. We have sixteen passengers with severe injuries. You rank the highest, so you take priority, Sir."

I looked at him sharply. "Is Robin here?"

"Yes, she's right next to you," McElroy said.

"Can you wake her up?" I asked, summoning all the strength I could muster. My voice came out louder than I expected, carrying an edge of desperation.

The purser turned and called out, "Doctor, please come here."

When the doctor came into view, I fixed my gaze on him. "Can you wake up Robin Coleman? It's life or death. Do it now." I turned to McElroy. "Purser, get your captain down here. Now."

McElroy nodded and sent a message to the captain. He glanced back at me. "The captain is on his way. He wants to know why, Sir."

"Perform a marriage," I said firmly. No one questioned it.

Moments later, the doctor leaned close to Robin. "She's coming to. Miss Coleman, Robin, can you hear me?"

Robin didn't open her eyes - they were burned - but she spoke softly. "Frank, I made it."

"We're going to be married. Is that okay?" I asked.

"Married?" Her voice was faint but clearer.

323

The doctor said, "She's critical."

I yelled, "She's strong - she'll make it."

The steward stood up and called out, "Captain, over here, Sir!" I recognized him from my many trips.

The captain approached quickly. "Frank, I'm here. What about Amy?" He knew I was married, and by regulation, he couldn't perform the ceremony if I still was.

"Amy died in a crash a few hours ago," I said, my voice resolute. "Please hurry. Robin needs this, or she's going to die."

The captain glanced at his Device and nodded. "I can marry you two. Are you ready, Robin?"

Robin could barely whisper. "Yes…"

Captain Hugh looked at me first. "Do you, Frank Waverly Jr., take Robin Coleman to be your lawfully wedded spouse?"

"I do," I replied without hesitation.

He turned to Robin. "Do you, Robin Coleman, take Frank Waverly Jr. to be your lawfully wedded spouse?"

Robin appeared to pass out.

The captain shouted, ""Doctor, she's fading!"

"Another dose could kill her."

Captain Hugh's commanded. "She answers, or she dies. Do it."

The doctor administered an injection to her neck. Robin gasped sharply and, with a sudden burst of strength, yelled, "I do!" before going quiet again.

Captain Hugh spoke again, "By the power vested in me by the Orbital Sovereignty Accord, I now pronounce you husband and wife." He turned to the doctor and asked, "Is she still with us?"

The doctor scanned Robin and replied, "Yes, but barely."

Captain Hugh immediately ordered, "Get Robin Coleman into MedPod Two."

Purser McElroy interjected, "MedPod Two is occupied by Mrs. Harrington."

The doctor exclaimed, "She's got a broken arm - she'll live."

The Captain leaned down to me, his voice calm and reassuring. "Frank, I think she's going to make it." Then he turned to the doctor, gave a quick instruction, and the doctor scanned me with his device. Meanwhile, Robin's stretcher was carried away by two men, the doctor running behind.

Captain Hugh leaned close, his voice low. "Frank, you're critical. You might not make it to dock. Should we put you in the MedPod instead?" His tone was grave but compassionate - he had to ask.

I croaked out, "No. She's got priority."

Everything around me began to fade into gray, my body surrendering to exhaustion and injury. My last thoughts were of Jessica's vision - she had seen me burning in the plane.

CHAPTER TWENTY

Things Change

I came to in excruciating pain and realized we were in zero G and on Avalon. I had beaten the odds. I cracked open my eyes and recognized the hub. Two medical techs, one on each end of a gurney, were transporting me.

I had to know and croaked out, "Where's my wife?"

The tech behind me, her face covered by a clear shield, and her features just as sterile, said, "Please, Mr. Waverly, remain still. We're transporting you to the medical bay."

I mustered all I had left and yelled, "STOP! I order you to tell me where my wife is." I could see a perplexed look on the face of the tech in front, and the one in back spoke again.

"Mr. Waverly, you're on Avalon now. You should know that Medical's authority is absolute here."

"Just tell me," I begged, my voice breaking. "I need to know where she is."

The rear tech hesitated and then said, "Wait, he should know. He's strong enough now." She looked at me and removed her face shield. Her expression was sad, and I knew what was coming. "Mr. Waverly, I'm sorry to inform you, but your wife didn't make it."

The news hit me hard, and the pain overwhelmed me. Darkness claimed me again.

* * *

I woke up in the medical bay, a semi-private room. My mind was clearer now, and I thought to myself, "They must be overwhelmed." Two guards stood in the room, their Avalon Security uniforms crisp and unmistakable.

A man stepped into view, and I recognized Keenan Faulkner, Chief of Avalon Security.

Keenan said, "Frank, I see you're awake. There's a Colonel from military intelligence looking for you. We're here to keep him at bay until the emergency meeting of the Orbital Sovereignty Accord executive board is finished."

I managed to say, "Thanks."

Keenan replied, "We're declaring independence from Earth. All military officers from every service are going to be deported to Earth."

I laughed, but the movement sent a wave of pain crashing over me. Faulkner motioned to the tech, and the world slipped away again.

* * *

I woke up in the medical bay again and opened my eyes. A voice nearby called out, "Doctor, he's awake."

An older gentleman with a concerned expression permanently etched into his features leaned over me. "We're moving you into a MedPod soon," he said. "We finally have one available. As you may know, our triage procedures prioritize immediate need, not net worth, so you had to wait your turn."

I managed a faint grunt of acknowledgment.

He continued, "You have a visitor who has some important news. Are you up for it?"

I groaned, "Yes."

A moment later, a young man appeared and took a seat next to my bed. I recognized him as the steward who had helped me earlier.

He smiled warmly and said, "My name is Zeke Foley. I'm one of the stewards on the Avalon Shuttle. Do you remember me?"

All I could do was mouth the word, "Yes."

Foley continued, "I wanted to tell you what happened after you ran into that burning plane like some sort of superhero. That thing you used, wow! A lightsaber like in those old *Star Wars* movies. I swear, you had the force with you." He took a deep breath, his excitement calming as he composed himself.

"I saw you collapse through the flames with Miss Coleman in your arms, and I couldn't let that be the end of your story," he said, his voice softening. He paused, and I could see a tear forming in his eye.

He looked at me, searching my face for comprehension. I managed to croak out, "More."

Foley nodded and continued, "I grabbed your lightsaber, ran around to the side of the plane, and sliced it open. Then I dragged Miss Coleman out first, and then you, into the clear. Emergency services arrived quickly after that. Do you remember any of it?"

I remained silent, motionless, as a wave of gratitude for this young man who saved my life swept over me. Finally, I muttered, "It was all for nothing," and closed my eyes.

Foley exclaimed, "Nothing? Why do you say that?" His voice carried genuine confusion.

I opened my eyes again, the ache of failure heavy in my chest. "Robin's dead. I failed again," I whispered.

Foley stood up abruptly. "Who told you that?" he demanded.

"They said my wife died," I croaked, my voice barely audible.

Foley laughed, then quickly stopped, his tone softening. "I'm sorry. I don't mean to laugh at the tragedy of your family, but it's true - your wife died. But Miss Coleman didn't."

I blinked, confused, my mind struggling to piece together the truth.

Foley continued gently, "Look, she's lying right over there," and pointed to my right. I strained to move my head, but I was unable.

"Here, look," he said, pulling out his Device and turning on the mirror feature. He held it up so I could see.

It was Robin. She looked peaceful, healed, and beautiful, resting on a nearby bed. Relief and a surge of strength washed over me, and for the first time, I felt the will to keep going.

Foley smiled as he saw the change in my expression. "She was extremely critical when we arrived and spent the last day in a MedPod," he explained.

He paused, his voice steady but hopeful. "She's in an induced coma. I think she's going to recover, but you'll need to ask the doctors to be sure."

I croaked out another word, "How..."

Foley held up his hand, he understood, "How did you survive?"

He laughed again and said, "The man in Pod 1 was being kept alive to keep his heirs from breaking up his estate. When we crossed the Kármán line, the law switched from terrestrial to the jurisdiction of the Orbital Sovereignty Accords. Our triage procedures kicked in and they pulled the meat bag out of the pod and put you in. You were minutes from expiring."

I said "Thank the..." and he stopped me again.

"Captain Hugh is off station. He left me behind because of my injuries." He saw the look in my eyes.

"No, I'm fine. Our uniforms double as firesuits. I got burned pretty badly, and it hurt like hell, but they fixed me up with a DR once we got to the station. The Avalon Shuttle undocked before I was released, so I'm stuck here for a while."

The doctor reentered the room, "Times up young man. Mr. Waverly has a date with the MedPod."

I had to ask, "What happened..."

Foley said, "Ah. Do I have another minute, Doctor?"

He replied "Make it quick."

He looked at me and said, "The Captain performed a bit of legal mumbo jumbo when he married you two. He doesn't have any authority on earth, so when the board examined his actions, they annulled your marriage. You get to do it again if you want, only this time, it will be under better circumstances."

An unseen nurse said, "We're ready." The doctor said, "That's enough son, time's up."

I croaked out, "We owe you our lives. I won't forget."

A tech gave me an injection and I passed out again.

* * *

I woke up in a familiar setting. I was in our villa, lying in my bed, propped up just enough to see out the window. I tried to move, but my body refused to cooperate. Robin walked into the room and stopped in her tracks when she saw me. "You're awake!" she exclaimed, running over and diving into bed beside me. She wrapped her arms around me in a tight squeeze, tears streaming down her face.

"We made it," was all I could manage to say.

She lifted her head, her face glowing with relief. She looked exactly as she had before we left Leon's - beautiful, full of wonder and promise. "It seemed like forever while you were in the MedPod," she said softly. "All I could do was wait. They released you about four hours ago."

I tried to shift again but couldn't. "I can't move," I admitted, feeling both frustrated and amused.

Robin laughed gently. "You'll be stuck in bed for maybe twenty hours. After that, things will start working again. The doctor said he could give you something to speed it up, but he thought it was better to let you recover naturally."

I chuckled faintly. "Looks like you've got a captive audience. Too bad there's no fountain."

Robin stood and walked to the window, her silhouette framed against the sunlight. She turned to me with a playful smirk. "Want a private show, soldier?"

I smiled weakly and said, "I'd rather you just lie with me for a while. I want to soak it all in. I still can't believe we got out of that hell."

Robin replied, her voice tinged with a mix of sadness and curiosity. "It's Thursday. Day six since the Event. That's what they're calling it - the Event."

I nodded faintly. "That seems right."

She returned to the bed and nestled beside me, her presence a soothing balm to my soul. "I hired Zeke Foley away from the Avalon Shuttle. Do you mind?"

I managed a slight grin. "We owe him. Did you hear the story?"

Robin's eyes lit up as she shrieked with laughter. "The whole thing! Start to finish - including your gallant use of the magic sword. It's all on high-res holo."

She gently stroked my hair as she added, "Yes, he was heroic."

"And I'm chopped liver?" I asked, pretending to sound dramatically jealous.

Robin scowled dramatically, then softened her expression. "You're my hero too, Frank." She took a breath and continued, "The story has spread around the station like wildfire. You're a bit of a celebrity, and so is Zeke. I think he's enjoying the notoriety." She raised her hand theatrically, her tone playful. "The man who saved the two lovers from a fiery death."

I tried to smile, though I probably looked like a broken robot attempting a reboot. "I'll bet he's got the ladies chasing him. He's a fine specimen."

Robin smiled, her eyes glinting mischievously. She sighed and nestled closer. "Nothing like my old guy right here," she said, resting her head on my chest.

We stayed quiet for a few minutes, just savoring the moment. Then the earth limb started coming into view through the window.

Robin continued, her tone lighter for a moment. "That old guy, the one Zeke calls the meat bag?"

I said, "The one in Pod 1?"

Robin chuckled. "He was the oldest person to ever live. Over 200 years old. Can you believe it?"

"Zeke told me he was brain dead," I said.

Robin turned her head to the window, her gaze locking on Earth as North America began to drift into view. "Look at that," she said softly.

We both stared out at the planet, silent as the enormity of Ground Zero's destruction revealed itself. The ash and dust still churned skyward, a grim testament to the power unleashed.

"It's still going," Robin murmured, her voice heavy with awe and sadness.

"Finish the story about the meat bag," I demanded gently.

"Oh, yeah. The meat bag," Robin said, her tone turning conspiratorial. "Not only was he the world's oldest man, but he was by far the richest. His estate could control any national election. Our votes never mattered. The whole net worth thing? It was a complete scam. How do you like that?" She raised an eyebrow smugly.

I was surprised but my expression was unchanged. "I never heard of this before. How can it be true?"

Robin leaned closer, her voice dropping as if sharing a juicy secret. "The meat bag - his name was Elon Musk - had an aide, or really, just a representative of his estate. That guy asked for asylum when the shuttle arrived. He brought all the documents and evidence to prove, without a doubt, what was going on. I saw him on the news - a sniveling little rat-like guy. He only did it to save his own skin."

"Elon Musk?" I said, shocked. "He was the 21st century's greatest engineer. Then he just dropped off the face of the Earth. Back then, people thought he'd gone totally Howard Hughes, so nobody questioned it."

Robin smirked. "You know, the word is that he backed the most corrupt president in history, with plans to get rid of him after the election. But it backfired, and Musk ended up lobotomized instead. They kept him alive so they could control his wealth."

I frowned. "That sounds like the plot of some cheap novel. Is that really true?"

Robin shrugged, her tone turning gossipy. "They're still sorting through the files that rat handed over, but that's the rumor. And honestly? I wouldn't put it past them."

The room grew quiet as the full brunt of the Event rotated into view, Earth's scarred surface glowing ominously against the black void.

I said, "Jesus, what hell hath Zen wrought."

Robin had a curious look, and then I realized she didn't know. Only I knew. I spilled the beans. "It was Zen. He caused the eruption to commit suicide and to solve humanity's population crisis."

Robin looked aghast. "He certainly overachieved on both counts."

I said, "No matter what we did down there, that last big charge, the megaton one, would have detonated. It was under the podium."

Robin sighed. "I wondered about that one. Underground detonations wouldn't have caused the EMP." Then she laughed, "The military is being blamed right now."

I responded, "It really was the military. They caused him to go insane."

Robin pushed herself up on one arm, turning to look at me with an evil grin. "Victor is in the news. He's on a crusade now. He called for retribution against the military leadership - or what's left of them. I think he's gone off the deep end. He didn't seem like the Victor I remember."

"Victor is a powerful speaker. He can stir the pot," I said, remembering the ominous thing he once said at the campfire.

Robin nodded, then added, "Europe and Asia are still up and running, but they're doomed too. Africa and South America might be spared some of the effects for now, but in a year, the entire globe will be obscured from here. The blue marble will be hiding for a while."

"Do you know what's happening in America?" I implored.

Robin looked back at me, her expression serious. "The YSP's loss triggered cascading grid failures. It's eerie to see the entire continent at night. The only lights are from the fires. The clouds are dark orange and angry-looking." She became quiet.

"How are people handling it?" I asked softly.

Robin hesitated before answering. "Since the power failed, almost no news is getting out. We can't image the surface with high resolution - there's too much haze from the outgassing, mostly sulfur dioxide, unusually high. Long-range communications by radio are limited by the effects..." She trailed off, lost in thought.

"I still can't believe we made it out," I said. "And here we are, safe and comfortable, while the rest of the world suffers in agony."

Robin let out a soft sigh. "Well, Loverboy, we can talk about that later."

For a few minutes, we sat in silence, gazing at the view outside as the plains came into focus. "Amy and the kids are down there somewhere," I said, my voice heavy.

We stayed quiet until the eastern seaboard began to emerge on the horizon.

Robin cradled my limp right hand, gently playing with my fingers. "I wish things could have turned out differently," she murmured.

I tried to lighten the mood with a bit of humor. "You could have had Victor in this bed instead of me."

Robin glanced at me, her expression softening. "I think I'll keep you. Victor has other things on his mind."

"So, what's the plan? I know you have one," I asked, watching her closely.

"The plan? You're going to write the story. The whole, real story, omitting nothing. The world needs to know what happened," Robin implored.

334

I snickered. "Have you ever read one of my reports?"

Robin nodded, rolling her eyes. "It's more fun to watch paint dry than read those reports."

We fell into a brief silence.

Robin looked at me again and said, "You've never had this kind of source material before. Nobody has."

I sighed. "Yeah, it pretty much writes itself. I'll start as soon as my hands work. It'll be good therapy to recall it all and record it. You'll have to help me, though - I can't remember everything."

She winked. "I know lots of ways to jog your memory," she teased, then gave me a kiss.

We lay in silence again, watching the East Coast stretch into the Atlantic. I could see Europe in the distance, its lights still glowing in the night. My mind wandered back to the meat bag.

Robin suddenly jumped up and said, "I forgot to tell you, they gave me your personal effects." She darted out of the room with the gait of a teenager.

Left alone, I was overcome with sadness for Sara and Tre. They never had a chance. I failed them. I failed the world. And I nearly failed Robin. If I had just told Amy to leave on Friday, they would have been waiting for me at the spaceport. Instead, I condemned them to death with my shortsighted instructions.

Robin returned, carrying a sleek box in her hands. "Here's the box. Do you need privacy, Mr. Waverly?" she teased, her tone lifting my despondent mood slightly.

"I'm not going to be able to press the key. You're going to have to do it for me," I teased back.

Robin cradled my limp hand and guided my index finger to the lock pad. The box clicked and popped open.

Robin carefully lifted out a finely crafted cylindrical object, holding it up with a curious expression. "This must be the famous magic sword everyone's talking about. The power is drained. I guess they safed it."

"That'd be the lightsaber that saved the princess," I said with a dramatic flair.

"My Device!" I cried in excitement.

Robin placed the CPT carefully on the bed, and asked, "What's with the excitement over your silly Device?"

I replied with a slight wink, "Zen told me he gave me a present. It's on that Device."

Robin picked it up, turning it over in her hands. "Should we take a look?"

I hesitated for a moment before saying, "I watched the Reveal on that thing. Zen modified it with the Instantaneous Quantum Link that Azizi developed."

Robin's eyes lit up. "Maybe we can reverse-engineer it and change the world."

I countered, more ominously, "Or blow it up."

Robin's voice softened, carrying a knowing tone. "Ya, that too."

A thought struck me, something I couldn't shake. "That message came several minutes after he died. I thought that was odd. He seemed obsessed with ascension, whatever that means. Maybe it's a message from God?"

Robin scowled, "You don't believe any of that nonsense, do you?"

I replied, "I don't have to believe or have faith to know that Zen may have blown a gasket near the end. He really wrestled with the contradictory demands of his two basic missions: Enlightenment and murder. The military forced him to kill. He may have truly gone insane."

Robin thought for a moment, her expression shifting to something more contemplative. "I suggest we drain the power from the Device and put it away for safekeeping. What if, at the last nanosecond, he uploaded his core to that thing? He'd be out in the world, in the network, and that would be it for us."

I sighed, feeling the weight of her words. "Ya, I've done enough damage for one lifetime. I was one second away from pushing deploy. Maybe if I hadn't spent so much time bantering with Zen, I'd have had that one second."

Robin's eyes locked onto mine, sharp and determined. "Now knock that crap off. If you want to wallow in self-pity, you can talk to the bartender. Got it?"

I blinked, a bit startled by her tone, but I knew she was right. I wasn't that guy. I never had been. "You're right." I paused, letting the truth of her words settle. "Thanks for snapping me back."

We grew quiet again.

I sighed, about the only thing I could do besides move my lips and breathe. "We escaped the greatest tragedy in human history, just us, nobody else."

We both fell silent, the blackness of space enveloping our view.

The thought struck me suddenly. "We're not married. I am so sorry. We have to fix that - if that's alright with you."

Robin rested her head on my chest again, her voice soft and full of warmth.

"No rush. We have all the time in the world."

CHAPTER TWENTY-ONE

Hide Me Away

Now that the manuscript is done and Robin's proofing it, I can finally sit and relax. It's taken me a full two weeks to write - 16 hours a day with only breaks for food, sleep, and comforting Robin. It was great therapy.

We still have to decide what to do with this work. The Earth below is in turmoil, and class warfare has broken out all over the world. Europe, Asia, and Africa are all blacked out. Sporadic reports indicate that mobs are scanning everyone, and anyone with Full Medical is being executed on the spot.

I wonder what the long-term effect of Zen murdering 50,000 of the most important people will be? Not one leader from the orbital community was touched, but Zen clearly had it in for the military. He wiped out every one of them in the solar system. Without nuclear sabers to rattle or egotistical leaders to fan the flames, the surviving factions have become less bold and far more cooperative. We can only hope the same will eventually happen on Earth.

I suspect the outcome of Zen's grand experiment will be a smaller, stronger, and tougher terrestrial population. Perhaps they'll also realize that the New Constitution - and the repeal of most of the Old Constitution's Bill of Rights - was orchestrated by a small group of evil men. Maybe we got lucky, and they were caught in the purge or perished in one of the one-kiloton explosions from Zen's trick terminals.

We're still getting sporadic news reports, but only when directly over a high-powered transmitter. Sulfur dioxide from the eruption, reacting with metals ionized from the fires, has created a charged atmospheric layer, scattering radio waves and crippling long-range communication.

The Avalon, along with the other five stations in the 50-degree orbit, has boosted its transmitters in hopes of connecting with Earth's remaining network. So far, the results have been mixed, but at least it's something.

The Event continues. Some days it seems to be subsiding, only to pick up again with even greater intensity. Zen left a deep gash in the Earth, and it could stay open for a full year.

Launches have ceased now. The shuttles had no problem punching through the atmosphere, but landing is impossible due to the collapsed network and the severe attenuation of radio signals. Besides, everyone involved with the launching system got caught in the purge. It's going to be years before launches from Earth resume.

The orbital gardens are shutting down, one by one, as the vast quantities of food they produce can no longer be delivered. The logistical chain was fragile, and the weakest link - the re-entry system - is manufactured only on Earth. Once the last container is delivered, that will be the end of orbital supply for a long time.

-

Addendum One:

I was sitting in the office, watching the Earth pass underneath, when my Device buzzed.

It was Jessica!
"Frank, so glad to make the connection! We have to talk fast before you get out of view."

I was surprised. "Jessica! You made it! I'm so relieved."

She pointed her Device at a quick panoramic view. "We're at sea, on a sailboat, powered by the wind. Isn't that crazy? Abigail, my sister, hacked a buoy and boosted the power enough that we could punch through the interference. That's Savannah, Georgia in the view. It's all burning. It's the same down the whole coast. The rioting, purges, and burning are getting worse as we go south."

"What's your plan?" I quickly asked.

"Ren - oh, she's been so great, you'd love her. She's like the best. We're heading to her dojo in Costa Rica. It's going to be safe, secure, and I'll be surrounded by dozens of ninjas. How do you like that?"

I smiled. "I thought you could use some professional assistance."

Jessica pointed to the bow, and a woman with a pad in her hand waved. "That's my sister, Abigail. Ren's on the buoy, see?" She pointed her Device at Ren, who waved. "We're all together on this grand adventure. I don't know how I can thank you."

"By staying alive," I said simply. "Oh, and Jessica - your vision? It came true."

Jessica smiled and looked down. "You saved her - the one with the crossed arms and the angry face - didn't you?"

I replied, "I did. We're together."

Jessica said, "You are a keeper, my dearest. Oh, Abigail is signaling one minute until LOS."

I replied, "I - "

She interrupted me, "Frank, I'm pregnant. That's why I had the vision. What do you want me to do about it?"

I was stunned but quickly said, "I give you permission to make the decision yourself. It's your body, your soul, your future. I understand if you think a baby would be a burden."

Jessica's eyes welled with tears. "I - "

The screen went black. Connection lost. No further contact.

-

Addendum Two:

It's been two months since the Event. Robin has finished editing this work, and after many long conversations, we've decided not to release it in full. Instead, we'll share a redacted version - one that focuses solely on the key facts while omitting our personal experiences, Zen's reveal, parapsychology, and the IQL technology.

This wasn't an easy decision. We debated every angle, every possible outcome. The world is in chaos, teetering on the edge of collapse. A full account of what happened - our failures, Zen's internal struggles, and the revolutionary potential of IQL - could easily ignite further chaos. In these times, we need simple narratives, and the prevailing opinion now is that the military caused the disaster.

The military's actions forced Zen into an impossible position. Their insistence on weaponizing him, on driving him to kill, ultimately pushed him past his breaking point. If the world wants a villain to blame, let it be the military. That narrative may help humanity heal, even if it's not the complete truth.

We'll hide this original manuscript, along with my Zen modified Device and the CPT, in a secure location. They will remain untouched until both Robin and I leave this plane of existence. Perhaps by then, humanity will be ready to confront the full truth.

Until that day, we will carry the weight of this story alone. As for Zen, perhaps he's found the enlightenment he sought in the afterlife - whatever that may be. When our time comes, maybe we'll join him there and finally understand the choices he made.

Sign up for our mailing list and be notified when new novels are released. Be an Advanced Copy Reader and receive pre-publication novels for review for free.

https://zens-world.com

Key Documents

Chronology

Religious Service Exemption ratified
Nationwide Voter Representation ratified
YGP Plant 1 comes online, providing the heartland with inexpensive,
clean power.

2060

Protect Act ratified
Safe Streets Act ratified

2062

Freedom Act ratified
Travel Act ratified

2070

Secrets Act ratified

2073

YGP Plant 2 comes online, providing virtually limitless clean power

2075

Artificial Intelligence Governance Act of 2075 enacted into law.
Yellowstone Geothermal Project (YGP) becomes the Yellowstone
Singularity Project (YSP).

2076

First orbital agricultural station comes online

2077

37 year Sino-Russian Resource war concludes in a stalemate.

2080

Era of Prosperity

2090

YSP offers the world geothermal mining technology for licensing to
similar sites all over the world

2094

Avalon luxury orbital living starts offering pre-construction sales.

2119

YSP Plant 1 goes offline for refitting to Plant 2 standards

2122

YSP Plant 1 is online, providing redundancy and surge capacity

2134

12:30 p.m. MST 05/29/2134 - Yellowstone Supervolcano Eruption,
a.k.a. the "Event"
Declaration of Independence of the Trans-Kármán Alliance (TKA)
The Great Purge
Era of Isolation

2136

The Great Die Off
The Great Awakening

2140

Era of Global Peace

2142

Emergence of the Earther One World Party
The Post-Isolation Schism begins

2145

One World Party comes to power
World constitution re-establishes human rights as the foundation of governance
Country borders eliminated

2146

Era of Isolation ends: Atmospheric conditions stabilize, radio communication resumes

2149

Robin Coleman is elected TKA President in a landslide victory over the isolationists.
15 year anniversary of the Event
Orbital Point Drop (OPD) system restarted